Tim Geary became a model while at Cambridge; his first novel, *Ego*, was about the international world of male models. *Spin* is his second novel. Tim Geary lives in Suffolk and is now a full-time writer.

Spin

Tim Geary

CORONET BOOKS
Hodder and Stoughton

Copyright © 1995 by Tim Geary

First published in paperback in 1995
by Hodder and Stoughton
A division of Hodder Headline PLC

A Coronet paperback

Bridge over Troubled Water © 1969 Paul Simon
Used by permission

The right of Tim Geary to be identified as the Author of
the Work has been asserted by him in accordance with the
Copyright, Designs and Patents Act 1988.

10 9 8 7 6 5 4 3 2 1

British Library Cataloguing in Publication Data

Geary, Tim
Spin
I. Title
823.914 [F]

ISBN 0-340-61369-6

Typeset by Hewer Text Composition Services, Edinburgh
Printed and bound in Great Britain by
Cox and Wyman Ltd, Reading, Berkshire

Hodder and Stoughton
A division of Hodder Headline PLC
338 Euston Road
London NW1 3BH

For my brother, James

Acknowledgments

I owe much to Jake Siewert in Washington and Nancy Curlee in New York for opening doors that may have stayed locked, though neither is to blame for what I chose to see. I would also like to thank Carolyn Mays, Felicity Rubinstein and Sarah Lutyens. Thanks too to Emma Hopkins and Nicola Turner in San Francisco, Ian Mills and Stuart Calder for their gruesome surgical tips, my parents for their ceaseless support and kindness and Philly and Philip Roberts for the unconditional friendship and generosity they never fail to show. The key to the villa is yours.

Prologue, 1978

I n a windowless room in downtown Manhattan, Annie
Marin closed her eyes and imagined the touch of
his hands. Beside her Janos the aloof Hungarian was
beginning to cluck once more and to her side, Faith
Stumpf was slouched on a harsh, metal chair sobbing at
the horror of it all.

Suddenly, there was a scream. 'No! Please, Johnny. It's
cold. I'm shivering from the cold, Johnny, don't let me die
from the cold. Please.'

There was a loud clatter as Brian kicked his chair to
the floor. A moment's silence was followed by one final,
broody screech from Janos, and then all was quiet.

Annie smiled. Oh, to be naked with that stranger! She
could only imagine the bliss.

'Annie?' came a voice.

Annie jumped in her seat and clamped a hand to her
racing heart. Her acting teacher, Bea Shellenburger,
was standing in front of her, a cup of coffee steaming
boisterously in her hand.

'What are you working on?' she asked kindly.

Too embarrassed to admit that she'd been dreaming of
the man with whom she'd collided on her way into class,
Annie lied. 'Ah, coffee,' she said. 'Just coffee.'

Three weeks earlier, on her first day at the world-famous
Cornell Williams Theater Academy, Annie had been

1

instructed to spend two hours imagining that she was holding a cup of coffee in her empty hand. The intent was for her to train her mind to sense the cup's weight and the drink's aroma, so that soon she could conjure up myriad emotions and sensations from the storehouse of her brain.

'Haven't you already done coffee?' asked Bea.

'Um, yuh,' replied Annie. She, like the others, had lied about mastering the exercise. 'But I was seeing how quickly I could get the sensation back.'

'OK, smart idea. You're doing well but I want some scene work from you and Faith. Yeah?'

'We'll do it soon,' promised Annie.

'Good,' said Bea before addressing the rest of her class, telling them to pack up and prepare for the scene studies. As Brian passed her, she asked how he'd been feeling.

'Angry,' he said in a trembling voice. 'Angry and cold. And maybe a little scared.'

'Well, keep working it,' Bea advised before strolling to the one student who remained wrapped in her sensory work. She touched her on the shoulder. 'Faith, do you need to talk?'

Faith Stumpf lifted her head and slowly brushed away the strands of long blonde hair that were veiling her heavily made-up face.

'What were you working on?' asked Bea.

Faith clasped together her hands and beat them softly against her chest. Eventually, after taking a few deep breaths, she answered, 'Loss!'

The students watched Bea circle their classmate on the spotlit stage.

'Were you remembering some loss in your past?'

'Mmm. When I was younger . . .' Faith bit on her upper lip and covered her face with her hands. She began to rock on the chair. 'When I was younger my baby rabbit died and I remember it hurt me so very much that even now . . .'

Bea clapped her hands. 'I want you to tell me a joke. Go! Now!'

Faith looked up, her face a jelly of commotion. 'I . . .'

'Anything to make us smile,' Bea insisted.

'I don't, I mean, I can't think.'

'OK,' said Bea, 'you're OK!' She drew up a high stool and pulled a packet of cigarillos from her mauve clutch bag. Once she'd lit up, she began her familiar lecture from behind a tumbling curtain of smoke. 'Why did I want Faith to make a joke? Anyone?'

'To prove she hadn't lost it over the stiff bunny?' suggested Tommy Hewitt.

Bea smiled because she fancied Tommy, but then she scowled. This was serious stuff; dead serious. In fact, it was her life. 'Yes and no. The reason why we put you on this emotional roller-coaster through your inner life is so you can visit the emotions that are hiding somewhere inside. Because once you know where they are you can use them whenever you want. It'll be like carrying around a tool kit full of anger and love and jealousy. But just as important as finding where those emotions are is . . . is what?'

'Letting them go again?' wondered Sophie English.

'Letting them go. Exactly.' Bea nodded vigorously and took a long drag. She exhaled. 'Cornell used to tell me that locked emotion is like a broken-down car on a freeway. It's like smoke trapped in your lungs. It could kill you.'

This notion didn't frighten Annie Marin as it did most of the students. To her, acting was simply fun, the most fun thing in the whole world. She walked away from her roles the moment she stepped from the stage.

'It's because we feed from this trough of life,' Bea was saying, 'that what we do is dangerous. But it's exciting too. It's,' she gazed into Tommy's bright blue eyes, 'it's sexy it's so exciting. And it's what makes our job the hardest, loneliest, most beautiful job under the sun.'

Faith Stumpf seemed to have tears in her eyes as she

3

gazed up at her teacher. She shook her head slightly, looking bedazzled by the enormity of this challenge.

For her part, Annie raised her eyes to the ceiling, as if to ask God why he'd made Faith her scene partner. She couldn't understand why Faith wanted to act if she found it so hard. Why couldn't she just imitate and pretend? Since her childhood, Annie had copied mannerisms and habits to flesh out the characters she had created. Now she was twenty, had anything changed? All that a grown actress needed, she believed, was the courage to be as foolish and faithful as a child.

These thoughts were still on her mind when the class came to an end. Although she longed to get started on her scene work, she hadn't been able to find a suitable piece. The problem was that she resented the five-feet-eleven-inches that made up her partner, Faith Stumpf. At five-six Annie had never considered herself small nor, with her ginger-brown bob and sweet face, anything but attractive. Yet Faith upset her. It had something to do with the way she leant towards people as she spoke, as if her breasts were too weighty for her to keep straight.

Now Annie saw Faith advancing. She waited until they were close before taking a crafty step back.

Faith straightened. 'Did you find a scene for us?'

'Not yet, no.'

'Don't you want to work with me?' Faith asked, fluttering eyelids so metallic blue it seemed they had been sprayed by Toyota.

'Sure I do. Problem is finding something to suit us.'

'Annie, *real* actresses make the work suit them. That's why I've chosen something.'

They'd moved into the hallway now, busy with students studying bulletin boards that were crowded with audition notices for NYU films, call-ups for non-union extra roles, ads for headshot photographers and favourable reviews, pinned there by the actors themselves, of

Off-Broadway shows featuring members of the teaching staff.

'I thought we'd do Shakespeare,' Faith declared. '*Romeo and Juliet*. I rather saw you as the nurse.'

'Oh, I don't know about that,' Annie said, with some indignation.

'You'd be great,' Faith declared, seeming to grow another inch as she handed a copy of the scene to Annie. 'You've kind of got one of those nursey faces. Still if you don't think you could manage, I . . .'

'I could do it! I'm worried it's not right, that's all.' Annie studied the script. 'I mean, Shakespeare isn't really for beginners, is he?'

Faith looked completely horrified. 'I am far, far, faaar from being a beginner. I have been an actress for most of my life. I've had SAG membership for fifteen years.'

Annie was impressed. Membership of the Screen Actors' Guild was something of which all aspirant actors dreamed.

'In fact, *I* was something of a child star.'

'No way! In the movies?' asked Annie.

'Well, TV mostly.' Faith paused to smoothe another coat of lipstick to her fleshy lips. 'Commercials and things.'

'Oh, I see.' Annie couldn't contain her giggle. 'Those kinds of things.'

Faith grunted and raised her nose. And then, quite out of the blue, she began to shout. 'The point, Miss, Miss . . . Titless, is that I came to this school to develop my art and broaden my range. Jesus!'

The students in the hallway turned to look. Though Faith's bottom lip had begun to quiver, she knew she had to keep control. So she composed herself, relaxed her clenched fists and continued. 'I had a nasty feeling that I'd come across people here who'd judge me because of my looks. But I was born with this face and body, Annie Marin, and I'm proud of it, and you have no right to judge me as some kind of, of, of hopeless tartlet.'

Only the receptionist, armour-plated behind her inch-thick spectacle lenses, was ignoring the scene.

Annie lifted her arms in dismay and began to protest her innocence. 'Faith, listen, I didn't . . .'

'You made fun of me.'

'I never . . .'

'In front of my fellow students!'

'I . . .'

'And I vow I'm never going to speak to you again!'

Faith threw her pages into the air and stepped, rather dramatically, out of the school and into the chill November wind.

Annie's daffodil-yellow bathrobe was one of the few possessions she had brought with her to Manhattan and this alone was what she was wearing now. The only daughter of parents who were in their forties when she was born, Annie had lived in the same house in a suburb of Pittsburgh all her life and had not had the courage to dislodge too much at once. Her childhood belongings remained where they had accumulated, jumbled in an order only she understood, anchors to a past that had been happy and crowded with love. What lay ahead was a different world, and if it proved fulsome and sour she would leave it without regret to return to the harbour of home.

Reclining on the embroidered quilt on her bed, biting on the nail of her forefinger, Annie listened to the ring tone. She pictured the phone in her best friend's house, on the fake-walnut cocktail cabinet, and thought how odd it was to be disturbing the sounds of a familiar space so far away. It made her, if only for a moment, homesick.

Someone picked up. 'Hello?'

'It's me!'

'Aaaaannie. Oh my God! How are you?'

Annie told Barbara about the studio apartment on the edge of Little Italy. She told her about Bea and the

acting class and about how she'd been dumped doing
scene classes with Faith Stumpf.

'She's your worst nightmare come to life,' Annie said,
tucking the phone under her chin as she began to clip her
toenails. 'She's really tall and thin and . . .'

'Tits?' Barbara enquired.

'Huge tits,' said Annie.

'I hate her.'

'And she's got these long red fingernails. It's like she's
been ripping open bodies or something.'

'Sounds like you're jealous,' concluded Barbara.

'Cut it out!' Annie slapped her palm onto the quilt in
frustration. 'She's just so stupid and self-involved. We
had this argument over nothing and in the end I was
the one who had to plead with her to come back. I
mean, Bra, why me? She's going to make me look
like shit.'

'No she won't. You'll be great, you always are. Anyway,
tell me about the men. Have you found one yet?'

'Oh, God,' Annie sighed, twisting to lie on the bed as
if this was the only position for such talk, 'I've found the
perfect guy.'

'But he's married,' Barbara decided.

'I don't think so.'

'You mean you don't know? Did you go on a date?'

'No. I ran into him.'

'That's it?' Barbara said, incredulously.

'It was enough, Bra. I know it's crazy, but it was. I was
late for class and I was running through the hall and it
was like he appeared from nowhere and I ran straight
into him and I swear to God he is the most, I mean
I don't even know how to describe him but just the
way he said sorry and smiled at me I thought, I don't
know, I felt like we were meant for each other. It was
incredible.'

'What did he look like?'

'Just think perfect and you'll get the picture. He's tall and strong-looking and, and he's got one of those sort of cute, boyish faces and his smile – I mean, no kidding, Bra, I would have done anything for him.'

'So is he an actor, or what?' asked Barbara.

'I don't know. He looked older. He had a suntan.'

'So? Don't actors tan?'

'Not in New York in November, they don't,' said Annie. 'I mean, it looked kind of fresh. Guys in Manhattan usually look more sick.'

'You're always doing this, Annie. Why can't you find yourself a real guy? Someone you can have and hold for a change. Especially hold. You only dream about these no-hopers because you're scared of getting involved.'

'Am not!' Annie insisted.

She climbed off the bed and walked to the mirror, as if to judge her own appeal in the eyes of this man.

'Prove it then,' challenged Barbara.

'I will. I'll go and find him!'

'Right, that'd be just like you,' said Barbara sarcastically.

'I will, Bra,' pledged Annie. 'I'm telling you, I feel like a new person here, like I can make everything work out right.'

'So go and grab your mystery man, then call me to say how it went.'

'You're on,' said Annie, feeling optimistic and bold. 'If you're lucky, you might even be asked to the wedding!'

'Still here?' said Bea Shellenburger.

'Yup,' replied Annie, doing her best to put a brave face on the hours spent in the Cornell Williams hallway. 'He's hopeless with time!'

It was late in the afternoon and still Annie hadn't caught sight of her dream man in the flow of students.

'I hope he's worth waiting for,' Bea said. 'By the way, did you and Faith find a good scene?'

'We're still looking,' Annie explained. 'Faith's a little bit – you know.'

Bea nodded, as if she understood. Then, holding her hand out flat and weaving it through the air, she said, 'If you're going to be an actress, Annie, if you're going to travel this twisting, turning, mysterious road, you're going to find some very strange characters along the way. Believe me, I did. Even when I was at the top.'

'When was that?'

'Let me finish!' said Bea sternly. 'You're going to have to play the Good Samaritan. You're going to have to hold out your hand and say, "I will help you." Can you do that, Annie? Can you help Faith?'

'I don't know. I'm not a shrink.'

Bea acknowledged the joke with another nod. 'What I suggest is that you go out and look for a scene that plays to your strengths as actresses. Because whatever you think, there are parts out there tailor-made for you both. I always say that negativity is like poison to an actress. It's Cleopatra's asp, it's Gertrude's cup, it's the rapier of Laertes, it's . . .'

But Annie wasn't listening any more because behind her teacher, she could see him clumping down the stairs, the man who'd invaded her heart and mind and made her feel as if she'd been swallowing nothing but air since their briefest of encounters. Though he seemed more pale than he had, and perhaps less muscular, he was still gorgeous. She felt a rush of blood to her cheeks.

Bea stopped talking, and after quickly glancing at the man whispered, 'You're right. He's worth waiting for,' before leaving Annie alone.

As the man reached the bottom step, he looked up from his book and straight at Annie. She smiled, and waited for him to speak, but instead he returned to his play and moved towards the door. Annie couldn't believe it. Surprising herself, she mustered up the courage to speak.

'Sorry about yesterday.'

He turned. 'Excuse me?'

'Running into you like that. I'm sorry!'

The man looked bemused.

'You don't remember?' Annie asked. 'It was right here!'

He shook his head. 'Wrong guy, sorry!'

'But . . .'

Feeling as if she'd been left by a lover of years, Annie stared after the receding figure. But then, as if her will was strong enough to pull him back, he reappeared.

'You know something?' he said. 'My brother Alex was in here yesterday, looking for me.'

Annie looked unconvinced.

'We're identical,' he said. 'He was here visiting. From Berkeley.'

'The tan . . .' Annie said, almost to herself.

'The tan!' he repeated. 'So I hope that explains it,' he said, raising his hand in a half-wave. 'See ya.'

Again, Annie stopped him from leaving. Perhaps Fate had planned this confusion. Perhaps this was her man. He was, after all, equally handsome, even if he didn't have quite the same effect on her heart.

'I'm Annie Marin,' she said, holding out a hand.

'Max Lubotsky.'

'Are you an actor?' she asked.

'No. I'm doing a play-writing class.'

'You are?' Annie enthused. 'That's so great. I'm looking for a play scene for me and my partner. Have you got one we could do?'

Max tapped a pen against his copy of *All My Sons*, and said, 'I guess there is one thing I don't find so terrible. It's about four people who get trapped in an elevator, try to make friends and end up despising each other.'

'So it's a comedy!' said Annie, at once regretting her goofy expression.

'It's not that serious,' Max promised.

'OK, then I'd love to see it. I mean, if I could. Do you, do you live near here?'

'No, I'm in Hell's Kitchen.'

'I know where that is!' said Annie, pleased with her knowledge of the city. 'In fact, I was wanting to go and check it out.'

'I won't be there all day.'

'Not at all?'

Max paused a moment but then relented and gave Annie his address and said he'd probably be there around five.

When he left she tried to picture his apartment and wondered whether she'd have a good time and stay for a drink or maybe some pasta and who knew what else except that the idea of being alone with him in a room with a bed was oddly exciting seeing how she didn't know anything about the guy except that he smiled rarely and had wide, strong hands that would feel great cupped over her breasts.

Just like Barbara always said.

Max Lubotsky could hear knocking. Was it at his door? There was no telling in this grimy shit-hole. Weird noises sounded at the oddest hours from the strangest places, and most often he ignored them. The knock came again, loud on the old door. He groaned, opening his eyes.

'Max? Are you there? It's Annie Marin. Max?'

He sat up. Who was Annie? He'd heard the name before, no question, but the face wasn't there.

'Max? You there?'

'Yeah. Hold it!'

He took his time, standing up and falling back down twice before he pushed himself up on those thighs that had been so in shape just a year before, racing down the

11

mountains in Tahoe, the edges singing on the icy snow, swooooosh, right past his brother Alex who hadn't had a chance. Always could ski better than him, Max thought. About the only thing.

He unbolted the door to a smiling Annie. She was holding watermelon slices.

'I'm sorry. Were you sleeping?' she asked.

Max nodded. The question made him think to run a hand over his hair. He could feel what it looked like, all snarled up and spiky at the front.

Chirpy still, Annie said, 'Can I come in?'

'OK.' Max stood aside, one hand on the door, the other tucked into the waistband of his pants.

'I brought some melon,' she said. 'You want some?'

She held it out to him and in seconds he was running to the bathroom and then she heard him retching as if he'd swallowed a distillery. The room filled with the stench of vomit.

Annie found him kneeling in front of the toilet bowl, really clinging to it, his right hand splattered with the puke. And though she wasn't so great at that sort of thing, she pulled the chain and helped him to his feet and to the basin where she cleaned his arm and, without words, led him to the bed, draped a blanket over him and tucked it in.

'Thanks,' he said, and then, 'I'm sorry,' before closing his eyes and drifting to wherever it was that Max Lubotsky took his mind after drinking half a bottle of Scotch.

It was dark when he woke, but he wasn't alone. Annie had stayed and in the previous five hours had washed the dishes and cleaned the oven top and swept the floor and wiped in the bathroom and scrubbed the coffee pot and cleaned the joint-ridden ashtrays and thrown out the trash so that now the room smelled less like a bar, though miracles weren't part of her service. And once she had slaved for this man she hardly knew, she'd hollowed out a space in the large turquoise beanbag to read *The Elevator*, a play in one act.

She was almost at the end when she glanced up to find him staring at her. She wondered how long he'd been awake and was suddenly embarrassed. What if he hadn't wanted her to sprinkle her values around?

By his bed she folded her arms, like a nurse. 'How do you feel?' she asked.

'So-so,' he replied, his voice croaky.

Max propped himself up on his elbow and took from Annie a glass of water. As he drank, she left to light the gas ring beneath the coffee pot. Having been mothered for twenty years in Pittsburgh where after high school she had stayed living at home, saving money for Cornell Williams by working days and nights at the Pittsburgh House of Prime Steak, it felt good to be mother now, as if adulthood had arrived.

After a few minutes, Max threw back the blanket and sat up, nursing his sore head. Then he looked at the apartment.

'Shit!' he said. 'What happened here?'

'Oh,' said Annie, nervously kicking the back of her left sneaker with her right foot. 'I cleaned up some.'

Max stood. His walk was unsteady and he looked as pale as a ghost, but Annie's effort cheered him. 'I can't believe this.' He walked to the open-plan kitchen. '*And* I smell coffee.'

Annie skipped past him. 'I know. You want some?'

'I'd love some. Thanks.'

'Watermelon too?'

He patted his stomach. 'I don't think so.'

They sat at an ink-stained butcher's block table strewn with sheets of paper. The writing, Annie noticed, was surprisingly neat. Such order in this chaos clearly displayed Max's priorities.

After a while, Annie said, 'I've never got drunk on my

own.' She took a large bite of melon. 'There doesn't seem any point.'

'Surely that depends on whether you're drinking to live a little more or a little less,' he said.

'More always. God!' She spat some pips into the cup of her hand. 'Who could ever want any less of life? Especially in New York. Ever since I got to Cornell Williams and saw how bad most of the students are, I've had this amazing feeling, like everything's going to slide into place.'

'You've got your life all planned out, have you?' asked Max a little scornfully, as he looked up from flaking grass into a joint.

Annie had been arranging the watermelon seeds into the shape of a heart but swept them together when he looked her way. 'No, it's just there's something about Manhattan that makes your dreams seem nearer.' She squeezed one of the seeds hard between finger and thumb. 'Like they could grow into something that matters.'

'It doesn't matter how near your dreams are if you haven't got what you need to reach them,' Max said. 'Tell me what do you do about that?'

'Simple,' she said at once. 'You work at it. One per cent inspiration, ninety-nine per cent perspiration, isn't that what they say? And we're still so young.'

'No! *You're* still young. I'm twenty-seven.'

'So big deal! Enjoy life now and write great things when you're older and wiser.'

Angrily, Max clonked his cup on the table. 'That is such bullshit. You think wisdom's some kind of reward waiting to be unwrapped when you get old? Most old people are sour and angry because they've been through life and found out what a pile of shit it is. It's only young and *un*wise people who do anything, because it's only the young who're stupid enough to have ideals.'

'So write something about that. About politics or something,' she said, though politics had never held much interest for her.

'Nah. I'm leaving that to my brother Alex. He's working part time for Senator Grant in California.' Max tore a strip of cardboard from his packet of Marlboros and began to roll it into a roach. 'He'd probably run for President if only we'd been born in the States.'

Annie started bouncing the basketball she'd found earlier in the broom cupboard. 'I think you like feeling sorry for yourself. My mom's always saying it's easier to do nothing than do something.'

'Well, tell her to write a play and see what happens when she tries getting any of those bastards interested,' said Max, pointing out of the window. 'I mean, it wasn't so long ago that an Arthur Miller première was the sexiest thing around. Now what is there? *Jaws*. Fucking *Charlie's Angels*. No one could give a shit about anything serious any more but I don't want to be writing advertising copy or trash novels when I'm fifty. Writing *matters* more than that.'

Annie had always thought that the world offered endless opportunity. There was little she liked less than to hear people listing excuses for failing to grip their potential.

'So it's all hopeless, is it? You can't write because you're too old, too disillusioned and too unlucky not to have been born thirty years ago when people liked plays? I mean, if that's what you really believe, you might as well kill yourself.'

'I might just do that,' he said, taking a deep drag from his joint.

'Don't say that, Max! Never even think about it.'

He tried to hold the smoke in his lungs as he spoke, so it sounded as if someone had a hand clutched to his throat. 'Why not? It's only through being aware of your death that you strive to do anything at all.'

'You're a gloomy bastard! Did you know that?' she said, tossing the basketball at him.

Max deflected it with a forearm and it bounced lazily into a corner.

'I mean,' said Annie, 'do you think if Arthur Miller was alive he'd kill himself instead of writing plays?'

Max banged the table with his free hand, believing his argument won. 'There! You've got it! That's what I'm saying. Arthur Miller *is* alive but he's invisible. There's no point him writing any more. No one's listening.'

'I'm listening, aren't I?'

There was a long silence. Max gently shut his eyes as he spoke. 'I don't know what you do if you're not the person you want to be. That's all. How do you live with that?'

Annie had never had to think about it. She'd always been delighted by herself. As an only child, her doting parents had taught her to accept what faults she had with perfect grace.

'I don't know,' she said. 'I guess you figure out a way to fall in love with yourself. I'm sure you could do whatever you wanted if you tried. I mean, I thought that elevator play of yours was great. You've just got to tell yourself you can do it.'

Max, who was a little stoned by now, suddenly laughed. 'It's that simple, is it? OK, I am going to write something that really matters. How's that?'

'It's good. It's very good. And I'll win the Oscar for the most sensitive, beautiful actress of all time.'

She joined him in his laughter.

'How long shall we give ourselves?' he asked. 'Ten years?'

'No,' she protested. 'Not long enough. Make it twenty.'

'Fifteen!'

'Fifteen it is.'

They both lifted their coffee cups and chinked them together. 'To 1993! Our year!'

*   *   *

Claustrophobic as she was, Faith had initially been reluctant to take part in a scene set in an elevator. But now, two weeks after she had been persuaded, she and Annie were sitting in class waiting to perform. Annie had spent more time with her partner than she'd have wished. The problem with Faith was that she wasn't content to wear her heart on her sleeve, she felt a need to exhibit the rest of her organs too. At scene rehearsal every day she bored Annie with her doubts, allergies, weaknesses and desires. This snowball of psychological phobias collected garbage along the way, so that even dilemmas troubling her scene character became subjects of concern. Now, as they sat in the back row whispering so as not to disturb Sophie English's monologue, Faith was sharing her thoughts.

'I think she was an anorexic.'

'Who? Sophie?'

'No,' answered Faith so loudly that Bea Shellenburger turned to scowl. 'Beth, my character. I think she had a what-d'ya-call-it, an eating disorder as a child. Do you think, maybe?'

Annie, her patience worn through by now, snapped her head to the side and glared at Faith. 'I don't know. Ask the writer, why don't you? Luckily, he's still alive.'

'I already did.'

Annie tried to suppress the shock as it scratched its nails across her heart. 'You did what?'

'I asked Max. He said Beth was mine now, and that I should do whatever I felt was right.'

Annie turned back to watch Sophie's endless monologue. Her mind, however, was elsewhere. Why hadn't Max told her he'd been talking to Faith? Did he have something to hide?

After their first eventful evening together, Max had become a looming figure in Annie's mind. When she wasn't with him, she wished she was. And when she

17

was, she wished she was closer still. Annie, impressed by the quality of his work, had taken it upon herself to nurture his talent by mothering the man. Almost daily she visited him at the apartment, sometimes returning with him from school, at others arriving later to cook a meal for them both. The results were soon evident. Max had begun a play about Jimmy Carter's failure as President, and though it was Alex who, from Berkeley, provided his brother with the political ideas, it was Annie who gave Max courage. She believed her ceaseless optimism was oxygen to his muse. She knew she was spoiling him but she had no doubt that something solid would come from their loosely constructed friendship. There would be rewards. It was only a matter of time.

'Who's next?' Bea called out.

Annie funnelled her swimming vision into focus. Sophie English, all talked out, was leaving the stage free for Annie and Faith to set up. Borrowing a couple of men who'd been asked to act as the other passengers in the elevator, they positioned themselves on the stage.

Annie was surprisingly nervous. The audience numbered no more than a dozen, but now she was acting in New York and it was what she had dreamed of. So what if it was a five-minute scene in a class? It was her first chance to shine, a first step on the road to fame, glory and happiness.

The actors stood in a two-foot-square space. Annie explained to the audience that the four had been trapped for hours and that only she had remained calm. The resentment that had been building between the women was coming to a boil. Faith, as the housewife, Beth, spoke first.

'*Did anyone feel that? I thought we moved.*'

Frantically, she began to press a button on the wall of the imaginary elevator.

'*Will you stop doing that?*' snapped Annie, who was playing the tough businesswoman, Diane.

18

'I'm not doing anything. I thought I felt the elevator move.' Faith fell to her knees and put an ear to the ground. *'I thought I heard something.'*

'Will you stop! You're making us jumpy.'

'I'm scared! Is that allowed?' Faith shouted. *'I'm a mother!'* She clutched, rather oddly, her breasts. A hand on each. *'And I'm scared I'm never—'* Faith began to breathe in large gulps of air, *'going to see my kids. We're all going to die.'*

'We're not.'

'But we're trapped!'

Suddenly, Faith started to scream. The two actors working with her looked on, impressed by her ability. But Annie was alarmed. This wasn't rehearsed. Faith hadn't finished her speech and yet she was trembling, her hands on her head, her eyes staring wildly.

'I've got to breathe,' she cried.

Leaping from her spot, Faith ran right out of the room.

After a few seconds Annie, her face shrouded in an I-told-you-so grimace, lifted her arms and let her hands slap down on the sides of her legs. 'That's not in the script,' she said. 'She screwed the whole thing up.'

Bea turned on the house lights and pulled up her stool. 'There's something to be learnt from this,' she began. 'As Cornell himself used to say to me . . .'

The next day, Annie was lying face down on her bed, drawing beards on a newspaper cartoon of Snoopy with one hand and holding the phone with the other. She was sharing with Barbara her tales of woe. 'And that wasn't the end of it. After the class she comes up to me all weepy saying she didn't know what had come over her and could we do something more serious together and bull like that. I can't wait to tell Max what a fucking weirdo she is.'

'Has he called?'

Annie hesitated, wondering whether to lie.

'No,' she admitted, 'he's always working.'

'I think he's gay,' Barbara said. 'Why else would he spend a night in the same bed and not touch you?'

Annie wished she hadn't told Barbara about that night. She had only stayed because it had been impossible to find a cab during the heavy rainstorm, and Max's bed was so large that they'd managed not to touch, even though Annie had longed to, even though she'd lain on her side staring at the back of his head, willing him to turn, wondering if he could feel through the mattress springs the pattering beat of her heart, a drumroll to a climax that had never come.

'OK, darling, listen to your best friend on this. Tell him he's gotta quit screwing you around and start screwing. Tonight. Go and tease him a little, and if that doesn't do it, forget him.'

Having hung up the receiver, Annie sat around a while wondering what to do. There wasn't much on TV, and she wasn't starting her waitressing job for another week, and she didn't like going to the movies alone. In fact, she didn't like being alone. More than anything she wanted some company tonight. Yet who could she call but Max? After six weeks in New York he was her only real friend. She hadn't wanted to spend time with anyone else and besides, she didn't want to miss him in the mood when he'd reveal his gratitude and love. It thrilled and excited her to wonder which day they would kiss, and she hoped every morning for that day to be the one. Now, though, Max wasn't at home. The only place she could think of him being was Ken Lu's, so she decided to go and see.

Outside, sheets of wind-blown drizzle were dancing flamenco in the streetlamps' bronze arcs as Annie paced towards Chinatown and the restaurant where she'd eaten with Max on their three nights out. She loved the neighbourhood at night. The glaring bulbs that hung, unshaded and swinging, above the street vendors' stalls transformed grocery shopping into vibrant street theatre. She passed seemingly endless market tables of brightly coloured vegetables and fruit, past bulging plastic sacks of energetic beansprouts, struggling fish made brilliant in the white light and hillocks of ginger as gnarled as arthritic hands.

Ken Lu's was in a tiny, dark block off the elbow in Mott Street. Annie ran a hand through her hair as she approached but suddenly stopped dead, spun back and hid, like a movie detective, behind a streetlamp tailored in posters. She couldn't believe what she'd seen. Slowly, keeping herself hidden, hoping against hope, she peered round the lamp and looked once more.

This time there was no escaping the truth, for there, cinematically framed by the polished steel of the restaurant's full-length windows, was Max with another woman. Had he not been stroking the woman's thigh, Annie might not have cared. Had they not been sitting at *her* table in *their* restaurant, it might not have hurt so much. And if the woman had been anyone else, anyone but Faith, then she might have been able to forgive him. But all she saw now was thievery. Whatever Faith was feeling, whatever nerves were applauding his touch, whatever happiness his touching her brought, whatever thrill she was feeling from the knowledge that Max appreciated her, wanted her, maybe even loved her, these things belonged to Annie. She had worked for them, sacrificed herself for them, even, without words, been promised them.

Her heart was pounding with fierce hatred for Faith. What was the dumb bitch finding to talk about in that vacuum of a head? She was jabbering away, all eye-shadow and lips, and Max looked as if he was actually listening to what she was saying. You could hardly tell who was the whore and who the writer.

As the drizzle thickened to rain Annie scurried to the shelter of a dark doorway. She gazed at Max's animated,

happy face. She wished she could hate him, but seeing him
with another only made her want him more. It made her
feel weak though she knew she had to be strong. She had
to be. She couldn't lose him after dreaming for so long.

So she told herself to be bold and, thumping open the
restaurant's smoky glass door, she ignored the welcoming
waitress and marched to the table by the window. Max's
hand jumped from Faith's leg as if he'd been stung.

'Hi, Annie,' he said. 'Want to join us?'

'No, I don't,' she replied, breathless. 'Anyway, Max,
how could you eat if you had to fondle both of us
at once?'

Max drained his face of expression. 'What do you
mean?'

'You know what I mean!'

'No, I don't! Faith and I were talking about my play.'

'Talking about your play? That's a joke. Hang on . . .'
Annie cupped a hand to her ear. 'You know, I can still hear
what you were saying.' She pointed at Max. 'You're saying
that no one's going to produce it because it's no good, and
she's saying she'd play the lead if only she could get over
being a fuck-awful actress.'

Max stood, briefly alarming Annie by his sheer physical
presence. 'Annie, I don't think Faith . . .'

'You don't think Faith what?' she screamed, furious at
him for taking Faith's side. 'You don't think Faith'll sleep
with you if I go on? God, Max, I wouldn't want that to
happen. I bet she gives the performance of her life, huh?
Lots of moaning and back-scratching and urging you on
and then a real big scream just a second before you come
so you'll feel good about yourself. Am I close?'

Max looked shocked, not because of the words but
because they'd come from Annie's mouth. What had
happened to the sweet girl from Pittsburgh?

'No,' he said. 'Nowhere near.'

Annie didn't seem to care. 'You know she's only doing

it so you'll climb out of bed and head straight for your whisky and cigarettes and prissy page margins and scrawl some starring masterpiece for her. I've actually found the actress stupid enough to sleep with the writer.'

'Hey, listen,' he said. 'Just, just fuck off. OK?'

'The great wordsmith speaks! Fine. I'm gone. For good, so don't expect me to run over tonight when you start puking up in the bathroom. Or any night!'

Then, as abruptly as she'd arrived, Annie left the restaurant.

Sitting back down, Max shrugged his shoulders and said, 'Must be her time of the month, I guess.'

Behind them a weighty man with an owlish face stood and, leaving his food uneaten and his coat on the chair, hurried to the door. Faith stared at him keenly.

'I'm sure I recognise that guy,' she said.

As Max hadn't a clue, Faith called over the waiter. He was more useful. 'He Mr Bernie Hermann.'

Faith's eyes lit up. 'Of course he is! Is he – is Bernie coming back?'

'Oh, yes! He come back.'

As Faith delved into her bag for her lipstick, Max asked her how she knew the stranger.

'I don't.' She held her compact mirror at arm's length to daub on a fresh layer of lipstick. 'But I saw him at the Soap Awards.'

'I thought he looked sleazy,' Max said.

'Sleazy or not,' Faith said, teasing her hair with both hands, 'he's Executive Producer of *Unto the Skies* and tonight he's going to find himself a new star.'

Like a crowded jumbo climbing against the wind, *Unto the Skies* rose slowly to its position as the most popular soap opera on daytime television. Beginning life as a half-hour show, it told the story of two families based near Chicago, the Sheridans and the Brenners, co-owners and partners in Brendan Air. Owned by the manufacturing conglomerate Gardner and Hyde, *Unto the Skies*, like the other soaps, was created to fill air space between commercials for the company's household products. It was a remarkably successful tactic, for the captive audience of unliberated housewives not only became hooked on the drama, they became remarkably loyal to the sponsor's products as well.

Once produced by Gardner and Hyde's production division, *Unto the Skies* was then loaned to the UBC network. UBC earned its profits from selling advertising space not only to Gardner and Hyde but to other sponsors as well. Though the formula gained strength in the 1950s, UBC had been unsuccessful in its two previous soaps and by 1963, when they bought *Unto the Skies*, they were desperate for a winner. In this tale of two successful, white, middle-class families, they found it, and by the mid-seventies the soap was attracting a daily audience that exceeded twelve million viewers, not including those viewers addicted in foreign lands where it was syndicated.

As Executive Producer, Bernie Hermann was responsible for the show's success. Working with his production team, he hired and fired the actors, writers, directors and technicians. Ratings were all that mattered, and since his appointment Bernie had transformed *Unto the Skies* into the most successful soap on daytime television.

It was no wonder, then, that Faith lit up at the sight of him. The soaps were seen as excellent training grounds by many actors. The work was regular, the pay was good and the exposure was terrific. The fact that an hour's worth of television had to be taped every day meant that production standards were not exactly high, but some actors thought this gave them the chance to shine. There was no shortage of applicants. Every day the casting director of *Unto the Skies* received up to three hundred unsolicited actors' headshots. Almost all were rejected, including, in the week before her dinner with Max, the back-lit headshot of which Faith Stumpf was so proud.

She had never lacked the will to succeed. It was the way that had proved elusive. Elusive, that was, until her trip to Chinatown when suddenly it seemed illuminated as the Northern Star, plum above the rotund frame of Mr Bernard Hermann.

Chinatown had lost its lustre. As Annie pushed past a man selling plastic gimmicks, the vendor covered one nostril with a finger and snorted mucus from the other. A string of it twisted and jumped towards her in the gusty wind and she leapt away in disgust.

Damn Max! Faith was the dumbest, trashiest bitch Annie had ever met. What was wrong with him? Had Faith cooked and cleaned for him? Had Faith been kept awake with dreams of him? How could this have happened?

Now even the spiralling sweet steam of soy bean custard was sickening to Annie. She was hungry and the rain had dampened her clothes as the evening had dampened her spirits. She didn't think she could face going home alone, but where else was there to go? She longed for the world to swallow her up. If only Max had followed . . .

Suddenly she felt a hand grab her arm. Excited, she spun around, but instead of Max she saw an older man.

'Get off me!' she screamed.

The man lifted up both hands in surrender and took a step back. 'Nice to meet you too.'

'Do you need something?'

'Yeah. You.'

Annie shivered and started to walk away again but he was following her, and talking, though he was breathless from the run. 'My name's Bernie Hermann. I produce *Unto the Skies*.' He handed her his card. 'I liked what I just saw in the restaurant. Was it for real? I hope not. I hope it was acting!'

Annie held the card between forefinger and thumb and angled it to catch the light. 'What am I supposed to do with this?' she asked.

'You take it home with you and tomorrow – or later tonight – you dial my home number if you want to come in for a test.'

'For *Unto the Skies*?'

'For *Unto the Skies*,' said Bernie, chewing on an indigestion tablet.

Annie giggled. 'You mean you saw me for two minutes and now you want to give me a job?'

Bernie shook his finger. 'I didn't say that. I said I wanted you to test for a new part.'

As she faced him, she saw a drop of sweat bulge and skip down his temple. She bit at the inside of her lip.

'I don't know. How do I know you're not trying . . .'

Bernie snatched back the card. 'You know what?' he said, 'I don't need this shit. There are a thousand bitches who'd get on their knees and blow me for a break like this. You've blown your chance instead.'

He turned without saying goodbye. Now it was Annie who was doing the following.

'I'm sorry. I'm sorry.' She wanted this now, more than anything. 'I'll do the test,' she said.

'No, you won't.'

She skipped in front of him, and he stopped. 'I'm sorry, I wasn't thinking. Can I give you my name in case you change your mind?'

Bernie nodded and took a calfskin notebook from his inside pocket. 'Shoot.'

'I'm Annie Marin. Like, like in the county.'

'Agent?'

'No. I mean I don't have one. Yet.'

'Home phone?'

Annie paused.

'Jesus Christ,' muttered Bernie, shaking his head and closing his notebook.

'It's 782–9800,' she said, too fast so she had to repeat herself.

He took down the number and clicked shut his pen.

'Do you think, I mean, will you call?' asked Annie.

'I knew it,' Bernie Hermann said, pinching her cheek with his plump, clammy fingers. 'You want to be a star!'

1

1993

The First Lady of the United States of America had her back to the wall and an earlobe between her teeth. Her ankles were shackled by her tight skirt and her underwear was gathered in wrinkles below her knees. 'That's it,' she whispered, 'like that . . . just like that.'

It didn't seem to matter to these two that they were denied the luxury of beds or baths or time, for the pleasure they got from their lovemaking warmed them for days. And by now much of their excitement came from fucking in odd, dangerous places, between public engagements, in her office, in her limo. Even now, while he was inside her, he closed his eyes to gild this pleasure with fantasy. He felt her tighten her grip on him and clasp her hands on his buttocks to pull him deeper inside.

Suddenly a high-pitched noise startled them both. Alex Lubotsky twisted his head and looked down. He was still wearing his suit trousers and could easily read the message on the bleeper attached to his belt. Call POTUS, it said. The President of the United States.

'It's Jack,' Alex told her. 'I've got to go.'

He withdrew, and turned to the mirror to flick his thick, dark hair back into place. His face betrayed nothing. When he kissed Susan she pulled him closer again, and pressed herself against him.

'Do you think you can make it on Friday?' she asked.

'I'll do what I can.'

Taking the battered leather briefcase he'd had since his days at Berkeley, and paying no attention to the guard outside the office, Alex walked briskly on the black and white diamond tiles of the Old Executive Office Building, where most of the White House staff worked. The corridor was empty but for him and his footsteps echoed in the high ceilings.

Rebecca Frear, the White House press secretary who'd been Alex's protégée during the Grant campaign, was waiting for her boss in the lower press room. She followed him into his office that was situated midway, as was Alex himself, between the press and the President. The vantage point was a good one if ever Jack Grant tried to sneak through the net to talk directly to the nation.

'Jack's in a terrible mood,' Rebecca said, closing the door behind her.

Alex slid a weary hand over his brow and sat on the corner of the desk. Casting an eye over his memos, he asked, almost distractedly, 'Did he hear about the CBS poll?'

'Not yet. I thought you'd like to tell him.'

'Love to!'

He glanced out of the window to the front lawn of the White House. A network reporter, microphone in hand, was concluding a stand-up beneath large camera lights. Alex wondered what great truths she was sharing with the nation this time. He sighed. What he'd give for a break; just a day on a beach miles from the White House press corps; just a night doing something other than wondering what shit the morning news teams were aiming at which fans. Maybe he would relax over Thanksgiving. The President was spending the vacation at Camp David and Alex was heading up to his brother's new house near Princeton.

Max! He'd almost forgotten Max.

'Becca, when my brother calls can you tell him I'll meet him at the Parrot on L at . . .' Alex looked at the clocks on the wall, one each for Washington, Paris, Moscow, Tokyo and Santa Rosa, California, his home town, 'at one thirty?'

'Sure.'

She would, too. Rebecca and Alex had spent only one night together, but she'd been willing to do anything for her boss since then. Though he'd apologised to her sweetly with flowers and lunch, and said the night had been a beautiful mistake, Rebecca had not given up hope. How could she when Alex Lubotsky was the most perfect man alive, and his smile alone made her feel like a schoolgirl?

It was a short and noiseless walk from the press room to the Oval Office, on soft blue carpet that insulated most of the West Wing's corridors. The first time Alex had visited these presidential offices, during the transition period the previous year, he had been struck by how insignificant they were. There seemed a deficiency of space surrounding the most important man in the world. After a lifetime of homage to the presidential myth, Alex would have preferred to have found solid oak doors, twelve feet high, opening into a grand, marble-pillared chamber with vaulted ceilings in which his footsteps would echo as he approached the President seated on a podium at the far end.

Instead, the business quarters had the feel of a hotel designed to flatter its guests into believing they'd been invited to a luxurious private home. There were some fine but unremarkable portraits of ex-Presidents hanging on the cream-coloured walls, and some sturdy pieces of antique furniture, and a multitude of well-polished, upholstered chairs and, in the Cabinet and Roosevelt rooms, a couple of handsome conference tables. There was, however, little grandeur to mirror the building's famous pillared exterior. Only the Situation Room had an aura of its own, and that because it was in use only

31

at times of crisis, and access to it came from punching in coded numbers known only to a few.

As Director of Communications in the White House, Alex Lubotsky did what he could to shroud the President in a similar mystique. He believed the public were turned on by the trappings of power. It did Jack Grant no harm to be wrapped in bodyguards, to have snipers saluting with gun muzzles from the White House roofs, to have streets closed for his motorcade and restaurants combed for his safety. Such entertainment was worth its tax dollar and confirmed the importance of the man.

Inside the Oval Office, President Jack Grant stood beside an unlit fireplace. The room, though it shivered with history, was made to seem curiously dead by being so neat and dusted and newly refurbished. Jack's wife, Susan, had wasted no time in changing the interiors after twelve years of Republican occupancy. Fresh yellows and pale blues predominated, and much of the artwork was Native American as if denying that the office celebrated, by its existence, the colonialists' past butchery.

Alex took a seat at the end of one of the two sofas. To his right was a sturdy desk, favoured by John Kennedy and built from the timbers of the USS *Resolute*. A portable cassette machine stood upon it. The President had been playing John Coltrane again, as he liked to if ever the ride became too rough.

Jack Grant picked up his can of Pepsi. 'News?'

'The CBS poll came through,' Alex replied. 'You're down ten.'

The President made no movement. The man had changed so much since Alex had known him first. When Grant had been running for the governorship of California in the mid-eighties, a ten-point fall in approval ratings would have made him livid. He would have blamed others, cried for heads, watched them roll. Now he took the blows himself, and they weakened him. He pulled up a chair and brought it close to the friend in whom he placed such trust.

'What do you suggest we do about these figures?'

The TV pollsters had attributed this further ratings fall to the so-called Cochabamba scandal that had been rocking the White House. The accusation that Jack Grant had turned a blind eye to money laundering and drug importation when he'd been Governor of California had done more to threaten the stability of the office of the Chief Executive than any incident since Watergate.

'I suggest we concentrate on the new jobs programme,' said Alex. 'We stage a media event here, we keep tough on crime and we basically press on with the business at hand. Also I'd like to see the First Lady head out with the Education package to deflect some of the press, and . . .'

Suddenly the President interrupted. 'Stop it, Al,' he said. His eyes were closed. 'Just shut up.'

Alex was surprised. He knew that whatever faults Jack Grant had, he was a great listener and that it was to his closest adviser and friend that he listened the most. Impatience such as this was so rare that Alex knew it would be foolish to make light of it.

The President opened his eyes, their redness suggesting another sleepless night. 'I want you to tell me what you would do if I was guilty of these charges,' he said.

'I'd take advice from Bob,' Alex replied.

'Forget what counsel would say,' the President snapped. 'I want to know how you *personally* would package a President guilty of turning a blind eye to Bolivian drug dealers.'

Alex paused, trying to read the President's face. Was this a confession? Was there truth to Cochabamba? The Director of Communications thought long and hard about his reply, wondering whether his future would depend on it. At last he answered, saying, 'I would consider it my duty to tell the truth, Jack. Whatever the price.'

Grant nodded. 'But say you didn't feel so honest. How would you package me to look as good as I could?'

Alex laughed a little, to ease the tension he felt inside. 'I'd suggest we dismiss the charges as scurrilous and focus on your agenda.'

'Thank you.'

The President stood slowly and, picking up a large paperweight as he passed his desk, he moved to stand by the heavily armoured window that looked onto the clipped tailoring of the Rose Garden. He began to toss the weight from hand to hand. 'Now can you tell me,' he said with his back to Alex, 'the difference between that response and the way you are in fact handling this problem, knowing that I'm a completely innocent man?'

'Jack, come on – we've all agreed that the most mature option is to let this one burn itself out. If we stay focused on important issues, the media will come into line.'

'Not if they're out to break my balls,' Jack Grant said, turning to slam the paperweight onto the surface of his desk. He returned to the centre of the room, to stand on the seal woven into the large blue and yellow rug. 'I've been hearing this for six weeks and I don't see any burn-out. Is this a burn-out?' He picked up the latest issue of *Time*, the cover of which showed a White House constructed from gleaming bricks of cocaine. 'Do you call a ten-point drop in my rating a burn-out? Because if you do, Alex, then I'm afraid we don't see eye to eye any more.'

'To be fair, Jack, it's really out of my hands if the media won't let go.'

The President sat again and drew his chair even closer to Alex. He looked worn out and the dark bags beneath his eyes seemed a permanent feature on a face that had aged years in the months since his inauguration. He spoke as if he was explaining an ethical dilemma to an eight-year-old.

'When I was at UCLA I had a football coach called Brad Thomas. I played tight end, as you know, and I didn't much care for our quarterback, so whenever I didn't connect with a pass that maybe I should have held, I used to fire off at him and accuse him of missing the sweet spot. And it was my coach, Brad Thomas, who made me understand that my duty was to catch that football. Period. That was why I was on the field. So if the pass wasn't perfect then I had to leap higher or run faster or time myself better. *You* are not doing that, Al. You are letting too many people intercept when the ball should be in your hands. And they're scoring so many touchdowns that soon we'll be out of the game. Now I cannot let that happen, and I'm not going to. I made a promise to the people of America. Not many people get the chance to say that. Even fewer mean it. But I intend to keep my word even if I have to make some tough and painful decisions in doing just that. Am I making myself absolutely clear to you?'

'Yes, Mr President.'

The President laid a hand on Alex's shoulder. Alex felt this was less a pat of reassurance than a confirmation from Grant to himself that he wasn't alone. He was being worn down by Cochabamba and by his failure to break the deadlock in Congress. As a friend, Alex hated to see it happen. As an adviser, he was becoming desperate to find a way to help.

'Now, let's see if we can't get something positive going out there,' the President said. 'Because I need a touchdown more than you can imagine, Al.'

This was the closest Jack Grant would come to threatening his friend, and Alex knew it. It was a final warning that, if things didn't improve, if the President's approval rating didn't start to climb, and soon, then Alex Lubotsky would be out of the job he'd dreamed of for as long as he could recall.

Vince Moscardini rarely sat down but now, travelling in the back of a New York cab, he had no choice. His lifeline was the mobile phone he kept for ever by his side. This call, to UBC's Vice President of Daytime TV, had been made when he was still on the sidewalk hailing a cab. He was jabbering as fast as ever. 'Am I allowed one word in here, Anne-Marie? Jesus! I'm talking ratings too. But what I'm saying, what I've been trying to say since,' he glanced out of the window, 'since 78th Street, is that Lanny Mason is as ugly as chicken-shit. He'll murder the ratings.'

'He was a hit in *General Hospital*, Vincent. You know that.'

'Before the knife, right? Before the lift. Now look at the guy. It's spooky. I mean, who did his surgery? Stevie Wonder?'

Anne-Marie Stillinger was beginning to despair. Since *Unto the Skies* had begun its slump in the ratings, the production team had been at each other's throats. One of the main problems was that all decisions were made by committee, and it was almost impossible to make everyone agree. New ideas were almost always stamped on, if not by the Executive Producer then by the headwriter, or by Standards and Practices, or by the PR division of Gardner and Hyde Productions. Even Anne-Marie had felt obliged to veto some suggestions on behalf of UBC. Now, though, it was only Vince Moscardini who was objecting to the hiring of veteran actor Lanny Mason as a new non-contract player.

Anne-Marie tried a new tack. 'Apparently Bernie Hermann loved what Lanny did,' she said.

'Bernie Hermann is dead, OK? I'm not Bernie. I'm tired of everything being Bernie this, Bernie that.'

'He had a knack for picking the right actors, Vince. You shouldn't forget who he found in Chinatown.'

Vince tapped a cigarette out of its pack and lit up, ignoring the NO SMOKING sign in the cab. 'Am I,' he asked, speaking slowly for a change, 'or am I not the Executive Producer of *Unto the Skies*?'

'Yes, Vince, you are.'

'OK. So can someone let me do my job? Because I get the feeling there's so many cooks in my kitchen we could feed the five thousand.'

'Didn't Jesus do that on his own?'

'Maybe, but he had the network on his side.'

The cab was slowing. Vince flicked the cigarette through the open window before fishing in his pocket for his gold money clip. 'I'm at the studio,' he told Anne-Marie. 'I'll call back.'

The driver twisted his head around. He was in his late thirties, blond, attractive. 'Excuse me,' he said, 'I'm an actor. You work on this show, right?'

'There's a ten,' Vince said in reply.

The driver took the money and handed his headshot to Vince along with the cab receipt. 'If ever you need . . .'

'Save your breath,' said Vince, sliding across the torn seat to the door. He tossed the headshot back into the cab. 'My guess is I'll be hiring removal men, not talent.'

Unto the Skies was taped five days a week, fifty-one weeks a year on the eighth floor of a building on 53rd Street on the east side of Manhattan. The production offices were on the seventh floor, their command centre Vince Moscardini's office, close to a reception area adorned with framed stills of momentous scenes from the show's history. As Vince passed through reception he saw his young co-producer, David Kellis. Grabbing him by the arm, he marched him into the office. Dave, accustomed to the producer's capriciousness, munched unconcerned on his honey-dip doughnut.

Vince lit up another cigarette, angrily snapping shut the metal lid of his Zippo lighter before saying, 'What I need to know, David, is who suggested that second-hand, third-rate douchebag Lanny Mason for a part on my show.'

'I don't know, boss.'

'Don't *boss* me!'

Vince threw his jacket onto the long leather couch and opened a concealed cupboard in the wall. He poured himself a black coffee from the overworked filter machine. 'I've got a show in a nose dive and some asshole wants a lush like Mason at the controls? This isn't Aeroflot. I should be thinking about ratings, for Christ's sakes, not ideas. Our ratings used to be like gold dust. Now what have we got?'

'Five point four.'

'Five point four. Exactly.' Vince picked up his phone receiver. 'We're crash landing, you know that? If we don't do someth—'

There was a quick rap on the door and the show's casting director popped her head into the room.

'Vince, can I . . .'

'You!' snapped Vince as he slammed the phone down. 'I need to talk to you, Cathy.'

'But I've got . . .'

'Say your prayers because . . .'

'Vince, please!' Cathy opened the door wider. A tall, slender man in his sixties with brilliant white teeth and highlighted hair was standing behind her in a sports coat and cravat. 'Lanny Mason dropped by and wanted a word.'

Vince's eyes flew open in time to see Lanny stepping past Cathy to clamp one of the producer's hands in both of his. 'Good to see you again, Vince,' he oozed. 'Very good to see you. You look well.'

'Lanny Mason?' Vince said, taking a step back to get a clearer look. 'Is that really you? My God, you look – what can I say?' He shot a glance at Dave and slithered out his tongue to wet his lips. 'You look a cut above the rest.'

'You're too kind.'

Vince jabbed a finger into Lanny's muscular abdomen.

'Don't I know it. So, Lanny, what can I do you for?'

Cathy stepped in. 'Did you get a chance to see Lanny's guest appearance on *Murder, She Wrote*?'

'You know what?' Vince said, 'I missed that.'

Lanny reached into the satchel he was carrying over his shoulder. 'I brought you a tape, just in case.'

'You did? That's great.' Vince fixed an arm around Lanny's shoulders and walked him to the door. 'Problem is I'm snowed under like Alaska at Christmas. So what I'm going to do is take a look at the tape and then I'm going to get back to your agent. OK?'

Lanny's new dentures performed another proud curtain call and he exited.

As Cathy passed Vince, he whispered to her, 'Get rid of that cunt then come see me.' As soon as they'd gone, Vince hurled the tape into the bin and loosened his tie. 'David, I want you on time for today's two o'clock. Everyone's coming, right?'

'No. Your favourite headwriter called to say he couldn't make it.'

'What? Are you serious? You know, he thinks the ice is thicker than it is. But he's wearing golf shoes! With spikes on! He should be hearing serious cracking noises. Like the rest of us are.'

'Oh, he's hearing them all right,' Dave said, wiping his hands on a napkin. 'But if you ask me it's not the ice that's cracking up. It's Max.'

When Max Lubotsky had surprised his twin brother with the news that he was on his way to Washington, Alex had been somewhat annoyed. He rarely had the time to take lunch, and when he did he ate in the White House mess, an unappealing dining hall where staff members suffered food cooked by the Navy.

Since his meeting with the President, however, he had been grateful for the excuse to get out of the West Wing. It wasn't a long walk to the Parrot Pub, but it gave him time to think over what Jack Grant had said.

Six weeks had passed since the Cochabamba allegations had first appeared in the *Los Angeles Times*. Alex's response had been to accuse the media of swallowing Republican lies. He expected the story to die. It hadn't, and not least because its plot was so easily understood by a public familiar with such storylines in the movies. In no time rumours, half-truths, accusations and lies had been blown like poppy seeds in the wind. Where they'd settled they'd germinated in fertile ground, to grow anew and reproduce so the truth had had to struggle for light in the shadow of these blossoming stories. Teams of reporters had been despatched to La Paz and Bogotá, Cochabamba and Lima in the hope of substantiating the *LA Times* scoop.

To these men and women, hunting in packs, staying in the same hotels, dealing out sources and gossip from the same pack of trumpless cards, a kind of journalistic nirvana was at stake. Since Nixon, the scalp of a President had become the ultimate prize, and now another chance had arrived. Furthermore, the people and the press, having elected Jack and Susan Grant on promises of moral virginity, had demanded the bloodied sheets to be hung from the balcony and were braying at such deceit. For his part, President Grant was convinced that the Republican press was still sulking about Watergate and had seen, at last, an opportunity for revenge.

To the relief of Alex and a White House staff trusting their jobs on the President's word, the investigative journalists seemed to be digging in barren soil. Yet newspaper editors and proprietors demanded a return on their investments and insisted on daily stories that, in the absence of hard facts, relied wholly on conjecture. The journalists began to report on each other's reports. *Time*'s cocaine-bricked White House cover was in response to a fifteen-page story in *Newsweek*. The TV pundits debated comments made by politicians who themselves were responding to stories that had been based on unsubstantiated sources. The President's character came under the closest scrutiny, with Republicans usually outlining why they believed Jack Grant capable of such crimes even if he hadn't committed them. In short, the media were having a party, leaving the President to pick up the tab.

When Alex reached the pub he had decided that the only option was to go on the offensive. The time had come to get dirty.

The pub was poorly lit by greasy fluorescent bulbs lined up behind the bar and glass lamps that spread across the walls a deathly glimmer. At first, Alex thought that Max must be late too. Yet as he approached the end of the room he realised that a man he'd dismissed as a stranger was his own twin. He smiled, to cover the surprise.

Though it had only been a year since the two had seen one another, the change in Max was marked. It wasn't merely that the thirty pounds he'd gained had aged him, nor that his shoulders were rounded and tired – even the pale skin and puffy eyes could be attributed to hard work without holiday. No, there was something more alarming and less definable to his aspect, a hollowness, a sense that his spirit had collapsed like a sandcastle beneath a wave. Of the two, Alex had always been the more athletic and physically self-confident, but Max had remained only a half-step behind and had never been lacking in vigour. Now he didn't even notice his brother until Alex was almost upon him.

'I'm sorry I'm late,' Alex said, shaking Max's hand. 'You want a beer?'

Max lifted his glass. 'Scotch, thanks.'

'At lunch?' asked Alex with some concern, for there'd been a period, not many years before, when Max had struggled to control his drinking. Although he had won the battle without becoming teetotal, there remained the danger that he might sink back again.

'Relax!' Max said. 'I'm on holiday today.'

They ordered food too, fries and pies that arrived pallid and limp from losing a battle with microwaves, and small-talked about Max's kids, Robbie and Matt, while he finished his drink and bought another, a double this time.

After a while, Alex said, 'Are you here researching for the show?'

'No, I came to see you. Is that so odd?'

'No. Well, yes! I mean, your timing is odd. I'm coming for Thanksgiving, aren't I?'

'I wasn't sure you'd make it. I'd like you to.'

'Well, sure! It's all planned. Anyway, I'm looking forward to seeing the new house. It'll be good to see Pam and the boys too.'

Ten years before, Max had surprised everyone by giving up his tongue-drooling chase after tits and ass. He'd fallen in love with an academic, now tenured at Princeton University, and the two had married within six months.

'Oh, Pam said to ask if you wanted to bring anyone. She says she won't believe you're single.'

Alex flicked the hair from his forehead and looked about him to see if anyone was listening. It was a new habit, a side-effect of his fame.

'Tell her I'm too busy for romance.'

Max pushed his plate to the side and spoke without looking up. 'You need to find someone, Al. I'd have liked that.'

'Hey,' Alex responded, laughing. 'Thanks for giving up on me! There's plenty of time.'

'Is there?'

'Of course. We're only forty-two.'

The answer seemed to satisfy Max and he leant back in the cubicle. With eyes down, he ran a finger slowly around the rim of his glass before downing the rest of his whisky. Alex had no need for a twin brother's intuition to see that something was wrong. He leant on his forearms across the table and, his voice lowered, asked, 'Is there something going on between you and Pam?'

'No, of course not. She's being wonderful, as ever.'

'How's everything on *Unto the Skies*?'

'Do you ever watch it?'

'I don't have the time, I . . .'

'You used to, Al,' Max said, avoiding his brother's eyes. 'Then again, a lot of people used to watch who don't any more. The latest rating has us down to 5.4.'

Alex began to laugh.

'It's not funny,' Max complained, his lips tightening. 'It really isn't.'

'I was thinking we could join forces,' said Alex, laughing vigorously, though Max was yet to smile. 'Jack could appear on *Unto the Skies* talking about drugs, you'd get record figures, and we'd kill two birds with one stone.'

This excited Max. 'You think he'd do it?'

'What?' said Alex, wiping a tear from the corner of his eye.

'Would the President agree?'

'No, of course he wouldn't. It was a joke, Max. Remember them? They're supposed to make you laugh.'

'Why does it have to be a joke? It's a great idea. Those pricks in production keep asking me for sensational stories. We could write the scenes together. Like old times.'

Alex rested his chin on his hand and smiled. 'That was fun, wasn't it? Writing those plays together? When do you think you'll get back to the serious stuff?'

Max stiffened in his seat. 'What do you mean, "get back to serious stuff"?' he asked coldly. 'I write serious stuff for sixteen hours a day. Jesus!'

'Hey, Max, cool it! Why are you being so touchy?'

'Because it bothers me,' he retorted sharply. 'I'm sorry we're not all holding hands with the President, but what I do, Alex, is change the lives of five million fans every day. I call that serious writing.'

'But it's still only soap opera, isn't it?'

'It's real characters in real situations. If you only bothered to watch it, you . . .'

'Don't give me that! Please. I was only repeating what you used to say. I thought the whole reason for joining *Unto the Skies* was so you could save enough money to buy a house and send the kids to school. You've done that now. You're free.'

'That's a joke! I can hardly take a crap without Vince Moscardini wanting to know why I made it that shape. I don't do what I want, I do what they want.'

'So quit, Max. Look what it's doing to you. You're obviously not happy.'

There was a long silence while Max lit a cigarette with a shaking hand. Then he said, 'I can't.'

'Of course you can.'

Max held his brother's stare. 'No! I can't.' He ran his hand over his forehead in a motion that mirrored Alex's earlier in the day. 'They've got me by the balls, Al. It's why I came down here. I need your help.'

Alex settled back in his seat. 'Go ahead.' He smiled. 'Isn't that what brothers are for?'

2

After a week of dank skies and gibberish from weathermen on how winter's chill had checked in to stay, the morning sun felt warm and welcome on Annie Marin's face as she completed her climb to San Francisco's Pacific Heights. She was one of thirty actors in a firm called Curtain Call who visited and cared for elderly residents in the more expensive neighbourhoods of the city. Though few of the firm's staff had skills in nursing, they all shared frequent bouts of unemployment as well as the ability to turn on sunny dispositions for lonely people. For their good wages they would cook and clean and chat and when one actor landed a part, another would take over.

Annie rang the doorbell of the rambling old house on Broadway that belonged to one of the most cantankerous of Curtain Call's clients. Mrs Dorothy was a small, wiry woman, with thinning hair and sharp eyes, who liked to dress in her dead husband's clothes.

'I thought you would be late as usual,' the old lady said now, 'but you're in time.'

'Am I? For what?'

'For the television!'

'I said I'd give the kitchen a good clean today. Remember?'

Mrs Dorothy rapped her cane on the floor. 'I remember! Just because I'm eighty-eight doesn't mean I'm senile, does it? Now, come along.'

Annie followed Mrs Dorothy's slippered clump upstairs. The television looked out of place in the musty room.

The eyelets of the net curtains were clogged with years of dust, the furniture was antique. The centre of the room was filled with a cumbrous, French four-poster bed onto which Mrs Dorothy climbed with her dog.

On UBC there was an ad for baking soda toothpaste, followed by a besuited black man in his early forties seated on a yellow sofa. Given the hour and the oddness of his haircut, he seemed inordinately happy.

'Welcome back to *America's Awake*. All this Thanksgiving week we'll be visiting some of the nation's favourite stars to see how they celebrate this most American of our holidays. Today Lisa Mercado is in the New York home of one of our best-loved daytime drama stars, Faith Valentine.'

'What?' screamed Annie. 'I'm not watching this! I hate her.' She stood. 'You know I hate her.'

'Do be quiet, dear. I want to watch. Now sit down and act your age.'

Annie obeyed. In truth, she was intrigued. She hadn't spoken to Faith since they'd graduated from Cornell Williams though she'd followed her career, reluctantly, whenever the actress had appeared in the news.

In New York, Faith was guiding Lisa Mercado through her ornate Upper East Side apartment. The rooms were as plush as their owner. In the dining room, the table was set four days early for the Thanksgiving feast. In its centre, a collection of fruit and vegetables nestled between the outstretched wings of a giant crystal swan. Either side of it were the same candlesticks that had been used in the wedding between Faith's TV character, Vanessa, and Jamie Sheridan, eldest son of William and heir to the Brendan airline. It was a detail upon which the two ladies lingered.

After commercials for laxatives and against abortions, Faith and Lisa seated themselves either side of a passionate log fire, on velvet-covered cabriolet chairs. With legs crossed, spines upright and tits up and out as if controlled with nipple wires by a lascivious puppeteer, the women mirrored one another.

Lisa functioned first. 'Remind us,' she pleaded, 'how many years you've been with *Unto the Skies*.'

'Almost fifteen, Lisa. Would you believe? I was very fortunate. I was talent-spotted while I was studying at Cornell Williams.'

'They couldn't spot talent on her with the Hubble telescope,' Annie griped.

Lisa Mercado tapped her research notes with a manicured hand and continued. 'Now, Vanessa wasn't originally supposed to be such a large role, was she?'

'No, she wasn't. But something clicked. Do you know what I mean? People love the way she makes them feel.'

'Bernie Hermann loved the way you made *him* feel, more like,' said Annie. 'Stupid cow!'

On camera, Lisa was laughing. 'You know, I was such a fan back then that I wouldn't miss an episode.'

'Oh, thank you. I love to watch, um,' Faith tilted her head and smiled, 'your show.'

'How nice of you to say so.'

'You're very welcome.'

'Christ!' Annie yelled. 'They'll be making out soon. You wait.'

Instead, Lisa wanted to get back to 'the early days'.

'I suppose you could say that *Unto the Skies* has been your training ground,' she said.

'Oh, yes. Absolutely you're right. And you know,' Faith leant forward and patted Lisa's knee, 'it's one of the best trainings an actress can have.'

'It's because you're not an actress,' Annie shrieked at the TV. 'You're a screwing blow-up doll.' She turned to look at Mrs Dorothy. 'Do you know what I was doing? I was touring. Boston, Denver, Miami, Buffalo, Cleveland, Kalamazoo, Nashville, Little Rock, Baton

Rouge, Birmingham, Reno, Albu-effing-querque, you name it, I was there. Acting! All she can do is move her lips.'

'Your bitterness is ugly, Annie.'

'I'm not bitter. I'm disgusted. She disgusts me.'

Annie stomped to the door. 'I wouldn't sink to her level for all the tea in China. In the world,' she said, hovering just inside the room.

Faith was talking about her two little angels, the children from her marriage to song lyricist Ned Hooper, and of the struggle she faced bringing up kids and keeping a full-time career. Family, she proclaimed, was as important to her as it was to Vanessa on the soap. 'The writers think of me when they work on my part. Do you follow? Vanessa and I have grown so very close over the years.'

'I've often wondered,' said Lisa, wrapping her face in benign curiosity, 'if you yourself have any say in how your character develops.'

'Well our headwriter, that's Max Lubotsky, who is a dear, dear friend of mine, and . . .' She paused, and smiled again. 'Where was I?'

'You were talking about your relationship with the writers.'

'Oh, yes. I, in fact, was responsible for getting Max on the show, so he and I, we do discuss many things. But in the end, Lisa, I am an actress. Are you with me? And actresses act! We make parts suit us, however they're written.'

'Can you see yourself maybe branching out in the future?'

'Oh, yes! And I mean it when I say that. I'm hoping,' she crossed her fingers and held them up to the camera, 'I'm hoping to realise my dream of performing Shakespeare in the Park next season with *Romeo and Juliet*. I was approached by . . .'

'That's it,' said Annie. 'I'll be in the kitchen.'

She stormed from the room and down the back stairs,

leaving Mrs Dorothy chuckling to herself. Annie stood in the middle of the kitchen and folded her arms. 'Stupid bitch!' she said out loud. 'Shakespeare in the Park? That's a joke. *I* should be doing Shakespeare in the Park. My Ophelia got great reviews.'

She poured herself a shot of Jim Beam, choked at its sharpness and picked up the receiver of the old phone fixed to the wall. She dialled her agent's number.

'Sam? It's Annie . . . Yes, I am at Miss Havisham's. Ha fucking ha. Listen we need to talk. I think . . .' She stopped. 'Really? A Zoë Dunlop movie? When's the audition? Next Wednesday? Oh sure, I'll go. Thanks, that's great. You know something, Sammy? I've got a hunch about this one. Yeah, I do. I think it's got my name all over it.'

There were five people in the Executive Producer's office: Vince Moscardini himself, headwriter Max Lubotsky, Paul Roberts from Gardner and Hyde, Anne-Marie from the network and Cathy from casting. It was the Tuesday before Thanksgiving and they were looking for a miracle.

Vince was more edgy than usual. On the advice of his doctor he'd taken to wearing a nicotine patch. He loved it, for if he continued to smoke as before he could now enjoy twice as much nicotine. So impressed was he by this stimulant that he'd also bought some caffeine supplements to take with coffee. Times as desperate as these demanded desperate measures and, while other executives succumbed to the cool hand of Valium, Vince was determined to push his body to its limit. Tranquillisers could come later, when the war had been won or lost.

'Who saw Faith with that dumb bitch Mercado?' he asked.

A few had. They all agreed that it had been a good network decision to get her on the show.

'Of course it was,' Vince agreed. 'That's why it's a

mystery I have to go to war with UBC whenever I want publicity. We're supposed to be on the same side.'

Anne-Marie was looking very eighties today, with her shiny, shoulder-length, henna-tinted hair and her navy business suit. She said, 'We think the show needs to prove it can stand up without our help.'

'It's been standing for thirty years. You're treating us like we're still in diapers.'

Paul Roberts, who as supervising producer sat in on the creative decision-making meetings of all G&H soap operas, was a soft-spoken man in his late thirties. The slight protuberance of his front teeth gave him a belea-guered air, and he liked to keep himself to himself. He wore thin-framed glasses and had a habit of arriving at the meetings with a thick pile of notes that he kept in an open folder on his lap. As Vince paced about the office he would try to peer over Paul's shoulders, but Paul was wise to the trick and kept what he could close to his chest.

'We agree with the network,' he said, 'in thinking you can't save a marriage by smiling for the cameras.'

'Thank you for that,' Vince said sarcastically. 'I'm a much wiser man. Still, an iota of support once in a while would be nice. Now, Max, what can you do to support me?'

Max pushed himself up in the couch. He could think of a million and one places he'd rather be than here, trying once again to plead for his own particular vision. 'I've been looking at ways of going deeper into the relationship between Vanessa and William. I feel there's a logic to someone finding their husband's father attractive.'

Vince butted in. 'So long as you're looking at ways of William going deeper into Vanessa, I'm happy.'

Max continued, 'I don't know where the story's leading, but Vanessa's always seen William as a father figure, and it would be interesting to see what would arise if her feelings became more complicated.'

'I see something of William's arising, yeah?' asked Vince with a laugh. 'In the bedroom.'

There was agreement that here was a story with potential. Max was surprised. The fight was usually harder. Encouraged, he continued. 'I also think that in advance of Paolo getting released from jail, we should have Carrie complicating her feelings towards him by becoming interested in another person.'

'This is beautiful,' Vince said with a clap of his hands, 'I like this.'

Paolo Lunardi, played by the debonair Stefano Benedetti, was a favourite among the female fans of the show. The character was a renegade, a pilot for Brendan Air who'd been arrested for drug smuggling and thrown into jail in the most sensational of the stories in the previous year. His wife, Carrie, had been traumatised by the trial and had fallen into a sudden coma when the verdict had been announced. The fans had been outraged and so, slowly and surely, she had returned to consciousness. By October, her recovery was complete but for one telling detail. Carrie Lunardi's memory was submerged in total amnesia.

The casting director, Cathy, wanted to know who Max had in mind for Carrie's lover.

'I thought her sister,' the writer proclaimed.

Vince almost spat his coffee over the carpet.

'You need help, Max. Believe me, you do.'

Anne-Marie was laughing. 'I'm not sure we're ready for lesbianism and incest at the same time.'

'Everyone's doing it,' said Cathy. 'Dykes are red hot right now.'

Vince licked a finger and made a hissing noise when he held it in the air. 'I don't mind it being hot. I like hot. But it's sick. S-i-k.'

'It's got a c in it,' Paul said quietly. 'But the idea wouldn't fly with my people, anyway.'

'I like the triangle,' said Anne-Marie, wanting to be conciliatory. 'Very much. But couldn't it do with being a little more subtle?'

Max drummed his fingertips against his lips and closed his eyes. 'Can somebody tell me what I have to write to please you all?' In the silence, he opened his eyes. 'Or is there going to be a problem with everything I do, because if that's the case I may as well give up.'

'Hey Maxy, Maxy, Max,' Vince said. 'This is talk time. Don't make it so personal. Only remember who's watching. Not everyone likes lesbians as much as we do.'

'But they weren't going to consummate their love, Vince,' Max said, his voice raised in anger. 'The point I was hoping to make was that if you have your memory wiped out, if you completely forget who you are then who's to say you wouldn't fall in love with someone very close to you? And maybe, *maybe*, even someone of your own sex? It's a fascinating idea.'

'Max, Darlene in Des Moines isn't going to like it. She wants Carrie to have a better man than Paolo, someone who'll give her a child and a great sex life. Why does it always have to be so complicated with you?'

'Because life is complicated.'

'And we're supposed to provide the answers,' said Paul, with a little toothy smile.

'No,' said Max, 'soap powder provides solutions. Soap drama should provide conflict.'

'Exactly,' Paul agreed, 'conflict that gets resolved in the same easy way that G&H powders clean dirty laundry.'

'Sure, but . . .'

'Can somebody tell me when this fucking symposium's ending?' cried out Vince, walking between the two men. 'What's there to talk about? No way is Carrie about to get laid by her sister. Period. Now, where are we headed with the court battle?'

The court battle was the latest instalment in the war

between the Sheridans and the Brenners over Brendan Air. The rivalry between the families had been the show's main theme since its inception, the rift becoming as deep as anything the Capulets and Montagues had known.

'I've done some work on this,' said Max. 'And I think William would be happy to give up the international routes to the Brenners . . .'

'Forget it,' interrupted Vince.

'Excuse me?' said Max, anger reddening his cheeks.

'Forget it,' said Vince. 'I don't like it.'

'You haven't heard what I've got to say.'

'It's not sexy, Max. You've got to start understanding that. There's nothing sexy about people settling out of court. Capisce?'

Whether the expression on Max's face was one of hatred or incomprehension, it was hard to tell, yet its severity sobered the mood. 'Why don't you write it then?' he said.

With tennis-match eyes, the others waited for Vince's reply. He laughed. 'Maybe I will.'

'Do that then,' Max shouted, rising to his feet. He threw his legal pad against Vince's chest. 'Write the fucking thing. I don't want anything more to do with this circus.'

'Maxy! Max. What are you doing?' Vince asked. 'Don't forget our little agreement!'

Ignoring him, Max walked to the door.

'Hey, people,' said Vince, trying to lighten the mood, 'what's he doing?'

'Escaping,' whispered Max as, feeling quite light-headed, he walked out of the room and away from the show that had been his life for the previous eight years.

'Jerry,' Annie called out, 'are you going to be much longer?'

From within the bathroom, Jerry grunted. Annie returned to the bedroom mirror. Beside her on the floor lay a heap of clothes yanked from the wardrobe in her desperation to find the perfect outfit for today's movie audition. Dressing for the role of a TV newscaster should have been easy, but when the director was the infamous feminist Zoë Dunlop, nothing, but nothing, was easy.

Zoë was a British director who had become a media darling with the release of *Tarts*, a Thelma and Louise tale about two ageing prostitutes visiting the wives of their most regular clients. Though a comedy, *Tarts* was heralded as the first major motion picture to show prostitution as it is, genital warts and all, and not as Hollywood wants it to be. Zoë was crowned a feminist queen, and whenever the role of 'women in the arts' was discussed, in print or on TV, she was wheeled out to add her voice to the debate.

'You'd better wear a nose ring, or something,' Annie's agent had joked.

Annie wasn't so sure. Feminists had been getting so glamorous recently. Just the week before she had seen Charlie Canon, the new feminist star, on a chat show, and all the time she'd been thinking how silky and thick Charlie's hair looked, and that she had nice breasts. What the feminist had said was anybody's guess.

'Jerry!' Annie banged on the door. 'Please, I've got to go soon.'

The door opened. Jerry was naked. For a forty-four-year-old he had a remarkably firm body, if a little on the skinny side. He kept supple through yoga and thin through dieting on macrobiotic food while Annie plundered the freezers of the Marina Safeway for Ben and Jerry's ice-cream. Annie complained that her lover went too far, that he had even lost girth from his penis, but her friends assured her that this was impossible and that she was simply yearning for a change.

'What do you think?' she said now, spinning for Jerry in the leggings and turtleneck beige sweater she had

54

eventually chosen. 'I think it's kind of male *and* female. Don't you?'

'So long as you're happy in yourself, babe,' Jerry answered, scratching at his pubic hair.

Happy! Sometimes Annie wondered what it would take to make her happy. Turning the clock back to the days when she and Jerry had truly been in love would surely be a start. Their passion had seemed so permanent then. Jerry had been her world. His uncomplicated acceptance of life's travesties had been a much-needed antidote to the sense of gloom that had infected Annie at the start of her third decade. Through him she had rediscovered a love of life that had been lost under the mountain of missed opportunities and unfulfilled goals. Even his lack of interest in her acting career (he disapproved of a profession that, to his mind, relied on self-aggrandisement and selfishness), *even that* had seemed a kind of liberation from the world she was used to inhabiting. The new perspective that Jerry had given her had made her feel as if she'd lived her first thirty years with eyes half-closed, and the more he'd helped her open them, the more she had fallen in love.

And now? Now she felt that she'd opened her eyes too wide. She saw more of this man than she wanted, so that only his faults were visible. She even hated following him into the bathroom in the mornings. She hated brushing her teeth in the minty, shit-tinged stench he left hanging in the shower's steam. The notion that she was filling her mouth and lungs with these vapours bothered her and made her wonder whether she was left with fetid breath for the rest of the day.

By the time she had applied her light make-up, Jerry was dressed and ready to leave for work. There was a small suitcase by his side. 'Have you found something to do tomorrow?' he asked. 'You could probably still come.'

'To your parents? No, I'll be fine.'

He shrugged his shoulders, not because he didn't care but because he didn't want to argue. At the door he wished her a happy Thanksgiving and kissed the air.

'Same to you,' she said as she watched him go. As the door closed behind him, she whispered, 'Wish me luck!' because he'd forgotten to, yet again.

From the window, Annie watched her lover walk down the hill. Often, now, she wondered what would have happened if he hadn't spotted her on that day five years before.

They'd met by chance. During rehearsals at the Exit Theater for a play about San Francisco in the sixties, she had nipped out of the theatre, in costume, to buy juice from the deli. Jerry, himself a child of that era, had fallen instantly in love with this creature after his own heart, and with the assured spontaneity of a recently converted Buddhist he'd approached her and asked her out to dinner at a place of her choice. It was not until later, when she had already begun to fall in love, that Jerry revealed that he'd liked the kaftan before its owner. At the time, Annie had thought this admission lovably quirky and honest. Now she wondered why she hadn't seen the confusion as a warning. Instead, she had done what she could to change herself into what she'd first seemed to be.

Now, at thirty-five, she wondered how she seemed to the world out on those streets. What would Zoë Dunlop think? Annie had lost most of her pride in herself. It upset her to look in the mirror, and she gazed with envy at the women on TV who seemed so perfect by comparison. Annie had thought that breasts so unspectacular wouldn't sag like tired helium balloons, and hips so slender should not have widened, nor should her buttocks have become lumpy and full. Though she had taken to Stairmasters and aerobics classes, her body seemed stubborn in its pursuit of decay and she didn't feel shaped-up at all, though Jerry said she looked better than before. 'More of a woman' had been his words, said as a compliment but taken as an insult, because Annie wished to remain a child. A child, at least, until she had children of her own. *If* she had children of her own. Jerry wouldn't talk about it, and the journey to that point with another man seemed impossibly remote.

She looked at her watch as if suddenly conscious of the draining sands. It was half past nine, time to go. Grabbing her pages from the script of *The Fur Bites Back*, she took a long, careful look at the apartment, knowing how much brighter it would seem if she was to return with a movie role assured. She closed her eyes and when she said a silent prayer, something mysterious sounded within her and made her believe that maybe this was the chance she had been waiting for, and that from today she could begin a new and better chapter in her life.

3

It wasn't easy to have an affair when always being watched, yet Alex's friendship with Susan Grant had been well established before they'd become lovers, and he was afforded considerable access to the First Lady without rumours and gossip being born. Even so, today was a rare treat, for they were in New York, alone in a hotel bedroom before a dinner in Susan's honour.

The First Lady was in Manhattan talking to city and state officials about the Education Bill that was her baby. She was accompanied by Alex because her appearances had become increasingly important to the Administration itself. As someone not implicated in Cochabamba, Susan was being used to put presidential policies back where they belonged, on the nation's front pages.

Of course, if the journalists could have seen the First Lady as she was now, she'd have made every front page in the world. She was kneeling on the bed, a bathrobe pushed up her back while Alex, trousers off but with his shirt, socks and tie still on, screwed her fiercely from behind.

'Alex,' she said.

'What?' he whispered with heavy breath.

'I'm going to run.'

'Me too,' he replied, happy to release himself now.

He pushed in as deep as he could and when he came the feeling shuddered through him from head to foot. His orgasms were always this intense with Susan, and they left his body feeling loose and pleased with itself.

He withdrew and, wincing as he snagged a pubic hair in the torturous rubber condom, flushed the evidence away before returning to his lover. She was lying on her back, the robe open. Though the two of them had made love many times, Alex could count on one hand how often he had seen her like this, as if she belonged to him, as if he could climb on her again and take his time with her body. Now he stroked a hand over her breasts and stomach and lowered his head to kiss the soft flesh of her belly.

'Better get dressed,' he whispered.

Susan sat up. 'What did you mean by "me too", Al? That you'd help me?'

'What?'

'When I told you I wanted to run, that's what you said. Me too.'

'I thought you were coming,' he said. Talking like this, because it was so rare between them, made him feel ill at ease. He stood. 'I thought that's what you said. What do you mean, you want to run?'

She climbed off the bed and slid the robe from her shoulders, surprising Alex with an embrace. He couldn't understand why she was being so casual. If they were caught now, their careers would be ruined. Susan lifted herself on her toes and kissed his ear.

'For the presidency, Al. I want to run in '96.'

Alex gripped her arms and pushed her back a step. He looked at her in complete amazement. 'That's insane! Jack will never step aside.'

'He's going to have to,' Susan said. 'He's guilty.'

Though Alex heard the words he said nothing. Instead, he entered the bathroom to collect Susan's clothes.

'Get dressed, will you?' he said, handing them to her. 'Mary could be here any minute.'

'Weren't you listening? Jack took hush money.'

Alex began to smoothe the wrinkled bedspread as if he wished to sleek away the hell that was Cochabamba.

He had never questioned the President's innocence, not seriously. There was something childish about the scandal. It was the stuff of an absurd Jeffrey Archer thriller and besides, Jack was a supreme politician. Alex couldn't imagine that Grant would have jeopardised his political future for mere dollars. He had always assumed that only the media were guilty.

At last, he looked at Susan. 'How do you know?'

'Just take it that I know.'

When Susan was dressed Alex regained some of his confidence. The two of them sat at a table over which they'd spread some papers before making love. Still, he found it hard to meet her eye. He didn't want to see her revel in the demise of the man in whom Alex had invested his faith.

'Let me get this straight,' Alex began. 'You are seriously thinking about a nomination?'

'Absolutely.'

He poured a tiny can of Coke into a glass and onto cubes of ice that babbled and cracked with surprise. 'Have you mentioned it to Jack?'

The bubbles prickled against his lip as he drank.

'No, you're the first.' She touched his hand. 'I wanted you to be the first.'

Alex turned her hand in his as if looking for an indication of her fortunes in the lines of its palm. Then he closed it into a fist and gently pushed it towards her.

'I'm sorry,' he said. 'I can't betray Jack.'

Susan snorted a laugh. 'You already have.'

'No!' Alex's stare revealed his self-belief. 'Never. Not professionally.'

'Just personally, and that's forgivable, is it? That's excusable.'

Having asked himself the same question at the start of the affair, Alex already knew his answer. 'Given Jack's history in that department, I think it is. What would not be excusable is if I turned my back on him after all these years and tried to destroy him because I felt I owed you something.'

'Fuck you, Al,' she said quietly but with some venom. 'Neither of you would be in the White House if it wasn't for me.'

'Bull! Jack was *always* going to be President.' Alex stood and walked away from the table. 'Always.'

'So was I. And I will, Al. I will.' She moved to him and flattened a hand against his cheek, knowing that he felt an allegiance to her body and that the well of romance that lay barely touched within him made him vulnerable to such affection. 'I want you with me,' she whispered. She kissed his cheek. 'I need you to show me the way.'

Softly, Alex lifted her hand from his cheek, and pressed his lips to it. 'I will, when the time's right. Maybe as soon as 2000, when Jack's through.' Now when he looked at her there was a familiar glint in his eyes. 'Think about that. The voters will love having a female President to kick off the millennium. *That's* a concept they'll be able to understand, like the decision won't be theirs. We could sell it as Destiny.'

'Come on, Alex! People aren't going to want the same couple in the White House after eight years. You know that. They'll be sick of my wardrobe and dogs and hairstyles and probably everything else. I wouldn't stand a chance in 2000.'

At the window, Alex pulled up the blinds to look out over the city. What would you do, New York, with a female candidate for President? She would probably fly in a place such as this, he thought, where Lady Liberty stood proud and feminine in the harbour. But what about in the South and Midwest? Some of the states there were even finding Susan's present role as First Lady a hard pill to swallow. They would never hand her the keys to the Oval Office.

'OK,' he said, turning, 'let's say you won the nomination. Have you even considered how hard it'd be running for President as the wife of a proven crook? People think of you as a team.'

'But people are never going to know the truth. Jack was too smart. I mean, even you didn't know. Right? And I'm only going to tell the rest of them if he refuses to step aside.' She grinned. 'That's why I can't lose.'

Alex sat on the edge of the bed and looked up at her.

'Would you really do that? Destroy everything we've fought for?'

'I'm not going to destroy anything. There'd be much more chance of throwing everything away if Jack ran again. Think about it, Al,' she urged him, sitting to stroke a hand on his inner thigh. 'We could make history. Real history.' She kissed his lips. 'You and I.'

'And if I say no?'

'Jack would never forgive you.'

'That's a joke,' Alex laughed.

'I meant if I told him about us.'

This hurt. For twelve years, Alex had been Jack Grant's most loyal, supportive aide. He couldn't imagine having to face the President with the truth that he'd been sleeping with his wife. Alex searched Susan's face for a smile, but he saw nothing but the fiercest ambition.

'You wouldn't,' he said.

'Wouldn't I?' she answered. 'Why not?'

As a big-boned and big-breasted member of the British upper class, Zoë Dunlop was an unlikely feminist. Yet it was with a feminist movie, *Tarts*, that she had won acclaim, a prize at the Venice Film Festival and ultimately the financial backing of AFM for *The Fur Bites Back*. The movie was to be filmed in a new studio complex outside San Francisco, and it was to Zoë's apartment in the city that Annie came for her audition at a little after ten in the morning.

She rang the doorbell, and waited. After what seemed an age, Zoë opened the door. Her red hair was in a fuzzy mess, and she was wearing nothing but a long Katherine Hamnett T-shirt and square, black-framed glasses. 'Yes?' she said.

'I got the wrong day, didn't I?' said Annie, rocking back onto her heels.

'Who are you?'

'I'm Annie Marin.' She lifted her copy of the script. 'I'm here for the audition.'

'Oh fuck!' Zoë heaved a great sigh. 'Um, you'd better come in, I suppose.'

The apartment looked hungover. The blinds were half-drawn, like drooping eyelids, and the air was stale from too much smoke and heavy-breathing red wine.

'Do you want some coffee or something?' said Zoë.

'Not if it's any trouble.'

Zoë lit up a Silk Cut and took a drag so deep it was as if she was an asthmatic desperate for relief from her inhaler. She closed her eyes and the thin smoke trailed her words as she spoke. 'I live in hope that one day I'll meet a Californian who can give me a straight answer. Now, would you or would you not like a cup of coffee?'

'I'm fine.'

'That's a no, isn't it?'

Zoë sat down. She wasn't wearing any underwear and Annie got a shaded flash of ginger pubic hair.

'What did you think of the script?' asked the director, her voice deep and croaky.

This wasn't an easy question. *The Fur Bites Back* was a horror film about fur coats coming back to life to seek revenge. The idea was amusing enough, but the story seemed to draw its inspiration from those seventies films in which birds and bees and spiders and bugs discovered new strengths and threatened the planet. Of course, in the end the furs were defeated and it all seemed rather pointless and predictable to Annie, right up to the last frame of an overlooked mink coat warming in a closet, finally discovering its pulse. Annie would not have given the movie a second thought had it not been for Zoë's involvement.

'I thought it could make a good movie in the right hands,' she said.

'Mine?' wondered Zoë.

'Yeah. I loved *Tarts*.'

'That's probably because I wrote it. This, on the other hand,' she grabbed a handful of manuscript pages and tossed them onto the floor, 'is unadulterated crap. Unfortunately, Joel-of-the-tiny-penis Ritchie and I do not see eye to eye on this. Ergo the state of me and my flat.'

'Excuse me?' said Annie.

Zoë rubbed at her eyes, trying to wake them up. 'I did ring your agent, love. I'm sorry if the message didn't get through to you, but I am, as of yesterday, the ex-director of the forthcoming aforementioned movie, blah-di-fucking blah.' She stood and clomped heavily on her bare feet to the small kitchen on the far side of the room. She clicked on the electric kettle and, as she unhinged a cup from a row of hooks, said, 'It wouldn't have taken an Einstein to know what I'd do with *The Fur Bites Back*.'

'What was that?' asked Annie, walking nearer.

Zoë tipped one spoon of coffee and three of sugar into the cup, upon which was a cartoon of a hippopotamus stripping out of a pink tutu. 'It's pretty bloody obvious to anyone with half a brain that the fur, darling, the fur is alluding to the fur between our legs. The little pustule who wrote this probably doesn't even realise that coats coming to life is a fantastic metaphor for women rediscovering their aggressive selves to fight against this prison that man, in collusion with the billion-squillion-dollar beauty and diet businesses, has put us in.'

Looking at Zoë now, unwashed, unaccessorised and

unashamedly dishevelled, Annie thought that the director
had been on the run from the beauty prison for years. The
question remained whether society would serve itself best
by locking her up again.

Zoë continued to rant. 'However, as the last two films
that AFM produced were buddy-buddy action jerk-offs for
Joel and his tiny-penis friends, they didn't like my idea.'

Annie thought it odd to hear these words garnished in an
accent so English. Somehow, it made them forgivable.

'Maybe they were just wanting a regular horror movie,'
she suggested.

'Fine!' Zoë said, the rumble of boiling water echoing
her malaise, 'so they shouldn't have chosen a feminist
director, should they? I still can't believe these people.
They think that because they've got fat wallets in their
back pockets and fat balls in their front they can get
anything they want.'

Zoë suddenly began to scratch her scalp with both
hands, as if she had lice or fleas.

'Do you think you could maybe, I don't know, compromise a little?' Annie asked nervously.

'Listen, love, have you ever tried talking to a man with
an erection?'

'No, I . . .'

'Well, believe me, film producers in LA are walking
erections. If you don't stroke them the way they want,
they'll move on to someone who will.'

'Oh, right!' Annie found herself reverting to the mannerisms of her childhood, as she did, involuntarily, whenever she was embarrassed or publicly confused. Now she
was biting a fingernail on her right hand while her left
arm was clamped across her chest. She swung a little
from side to side as she nibbled. 'I suppose I'd better
be going then.'

'Yeah! Listen, love, I'm sorry you wasted your time. I
promise I'll keep you in mind for next time. OK?'

'OK,' said Annie, failing with a smile before leaving.

She wandered aimlessly down the hill, feeling completely dejected. She'd been so certain she was right for the part but the big break had proved a black hole. She was thirty-five, unmarried, seemingly unemployable and definitely unhappy. Was this really all there was to life?

She thought of Faith Stumpf. What had she done so right that Annie had done wrong? In the end, was it simply a matter of who you slept with? Maybe it was time to start putting out. Only talent between the sheets seemed to be rewarded these days.

Thinking of Faith, she was reminded of Max. He had touched something deep within her. It wasn't simply that her love for him had survived because it had been unconsummated. No, there was more, for he was one of the few people who had made a difference to her life. When considering acting roles, Annie had often tried to judge the opportunity through his eyes. It was as if he'd passed to Annie his own refusal to compromise when he'd abandoned his intent and become a writer of television garbage. It was she who'd stayed true to his principles.

She wondered which one of them had been right. Probably Max! Annie imagined him living a life of luxury with his wife and kids, laughing in the lather of soap opera dollars, while she kept up the struggle to make a difference as they'd promised the world they would. That hope seemed so long ago. As Annie looked across the city and over to the glimmering bay, she thought the only difference that mattered now was that Max Lubotsky was probably very happy while she, of course, was not.

In New York, Alex hired a car and drove to New Jersey, arriving at his brother's home near Princeton by midday. From the elegant white porch of the nineteenth-century house, a large lawn sloped to the banks of the Delaware. In 1777 Washington had crossed this river, handing the

British a surprise defeat not far from where Alex was standing. Wanting to stretch his legs, he sauntered to the river's edge and onto a small jetty floated on oil drums to which a paddle boat was tethered. Crouching down, he lifted the rope to release a scummy cluster of branches and leaves into a current that had been witness to so much history.

Alex himself had wanted, for as long as he could remember, to be a part of that history. Though close with President Grant, he feared their Administration would never be given enough time to see through the policies that could reverse the nation's decline. Time! It was the one thing that the media, with their greedy, selfish love of quick fixes and immediate answers, was loth to provide.

From where he was standing looking out over the wide river, Alex understood the time it had taken to build America and how quickly it was falling apart. He couldn't fathom what was wrong with everyone else. Why couldn't they see that Grant needed time? Nothing concrete would be achieved if he had to run a presidency of feel-good soundbites, if his every utterance was torn apart by partisan and minority interests. Alex wished that every American could be brought to this river to be filled with an interest in what had happened two hundred years before. Maybe then they wouldn't be so obsessed with the previous two hundred minutes. Such impatience, he thought, provided the most unstable of foundations for the future. Making mistakes, as Grant had surely done, was simply a vital part of learning how to get it right.

And yet if Grant had made the mistake of Cochabamba he deserved no more time and patience. Alex had been awake most of the night wondering whether Susan had been telling the truth. If so, then his only hope of carving a significant place in history would rest with her. She had already assured him that if he could get her elected to the presidency, his reward would be a top Cabinet post.

'Are you hiding from me, stranger?'

Alex spun round. Max's wife, Pam, was calling from the porch. By her side were her sons, Robbie, who was seven, and Matt, five. They ran to their uncle, their excited steps rocking the jetty on which he stood.

'Whoa, guys! You want me to fall in?'

'Daddy did, last summer,' said Matt.

Alex picked Matt up, finding it spooky how he'd hogged the Lubotsky genes. Matt looked exactly like the twins had at that age. Now Alex carried him in his arms as he moved back up the lawn, the curled leaves crisp under his feet.

'So, guys, how do you like this place?'

'It's neat,' said Matt.

'He's a cry-baby,' Robbie said. 'He thinks there are ghosts in his room.'

'Do not!' Matt insisted.

'You do too. You said.'

'I'll take a look,' said Alex. 'I can always tell.'

'Can you?' said Matt, obviously impressed.

He stuck his tongue out at his brother. At the porch Alex gave Pam a warm hug, and the kids ran back to their Sega.

'I can't believe you've been here almost a year,' he told her. 'I should have come sooner. It's beautiful.'

'Thanks. You don't look so bad yourself. Running the world obviously suits you.'

'You think so? I thought it was killing me.'

He closed the door slowly, careful with the corn wreath hanging on the knocker for Thanksgiving.

'You look like Max's younger brother now,' she called over her shoulder as she led him through to the big, airy kitchen.

'I am, by a minute.'

The kitchen was decorated with bright green-and-yellow

floral curtains and wallpaper. It extended into a conservatory at the back. The new white units were lit by long rows of miniature spotlights, making it seem like a showroom display. Food lay chopped and prepared on almost every counter. For this one day, gluttony was sanctioned, compulsory even. For Thanksgiving to be a success, families had to stuff themselves so full of turkey that they couldn't move. It was the only way to force them into spending a few hours together.

Alex watched Pam bend down to take a saucepan from a low cupboard by the stove. He realised she wasn't wearing underwear beneath that little blue skirt, and liked what he saw of his brother's wife. It made him think of Susan. Though she and Jack no longer slept together (it was the President himself who'd chosen to share this fact), Alex found himself increasingly jealous. It was disarming. He had never imagined he might actually fall in love with the President's wife.

'Max is picking up my parents,' said Pam. 'He'll be back soon.'

'How's he doing?'

'Oh, he's . . .' she stopped, checking herself. 'He'll be fine.'

Alex sat on one of the pine stools by the counter that divided the eating and cooking areas of the kitchen.

He said, 'Max seemed very edgy when he came down.'

'You make him edgy.'

'I do?' Alex jerked his head back in surprise. 'How?'

With the turkey basted Susan unknotted her apron, helped herself to a cup of coffee, and joined him. 'Oh, being where you are, doing what you're doing. I think Max secretly believed that he'd be the one changing the world!'

'Who knows? He still may, especially now he's escaped from that soap. I suppose he sorted out the money problems, did he?'

'Money? Oh, he refuses to talk to me about that. I think he inherited all those old-fashioned ideas from your dad. You know,' she tipped back in her chair and, holding one of Robbie's crayons in her mouth as if it were a pipe, tried to imitate the old man, 'money is a man's business, son! Max is such a stubborn ass that he forgets that I'm the one who's good with figures. Still,' she said, looking puzzled, 'I thought money was the only thing he *wasn't* worried about. Did he tell you something?'

'No.'

Pam shook the crayon as if she was wagging a finger. 'You're a better liar than Max, but you're still lousy.'

Alex laughed. 'Lucky for me you're not in the White House press corps then. They believe everything I say.'

'You're changing the subject, Al.'

Alex hesitated before saying, 'Why don't you ask him about it? Yeah? I'm sure he didn't want to concern you, that's all.'

Keen to talk of something else, Alex fished from his case the claret he'd brought for dinner. He handed the bottles to Pam, telling her it was the vintage served to Mitterrand on the French President's last visit.

'Thanks. It looks wonderful,' she said, adding, as she placed the bottles by the oven, 'We'll have to make sure Max doesn't hog it to himself.'

'He's not drinking again, is he, Pam?'

At the sink, her back turned to Alex, she said, 'No. I mean, nothing like before. It's just there's something . . . Maybe I shouldn't say.'

'I'm his brother, Pam. Come on!'

'I don't know.' She turned back, wiping her hands on a cloth. 'You know how Max is with you. He's always trying to make everything sound so perfect when you're around. He doesn't want you to think badly of him.'

'When have I ever done that?' The slight whine in his voice made him sound younger.

'Always. You don't notice you're doing it. I don't know. Maybe you two could sort it out. He'd like that. He thinks you don't rate him, Al.'

'God! If anything he was the one who used to make *me* feel small. He was always the smartest.'

'But you got all the girls,' Pam said with a smile.

'He got you, didn't he?' Alex said, flirting with his eyes. 'And look at me. All alone!'

She threw the tea towel at him and he let it land on his head as an admission that his self-pity was largely contrived.

'Alex Lubotsky! You could pick anyone you wanted and she'd be yours.'

'Not true. Not anyone.' He drank from his cup and averted his eyes, thinking of Susan but keen not to be drawn on this subject. 'Did Max tell you what he was going to do now?' he asked.

'No. He's been very quiet.'

'I'll get it out of him. I can't wait to have a talk with him about something other than *Unto the Skies*. He never seemed to be able to walk away.'

'Tell me about it! Can you believe he started calling out the name of one of the characters in his sleep? I thought he was having an affair at first.'

Behind her, Alex heard scampering feet. Matt ran into the kitchen. 'Did you see my room yet, Uncle Alex? It's bigger than the one before, much.'

'The whole place is bigger. It feels almost as big as the White House.'

'Have you been inside the Oval Office?' asked Robbie.

'Sure have.'

'I want to show you my room,' Matt said, pulling his uncle's hand. 'Come on!'

With his arm stretched out to the leaning Matt, Alex said to Pam, 'I won't be long. Then I'll come and give you a hand. That's if Matt doesn't pull it off first!'

She laughed. Alex was glad to see her happy. Sometimes he feared that Max's moodiness brought her down.

'Be as long as you want,' she said. 'Max never has enough time to play with them.'

'He will. Even if I have to make him,' Alex promised as he was tugged away, leaving Pam to prepare the pumpkin pie.

Robbie and Matt gave him a lightning tour of the house. He pronounced Matt's room totally free from ghosts and broke the house rules by peeping round the door of Max's study. In the top-floor playroom, the two brothers sat Alex down to explain the intricacies of their latest computer baseball game. So noisy was it that not one of them heard the car pull into the driveway or the sound of a man at the door. The only thing they heard was the anguish in Pam's terrible scream, and the thud of her body as it fell heavily onto the wooden floor.

Mr Saul Weissman, of Weissman's department store fame, and his wife Patty were longtime friends of song lyricist Ned Hooper, and guests at his table for Thanksgiving dinner. Joining them were Johnson Bell, who played patriarch William Sheridan in *Unto the Skies*, his wife Shirley, Saul's son Nathan, and his wife Liz and Ned's two little angels, Billy and Kim. The hostess was Ned's glamorous wife, Faith. For so few people, they were making an inordinate amount of noise, clamouring to be heard over the clinking of glasses and cutlery and the conversations of others. It was the kind of scene about which jailed men dream.

An eighteen-pound bird with oyster stuffing had been cooked and prepared by the Hoopers' maid, Consuela. Its sumptuous aroma barely overpowered the sickening fog of cologne that Saul Weissman and the rest of the men were wearing. He had brought with him bottles of Eden, the store's new cologne, as Thanksgiving gifts.

'Tell me, Faith,' said Patty Weissman. 'Is everything going well on your TV show?'

Faith patted the corners of her mouth with her napkin and talked more loudly than necessary. 'Well, Max Lubotsky, who was a dear friend, has left the show and we're getting a new headwriter and honestly I'm not too unhappy. I didn't think Max was taking Vanessa as far as she'd like to go.'

'Which is into my bed,' said Johnson Bell languidly.

'That's my wife you're talking about,' complained Ned, holding up his knife in a playful threat.

'Anyway,' continued Faith, her lips tense from the interruptions, 'I'm hoping our new headwriter will bring us into line with the more upbeat shows. We've been around so long we're a little, shall I say, stuck in the mud?'

'Does that mean you need more sex?' asked Nathan.

'She shouldn't have married a man thirty years older than her then,' Saul Weissman said.

'I meant on the show, Dad,' Nathan explained, his voice laden with disapproval.

'And Billy and Kim don't like to hear such language. Do you?' asked Patty.

Billy, the seven-year-old, had his hair greased back for the day and was wearing a grey suit and red bow tie. He shrugged his shoulders. 'We've seen it all on the soap. We watch it with Consuela when Mom's out. I have to tell Kim what they're doing when they get into bed. It's funny.'

'She knows it's only play-acting,' Faith told Mrs Weissman while stroking her daughter's cheek. 'Don't you, darling?'

'Mom was in bed with that Italian man,' Kim announced.

Johnson Bell touched Liz Weissman on the arm and, in his luxuriant voice, said, 'Paolo Lunardi is our resident stud. He's tempted all the female characters under the covers except,' Johnson looked confused, 'except, I thought, Vanessa.'

'Mom was in bed with that Italian man,' Kim said again.

'They know that!' said Faith sternly, pushing her daughter's plate closer to her. 'Now finish your vegetables or you won't get any pecan pie.'

Kim giggled and hid her face behind her hand. 'You told me not to tell Daddy before.'

At once, the smile slid off Ned Hooper's face.

'Kimberley gets very confused,' said Faith. 'Don't you, darling? When you see me on TV.'

'Nope, don't, don't, don't.'

Faith laughed and shook her hair. 'Sometimes I think I shouldn't be letting her watch! Too young,' she mouthed at Patty before clapping her hands to change the subject. 'Now, who's for more turkey?'

'I never say no,' said Saul.

'Nor does my wife,' Ned said. 'By the sound of it.'

'You're a lucky man. Very lucky,' Saul said.

'My wife hasn't said yes since Nate was born. Or do I mean conceived?'

'He gets worse every year,' Patty told Shirley.

'How do you know?' Saul said. 'You never try me.'

Throughout this, Ned and Faith, at opposite ends of the table, were staring at each other in silence.

At last, Faith broke the stare and said, 'Please help yourselves, everyone. There's so much food here, and I do want everyone to have a good time. Neddy, dear, can I give you any more?'

'No,' he said. 'Why don't you go on giving it to everyone else instead.'

In her quiet apartment on Leavenworth Street, Annie flipped through her phone book one final time before hurling it across the room. They've all deserted me, she thought. For the first time in her life, she was spending Thanksgiving alone.

She poured herself another vodka, topped it up with orange juice and ice and sat back trying not to think of

turkeys and happier times. In front of her was a crispy
duck that was no longer crispy. She pushed it to one side,
clearing a space onto which she spread the contents of
a bag of fortune cookies she'd had delivered with the
meal. Then, having gripped the vodka bottle between
both hands, she closed her eyes and lifted it above her
head to thump its base hard on the table below.

Brittle fragments of cookie spun in the air and skidded to
the floor. Annie opened her eyes to see two paper fortunes
exposed. *A surprise will titillate and frighten you*, the first
read, *but you will accept it*. Titillate and frighten suggested
a strong stranger with an oversized hard-on. Well, there
was hope in that. The second was less cheering. *Your
sparkle never fades. The party begins when you arrive.*

'Great,' said Annie out loud. 'Some party!'

She dug a fork into the cool rice, took a mouthful, and
tried something new. Again with eyes closed she moved
her outstretched hand over the table, concentrated hard
and then grabbed at a single cookie.

'This one!' she said. She snapped it open and read,
Your energy is at peak. Channel it into fun activities!

'Thanks a lot!'

She stood. The streets were lifeless. All the fun was
being had behind doors closed on happy smiles and
smells and plates laden with succulent turkey and squash
and sweet potatoes and stuffing and carrots and pecan
pie and . . . This was no good. She decided to try
one more cookie to decide her future. She was after
something encouraging such as *The lottery numbers will
come to you* or *Secretly JFK Junior has his eyes on
you and will shortly propose*. She stared long and hard
at the crisp little shells. There was one she thought
looked rather shy at the back, and the corner of its
fortune was peeping through the crack in the pastry.
You! she thought. She grabbed it, snapped it open and
read.

It was a simple promise: *541 is your lucky number*, it said. *Believe in it!*

'Wowee,' said Annie, tossing the fortune aside and thinking that even the cookie gods were against her.

4

Pam Lubotsky had fainted and fallen as soon as the police officer had told her the news. Even now, two days on, she looked barely conscious.

They had been given no satisfying details, simply these bare facts: Max's car, travelling at an estimated seventy miles per hour, had left the road on a corner four miles west of Trenton. Max had died instantly as the car was crumpled against a concrete barrier. The police could only guess that he'd been distracted, lighting a cigarette, fumbling for a CD, peering at something by the roadside. The possibility that he had suffered from cardiac arrest could not, of course, be ruled out before the autopsy, nor could technical failure in the car. The hideous thought that had gripped Alex's heart, however, had not been spoken aloud.

After much debate, the boys had been collected by their aunt and were staying in North Carolina. Alex had remained with Pam. She had not been outside since returning from the hospital. There, with Alex holding her hand, she'd identified Max's body, thinking that she'd never seen his undamaged face looking so serene and calm.

Now she was returning from the mailbox. It had been a traumatic experience opening Max's post the day before. The way in which the correspondents had addressed him in the present tense, wishing him well and hoping to hear from him soon, served only to deepen the sense of a life ended before its time. Included among the computerised bills and junk mail had been handwritten letters from dedicated *Unto the Skies* fans. Unusually kind in their tone, the knowledge of how pleased they would have made Max had brought tears to Pam's and Alex's eyes.

Now, from an upstairs window, Alex watched her as she flicked through the bundle of mail. Suddenly she stopped walking and all but one of the letters fell from her hand. He saw her rip open the envelope and within seconds she collapsed, the letter still gripped in her fingers. He raced downstairs and into the garden.

'Pam!' he cried out. 'Pam! Are you all right?'

She didn't reply, and when he reached her she had curled into a ball, her eyes open, her breathing erratic.

He knelt down beside her. 'What is it?'

She said nothing but let him help her to her feet and together they walked back into the house, the discarded letters mingling with the scattered leaves. Pam was clinging to Alex as if he'd rescued her from quicksand. Her body was shaking and he could feel her tears wet on his neck.

In the house he sat her in an armchair.

'What happened? What is it?' he asked her.

She said nothing, but opened her hand as if surprised she could do so at all. The letter was wrinkled and torn, though when Alex spread it open he noticed that Max's handwriting was characteristically neat.

Pam, you were my dream come true. I will always love you as I love you now. I'm sorry that I let you down. I hate myself for that, and for so many other failings. I tried as best I could. It wasn't enough.

This I know: my fingertips feel raw from clinging, and my nails are ripped back. Heaven will be falling free. I will be smiling. For once you won't have to do that for me. I love you. Smile for yourself now.

Wherever you are, whoever you are with, I will be with you too – happy, only if you are.
Max.

On a separate piece of paper he had added these words:

I don't need to tell you how I treasure the boys. I know they will be all right with you. They are young enough to live with this. I could not have waited longer. They must never understand, never know. I fear contagion in this act, and they <u>must be immune</u>. Destroy this, then. Please. This was an accident.

You will be better without me. In the third drawer of the desk you will find a letter explaining what I owe to whom. The insurance will cover it all, and much more.

If only I'd loved myself half as much as I love you, I would not have been afraid. Forgive me. Please.
Max.

Alex looked at Pam. The blood had drained from her face and her eyes and lips were swollen. A hair was tickling her cheek, stuck there with tears. He lifted it away.

'Why didn't he talk to me?' she whispered, moving nothing but her eyes. 'If he loved me, why didn't he talk to me? Mmm? Why? He wouldn't have done this to me if he'd loved me. Would he? He wouldn't have done this.'

Alex squeezed her hand. 'He did love you. It was himself he didn't love. You knew that when you married him, didn't you? Pam? Didn't you?'

She pulled her hand away and clenched it into a fist. 'But he told me I was enough. He always said I did his smiling for him, he said that made him happy enough. I thought I was helping him. I did, Al. I should have done something more.'

The tears were streaming down her face as she rocked back and forth in the chair. Alex held her.

'You did everything you could.'

When Pam looked up at Alex she seemed to be seeing him for the first time. 'You look like Max,' she said. 'Just like Max.'

'Don't . . .'

'No.' She touched his cheek with her fingertips, as if to see whether it was warm. 'I mean now. You look like him. The way your face is so stern. He wasn't always like that, was he? Al? Did I make him so sad?'

Alex took Pam's face between his hands and tilted her head so she would look into his eyes. 'When he brought you out to California to meet me – remember, when you'd first met? – he was the happiest man alive.'

She took a long, deep breath. 'So what went wrong?' she said. 'What?'

What answer could Alex give? That life itself had disappointed Max? How could he say that to Pam?

The silence of the room seemed to envelop them until nothing around seemed alive. With Pam's head cradled on his chest, Alex closed his eyes and they rocked together, saying nothing, and wishing for nothing in the world but the sound and sight of Max coming through the door.

The actors and actresses who played the forty-five characters in *Unto the Skies* were well accustomed to symbolism in their scripts, and few of those arriving at work on the Monday after Thanksgiving took the news of Max's resignation and death as merely a sad accident. To most it signified something deeper, that the troubled soap had suffered a fatal blow. Most feared that they would soon be out of work. Some dealt with the disappointment by telephoning their agents and warning them to keep their eyes open and their ears close to the ground. Others carried their gloom within them.

Whatever the reasons for the pervasive mood of despair, all spoke of their terrible loss, competing with one another as to who'd known Max the longest and best. Only Jackie Clapton, an extra playing a maid in a hotel scene, admitted that she had never met the writer, though she said she'd watched the soap for years and *felt* as if she knew him.

Others agreed that he was a man who had put his soul into the work, and did what they could to comfort her.

In her dressing room, Faith Valentine was standing in front of the large mirror studying her expression and body language. When Vanessa, her character, had suffered the trauma of a miscarriage, Faith had wished she'd been able to remember precisely how she looked and felt when someone she knew died. She would have to absorb this now, add the tool to the kit.

Almost alone among the cast members, she had been a friend of Max. They'd been lovers for a while, for a few months in '79, and it had been she who had persuaded Bernie Hermann to hire Max as a writer. One of the hazards of being a soap actress was that she could be written out of the script at any time for any number of reasons, and so it was with considerable guile that she had positioned a friend in the headwriter's slot.

A call came through the PA system summoning the cast and technicians to Stage Four. At her mirror Faith practised a couple of faces, settled on an expression of vulnerable, almost scared, bewilderment and high-heeled it to the large, windowless studio where fifty or so people had gathered. Faith spotted Johnson Bell and trotted to stand behind him.

'Are you all right?' he whispered. 'You look a little shook up.'

As she took one of Johnson's hands in hers, squares of light were reflected in her long, red nails. She sucked at her top lip hard enough to bring a tear to her eyes and said, 'We went back such a very long way. We talked of marriage, you know. Once.'

'It's a loss to all of us,' said Johnson. 'And to the soap opera world.'

Close to them their esteemed Executive Producer, Vince Moscardini, was clapping his hands. 'People! Hey, you grips back there, can you keep quiet a second? Now,' he clapped his hands again, 'let's begin with a minute's silence.'

They bowed their heads. After twenty seconds, Vince began to talk. 'I know we're going to miss Max, but the show goes on, OK? We've asked young Bob Fein to step in as headwriter. He and me, we agree on how we're going to pick this baby up. Nothing too radical, no plane crashes, just some fast-paced drama. Bob doesn't think he's Shakespeare. Not like Max. So don't worry about a thing. What you should be doing is patting yourselves on the back for getting through the rough times. We're a long way from being dead too, if you know what I mean.'

A few of the cast looked at Vince in disgust, but the majority were happy to know that the show wasn't to be axed.

'Now I'm going to leave you in Howard's hands.'

Howard Gains, the day's director, said, 'Let's dress Three and Five at ten thirty,' and the assembled crowd split up to continue with the manufacture of fantasy.

Alex Lubotsky was at his desk in the lower press office when the door opened and President Grant came in. It was the day after Max's funeral.

'Is this a good time?' the President asked.

Alex nodded.

'I was so very sorry to hear about your brother.' He put a hand on Alex's shoulder, something he did to every man whose trust he was trying to win. 'How are you feeling?'

'I'm fine, considering.'

'If there was something I could do . . .' said the President, shaking his head.

'Thanks.'

'Susan sends her love, by the way. She says you should stay for dinner next week.'

Suddenly, Alex longed to see her. Even in the intense

passion of their lovemaking she calmed him. He wished he could hold her now. He didn't have anyone else, no one but someone else's wife.

Alex and Jack sat in the wide black leather armchairs that had been a gift from the Italian President. There was surprisingly little noise in the compound that day, with only the hum of the electric clocks boasting time's march.

'Alex,' Grant began, 'I think you need to take a break.'

'Now?' Alex said with a dismissive laugh. 'That's impossible. Besides, it's good I'm so busy.'

The President leant forward in the chair, resting his forearms on his thighs. He was wearing his most sincere expression.

'I don't want you to think that I'm being insensitive to your feelings, but that wasn't a request,' he said. 'I'd like you to take that break.'

'I *am* this office, Jack. I can't walk away and expect things to run themselves.'

'I talked to Susan over the holiday . . .'

Alex felt his stomach tighten. He wanted to escape. Though usually so circumspect, for all the time he'd been seeing Susan he had blocked out the thought of what would happen if Jack discovered the affair. Now it seemed as if she had carried out her threat.

The President continued. 'She and I were discussing the possibility of you helping to coordinate her affairs.'

Alex was shocked. 'In what capacity?'

'As her Chief of Staff.'

'I couldn't,' he said, relieved that his secret remained safe. 'I mean, I couldn't find the time.'

'We thought you would do it instead of this.'

Slowly, Alex began to understand what Jack was saying. 'Am I getting any say in this, or . . .?'

'It isn't open for discussion, no. I'm sorry, but we feel we need to make a determined effort to reverse the ratings and we think we should start with this office.'

Alex felt the blood rise to his face. 'Who's we, Jack? Who's after me?'

'No one. I admit there are others who feel as I do, but it's my decision in the end.'

'To fire me,' Alex said, not really believing what he was hearing.

'To use your skills elsewhere.'

Alex shook his head. 'Fuck you, Jack! Can't you even be straight with me after fifteen years? What's behind this?'

'I'm being perfectly straight with you,' the President insisted. 'I don't think Communications is the right position for you. You know you don't have a great relationship with the press at the moment and besides, you yourself have been saying for some time that Susan should be used to promote the agenda, especially while the media are trying to scalp me. I consider what she's doing to be central to the future of this Administration. I wouldn't offer the job to someone I didn't trust and respect.'

Most people would have fallen for Jack's charm, but as one of his trainers, Alex knew him too well. 'So I should be looking at this as a promotion, should I?'

'You should look at it as a chance to serve your country.'

'Right!' Alex paced over to his desk. He could see his hand shaking. 'Susan isn't even an elected official. I'll be as important as her dressmaker.'

'Not at all. You'll be playing a strong role in shaping Administration policy.'

Now Alex couldn't contain his anger. He had reached the place he had always longed to be and Jack Grant was threatening to take it all away. 'That's bullshit. Susan's staff do not sit in the Cabinet. They don't even appear at the staff meetings. You're cutting me out. Why can't you face telling me the truth? You know sometimes, Jack, I wonder whether you've forgotten what it sounds like.'

As soon as the words had crossed his lips, Alex regretted them.

The President had lowered his eyes and was twisting his fountain pen in his fingers. He took some time to respond, and when he did so it was in a soft voice. 'What are you accusing me of?' he asked.

'Being too good at your job, I suppose. Or too keen to hang on to it. The problem is that I've been trying to defend you here knowing that facts have a nasty habit of coming to the surface.'

Now the President looked hard into Alex's eyes.

'You're accusing me of lying, aren't you, Alex?'

'No.'

'Aren't you?' Jack said, his voice raised.

Alex laid his hands flat on the desk's warm leather surface. Slowly, he told the President that he had heard some things that he hadn't wanted to hear.

'What on?' Grant asked. Though he was motionless, Alex could sense the anger inside. 'What on? *Hard Copy*? *A Current Affair*?'

'No, Jack. Somewhere much closer to home.'

President Grant shot to his feet and moved to within a foot of Alex. He pointed a finger in a mannerism that was second nature to him now, though Alex could remember teaching Jack how and when to assert himself during the gubernatorial elections in 1984. So much of the President's image had been created by Alex over the previous twelve years that he could hardly remember what the man underneath the façade was like. Now Jack stood with his finger raised, his voice lowered and his eyes fixed on his Communications Director. He was so close that Alex could smell the coffee on his breath.

'If you had any doubt about my integrity you should have talked it through with me. And if you couldn't accept my word then you should have stepped down. The fact that you did not, Alex, is reason enough for me to want you out of this job. It also makes me wonder how suitable you'd be working with Susan.'

Alex said nothing. Already he hated to think what the media would make of his dismissal. They'd been gunning for him for months. How much worse would it be if he was seen taking such a lowly position as Susan's Chief of Staff? Yet to refuse the post might mean that he'd play no further part in the Administration. The sudden realisation that he might be left with nothing scared and chastened him. He walked to the window and leant on the sill.

'If I have to go, have you already thought who might replace me?'

'Curt Wallis.'

'No,' said Alex, truly amazed. 'Are you being serious? *The* Curt Wallis? He used to sleep with Reagan, Jack. That's like, I don't know, like asking Polanski to direct a biopic of Manson. Think what he'll do to you.'

'He'll sell me. That's all. He's joining us to sell the package, not to tell me what to put in it. Everything I did was too close to your heart. You can't see clearly enough when you're fighting for yourself. I think that's where we went wrong.'

By saying 'we', Alex knew that the President was including himself in the mistakes that had been made. In a sense, he thought it gave Grant even less right to shuffle him out of this crucial post. Yet still he softened his tone and asked, with a certain amount of resignation to his voice, 'What if I say no to Susan? What else is there?'

'I don't know. I thought that since you and Susan were close friends you . . .'

There was a knock at the door. Rebecca Frear came in.

'I'm sorry, Mr President, but I've got a Mrs Lubotsky on the phone for Alex. She sounds very upset.'

'Didn't you tell her I was busy?' Alex said, taking his anger out on the press secretary.

'I'm sorry, she sounded so . . .'

'Take the call,' the President said, walking fast to the door. 'We'll finish this later.'

When Grant had gone, Alex slumped into the chair behind his desk and picked up the line. 'Pam,' he said gruffly, 'I was in with the President.'

'Oh, my God, did I . . .?'

He could tell from her voice that she had recently been crying, and at once regretted his harshness. 'Don't worry. What's up?'

'They didn't pay him, Al,' she said. 'Nothing. I called them and found out. For a year they didn't pay him. He had all these debts and loans he didn't tell me about and it's because they hadn't been sending him any cheques. And when I called that bastard Vince Moscardini he told me that Max had signed a contract. Did you know about that? Did he tell you that? You said you knew something about money.'

Alex coiled the telephone cord around his finger and leant back on the chair's legs. 'He, he just said that things were a little tough.'

'Did he tell you about the contract, Al?' Pam was sounding desperate now. 'I need to know.'

There was a silence before Alex admitted the truth.

'Yes, he did. When he came to Washington.'

Over lunch at the Parrot, Max had explained that, eight months before, Vince Moscardini had given his headwriter a choice. Max could either leave the show or accept a scheme whereby he would receive his salary (plus a substantial bonus) only if the show's rating climbed above 7.0 within a year. If Max failed, he would receive nothing. Max, confident of success, had accepted. Though four months remained before the deadline, the rating was falling still when Max arrived in Washington looking for Alex's help. He had said that he needed some cash to help with the mortgage. It was this request that Alex had denied, not only because his savings had recently been tied up, but because he believed in his heart that Max might not strive for the rating if the wolf was lured from his door. It was a decision that had been haunting him every hour of every day since the crash.

Through her tears, Pam said, 'Why didn't you tell me, Al? I could have done something if you'd told me.'

Alex longed to reach out and comfort her by shouldering the blame himself.

'Pam,' he said, 'I'm coming to Titusville.'

'No, don't. I mean, why? I thought you were busy.'

'I need to sort some things out.'

'Alex, I'm sorry,' she said, talking through her tears. 'It's not you I'm angry with. It's them. I didn't mean to shout. I'm sorry.'

He closed his eyes. 'It's OK,' he said. 'I've been shouting at me too. Listen, I have to go now. I'll see you this afternoon.'

As soon as Alex hung up he rose from his chair, smoothed his hair and headed for the door. He knew that if he lingered, he would lose the courage to face these next few minutes. At the door, Rebecca asked him a question, but he shrugged her off, saying he'd be back.

He walked the short distance to the briefing room. It had been the White House swimming pool, but Nixon had covered it over and now it served as the place from which the Administration briefed the world. It amused Alex how like a private movie screening room it was, with its sprung, blue chairs facing the podium. In front of the podium, microphones and lights were attached to the ceiling and at the far end of the room, the cameras awaited their subjects. The chairs were empty, but a handful of technicians were fiddling with equipment and monitors in a space behind the cameras, feeding in footage of the Vice President in South Korea and waiting for Jack Grant to make an appearance in a little under four hours' time.

Alex walked to the press booths, past the rows of telephones attached to the walls and the scruffy alcove housing the soft drinks machine. Though most of the nation's top publications had desks here, it was hardly spacious – merely a number of small desks crudely divided from one another. Alex was looking for Bill Kale, a veteran reporter who had covered the Administrations of every President since Eisenhower. Kale wasn't there, but through the window Alex could see Roderick Hall, the CNN White House correspondent, sitting on a high stool on the lawn. The lights beneath the umbrellas were on, Roderick was made-up and illuminated, but he wasn't on air; not yet.

Alex looked about him, foolishly worried that if he was seen, his thoughts might be read. But then, feeling as excited and scared as he ever had, he left through the small door in the centre of the room and walked, with his heart racing, out onto the lawn and towards the unsuspecting CNN team.

A coast away, Annie Marin was paying a visit to her agent. She found him talking on the phone in the tiny room on Fillmore, his feet up on the desk. He was chatting about the holiday but, seeing the way that Annie was pacing about, he hung up and came to kiss her.

'And how was it for *you*, darling?' he asked.

'Did you know about Zoë Dunlop being pulled off that movie?' Annie replied.

He folded his arms and stood as Annie was standing. 'Thanksgiving was fine thanks, Sam. How was yours?' He turned the other way. 'Why how nice of you to ask! Kyle and I got on like a bush fire and . . .'

'This isn't about you, Sam,' Annie cried. 'It's about me!'

'*Now* you're sounding like an actress.'

'Can you try sounding like an agent for once? I'm not in the mood for gossip.'

'Is this real? Are we having a teeny tantrum?'

'No, a big tantrum. Just tell me if you knew about Zoë and that movie.'

Sam poured himself a cardboard cone of water from the cylinder. He offered one to Annie, who shook her head. 'Did you get to meet the divine Miss Dunlop?'

'I got her out of bed.'

'But did she get you *into* bed, that's the question? Did she treat you to a flash of her ginger pussy cat?'

Annie reddened. 'You still haven't answered me.'

The phone interrupted them. Annie heard Sam giving one of his actresses details of the part she had won on a new sitcom to be filmed in the city. When he hung up he became more serious. 'It's not everyone who gets the chance to meet Zoë Dunlop, Annie. You met, you bonded, and even if you didn't fuck she feels she owes you one, and that's much more than you had before.'

'She liked my acting before, and she likes my acting now, Sam. You shouldn't have to play games with me to get me a job. I'm sick of this. I'm not asking for the world. All I want is a job. Any job.' Though she hadn't been expecting them, the tears suddenly welled up. Annie wiped them away with a tissue. 'God!' she said, grumpy with herself. 'I hate overemotional actresses.'

Sam curled an arm around her shoulder. 'I wouldn't represent you if you were any other way,' he said before kissing her on the forehead.

Annie flopped on the couch. It was hot, warmed by sun rays magnified through the skylight above. She donked her feet onto the table. 'What did I do that touring for, Sam? So I could do voice-overs for diaper ads? All that work should have paid off by now, shouldn't it?'

'You need to get seen in LA and New York. There's not enough going on in the Bay Area. It's not all my fault, sweetie.'

'No, I guess you're right. Maybe I'll do that. But then

. . . oh, I don't know. Maybe I'll do something else. I'm too old for this shit, Sam. I really am.'

'No, you're too good for this shit. We'll sort something out, I promise.'

She looked at him with an expression bereft of hope, and then said, 'We'd better, Sam, or I'm going to give the whole thing up.'

Robbie and Matt Lubotsky ran to meet their uncle when his car pulled up outside their home.

'We saw you on TV,' Matt screamed. 'You're on all the TV.'

'Am I?' he laughed.

'You look just like you.'

'Well, that's good.'

'They had a picture of Daddy, too,' said Rob sullenly. Though he looked less like Max than Matt did, Rob had inherited much of his father's glum nature. It worried Alex. 'Did they?' he said. 'That's because he was a famous man too!' He ruffled Rob's hair and was about to say something more when he saw Pam standing at the open door, her arms folded. 'Hi!' he said. Grinning, he waved at her. He was surprised at how good it felt coming here, leaving the world's worries back in Washington. This was the life that he had missed out on in pursuing his dreams. 'I guess you've heard,' he said, proudly.

Pam glared at him before retreating into the house.

'Uh-oh!' Alex said to Rob, and then he produced a football he had bought for them, and promised he'd be out to practise some passes as soon as he'd chatted to their mom.

In the hallway Alex saw the phone off the hook. The TV was on in the living room, and he could hear his name being mentioned. He found Pam in the kitchen. She didn't look at him as he came in, nor did she welcome his kiss.

'How are you feeling?' he said.

'You're on every channel,' she replied coldly.

'I knew they'd lap it up,' he said with a grin. 'What are they saying?'

'That depends on who's talking. The White House say you were fired. Reporters think you resigned.'

'And you don't think I should have done it! I can tell by your voice.'

She stared at him. 'It couldn't matter less.'

'Is something . . .?'

Angrily, she cut him off. 'My children matter, Alex. You could have warned me. The phone's been ringing off the hook with people asking if you're here and wanting to know personal things about Max. They're saying you quit because of his death. And now the boys want to know why their Daddy's picture is on CNN. It's unbelievably selfish. You think the whole world revolves around you, don't you? God! You're so like Max it sickens me.'

Alex bowed his head like a naughty schoolboy. For the second time in one day his judgment was being questioned.

'It's not as if I decided to put you through anything, I really didn't think . . .'

'Not thinking about it doesn't make it go away, Al,' she said sharply. 'I thought you were coming here to help me get over things, not to rub them in my face. How do you think it feels having my husband's death discussed on every TV station in the world?'

He was silent, wondering why he had been so obtuse. Was it because the world sometimes did revolve around what he said? Or had he become so accustomed to control that he'd forgotten that not everyone read, or approved of, his script?

'Listen,' he said, standing up. 'I'm going to stay in a hotel. I don't want to drag all of you into this.'

'It's too late,' she said, sitting at the table.

She looked completely drained, and he hated himself for being partly to blame.

'Why did you do it?' she asked, her voice no longer accusatory. 'You always said it was the closest you could come to being President.'

'It was.' He leant on the sink and peered out into the garden. 'Jack fired me.'

There was a pause, and then Pam said, 'So you decided to make it look as if you'd walked out. Was that it?'

'Yeah.'

'So like Max!' she said, almost whispering.

'The President was going to make an announcement this afternoon, I had to do something, I . . .'

'You had to shoot first? You had to save your own skin? I thought you cared about Grant. I thought you respected him.'

Alex didn't reply. When he announced his resignation to CNN he believed he was giving the President nothing more than was deserved. After twelve years of loyal service to Grant's cause, Alex had felt he was being tossed aside and he'd wanted immediate revenge. Yet as he drove further from Washington, past Baltimore and Philadelphia, listening on the radio to the excitement his words had caused, he began to understand that the bridges were burning behind him, that there could be no way back now he'd caused such mayhem.

In his resignation interview, Alex, well known as the President's closest adviser in the White House, insinuated that Grant was a man hiding skeletons in his closet. Now conservative Congressional pressure for an investigation into Cochabamba would be immense. The President would have to prove his innocence, and risk being crucified, with Alex as the unlikely Judas.

They heard the front door open and the kids rushed in. 'Mom, there's someone here wanting to see Uncle Alex.'

'Who?' Pam asked.

'He wouldn't say.'

'He had a funny voice,' Matt told them.

'That was English, stupid,' said Robbie viciously.

There was a knock at the door and Alex tightened the knot in his tie and took a step towards it.

Pam stepped in front of him. 'Don't you dare go to that door,' she said. 'Do they know for sure you're here?'

'No.'

'Kids, did you tell him?'

They shook their heads.

'So let me do this,' Pam insisted. 'I am not having this place crawling with reporters.'

'Good idea. And Pam . . .'

'Yes?'

'I'm sorry. I'll make it up to you. I promise.'

She made no acknowledgment of the apology as she walked away. Alex stepped round the corner so that he wouldn't be seen. Matt pulled at his jacket sleeve.

'Are you coming here to live?' he asked.

'Sshhh,' said Alex, putting a finger to his mouth.

Matt repeated the question, whispering this time.

'I don't know,' Alex whispered back. 'We'll have to see what Mommy says.'

5

In an interview with *Soap Opera News*, Cathy Hirsch said that when sifting through up to three hundred headshots a day for *Unto the Skies*, she looked for 'the life behind the eyes'. However, when model Stefano Benedetti sauntered into her office, it was life behind the overworked zipper of his black Levis that she looked for, and found, and within ten minutes the dark Italian's impressive six-feet-three-inches lost their role as his most persuasive statistic.

A week after this encounter, in August 1992, Stefano was hired as a contract player in the role of Paolo Lunardi, pilot, heartthrob, soon-to-be-son-in-law to William Sheridan, and now jailbird. He fast became the most popular male star on the show and the bad boy good women loved to hate.

Was it any wonder, then, that off set, women should have fallen for the actor, a man with the features of a choirboy, the bearing of a boxer and the confidence of a person utterly in love with himself? It was a hazard of the job that soap fans became incapable of separating fact from fiction, but in Stefano's case the confusion was all too real. He *was*, to all intents and purposes, Paolo, nurturing the reputation of an irresistible lover, seducing women with his character's lines and eschewing romantic commitment because Paolo wasn't the marrying type. For a few of Stefano's off-screen lovers, the arrangement was ideal.

Faith Valentine, devoted mother, wife to Ned, and

97

supreme star of *Unto the Skies*, had first spread her legs for the star on the pool table in his apartment in New York's meat-packing district on December 9th, 1992, the very day that he was voted Soap's Sexiest Stud. Neither had intended the affair to last, but a year on it was still going strong. Now Stefano was in Faith's dressing room, sideways to the door, his leg a barrier across it.

'I know you want to come back with me,' he said, combing his hair in readiness for the fans outside.

She kissed him. 'Of course I want to, sweetheart. You know how you make me feel.' She wiped the lipstick from his cheek with her thumb. 'But we can't. Ned's been watching mc like a hawk ever since that fucking child opened her mouth.'

Stefano lowered his leg, the toecap of his cowboy boot clicking on the wooden floorboards. Though unaccustomed to rejection, he wasn't about to plead. He could always turn to one of the other women in his telephone book to quieten the simmering and impetuous Latin muscle between his legs. It was a shame, though, that there was no one else like Faith.

'It's no problem for me,' he said. 'I'll see you tomorrow, yeah?'

He winked at her, blew her a kiss which she caught in her hand and returned to his dressing room to collect his thoughts, because he had a few, and his telephone numbers, of which there were many.

Faith was not, as she'd told her lover, heading home. Instead she hailed a cab to take her downtown, to 10th Street between Second and Third, a quiet, austere block in the yuppie part of the East Village. Standing between the stone columns of a handsome turn-of-the-century portico, she ran a painted nail down the list of names and pressed the bell of apartment number five. A man answered.

'Bob? It's Faith, Faith Valentine.'

Bob Fein was Max's twenty-eight-year-old replacement

as headwriter for *Unto the Skies*. He looked almost unnervingly normal, like a living illustration from a biology textbook, but clothed in a Nirvana T-shirt sprinkled with cookie crumbs. He had a solid, clean face and perfectly straight, dark hair that he swept in a parting. He and Faith had met once only, at a Christmas party, and so he was surprised that she knew where he lived. Now he listened to the sharp click of her high heels as she climbed the black-and-white-tiled staircase.

'This is quite a surprise,' he said.

'I hope it's a nice one,' Faith replied.

She had dressed provocatively in a top with a neckline that plunged in a deep, wide V to her midriff. On her way up the stairs she had tickled her nipples and now they were pouting attentively. Bob's eyeballs spun like fruit-machine lemons as he held out his arm to welcome her inside. She followed him down the herringbone parquet corridor, past the bedroom and into the sitting room.

'Do you live here alone, Bob?'

'Yes, I do.'

Faith span around and held her arm out, as if she was selling the property. 'It's lovely. Very, what's the word – come on, you're the writer.'

'Untidy?'

'No, European! Very cultured.'

She was referring, he supposed, to the teetering towers of books that covered one of the walls, or perhaps it was the view of the back of St Mark's church through the window. 'Can I get you something to drink?' he asked.

'Do you have cranberry? I'm still recovering from Thanksgiving.'

'Me too,' Bob said, moving into the kitchen.

He returned with the blood-red drink. Faith was on the couch now, her right leg flopped loosely over the left, her short skirt riding up her thighs.

'I hope I'm not disturbing you,' she said.

'No. I mean I was writing, but that's fine.'

He wondered whether she could smell the static fuzz of warm television still lingering in the air.

'I won't stay,' she said, 'but I was passing and when I saw your name I thought how nice it would be to get acquainted.'

Bob sat on a stool the other side of the room.

'Dear Max told me how he liked your scripts more than any of the other associate writers.'

'Did he?' Bob said with evident surprise. Max had always insinuated that of his five co-writers, Bob was the least talented. Certainly Max had gone to considerable lengths to doctor the scripts that Bob had sent. 'He never told me.'

'He didn't? Well, to me he said you were good with dialogue. Especially for the women.'

Bob rubbed the back of his neck with his palm and frowned. 'He never mentioned that either.'

'With some of the other writers the words don't come out like the way we normal people speak them. I always feel confident with you.'

'Thanks! I suppose I find it easier to write for someone like . . .' He stopped because his mouth had gone dry and he had developed an odd little tickle in his throat when Faith had leant forward on the couch. He was sure that if she only spread her arms, the fabric of her top would give way and those oversized breasts of hers would erupt into the room like driver's airbags in a crash.

'Someone like me?' she suggested.

'Yes.' He nodded. 'I mean, you've been on the show for such a long time that I feel I know what Vanessa would say and do.'

Faith carefully placed her drink on the low coffee table and clasped her hands together. 'That's dangerous, Bob.'

'How so?'

'Well, although I had the *deepest* respect for Max, I

felt that he never took Vanessa far enough. She's so, so . . .'

Bob was going to suggest 'busty' but settled on 'dependable' instead.

Faith liked the word, and almost physically grabbed it with her lips. 'Dependable, yes, and I think she's also, how can I say it? – predictable. She should be more assertive. I'd like that, and I know my fans would like that. I've been playing the second fiddle to all of the Sheridan men, you know, for a very long time. Vanessa should stand up for herself, become more, more . . .'

'Bitchy?' said Bob.

'I prefer "dynamic".'

'She's about to be having this thing with William, don't forget.'

Faith swatted at the air. 'Oh, I know. But is that thrilling? Hmm? Is it? He's an old man, Bob. An old man.'

'Yes, but . . .'

'Yes but nothing. Vanessa needs to take charge more.' Faith clenched her fist. '*Unto the Skies* is screaming out for a strong female character.'

Bob, suddenly noticing how filthy his toenails were, stood and kicked his feet into a pair of sneakers as he said, 'I'll bear that in mind.'

Faith rose, approached, and leant. 'I don't mean to tell you your job, but I've grown with Vanessa, Bob. I have. I feel we want the same things from life. I don't like her being too sappy.'

For a moment, as she moved her head towards his, Bob felt as if he was in an episode of *Unto the Skies*. This was exactly how he knew Faith – in close-up, her lipstick fresh and glistening, the many muscles of her face twitching almost imperceptibly, each one vying for attention.

The illusion was broken by the sound of the door buzzer.

'Must be my girlfriend,' said Bob, rubbing a hand across his forehead as he took a step back.

'I'd better be on my way,' said Faith, leaving the cranberry juice untouched, just as drinks were rarely drunk during the show.

They walked together to the door. Faith squeezed Bob's hand in parting. 'I'm glad we could meet like this,' she said. 'I'm sure I'll see you in the studio soon.'

'I'll probably keep low for a while,' he replied, 'but, yeah, I'll be there.'

Faith smiled. 'I look forward to it.'

Then, after another quick squeeze of his hand, she left, smirking at Bob's girlfriend as the two of them passed on the stairs.

In San Francisco, Annie was lying on the sofa slurping on a strawberry-banana smoothie and watching the morning news when Jerry came home to work at his computer. He kissed her lips and then her breasts, his hands moving over her body.

'Jerry,' she complained, 'I'm watching.'

Jerry twisted to see the TV. 'Why? You'll have forgotten it all by tomorrow,' he said, as he stroked her thigh.

'No, I won't,' she snapped. 'It's interesting.'

Jerry sighed and rose to his feet. 'You realise that television is in the business of keeping you immature by denying any chance of self-awareness, don't you? You're collecting information at the expense of wisdom.'

'You talk a lot of baloney, Jerry. You know that?'

'You used to agree with me.'

'Well, now I agree with the rest of America, so can you let me listen?'

'Nice to see you too,' he said, leaving for the kitchen to fix himself a rice and black bean salad.

Annie returned to the press conference, live from New York, on Alex's removal from office.

Having calmed down, Alex had greatly softened his criticism of President Grant and taken instead to haranguing the media. He felt it was his only chance at redemption in the Administration's eyes.

'As I mentioned before,' he was saying, 'I feel that my authority as Communications Director was undermined by Cochabamba, not because I didn't believe the President – I do – but because everything the Administration says or does is torn to shreds. Let's look at the facts. Cochabamba is no Watergate. It isn't Iran-Contra. It isn't an S&L. This is a lie that's been picked up by insidious right-wing media interests and told so many times that it's beginning to sound like the truth. Now that's not good for the country.'

'Are you trying to argue that investigative journalism is unpatriotic?' asked a reporter from the *Wall Street Journal*.

'Not at all, Bernie. What's unpatriotic is having a conservative machine intent on using lies to discredit the people's President. The flak President Grant is getting from partisan journalists is making his job impossible. Frankly, I consider it to be a no-win situation at this point in time, and I am no longer prepared to be a part of that.'

'Don't you think you're trying to blame others for failings within the Administration?' asked Bob Bayley.

'Bob, you find me an Administration that hasn't had teething troubles. Even Reagan's was in turmoil for months. What I am objecting to is the fact that none of you is focusing on the agenda. What's more important to you people?' he asked, real anger in his voice. 'Positive policies designed to cut the deficit, reduce homelessness and crime and restore a decent life to millions of Americans, or these scandals that have no foundation in the truth? We've sunk to a level of hostility where it's impossible to relay serious information to the people. Now I can't operate in a climate like that, and that's the reason I'm getting out.'

'Although you appear to be supporting the Grant Administration,' one reporter asked, 'wouldn't you agree that you've inflicted a potentially fatal blow on the President by withdrawing your support?'

Alex flashed his killer smile. 'Philippa,' he said, 'you know I haven't done that. I fully support Jack Grant and the policies that he will be carrying forward for the next seven years.'

Roderick Hall from CNN, the man who'd broken the story, asked, 'So when you said to me yesterday that doubts about the President's integrity had made your position untenable, that wasn't a direct attack?'

'How many times do I have to repeat myself? What I meant was that it was the doubting itself that made my position impossible, not the integrity of the President. Now I'll take one more question.'

It came from Sarah Thomas. 'Are you willing to confirm that you turned down a post as Chief of Staff to the First Lady?'

Alex paused before speaking. 'I am willing to say that Susan Grant is a wonderful asset to the Administration and a role model for women in the whole nation. We're lucky to have someone of her stature in the White House.'

'But did you . . .?'

Alex stood. 'Thank you all for coming. Thank you.'

In the kitchen, Annie found some wild rice on the stove and Jerry standing on his head. There was a greasy smudge on the pink-and-green-chequered lino and the paint was scuffed in the corner from this near-daily routine.

Standing beside him, Annie tickled his hairy calf and said, 'Sorry I snapped at you back there. I'm a little upset about something.'

'What?' he asked, though he didn't right himself.

'I heard on the television that a friend from acting school was killed in an accident. Max Lubotsky.'

'I don't remember his name,' said Jerry, the veins on his forehead bulging like greedy maggots.

'I think about him sometimes.' Annie shuffled over to the fridge. 'He was you before you came along. Not that we ever . . .' She took a deep breath. 'I mean, he was the first person who made me see things in a different way. I always had this feeling we'd end up working together one day. Still, I guess nothing works out the way you think it will, does it?'

'The mind's like an eye that sees but cannot see itself,' said Jerry. 'You can never know the future, Annie. You've got to let your actions take you where they may.'

'Mmm.'

Needing something more than spiritual consolation, Annie opened the freezer door to look for the Choc Chip ice-cream before remembering that she'd finished it on Thanksgiving. Now there was nothing inside but a box of spinach, a year old at least and layered with crystals of ice. It was sitting alone on the rusting, broken grate. Annie thought that if she could see her future, it might look a lot like this. She slammed the compartment door with a rubbery thud and went to the stove to stir Jerry's rice because she could think of nothing better to do.

'Jerry,' she said. 'What would you think about me going to New York for a while? See if I can't find a good part.'

'Can't you do that here?' he said.

'You know how badly it's going here.'

'Maybe you should do something else, then.'

'Give up acting?'

Jerry let his legs clump to the floor, where he sat looking up at her. 'Why not?'

'Because it's all I've ever wanted to do! That's why,' she answered.

Though she herself had considered giving up, it hurt coming from another. It seemed insulting.

Jerry said, 'Maybe you should accept that it's not the path that was intended. I've thought that for a long time.'

'Oh, have you!' Annie said angrily. 'Well, thanks for telling me!'

'I meant that maybe you made the wrong choice.'

'Maybe I did, Jerry,' said Annie, staring at him. 'Maybe we both did!'

Without waiting for a response, Annie left the room and continued out of the apartment and into the generous December sun. She climbed Washington Street, past the wheezy tram cables buried like tendons in the asphalt, right up to the crest of the hill by Lafayette Park. She found it almost impossible to be angry while revelling in this view over the bay. As she watched the pot-bellied sails, pregnant with the western breeze, carrying sailors criss-crossing in boats untethered from the marina below, she felt her complaints being absorbed by the water itself. Above her, the sky spread out like a sheet of old blue writing paper, bleached at its edges where it tucked into the horizon, and to her left the Golden Gate Bridge looked regal. Annie liked the feeling that it protected the city and its people from a world beyond that wasn't as privileged or fine.

Could she really leave this behind? Even though she often dreamt of Manhattan, and even though she had believed after Cornell Williams that she would stay for ever, the prospect of returning frightened her. She was not good at cutting ties. If she was, she thought, she would have left Jerry months ago.

And yet when he truly annoyed her, or bored her for too long with his sanctimonious piffle about the inner self, she would remember how happy he had once made her. She would remember days spent sailing in the bay, or riding up to Mendocino, or climbing in Yosemite where they'd camped out and held one another under chill skies with the wolves barking in the distance. She would remember nights spent talking and learning and loving him as if they'd been born for those moments, and for each other. And she would remember lying beneath him, feeling him inside her, and looking deeply into his eyes and promising that she could never, would never, love another man.

And when she remembered these moments, leaving him seemed selfish and defeatist. They made her wonder whether she alone was to blame. Had her own sadness chipped away the varnish that had hidden Jerry's faults? If she could find a way to be happier in herself, would she be happier with him? It was still too soon to give up, she decided. She could be mature enough to see past the niggling things that annoyed her. She would get herself a job, any job, and give the relationship one more chance.

She turned back home, stopping by a liquor store for a bottle of wine, strangely convinced that a little hope and a little drink might be all that was needed right now.

6

Can you trespass on a dead man's space? Max Lubotsky's study had been a forbidden zone to his family. The boys had rarely dared venture inside and even Pam had shied away, conscious of how she disturbed his work. Now, four days after the press conference, Alex was in the study for the first time since Max's death.

It was a cosy room, painted dark green. Beneath the blue frame of the sash window sat a large, New England pine desk and beyond it, through bevelled panes, was an encouraging view of the garden and broad river. Although few rooms in the house had absorbed the identity of their new owners, the study seemed to have belonged to Max for years. It was probably because of his books. They filled the shelves from floor to ceiling, their bent and battered spines proof of his keen and vibrant hands.

Max had been a voracious reader. On the shelves beside the desk Alex found the books of which his brother had been most fond. They were plays, mostly. Shakespeare, of course, and then the Greek tragedies of Aeschylus, Sophocles, Euripides and Aristophanes beside a well-used copy of Aristotle's *Poetics* held together with masking tape. There were many twentieth-century works but it was Arthur Miller's early plays that had been positioned closest to hand.

Alex used his fingertip to angle a copy of *Death of a Salesman* from its neighbours. The musty paper was warm and soft to touch and this edition was dated 1951, the year the twins were born. Staring at the book, Alex remembered the excitement with which Max had spoken of it. Back when the play was inspiring his life, it would have seemed absurd to think it could inspire his death as well. And yet the similarities were too distinct to be ignored. Max, like the salesman, Willy Loman, had lived a life blaming others for a dissatisfaction with himself until, like Willy, he had killed himself, hiding the reasons by using life insurance as an excuse.

Alex closed the book and slid it carefully back into place. He doubted that he would have the heart to break apart this collection. He felt responsible for too much destruction already. Looking over the desk, he saw a framed photograph of the twins on a see-saw, aged five. He stretched to pick it up, and ran his hand across the dusty glass. In the picture he was at the top, his arm straight and held out in a confident wave. He was smiling at the camera while Max, his knees bending to push himself back, was looking at his brother instead. Though strangers would have been unable to tell the two apart, to those who knew them the photograph spoke volumes.

The Lubotsky twins had been inseparable in their youth. Though Alex was stronger and more assured, he had considered his brother his equal, treating him as such. Even in their twenties, when physically detached by a continent's width, the two had remained genuinely close, writing to one another, working on ideas for Max's plays, both excited by the potential of the other.

It was not until the early 1980s that Alex and Max grew apart. Then, while Max was struggling to establish a career as a serious playwright on the East Coast, Alex was carving himself a golden future in the West, allied to the young Senator Grant. He became Grant's most loyal aide, helping him to the Governor's Mansion in 1984, and then sharing with him the presidential aspirations that were kept secret from the country until the race began in '91. It was because Alex devoted himself to

Governor Grant that he found so little time for his twin brother.

Of course, this was a pattern mirrored by millions of siblings across the world, but the split affected Max in a peculiar way, for he began to feel inadequate in his brother's widening shadow. Perversely, his appointment as headwriter for *Unto the Skies* made things worse, for Alex considered the job nothing more than a fleeting, easy means for his brother to make some quick cash. Whenever they were together, Alex would joke about the medium and taunt Max by assuring him that Shakespeare would have taken the job if only he'd been around for network TV. What Alex failed to notice was that his jokes never made Max smile.

Now he opened the slim drawer in the centre of the desk. It contained nothing but a large, red, hardback notebook. There was a set of them on the top shelf, maybe ten in all. He lifted the book from the drawer and opened it. The page was filled with Max's handwriting and it was obvious this was his diary. After a moment's hesitation during which he decided that Max would have destroyed the journals had he not wanted them seen, Alex began to read.

July 19th, 1993.
Good meeting with bastards at G&H. All of us sure of higher figures in the school vacation with the Timmy and Karen stories going strong. Am feeling great about it all – well, better anyway! Am caging the demons again and feeling sure we'll be up in the 8.0s by Christmas, then big celebrations and gifts and windfalls and smiles all round! Pam could do with a break from me being so miserable. Maybe we'll go away. It's time I took the boys somewhere special. Virgin Islands? Away from it all, at least. Maybe Alex too? – Some chance.

Idea: could Brendan Air start a travel business? To rival the Brenners? Think think think.
Hopefully, it's sliding into place, at last.

Alex pushed the journal away, unable to face any more. What had happened since July to destroy all that hope? Why had Max given up when there were still four months left before he would lose his salary? What should they all have done? What? What? How could they have stopped him?

Alex could not help blaming himself. If only he had given Max the money in Washington, then Max might have still been alive. But hadn't he tied up his savings in government bonds and in a mortgage of his own? And yet, to have lent the money would have been to put faith in Max's ability to turn the show's fortunes around. Perhaps that was all Max had been after. Belief from a man who'd been so impressed with his own success that he hadn't found time to celebrate that of his brother.

Oh God! Alex didn't know what to think any more. He had been doing so much thinking in the vacant hours since the death. All that he knew for sure was that Max had once mattered to him more than everything in the world, and now he'd watched him fall over the edge and done nothing. Or maybe he had done something. Maybe he'd helped to push.

The ringing phone startled him. He snapped shut the journal and returned it to the drawer, suddenly embarrassed at reading it. He could hear Pam's feet on the staircase, and then she called. He wiped at his eyes, wanting to stay strong for her.

'It's for you!' She opened the door. 'A mystery lady.'

Pam winked and gently shut the door. He cleared his throat, then lifted the receiver to his ear.

'Alex Lubotsky.'

'Al, it's Susan.'

Alex had not spoken to the First Lady since his sudden departure from DC.

'Where are you calling from?' he asked.

'Don't worry, it's a secure unit.'

There was an awkward silence before Alex said, 'Susan, I'm sorry that . . .'

'Don't be sorry, Al, or I'll start thinking you didn't do it for me. When are you coming back to Washington?'

Her attitude startled Alex. 'Back? I'm not sure.'

'We need to talk about my campaign.'

'We already talked about it. You know what I said.'

Right now, Alex felt he would never have the will to return to Washington. He leant back in the chair and began to draw on an envelope with his outstretched arm, filling an uneven rectangle with the stars and stripes of the American flag.

'That was before everything happened,' Susan argued. 'You haven't got anything to lose any more.'

'Haven't I?' he said wearily.

'No! Especially not now,' she said, the sound of her words flattened by a smile. 'I told Jack you'd agreed to run my campaign.'

Alex felt the blow deep inside him. Although his resignation had damaged the Administration, a part of him had clung to the hope that Jack Grant would invite him back on better terms. Now, there would never be a chance. It felt as if he was paying three times over for the success he had so far enjoyed.

'What did Jack say?' he asked, his heart thumping. 'Did he believe you?'

'I don't know.'

'It doesn't sound as if he backed down like you said he would.'

'Not yet, but he will. He knows I've got him by the curlies. What he doesn't know is how hard I plan to pull.'

Alex leant forward on his elbows, his shoulders rounded, his neck sore. 'Have you really thought this through? I mean, it's hard enough getting elected to the Senate if you're a woman. It's not like people couldn't care less what sex you are. I'm not convinced America's ready for you.'

Susan Grant replied straightaway. 'Then you make them ready, Al. It's all I'm asking you to do. If you can find a way, I know we can beat them all.'

With headwriter Bob Fein as his new ally, Vince Moscardini was on the offensive. The latest figures for *Unto the Skies* had shown a further fall in the ratings into the real danger zone, and it was recognised that the show would live or die on its performance over the next couple of months. Though Vince could be seen pacing the corridors muttering that he was up to his ass in alligators, in truth he was confident that the soap would survive. All that was needed was a new image to feed to the media. If they swallowed that, then the product would need no changing at all.

Right now, pumped-up, gum-chewing, and with the glint of a border collie eying up the black sheep of a frisky herd, Vincent was talking in his office to reporters from the three top soap opera magazines, and a journalist writing a feature on daytime TV for *The New York Times*.

The producer was toying with a wooden banana from his bowl of decorative fruit. 'My point is that just because *Unto the Skies* has been around thirty years does not mean we should be stuck in the mud. This isn't *Jurassic Park*. Bob and me, we feel alike on this.'

Jayne-Anne Lipke, from *Soap Opera News*, suggested that network television needed a traditional soap opera, brimming with old-fashioned morals, and that *Unto the Skies* fulfilled the role better than its rivals.

'I hear you on that, I do, but you go out there,' Vince darted a finger towards the window, 'and try selling that to the viewers. You know what I'm saying? This isn't a charity. I'm not producing *The Waltons* here.'

'Does that mean you'll be making the show sexier?'

Bob Fein spoke up. 'Our definition of sexiness does not necessarily involve the characters stripping to their underwear. I hope to make the storylines more glitzy. I'm particularly excited by working with Faith Valentine who I think is an actress whose full potential has yet to be realised.'

'He means you'll see more of her jugs,' Vince explained.

'Would it be fair, then,' asked the young man from *The New York Times*, 'to suggest that you'll be moving away from the drama of characterisation to a more fantastic view of life lived . . .'

He was interrupted by a buzz at Vince's intercom. 'Max Lubotsky's brother is here to see you,' said the secretary. 'He says it's urgent.'

'You mean *the* brother. The White House guy?'

'Yes.'

Vince tightened the knot on his tie and said, 'Ask him to wait a mo, yeah? Then I'll see him.'

A second later the door crashed open. Everyone turned in surprise to see the man who stood for ever composed at the President's side striding into the office looking distinctly dishevelled.

Vince stepped forward, his hand outstretched. 'Hi, I'm Vince Moscardini.'

'I want to talk to you,' said Alex, his staring eyes making him look almost mad.

'Sure. Let me wrap up this meeting and I'll be happy to.'

'No, *now*!' Alex said sharply. 'Take it that this meeting is finished.'

Vince looked so shocked it seemed he was mimicking the ham acting often seen on the soap. 'Excuse me, but this isn't the White House. This is el realo worldo and

I'm in the middle of something. Now if you could wait outside . . .'

As Vince put a hand on Alex's back to usher him from the room, Alex swung around and pushed him away.

'Don't touch me,' he snapped, his voice shaking with anger. 'Don't lay a finger on me.'

Vince took a step back and held up a hand. 'OK, OK.' He twisted his head to Bob Fein. 'Move everyone to the conference room. The people in here seem to be making Mr Lubotsky a little hot under the collar.'

'It's not the people, you smug little shit. It's you!'

Bob Fein and the journalists stood uneasily by their chairs. Had the intruder been anyone but the renowned Alex Lubotsky, they would have surely intervened.

'Hey,' said Vince, shielding himself behind his desk, 'I don't like strangers gate-crashing my meetings, and I don't like being mouthed off at. Capisce? If you weren't Max's brother I'd have you thrown out. Jesus! Let's sit down and talk about whatever it is that's bugging you. Like reasonable men.'

Alex leant over the desk and grabbed Vince's tie. 'I wouldn't sit down with you if my life depended on it,' he said, tiny globules of spit landing on the producer's face. 'I've read way too many despicable things about you in my brother's diaries.'

Vince straightened up, pushed Alex away, and called out to Bob who was shepherding the others from the room. 'I changed my mind. You guys stick around. Mr Lubotsky is leaving. You know,' he said, staring at Alex, 'you're as screwed in the head as your brother was.' Vince smoothed down his hair, and added, 'Remind me never to take a ride with you.'

'You fucking prick!' shouted Alex. 'No wonder Max killed himself if he had to work for you.'

'Killed himself, did he?' said Vince, looking at his assistant. 'See, Dave? You owe me ten bucks!'

Alex suddenly looked around him in the room. What had he said? He turned towards the window, wondering how to get himself out of the hole into which he had just tripped.

'I didn't mean that.'

'And I don't give a shit,' said Vince. 'Now are you going to leave or do I need Security?'

Alex turned. Beyond the open door, an audience of office staff stood self-consciously still, like film extras under instruction. They awaited Alex's lines, but he could no longer think straight.

'Listen,' he said, 'I didn't mean that Max . . .'

Talking into the telephone receiver, Vince began, 'Security, I need . . .' but before he could finish, Alex had decided to leave.

Vince dropped the receiver into place. 'Can you believe that?' he said when Alex had gone. 'He just accused me of killing his brother!' Then, to Bob, he added, 'I hope you were taking notes. That's the kind of action I've been talking about.'

There was an uncomfortable silence before one of the reporters, a young girl on only her second assignment, giggled and said, 'Was that a set-up?'

'She's a smart girl,' said Vince, wiping at the sheen of sweat on his forehead. 'Well spotted! Now people,' he said, pausing to light a cigarette. 'Remind me where we were at.'

A few days later, Alex returned to Washington DC. It was two weeks since he had left and he began his morning as usual, walking to Starbucks on Dupont Circle for coffee. On the face of it, nothing was different. However, as he paid for his *latte grande* he sensed that the server was eying him not with the customary awe but with a degree of disdain, and it took just this one glance for the horrible truth to become evident. He was no longer impressive even to a coffee-shop waiter. He was no longer the star he had been.

Success and standing in Washington were entirely dependent on who and what you knew, and if what you knew was new, and from the top, then you belonged to Washington's elite. Nothing beat fresh knowledge. If one knew, or could make others think one knew, what the President was thinking, how the Ways and Means Committee would swing or who was to be appointed to what, then one was treated as royalty in the nation's capital. As both White House Director of Communications and a close personal friend of the President, it had been understood by all that Alex was most definitely in the know. Almost no one could know more than he, and so he was rarely tested on his actual knowledge. Rather others, keen to barter snippets of information in order that they could remain knowing the latest knowledge, would come to him looking for his spin on what they'd already heard. In return for his wise opinions they would keep him informed on what was being discussed in the House or Senate or among the lobbyists, thereby adding to his legendary knowledge.

Today was different. Today no one had stopped him in Starbucks, no one was crossing the street to talk to him nor rolling down the window of their car to wish him a good day as he headed to the White House. He felt uneasily mortal in the city where he had been accustomed to feeling like a god. And what irritated him the most was that he himself was to blame. If he had graciously accepted the post as Susan's Chief of Staff, and if the Administration had worded the announcement to make it look like a transfer of authority as opposed to a demotion, then he would have remained in the corridors of power. Outsiders wishing to be insiders would have been desperate to discover what had prompted the shuffle, and why. As his friend, Alex's access to President Grant would not have been questioned.

His telephone calls would have been answered and, most important of all, he would have remained at the White House.

Alex reached the gates of the West Wing driveway and stepped into the white cabin. 'Hi, Davey.'

The uniformed guard, a young man with acne and a brutal crew cut, nodded. 'Mr Lubotsky, sir.'

'I forgot my pass,' he said in an offhand manner.

The guard typed Alex's name into the computer. 'I'm going to need clearance, sir.'

Alex handed the guard his driver's licence.

'I'm going to need more than that, Mr Lubotsky, sir.'

'You are? Oh, so call Rebecca Frear in Communications and tell her I'm here, would you?'

To Alex's great relief, Rebecca gave authority and he passed through the metal detectors to meet his ex-assistant on the lawn in front of the briefing room. She shook his hand, though he had been expecting a kiss.

'Did you get my fax?' he asked, though he had not sent one.

'No. Are you meeting someone?'

Alex was about to speak, but hesitated. Didn't he belong here? Why should he need a reason to walk into the White House? He had worked twelve years for the luxury of calling it his office.

'No, I thought I should clear out what's mine.'

'That had to be done for Curt Wallis.'

'Of course, couldn't keep Saint Curt waiting,' said Alex irascibly.

Rebecca remained stony-faced. Alex looked over her shoulder, trying to see through the window of his old room.

'Where are they all, my things?'

'With Security. They're planning to send them on.'

Alex glanced to his left. A tour group was mingling outside the main entrance to the East Wing, being herded together for the trip around a few of the grand state rooms. They were the usual gawping, plaid-clad crowd, enriching Kodak as they filled roll upon roll of film with a façade seen in millions of photos appearing in their newspapers every other day. Alex stuck his teeth out and made himself a little cross-eyed. 'Maayam, 's there any chance I can gayat to see the President?' he asked in a Southern drawl.

Rebecca was unamused. 'Are you being serious?'

'Yes, Rebecca,' he said, irritated by such arrogance in the woman, the girl, whom he had picked out himself from Grant's election staff. 'I am being serious. Is he here?'

'Yes he is, but . . .'

'But you don't think he'll see me,' Alex said, correctly completing her sentence.

She closed her eyes and nodded, and then turned to see if anyone was watching before briefly touching his arm. 'Alex, please! You know we didn't want you to leave. Especially not me,' she added, glancing away with embarrassment. 'But you didn't exactly do us any favours by going the way you did. You're hardly the most popular person around the press office. I suppose you've heard they're planning more hearings on Cochabamba, haven't you?'

'Yes,' said Alex.

He had gone too far with his resignation interview, and he knew it. The knowledge that in the previous month he had betrayed the two men who, aside from his father, had done most to shape his life had damaged a previously rigid sense of self-worth. Truthfully, he had hoped to come here to apologise, to Jack, to Rebecca, to the Communications team, but now he realised that they weren't interested in his apologies. What mattered to them was how Alex had made the President look then, and how they would make the President look tomorrow. As an ex-DOC and ex-buddy of the President, Alex no longer had a part to play.

'You know Jack fired me, don't you?' he said, wanting to be understood. 'I was out of here anyway.'

Rebecca nodded. She had loved Alex, as a man and a professional, and it wasn't easy knowing she now possessed the power that he craved.

'I was going to say goodbye to everyone,' he continued. 'Is Curt in?'

'Yes, he is. I think it'd be better another time.'

Alex smiled gamely. 'Do you know if Susan's about?'

'She's here somewhere. I don't know exactly.'

'I'll go search her out.' He rubbed his hands against the sudden cold and together they walked to the West Lobby portico. 'Listen,' he said genuinely. 'I'm glad Curt kept you on. You deserve it.'

'Thanks, Al,' she said, relaxing now. 'I was glad too. Even,' she added, lowering her voice, 'if it's no fun any more. Anyway, what about you? Are you staying in DC?'

'I don't know. I'll call you.'

'Please do,' she said. 'I'd prefer to see you somewhere else. Curt's being difficult with me as it is. He thinks I'm still on your side, somehow.'

'Aren't you?'

'Al, you know I . . .'

'Don't worry,' he interrupted. 'I'll give you a call at home.'

She kissed him and smiled before walking into the West Lobby where he could no longer follow. Instead, he set off towards Susan's office.

There was little explicit security within the White House complex. Once clearance had been given and bags and bodies X-rayed for weapons, badge-holders were pretty much free to wander around. Of course, there were the little details that made the compound safe – the hidden fortifications, the electronic and infrared eyes, the pressure detectors buried in the lawns, the steel mesh within the walls, the visible snipers on the roof, the Presidential Protection Detail, or PPD, who thought they looked plain in their clothes but who were unmistakable with their necks sturdy as oak and their earphones squiggling from under their collars. There was, however, no one to question Alex as he crossed the driveway to enter the hulking granite Old Executive Office Building where Susan had set up her offices.

As he climbed the steps, he passed Vice President Shaw coming down, flanked by Protection. Shaw nodded in that slightly gormless way he had, as one would to an acquaintance whose name had slipped the memory. He did not stop to greet Alex, aware as he was that his only duty as the Veep was to hate whom the President hated, love whom he loved, and question nothing he did along the way, however dishonest or immoral he knew it to be.

The guard stationed outside Susan's office recognised Alex and, with a glance at his pass and an ignorance of his lowly station, allowed him inside. Susan's Chief of Staff, Mary, smiled warmly when Alex came in.

Alex had known that Mary would go far, not only because it was perfect for the First Lady's image to have her office headed by a brilliant black woman, but because she made people warm to her while giving nothing away. It was certainly rare to have achieved so much power in DC without gathering enemies, a feat that Alex had not been able to match.

'You're the first person who doesn't look like they want to bite my head off,' he said. Mary raised her eyebrows. Smart bitch, thought Alex. *Say nothing!* 'Is Susan busy?'

'She's about to be. We've got a delegation from the Children's Defence Fund ready to descend from the Hill.'

'Funny, I always felt I was *as*cending when I left the Hill,' Alex said. 'Out of the swamps!'

'Right, and too many people knew it,' Mary said, adjusting her jacket as if to suggest that in Washington

you always had to take care to appear as others wanted
you to be. Alex, keen to remain his own man, had made
too many enemies in Congress.

'If you could wait here,' Mary said, 'I'll have a word
with her.'

After a few seconds, Mary reappeared and said, 'She
can give you five minutes.'

Susan was waiting for Alex on the other side of the thick,
panelled door to her office. He took her in his arms to
kiss her.

'Don't,' she said, gently pushing him away with her
fingertips on his cheek. 'My lipstick!' She took a step
back. 'Does Jack know you're here?'

'No. I came to see you.'

He fingered a curl of hair off her forehead.

'Are you back in DC for my campaign?' she asked,
though there was no affection to soften her voice.

'Why do you always talk to me as if I'd said yes?' he
asked, with undisguised petulance.

'Because I know you. Because already you can't keep
away. You're too fond of the way it feels.' She wandered to the window with its view of the Residence
and beyond, to downtown DC. 'I used to watch you
sometimes, swaggering around the driveway like a boy
who just got laid for the first time.'

'Screwed, more like,' he said, joining her, but then
stepping away aware that, from somewhere, a pair of
binoculars might be trained on the window.

'Don't be childish, Alex. You screwed yourself. You
really did.'

'Susan!' Alex protested. 'Jack fired me.'

She turned to him. 'He was being smart for a change.
He was protecting you from the press by moving you. But
you were too damn arrogant to see that. The rest of us
could hear the knives sharpening every time you walked
into that briefing room. They hated the fact that you were

rude as hell at the party, but always left with the girl.' She looked at him. 'They hated that.'

Self-consciously, Alex ran a hand through his hair. If he had known what the day would hold, he would never have come. He laughed to cover his shame. 'I feel like, I don't know, like I've been wandering around this place with a sticker saying "JERK" on my back. It makes me wonder why you'd want me anywhere near your campaign,' he said, wanting to hear the familiar chorus of praises being sung again.

Susan dutifully obliged, striding back to the desk as she spoke. 'Because that's what you're great at, Al. Winning campaigns is about proving you're smarter than the press. But when you're in the White House you've got to get into bed with those people and make them think they're better and smarter than you. I could have told Jack you'd be no good at that. In fact, I probably did.'

'I thought he did everything you said,' he joked, smiling.

'See?' she said, gesturing towards him. 'It's that smile of yours – all wrong. It makes you look like you're up to no good, like you're hiding the one piece of information that'll make a good story. When you're running Communications you need a smile that says, "Here, take everything I've got." That's what Wallis has. It's a kind of gigolo smirk. It doesn't come out right with you.'

'So you're saying I can't work for my country because I don't have the right smile?'

'You can work for your country all right, if you work with me. Get me into the Oval Office, and I promise you any job you want.' There was a knock at the door. 'Except Communication!' she added.

Mary popped her head round the door, and said, 'They're on their way.'

Knowing he had to leave quickly, Alex embraced Susan.

'I'll think about it,' he said. 'If you can swear that Jack won't fight us, I'll definitely think about it.'

She leant in to him to flick at his earlobe with her tongue. 'Trust me,' she said. 'Just trust me.'

He left by the front entrance to the OEOB, across paving slabs cut like a chequerboard. It was odd that he'd never thought of that before. Now he knew that he needed to put himself in a position from where he could leapfrog his rivals. If he supported Susan, could he find himself returning to the heart of power?

On Pennsylvania Avenue, he turned to face the dour and unattractive building and felt the pangs of which Susan had spoken. To the left of it he saw, through leafless trees, the White House gleaming, its chandeliers glistening beyond bullet-proof windows. Even under today's listless clouds it looked splendid, as if the President himself was exempt from the muddy business of politics.

Deep down, though nothing had led him to believe it, Alex had imagined that something might have occurred on this visit that would have lifted his heart. A pardon from Jack Grant, a gift of thanks from his office, or at the very least, a fond farewell from staff who owed their jobs to him alone. When, less than a year before, he had first stepped through those hallowed gates as a member of an Administration that could change the nation, Alex had not expected a farewell such as this – a weary trudge on the tarmac in a soft, unexceptional shower of rain. Even Nixon, impeached and disgraced, had seen his staff line up in honour. So what if I wasn't President? Alex thought to himself. I cared as much and tried as hard and did nothing illegal or wrong. He didn't feel he deserved this.

Now as he walked briskly away he was determined not to look back. He crossed the street. From the blank, colourless sky rain was dripping lazily, weighty drops mixed with the drizzle. The umbrella vendors were emerging, as if from some massive subterranean warehouse, to occupy street corners. Alex bought himself a flimsy five-dollar contraption made in South Korea while Northeast Washington slumped with the unemployed. As he rounded the corner at Dupont a wicked gust tore it inside out, ripping the canopy from its ribs and spreaders like a zeppelin fractured at its mooring. He threw it into a bin and chose to see out the rain in Starbucks.

Another steaming *latte* in hand, he spread the paper in front of him. He saw, as often before, his name. However, because he was so accustomed to receiving all articles of importance from the the Office of News Analysis in the White House, he had almost dismissed the piece unread when he was shocked to realise what it was about. As he furiously read, his heartbeat quickened and, when he had finished, he leant forward on his elbows and screwed the paper tight and hard in his fists, despising himself for what he feared he had done.

7

'**V**ince?'

Vince Moscardini shot a glance at his production assistant. 'Yeah, what do you want?'

'I thought you should see this. It's Jayne-Anne's article in *Soap Opera News*.'

Without lifting his head, Vince snapped the fingers of one hand and gestured for the page to be handed to him.

'Does she love us?' he asked, 'or what?'

'Well . . .'

'You ask me, I say she's a dyke.' A frown spread like a fault line across his brow. 'I can never crack her, you know what I'm saying? But she loves the show. Boy does she love the show. Always has.'

Dave handed the photocopied sheet to his boss. 'Maybe you mean "always did".'

'What?'

'You'd better read it.'

Vince lowered his eyes.

SOAP OPERA NEWS, Volume 4, Issue 39.

Editor's Notes
    by Jayne-Anne Lipke

UNTO THE SKIES LIFTS OFF AGAIN, BUT
WILL IT STAY CLEAR OF THE TREES?

Close your eyes and travel with me. Because we're going back in time.

Remember when you were younger and William Sheridan, played with such grace and authority by the wonderful Johnson Bell, was just the handsomest man on TV? And how you loved him and wanted him to win the battle for Brendan Air, that he was fighting against that scheming but foreverly forgivable rogue, Jim Brenner? Remember the joy we felt when Mary Sheridan produced the child she'd been dreaming of and how it tore us all apart to see that child kidnapped and held to ransom by the brutal Sicilian mafia? But what scenes of joy there were, what joy we felt when little Jamie was returned to his mother's arms only to be told that there was another bundle of happiness on the way, a lovely little girl who would be christened Carrie. They grew up in a loving, sharing environment, innocent of the rivalry controlling their parents' lives. The Sheridans were a family like families used to be. We watched the children grow and develop into the whole, mature characters they are, so ably played today by the beautiful Ally Springer and the brooding Philip Shaw.

Max Lubotsky, the late great headwriter of *UTS*, was not only a friend of mine, he was also a man of virtue. When he joined *UTS* he could see that its appeal lay in the enduring humanity of the show's characters, the ordinary-but-uniqueness of the residents of Hill Way. Max did not shower the soap with cheap and tacky gimmicks or gratuitous sex scenes that we find in other, I'll-not-name-them, shows. He was a student of drama and of life; and we became students of him. Thank you, Max. We all miss you.

Many of you who were loyal fans of the show will know that for years Bernie Hermann was the Executive Producer. He was a man who had faults, a man who thought nothing of sweeping aside actors or writers or directors he did not like. But just as Shannon de Salle, the longtime bitch of the show, has always been loyal to her family through all her schemings and connivings, so Bernie was loyal to *UTS*. He had its best interests at heart and he performed amazing feats on its behalf.

Max joined the team at a difficult time. Luke and Laura of *General Hospital* were enthralling our nation, and some of Soap's younger cousins were bouncing into the fray, keen to win audiences with their glitzy, glamorous ways. It would have been easy for *UTS* to slide down that slippery path. But it did not, my friends. We were thrilled as the tension built between the characters. Nothing was done for ratings alone. The handling of Vanessa's miscarriage was one of the most life-affirming pieces of television I have ever seen, played with tear-making intensity by the stalwart Faith Valentine.

Then something happened, and that something was a heart attack for Executive Producer Bernie Hermann. The blood drained from the show with the death of that man. It became colourless and drab, trapped between a rock, the rock of tradition and excellence, and a hard place, a place where there's a disease called impatience, the impatience of a teenager to sleep with her man, the impatience of today's soap opera viewers wanting action and excitement all the way, the impatience of a man called Vincent Moscardini.

I have been the senior editor of this happy magazine for six wonderfully fulfilling years. We pride ourselves on our tough fairmindedness. We understand that one viewer's soda is another's poison. But I feel the time has come to speak up. Please tell us, Mr Moscardini, what are you doing?? We know that the ratings have not been kind, but perseverance must be the key.

In an exclusive interview with the Executive Producer and the show's new, young headwriter, Bob Fein, I was told that *UTS* is about to become ballsier and raunchier. 'Take it that if this show was a pair of breasts,' I was told by Mr Moscardini, 'we'd be pumping in the silicone.'

Silicone? Ballsier? I ask you – is that why *UTS* has graced our screens for more than thirty years? What made it a leader in daytime TV? What made us care about the Sheridans and Brenners? No, I say, and I can hear my voice echo in living rooms around the nation. *UTS* deserves to be different. In this more caring, sharing age we are thinking again about families, about real love, about the bridges that unite human beings to each other. Mr Moscardini is burning those bridges and I worry that we will never get back to where we came from. He burnt the bridge on which that fine writer, Max Lubotsky, so proudly stood. Max died in the fall. Questions have been raised by none other than President Grant's close friend, Max's twin brother, Alex, about Vince Moscardini's culpability. I'd like to hear some answers to that, as I'd like to hear an answer to this: Mr Moscardini, is nothing sacred any more?

Write to him, and write to me, and tell me what you think.

Vince screwed up the paper and threw it against the wall. 'Think? I'm going to tell her what I think.' He screamed through his door. 'Kelly!'

His secretary ran in. 'Is something wrong?'

'Yes. Call *Soap Opera News* and get that bitch Lipke on the line. Tell her it's urgent.'

Kelly sauntered out, chewing gum.

'Vince,' said Dave, 'I don't think . . .'

'Good. Keep not thinking. It suits you better.' He

thrust his hands in his pockets and began to pace in front of the window. 'That Fein dork is finished as headwriter. Go tell him.'

Dave didn't move. 'Do we have a replacement?'

'Yeah. Me. Everyone else is clueless.' He squeezed a palm around the nicotine patch on his arm. 'I'm the sails and the rudder of this ship. I'm the hull. I can't trust anyone else.'

Kelly buzzed through and said, 'Miss Lipke's secretary says she'll have to call back later. She's out.'

'Out!' said Vince. 'She doesn't know how out she's about to be. I'm going to tell the world she's a fucking pussy-licker. That'll push her off her moral high horse.' He ripped back the ring-pull of a soda, took a long swig and burped. 'Do me a favour and scram, Dave. I feel like I'm in an elevator with you standing over me like that.'

Dave, who was on the other side of the office, said, 'Do you want me to call Bob Fein?'

'Yes. I mean no. I mean hold off on that until I've thought things through.'

Vince paused and seemed unusually pensive. Maybe, thought Dave, even remorseful?

And then the producer spoke. 'You know something, Dave, there's nothing I hate more than a dyke still in clothes.'

Alex returned to Titusville from Washington the day after the article appeared. Pam offered him a withering stare when she answered the door. Alex lifted a large bunch of flowers in front of his face.

'Why is it that I want to kill you every time you arrive?' said Pam without humour.

Alex lowered the bouquet, suddenly embarrassed at such an easy gesture of apology. She took them from him.

'The insurance company called this morning,' she told

him. 'They said they'd seen *The New York Times* article and are "withholding payment pending a further investigation".'

'Oh, Pam, I'm so sorry.'

'Christ!' she snapped, turning from him and striding towards the kitchen to find a vase for the flowers. 'I know that. You keep telling me.'

Alex took a tentative step inside and gently shut the door. The house seemed unusually quiet, as if the walls themselves were condemning him for his outburst against Vince Moscardini. If he had known a reporter from *The Times* was there, and if he could have guessed that an article would be written detailing his public admission of Max's suicide, then he wouldn't have said a word. But that was not good enough. He had made a mistake worse than any made while working for Grant, and now he had to watch others live with the consequences.

'Did you close that door yet?' Pam called out. 'It's freezing.'

He touched a cold radiator and said, 'You should have the heating on in weather like this,' as he moved to join her in the kitchen.

'And pay the oil man with what, Alex? These flowers?'

'I'll pay. That shouldn't be an issue.'

'Well, it is an issue,' she said frostily. 'This isn't a Democratic Administration. I can't spend just for the hell of it. Especially not now.'

'Look, just because the insurance people called doesn't mean . . .'

With her back to him and her hands resting on the side of the sink, Pam said, 'I don't want to talk about it. I know it was a mistake. I know you'd take it all back if you had half a chance. That's all I've been hearing for the last God knows how long. But it doesn't change anything.' She threw down the stems she had in her hand and looked at him. 'I don't know, you must have been in politics too long or something. You can't seem to get it into your head that sometimes when you make a mistake you can't make it go away just by finding excuses for it.'

'Point taken,' he said quietly, though in truth he knew that he'd been explaining his mistake to Pam as a means of explaining it to himself.

It had been so unlike him to lose his head, but the moment he had seen Vince, all the resentment and anger and guilt over Max's death had boiled out from within. He had become convinced through reading Max's journals that Vince was the catalyst for Max's death. Oh, he knew that his brother had never been a happy man, but now Alex believed it was the cynical deal with the producer that had pushed him over the edge.

In the journals, Max had revealed the depth of his obsession with the show. He had begun to see the weekly ratings as a judgment on himself, and as they had fallen so his despair had deepened. The fear (created by Vince Moscardini) that he would never be paid his salary only made things worse and, after Alex had refused him the loan, Max had begun to speculate on how Pam would benefit from the million-dollar insurance payout. It was a fact that had given some happiness – that in the end no one could say that he wasn't worth that much.

Sensing now that Pam needed to be alone, Alex returned to Max's study. Since discovering the journals, he had spent many hours learning about his twin. He felt closer to him now than he had done for years and it made him determined not to turn his back again. He had not started well, but if the insurance payout was denied, he knew he would support Pam and the boys until the difference was made up. There were plenty of highly paid jobs he could walk into – in the media, as a consultant, among the lobbyists – and he didn't need much for himself; not while he remained alone.

For the moment, however, Alex was occupying himself by sorting through Max's personal papers. Some he threw out, some he filed, others he put aside for Pam to read. He was undecided about the painted linen chest full of letters from fans of the show. Alex had glanced at a few and been amazed by how passionate most were. It seemed that these viewers deemed *Unto the Skies* more important than their real lives. He had found one letter demanding that Max pay for a dress the viewer had bought for a screen wedding that had been called off at the last minute. The woman had written how she had bought wine as well, to toast the happy couple.

Alex opened the chest once more, and was drawn to one letter, dated September 9th, 1988, on which Max had written some comments in red crayon.

Dear Writers of <u>Unto the Skies</u>,

As a viewer of <u>Unto the Skies</u> for more than ten years, I hope you will take a <u>good long look</u> at this letter to you. I am most deeply troubled by the actions of some of the characters, namely Carrie and her brother, Jamie. He should not be overly cruel to the young girl, namely Suzanne, who he is falling for, though it is clear to me LIKE DAYLIGHT that they are wrong for each other and I feel it is cruelty on your parts to make her suffer with him as she has been, like a mouse and cat playing before the kill. It breaks my heart because the girl is a beautiful sweet thing who will go very far and Jamie is wrong wrong wrong for her. I hope you will please listen to me on this. I wrote once before about Pierce's profanity (maybe you remember) and I was glad to see that he stopped being so GODLESS like are many of the other characters. But Jamie is too immature for marriage to the sweet girl. He is not a man yet, not like Carrie who is both very strong and very feminine too, especially with her new hairstyle *which is beautiful and I have tried to copy though I am older by some years!!*

This is also what I wanted to say. I love Carrie like she was my daughter and I feel she is too under the wing of her father, namely of course William Sheridan who has been very shining as an example of good fatherliness but feel there's a time for letting go and <u>that time has come</u>. For a woman to understand her own mind she must be very able to live on her own and be thinking her own thoughts. I am not blind that I see that Mr Max Lubotsky is writing this programme and he is a man and men do not understand that women of all ages want to be independent and free. I myself have parted company with my husband who was a rat and a hog and I am a happier and safer woman away from him and I do thank the good Lord for giving me the courage to do this. I would like <u>to talk</u> to Carrie about these things. Could this be arranged? Until then, I ask you to give her something to be proud of.

I love <u>Unto the Skies</u> more than anything and I don't like mistakes being made. Give Carrie a chance to make something of her life. In honesty the time is almost too late, but do it now. Vanessa is a wonderful character. I want to thank you for making her so positive. She is a role model for me, and must be for many women.

Before I go I would like to say that the actor playing the part of the lawyer, Kelvin Cross, has an unattractive amount of hair to his chest, and should not be allowed to play bedroom scenes; these bring the show into the gutter as it is.
Sincerely,
A worried but loyal and ever-hopeful viewer.

On the back of the letter, Max had written:

Am getting more convinced that the best stories I

write are the ones involving female characters. (Think Medea!) Yet another letter today raving about our treatment of Vanessa while criticizing Carrie for being too weak. Perhaps soaps actually provide women with positive role models. I should make Carrie stronger. I can do some good by giving women a stronger sense of themselves. Prime-time female characters are way too stereotyped. As mothers, wives or bimbos they're not representative. We can, I can, do something different. We're watched by millions of women and I've got to be responsible for that. Keep watching . . . Max the feminist is coming!

Alex read the paragraph again, and then a smile broke across his face. 'I couldn't,' he whispered to himself. 'Could I, Max?' He sprang from the chair and shouted down the stairs. 'Pam, what time's *Unto the Skies* on?'

'It just started,' she answered. 'Why?'

'Because I've got some serious catching up to do,' he said as he ran past her to turn on the show.

Because they ran that kind of city, the good officials of San Francisco had decided that its residents needed a free information system that could be accessed by simply dialling a few numbers on the phone. Recorded advice was provided on HIV and AIDS, herpes and indigestion, divorce, depression, drug abuse and global weather. Among the many other pieces of information considered essential were the changes in the stock indices from the Nikkei to the Dow Jones, as well as the predictions made by those astrologers hired for their priceless insights. One of the most popular services was the daily update provided on the loves and losses of the characters of every single soap opera broadcast on the nation's TV screens.

The Bay Area Telephone network was responsible for this service, and had recently employed a number of voice actors to read the scripts that were written each day. Annie's agent, Sam, had spent the best part of a morning persuading her that she should audition for one of the vacancies. He understood, he'd said, that she had not studied Shakespeare in order to sound sincere while giving advice on vaginal discharge, but this was a cushy, well-paid job, and in no time she could save enough cash to support her search for a more fulfilling role.

It was with that in mind that Annie had auditioned and secured the part. Now, a week on, she was sitting in a sound booth in a recording studio on Turk Street, a script in front of her.

'Whenever you're ready,' said the producer.

Annie adjusted the microphone, and began. 'Hello, and welcome to your latest *Unto the Skies* update for today, Monday December 20th, here on the BAT network.'

When being played down the telephone wires, the recording would be interrupted for some jazzy muzak, but for now the commentary was read uninterrupted.

'When Vanessa tells Jack that she fears her marriage won't survive, he boldly tells her that he has been in love with her for years. She asks for time to think, evading his probing questions about her feelings for William. Carrie swears to Paolo that she will love him for ever as the couple share a moment of romance before his return to jail. Despite all of her best efforts, Shannon's long relationship with Dale has clearly hit the rocks and her confusion is heightened since the two have shared so many pleasant times.'

Silence, then a voice came through Annie's headphones.

'What's the problem?'

Annie looked out of the booth at the producer. He

was a short man with a bald patch and a ponytail. She felt a sudden urge to get up and punch him.

'Er, nothing,' she said. 'Nothing.'

What other answer could she give? She couldn't say that she hated herself for taking this stinking, fucking job. She couldn't tell this stranger that it pained her to read the story of *Unto the Skies*. And most of all she couldn't admit that, despite all her best efforts, her long relationship with Jerry had clearly hit the rocks. She had tried so very hard over the past few days, but there seemed to be nothing left to say or do. Annie knew that as soon as she had the courage to leave – after Christmas, maybe, when it wouldn't be so hard to be alone – she would.

'Start the sentence before you left off,' the producer said. 'And try to be happy when you read it. It sounds like you don't care.'

'Oh, I do,' said Annie, her face so sullen it was as if she'd forgotten how to use the muscles that made her smile. 'Really I do.'

'OK, tapes are rolling.'

Annie mustered all the enthusiasm she could, and began again.

'Shannon's long relationship with Dale has clearly hit the rocks and her confusion is heightened since the two have shared so many pleasant times. Mary invites Vanessa to spend the weekend, unaware of the feelings that William is having for her. Believing him to be tired from too much work, she sends him into the bedroom innocently unaware that Vanessa is inside the house. Jamie and Pierce tell Wayne that there still might be hope for Dale's dreams for the business. And that's what happened on today's episode of *Unto the Skies*.

'Was that better?' enquired Annie.

'It'll do,' the producer said unconvincingly as he turned

to the next page of script. 'Now let's go to *As the World Turns*.'

With an explosion of glitter and jingling bells, Christmas blasted the American people over and beyond their continent. Packing bags with unwanted presents, families congregated in worship of their collective wealth and vowed to bond with relatives, however thin and rancid their blood ties might have become. For many, television provided hours of blissful escape and helped to forge friendships among in-laws and cousins struggling to find any other common ground. Suddenly it didn't matter who came from where, or what they did and why, when they could discuss the merits and flaws of characters they knew as mutual friends.

Of all the Yuletide programmes sprinkled like dandruff over the shoulders of the nation, few provided more opportunities for informed gossip and speculation than the daytime soaps. People unable to dredge up any interest in the real lives of their relatives would spend hours debating the decisions and mistakes made by favourite characters. Those left alone kept despair at bay by sharing their holidays with loved ones on TV.

The producers, writers and directors of the nation's soap operas rarely missed out on the opportunity to have their characters celebrate Christmas on air. It gave them a chance to display their exaggerated virtues or vices to the full. *Unto the Skies'* Christmas episodes were the last written while Max was headwriter. Each one was watched by his brother with the greatest curiosity.

Alex had been working like a man possessed, sixteen, seventeen, sometimes eighteen hours a day, and this throughout the Christmas holiday, so that Pam had begun to worry that he would get sick, as Max had done. Or had the sickness already taken hold? It had seemed when Max was alive that his obsession with *Unto the Skies* was a kind of cancer. The tumour had become alarmingly, visibly malignant as the show had taken over (and finally taken) his life. Now Alex seemed afflicted. He was taking little care of his appearance, sleeping and eating less, and had begun to lose interest in the real world as the imaginary one took hold.

Alex himself felt vitalised by his efforts. He knew he was working against the clock – his meeting with UBC's President was on January 3rd, only two days away – and he was excited to be learning so much so fast. He felt too that Max was guiding and teaching him. He had finished most of the Greek plays to which Max had constantly referred, and in so doing had begun to understand dramatic parallels with the soap operas that once he'd laughed at. From the library he had borrowed books on TV writing penned by writers who had failed at TV. He had pored over the pages of the soap opera magazines and studied the past histories of the Brenner and Sheridan families so vital to every current plot. And he had been studying, with complete fascination, the diaries that Max had kept for the last eight years of his life.

It was these journals that charted Max's obsession with *Unto the Skies*. There was barely an event in his real life, whether his drinking or the birth of his sons, that had not been deconstructed for its value to his writing. The pages were peppered with characters' names, helping Alex build a picture of which characters his brother had loved, and why. He could clearly see what Max had tried to achieve and these goals became his own motivation. He was determined that Max's industry should not go to waste. And in the long, quiet hours spent immersed in a world once inhabited by his brother, Alex really believed that he wasn't alone. He believed that the two of them were working together once again.

He turned his gaze to an index card that Max had pinned beside his desk. Upon it was a quote from Max's dramatic bible, Aristotle's *Poetics*. 'Agitation or rage,' it ended, 'will be most vividly reproduced by one who is himself agitated or in passion.' It seemed to explain why Max had been obsessed with the show, and why his brother had begun to hear in his head some of the voices belonging to the forty-five characters of *Unto the Skies*.

Now it was Pam's knock on the door that he heard. He called for her to come in.

'How's it going?' she asked.

'I'm getting there. Slowly.'

His back cracked as he stood, and an arrow of pain shot up his spine. He put his hands on his hips and arched backwards.

'You look beat, Al,' she said. 'Why don't you call it a night?'

'What time is it?'

She said, 'Almost twelve.'

He looked at her. The light from the desk lamp, made caramel by its reflection on the desk's grainy wood, etched out the contours of her trim body against the teak bookshelves behind. She was wearing a simple charcoal sweater, tight to the body, and the whiteness of her skin against it made her throat look creamy and soft and provoked in him thoughts he would have preferred to deny. His heart kicked itself as he took a step towards her, but his mind sped forward to imagine her naked, her thighs milky as her neck, the pubic hair dark like the wool of her sweater.

His mouth dried in the chemistry of his unease and, as if sensing this, she stiffened when he leant forward to kiss her goodnight. Perhaps it was unfamiliarity with such solitude that made his body yearn for her and enjoy the cool softness of her skin against his cheek. But he knew he had to resist those feelings he could not prevent. He leant back against the wall.

Angling her head down and away from the light so that

half her face lost its definition in shadow, Pam said, 'It's strange how like Max you are.' Though thirty-nine, she seemed girlish in the way she blinked up at him.

'Don't you think it would have been stranger if we hadn't been alike?' he said.

'Of course. I was thinking more . . . I mean, I never noticed it as much as I do now. You never seemed as gentle as he.'

'It was that job of mine. I was trying not to be eaten alive.'

'Mm, that must have been it. Well, um, good night then,' she said, and she moved to kiss his cheek before pulling her neck back sharply to say, with a nervy laugh, 'We already did that, didn't we?'

'Is there a law saying we can't do it again?' he asked. 'As a matter of fact,' he added, opening his arms, 'give me a hug. You look like you need one.'

She hesitated for a second, but opened her arms and leant into his strong embrace. He moved his head back to look into her eyes, their bodies together still.

'You're OK, aren't you?' he asked, in a half-whisper.

She nodded, though tears seemed close. 'I miss him, Al. I really miss him. I didn't know how I was going to get through last night. It was like rubbing it in – here's a new year that Max isn't going to see. Let's have a party to celebrate! It was so hard thinking that he'll never see 1994. He's just gone. And there's nothing any of us can do.'

A tear furrowed a line to her lip and stopped. Softly, Alex wiped at it with the side of a finger and at once Pam clasped her hand over his and began to kiss his fingers, closing her eyes as she did so. When she took a finger and sucked on the tip, Alex gently pulled his hand away.

'Pam, I don't know if . . .'

'I'm sorry,' she said, her eyes wide open now, as if

she had seen something horrible and shocking. 'I didn't mean to. I'm sorry.'

'Don't be,' Alex whispered. 'Come on.'

He laid his arm across her shoulders and walked her into the bedroom where he closed the curtains. Then he joined her on the bed and took her trembling hands in his. For a while they were silent, but when he heard that her breathing had calmed he said, 'Why don't you get into bed and I'll bring you some tea? That camomile will help you sleep.'

She nodded, and when he returned with the steaming drink she was sitting under the covers looking less terrified than she had, though her sadness tore at his heart.

'Thanks,' she said, taking the cup.

'Will you be all right?'

'Yup.'

'I'll be up for a while yet if you need me,' he said, retreating to the door. 'Just shout.'

'Thanks, Al, really. You've been wonderful.'

'It's about time I did something right,' he said, and he was almost out of the door when she called him back.

'It's going to be worth it,' she said. 'Isn't it? All your work?'

'I hope so,' he replied. 'But we'll have to see.'

FLICKS MAGAZINE, January 12, 1994.

Out Takes
        by Jimmy James

In a move predicted on these pages last week, AFM have filed a lawsuit against the hot young British director, Zoë Dunlop, for breach of contract over *The Fur Bites Back*. AFM's President, Joel Ritchie, said yesterday that Miss Dunlop had approved of the script (cowritten by *Rifleman* screenwriter Tom Shacklinger, and *Feet of*

Clay's Don Peabody whose credits also include *Mirage*, *Schoolmaster*, *Mad Mad Holiday* and *Doughbrain*) way back in January of this year. AFM insist that at no time had she shown any desire to make changes to the script. For her part, Dunlop says that she was unhappy at the way she was being treated by AFM executives. She claims that she'd made her wishes explicit concerning the film's style.

A spokesman at AFM said that Dunlop, who made her name last year with the acclaimed feminist flick *Tarts*, has done a U-turn in wanting to make *The Fur Bites Back* into a politically correct attack on America's beauty and fashion businesses. In a statement issued from her San Francisco home (Dunlop has little regard for our city of angels) the fired director questioned AFM's decision in hiring someone who had a pro-woman track record. She has been outspoken in her criticism of the way women are treated in Hollywood, both in the lack of strong parts and in the inequalities in pay. Referring to Macaulay Culkin, she said it was criminal that a child should be paid more than any female star has ever received. This outspokenness will surely be a tack for her attorneys to favor, especially as Dunlop was, in her own words, 'swamped with suitable material' after *Tarts*. Given that, she said in characteristically strong language, 'why would I have agreed to direct a macho, misogynistic heap of s**t like *The Fur Bites Back*?'

However, AFM executives are claiming that Dunlop was trying to have her cake and eat it too by hijacking a project that was always destined to be a horror spoof. The movie, due to go into production in March of next year, will now be directed by Billy Ray Spirano, who teamed up so successfully with Shacklinger on *Rifleman*. How big a setback to Zoë Dunlop's career this run-in with a major studio will be is an interesting question. The latest gossip has her running back scared to England where there are plans for a movie version of Indian supermodel Mit Yager's bestselling lesbian novel, *Goa*.

8

The President was late. With a brisk curl of his fingers Alex called over the waiter and asked for a second glass of Sancerre, having downed the first as if it was water. He wanted to steady the slight shake in his hands, unsure why he was so nervous. After all, Barry Shermer was hardly the President of the United States. He was merely the head of one of America's biggest TV networks.

If he had given it much thought, Alex would have realised that he was uneasy because, for once, he was selling ideas that belonged not to another man, but to himself. From the start he had invested his soul in the notion that he was about to present to Shermer, and since then he had been driven by an instinct that had been watertight in the past. It was the same instinct that had told him to focus on attacking the incumbent President's social record during Grant's victorious campaign. The same that had made him follow Grant from 1978.

And, of course, there was the fact that he was doing this for Max. Sometimes when the house was quiet and Pam and the boys were in bed, Alex felt a presence beside him in the study; nothing dramatic, no flying books or windows clapping in a sudden draught of cold air, but rather a strength of purpose, a conviction that would sweep through him when he began to doubt himself. This was *their* project, and Alex knew that he would be letting Max down if Barry Shermer were to say no.

He hoped with all his heart that it wouldn't happen. He missed being out of the fray. Sitting here, in the bright lights of Jules' Bar and Grill on Park Avenue South, he was conscious that while some of the diners obviously recognised him, few treated him to anything more than the double-take strangers would give when they saw a face they knew. In Washington, at Galileo's or Nora's or Palm, he'd had a regular flow of admirers coming to the table, genuflecting, offering him drinks, information, gossip. If the diners in this New York grill cared who he was, or had been, they made damn sure they didn't show it. Alex wished to be too important for that.

Shermer arrived ten minutes late. He looked like a convict with his short hair, thick neck and round face, but Alex knew him as a gentle man. The two had become friends in the mid-eighties in California when the affiliate station Barry had been running declared its support for Grant's gubernatorial election campaign. Alex had wondered then whether Barry was too keen a listener to make it to the top. Such a desire to pay attention to innovative ideas was hardly a requisite talent for network TV executives. They were considered much more reliable by the all-powerful sponsors if they continued to churn out predictable and generic shows. Barry's predecessor at UBC, so the story went, had a standard response when rejecting every original idea. 'This,' he would say, 'sounds way too like something we've never tried before.' Had Shermer fitted this mould, Alex would never have approached him.

'You were being very cagey on the phone with me,' Shermer said after the two had ordered their food. 'I'm keen to hear what you've got up your sleeve.'

Alex tugged at the cuff of his shirt as if he was about to produce something, but he was just fidgeting. Though he had relaxed with presidents and kings, here and now, he was a nervous man. He decided to come straight out with it. That was the way with a man like Shermer.

'I want to become headwriter for *Unto the Skies*,' he said.

Shermer's expression revealed nothing as he reached across the table, selected a toothpick and bit on it. Then, with the wood still between his teeth, he stared hard into Alex's eyes and asked, 'Why?'

'Why?'

Very slightly, Shermer nodded.

'Well, my brother Max had a – an understanding with the producers that he didn't manage to resolve before he died. I want the chance to honour that.'

Shermer flicked the toothpick into the thick glass ashtray. His face remained as granite. 'Why?'

'I felt,' Alex paused and glanced to his side to see if anyone was listening to what he was about to confess, 'I feel responsible for what happened to him, if you want to know the truth. I think I owe it to him and to his family.'

'So this is about money?'

'To a degree.'

'Weren't you recently offered a substantial contract to appear in *Window on Washington*?'

Alex scratched at his eyebrow with a thumb. 'Yes.'

'A sum of money, and correct me if I'm wrong, greater than that which you'd earn for writing the daytime drama.'

'Yes and no. It was a generous offer . . .'

'I know,' said Shermer, 'I made it.'

'Thank you,' said Alex, 'but what I was hoping to do on *Unto the Skies* was negotiate with the production company to be paid what they owed Max. I feel it's a matter of principle.'

They paused while their food arrived – bresaola for Alex, a pine nut and arugula salad for Shermer – and then the network President spoke again.

'Obviously,' he said, 'a deal was done between G&H

Productions and Max that I know nothing about. Nor should I have done. As you probably know, what my network does is purchase these dramas as finished products. Besides, I am, personally, not often involved with daytime drama decisions. I've got a very able head in Anne-Marie Stillinger.' Shermer stabbed at a shaving of parmesan in his salad, and continued. 'However, because it's you, Alex, and because you are an old friend I can trust, I am going to hear you out.'

He closed his lips on the heavy forkload of food.

'As I said, Barry, there was a sizeable sum of . . .'

Shermer held up his fork, and Alex paused for him to swallow the salad. 'Forget the money side of it,' Shermer said, dabbing at his mouth with a napkin. 'I don't believe that's why we're here. What I want to know is why, of all things, you want to get involved with a soap opera. I'm not interested in letting you use my network to fight your political battles, if that's what you're intending. I'm not interested in that at all.'

'I want to write the best possible scripts, Barry. That's all.'

'I see. So can you now please tell me why I should allow a literary novice loose on the longest-running show on my network?'

'Because it's not going to be running much longer without something pretty big happening. Is it?'

Shermer glanced at the neighbouring table, looking for eavesdroppers. 'I wouldn't say that.'

Alex, too, lowered his voice, which gave the conversation a kind of urgency, as if they were prisoners about to make their run. He knew that this was the argument that could win him the job. 'Look at its ratings, Barry. Three years ago you had an 8.2 almost every week. That was, what, a thirty, thirty-one point share of the audience? Last year you were in the fives and sixes, and you'd lost maybe ten per cent of the viewers, mostly to

CBS. Now *Unto the Skies* is lucky if it makes a four. You're haemorrhaging viewers.'

'And you think you can stop the flow?'

'I do.'

Barry Shermer took a long drink of his sparkling mineral water. 'You know, I liked Max a great deal, and I believed in him too, most of the time. But I sat at a table like this with him and that – Vincent Mascarpone.'

'Moscardini,' corrected Alex with a smile.

Shermer waved his hand. 'And Max looked me in the eye and said that very same thing. He promised me that what he was going to write would turn the ratings on their head. That was about a year ago.'

'This is different.'

Shermer smiled. 'He said that too.'

'No, it is, Barry. It is different. Believe me. I've done a lot of work on this. I am going to get people to tune in to *Unto the Skies* before a word of my script is spoken.'

'Very interesting,' Shermer said. 'And how is this miracle to come about?'

I've got you! Alex thought. *I've got you!* He relaxed in his chair, feeling all that remained was to reel his catch in. 'That is exactly what you're about to find out.'

Vince Moscardini was so high on stimulants he barely needed the elevator to lift him the twenty-eight floors to Barry Shermer's handsome office in Manhattan's UBC Tower. He had woken feeling groggy and thrown back a few caffeine tablets with his coffee as he'd thrown out that little slut of an actress who'd beavered her way into his bed the night before. Now, with the pills making his heart feel skittish, he wished he had settled for a good night's sleep instead. He hated to be conscious of his heart. It reminded him of his mortality, and he considered himself too important to die.

However, the question remained whether he was too

important to be fired from the show. Somehow he couldn't imagine the network or the production company looking for a new Executive Producer at this stage. Yet why else would the boss want to see him?

As the elevator doors opened, he shook his shoulders like a boxer warming his muscles and then announced himself to the receptionist seated in front of an elaborate Christmas decoration encompassing the most famous symbols of UBC's top shows. He'd made himself even more nervous by being half an hour late.

He was told by the receptionist to go straight through to Shermer's office. After a quick knock on the door he entered and was about to speak when he stopped dead, amazed by what he saw. The room was crowded with familiar faces – Shermer himself, Anne-Marie Stillinger, Paul Roberts with David Wolf (who was Paul's boss from Gardner and Hyde Productions) Bob Fein (*Bob Fein!*) and there beside Shermer, looking like he'd have the big man's children if he hadn't done so by now, was Alex Lubotsky, the prick who'd insulted him, who'd turned *Soap Opera News* against him, who'd even threatened to ruin him. Vince stood in amazement before Shermer walked to his side.

He took hold of his elbow. 'Vincent, I think you know everyone. Why don't you take a seat?'

'Sure, I can do that.'

Shermer sat again beside Alex. Alex had been amused to find the furniture arranged as it was in the Oval Office, with two large sofas opposite each other, then some winged chairs (red leather in Shermer's office, yellow fabric in the White House) forming a semicircle with an imposing desk at one end. He almost felt at home.

'Now that Vince has deigned to join us,' said Shermer, 'we can start.'

Vince held up his arm and tickled the air with his fingers. 'Could I get a coffee first?'

Shermer paused long enough to embarrass Vince before buzzing his secretary in.

'I was working late last night,' explained the producer as he glanced about him and wondered if everyone seemed so serious because they knew something he did not.

'Now,' continued Shermer, 'there's no one here who'll argue with the fact that *Unto the Skies* is in a great deal of trouble and . . .'

'Excuse me,' said Vince, 'but can the past tense get a look-in here? I'd say it *was* in trouble, but the changes I've made bringing Bob in and spicing up the storylines have knocked some shape into the show. We're moving very fast to where we want to be.'

David Wolf, head of G&H Productions, shook his head. 'No,' he said.

There was a silence before Vince, shifting his weight from one buttock to the other, said, 'No, what?'

'No, Vincent,' said David. 'Just no.'

Barry Shermer stood up. 'I think David and I share the feeling that *Unto the Skies* needs more than fine tuning. We need to do something more radical.'

'Hey,' said Vince, getting even more jittery, 'I can be radical. Sure I can. I mean, I mean I used to be all for Castro, you know?' He fired into the room a salvo of nasal laughs. 'I mean, I've been holding back. For you. What I mean is I've been restraining myself, like I'm a jack-in-the-box but I'm the one sitting on the lid. So if you've been in here talking about getting somebody else to produce the show, what I'm saying is that I can *be* someone else. You want a radical producer, that's me. You want someone to win viewers with tradition, that's me. I've been holding back 'til now.'

He stopped to take his coffee, brought in a delicate cup and saucer that troubled him no end. Under the gaze of the others he tried to balance it first on his knee and then on the arm of the chair before giving up, tossing the saucer onto the carpet and leaning back with the cup clenched in his hand.

Anne-Marie Stillinger spoke. 'Actually, Vince, we weren't talking about bringing in a new producer.'

'No? So what's going on?'

He looked across to Shermer, who was still standing.

'I think I was about to tell you,' Shermer said. 'Now as you might imagine, I have for some time been questioning UBC's commitment to the show. I had set a ratings figure that would have been the bottom line.'

'Don't worry,' said Vince, 'we've bottomed out on the ratings, no question.'

'Be that as it may,' Shermer said, 'the feeling is there's nothing much to lose and everything to gain if we can put *Unto the Skies* back where it belongs.'

'Exactly,' said Vince.

'And that's where Alex Lubotsky comes in. David and I agree that Alex should become the new headwriter.'

Vince opened his mouth in amazement. 'You do?'

'Yes,' David Wolf said.

'Oh! Well, I don't,' Vince said. 'And correct me if I'm wrong but this is my territory. Because either I'm Executive Producer or I'm some kind of noodle-head. Right? I mean, no disrespect, but does Mr Lubotsky know shit about writing soap operas?'

'I'm learning,' Alex said calmly.

'Learning!' Vince said sarcastically. 'That's beautiful. That's like asking a kid who's had one driving lesson to race in the Indy 500. Since when did my show become a fucking retirement job for ex-politicians? Uh?'

There was a long silence during which everyone stared at Vince before Barry Shermer said, 'Vincent, would you mind having a word with me out here?'

'No.' Vince stood. 'No problem at all.'

Shermer guided Vince to a small screening room. They sat beside one another in the stark, fluorescent glare.

'Vincent, you and I have different methods of conducting business, but I do understand that a certain – ebullience is no bad thing for a producer. I am not blind to your qualities.'

'That's good to hear. Because I felt I was about to be forced into a dumb decision.'

'However,' Shermer said, pausing as he softly rubbed his earlobe between forefinger and thumb, 'there are things you've done as Executive Producer which I simply cannot condone.'

'Well, sure there's . . .'

'Let me finish,' Shermer said sharply. 'That includes the underhand deal you concocted with Max Lubotsky. Alex knows about it. What he does not know is that you've been paying Max's cheques into an account under your name.'

Vince was fiddling with his watch as he answered, saying, 'I was keeping it safe for him, Barry. For, for when the ratings climbed up.'

'How kind. That, however, is no longer relevant, given the circumstances. What is relevant is that Alex Lubotsky *will* be joining the team where Max left off. He is prepared to accept the same terms, namely that he'll have four months remaining to lift the ratings. If he's successful, you will – and there is absolutely no space for discussion on this – you will pay the full amount that had been due Max. I believe that was considerably more than his negotiated salary. Is that understood?'

'Barry, Barry, Barry! You've got to admit this is weird. I mean, Alex Lubotsky? Come on! You hear things in the TV world, right?, and I've heard that he totally lost the plot.' Vince moved closer to Shermer as if sharing confidential information. 'That's why they threw him out of the White House. They were calling him Alex Lobotomy. I mean, do we want this guy on board?'

'You don't think he'll lift the ratings, then?' Shermer asked.

Vince shook his head. 'No way.'

'OK,' said Shermer, happy that Vince had sauntered into the trap, 'then you're in a win-win situation. If he fails, you walk away with two people's salaries and if he delivers, then the show won't get axed and you, Vincent, you will keep your job.'

Vince took a deep breath. 'I think you're forgetting that I care about this show. I don't like to see anyone running my baby off the cliff.'

'Vincent,' Shermer said, looking down at his hands, 'care or not, you've presided over the worst months in the show's history. I have every right to kick you out tomorrow, but I am not going to do that. Not if you give Alex the chance he deserves. Understood?'

Vince unwrapped a slice of chewing gum and slid it into his mouth. He screwed the silver foil into a ball and flicked it onto the floor before thinking better of it and bending down to pick it up. Then he said, 'OK, if that's what you want. But don't say I didn't warn you.'

'I won't.' Barry Shermer rose to his feet and held out his hand. 'You're going to like what Alex has come up with,' he added. 'In fact if you ask me, *Unto the Skies* is on its way to the stars.'

'So where's your space cadet now?' asked Barbara.

It was seven p.m. on the West Coast, and Annie was chatting on the phone to her oldest friend.

'He's in San Rafael working on this Meditation CD Rom thingummy for the Buddhist Retreat. They're getting uppity because it's late.'

Barbara was shocked. 'Since when did Buddhists have deadlines? These are the guys who've spent the last six thousand years trying to figure out that one hand clapping doesn't make any sound. Tell them to give Jerry a break.'

'I'm not sure he wants one. He spent a night there last week, and it's only a half-hour drive.'

'You don't think he's . . . Annie? Do you?'

Annie laughed. 'No, I do not think Jerry is having an affair. Not that we're doing it nowadays. The last time he . . .'

Suddenly, there was a howl from the other end of the line, followed by the sound of a plate or cup smashing, and Barbara's exasperated cry. Though Barbara was obviously holding the receiver away from her face, Annie could hear every word.

'Nicky, didn't I just tell you to stop doing that? Didn't I? It's past your bedtime as it is – no, you can't! Where's Bob, anyway? MICHAEL!' she squawked. 'Where's Bobby? So can you go and check on him, please? *No* I did not make this call. Annie called me – *yes*! Nicky, WHERE are you going without clearing that up? You know very well where it is, Miss Lazy-Bones – Unh-huh, that's right. Michael, Mi-MICHAEL! Help Nicky with the Dustbuster.' The voice was clear and close now, when Bra said, 'Annie, I'm sorry. It's a madhouse here tonight.'

'I could use some of that madness here,' she replied, her eyes ambling about the dull room.

'You wanna swap?'

'Yes. Yes, I do.'

'Oh, Annie! I hate hearing you so glumpy.'

'Glumpy?'

'Oh, that's Bobby's word for being pissed off and glum and moody all rolled into one. It's what happens when you have four kids driving you insane.'

'Or else having no kids to drive you insane.'

'You, sunshine, are not glumpy, you're broody! Have you talked to lover boy about it recently?'

'Yes,' said Annie grumpily. 'And he was just so god-damn *Jerry* about it. Listen to this: he said we don't have a right to bring new life into a world like ours. He said he doesn't want our child to have to worry about guns and AIDS and drugs. He doesn't think there's any innocence left in the world.'

'Try telling him you want a little boy because the world deserves more people like him. Most men think that anyway.'

'I tried that, but what can I do? He believes in reincarnation.'

'Great! What's he going to come back as? A bedbug?'

'Bra, be nice!'

'Why? You deserve a say in this. Have you tried the pill down the toilet routine?'

'I'm not going to trick him into anything he doesn't want.'

'Well, you've got to do something. You've got to decide what you want the most, and if it's a kid and if Jerry won't have one, then you'll have to find someone who will.'

'You're right.'

'Annie, when have I ever, ever been wrong?'

In her Washington office, FLOTUS, the First Lady of the United States, was staring at her lover as if he was insane. It was January 7th, and Alex had come to share his idea.

'You're doing what?' she said, unable to believe what she'd heard.

Alex uncrossed his legs and leant forward in his chair. 'I am taking over at *Unto the Skies*,' he repeated, smiling this time.

'And you think this is funny? You think this is something I should be happy about?'

'Yes.'

Susan shook her head. 'I should have known you wouldn't have the guts to run my campaign.'

The smile on Alex's face widened into a grin. 'I kept telling you that I hadn't made my mind up.'

'I know,' she snapped. 'But I had this notion. God

knows why, but I had this feeling that you might rise to the challenge. I thought that's what made the world go round for you. And I thought,' she looked away from him so her face was in profile, 'I thought we had a good history together. Didn't we?'

'Anyway,' Alex continued, apparently ignoring her, 'I gave it a lot of thought, and decided you were probably right. I don't have much to lose.'

She swung around to face him. 'Right! So why take this pointless job? Out of spite?' she asked angrily, but then, suddenly, her expression changed. 'Unless . . . why do you keep smiling, Al? Have you been pulling my leg?'

'No, but I am taking on your campaign.'

'How?'

'By introducing a female Senator running for Governor onto the soap.'

'And this is meant to help my campaign?' Susan said, furrowing her brow.

'Not only meant to, it will.' He moved to her side of the table, perched on the edge of the desk and took her hand in his. 'Listen, *Unto the Skies* gets hundreds of letters each week. If I make this character discuss your agenda issues we'll be able to find out how people respond even before we begin to campaign. We'll be trying out ideas without being accountable for them.'

'But, Alex, sweetheart, a few mindless soap fans don't make up a whole country.'

'No, but four million people watch this show every day and when we get the PR rolling that's going to go way up – who knows where? Maybe to eight or ten million. Now that is a lot of people and they'll be target voters, all of them. They're going to be family-orientated, traditional women who are going to need a lot of convincing that it's possible for you to run for President without growing a dick in the process. My character is going to be baking cookies and bringing up kids at the same time as holding her position. That's what they'll want to see.'

Susan snatched her hand away and stood. 'But don't you realise how hard I've worked to get away from that image? You know how uncomfortable I am playing the sweet wife to Jack. I don't want the word "wife" to stand for Washing Ironing Fucking Etc. It isn't my style.'

'Did I say it had to?' Alex asked smugly, taking her swivel seat. He lifted his feet on to the desk, trapping the First Lady between his legs. 'What I *am* saying is that if I can create a popular female role model who is also an astute politician then people will love the idea before you begin. It'll expand your power base.'

'You've convinced yourself this is a great idea, haven't you?' she said with apparent amazement.

'Why not? It's been done before. Greek playwrights tackled all kinds of political and philosophical issues. I've been reading them and they're not a million miles away from soaps.'

'Are you kidding? I presume you've watched this drivel,' Susan said dismissively, lifting his leg so she could move away.

'Listen,' implored Alex to her back, 'if this idea works by your announcement next year then that's great, if it doesn't,' he shrugged his shoulders, 'then who cares? No one will know we tried. How can you argue with that?'

'I say it could cause a lot of problems.'

'Uh-uh. I've got it all figured out.'

Alarmed by a crescendo of advancing police sirens, he walked to the window to see the flashing lights that heralded the return of the President's long motorcade.

'Damn,' Alex said under his breath. He couldn't relax on the White House grounds while Jack was around.

'Don't worry,' Susan said, walking to him. She cupped a hand behind his neck and drew him into a kiss. 'Jack won't come up here,' she whispered. 'He doesn't even come to me in the Residence.'

She kissed him again and slid a hand between his legs, gently trying to excite him.

'No, don't. Don't,' he whispered, kissing her on the cheek and breaking the embrace. 'I have to get back.'

Susan looked wounded and swung away from him so that he couldn't gloat. 'The little widow is beckoning, is she?' she said, her voice steely. At the desk, her back to him still, she straightened a framed photograph of herself with Jack, guests at Buckingham Palace. 'I'm surprised her neighbours aren't talking.' Now she turned to look at him. 'Or are they?'

Alex refused to reply. He was taking from his case some pages of dialogue, written for *Unto the Skies*. 'These are some of the speeches I've written for the Senator figure,' he said. 'Will you look at them?'

She returned to him. 'Am I right? Are you falling in love with a suburban widow?'

His eyes were hard when he replied. 'Pam is my brother's wife, Susan. You should know me better than that.'

'I didn't realise that screwing the wife of a dead man was worse than screwing the wife of a living President.'

Alex wanted to slap her for that. He felt the anger surge through his arm, and though he would never hit her, never hit any woman, he hated her for this, for being so proud of herself.

'I'm going now,' he said calmly. 'And for your information, I'm moving to Manhattan, to be close to the show.'

'Al, I'm sorry,' she said, dropping her shoulders, moving to him. 'But I miss you being here. Don't you miss our times? Don't you miss me?'

He closed his eyes and took a long, deep breath. Then he kissed her, once on the lips, and turned to leave the room, thinking that if this campaign was to work, there could be no place for the candidate either in his bed or in his heart.

9

Anne-Marie Stillinger, Vice President of Daytime TV for the UBC network, arrived at Vince Moscardini's midtown apartment with good news. The meeting had been called at the producer's home for fear that Alex's appearance at the studio would start unwanted speculation and rumour. The team was wary of the media hearing of the unusual appointment too soon. The most likely way to ensure high ratings was to release the story very soon before Alex's first episode.

The meeting, restricted to the essential few, was being attended by Paul Roberts, Alex, Cathy from casting, Vince and Anne-Marie. They were sitting in Vince's living room. It would have been an unexceptional white rectangular space had it not been for the wide mural of a movie shoot in progress. In the centre of this was Vince himself, standing proud and handsome before a director's chair sporting his name. An actress bearing an uncanny resemblance to Julia Roberts was listening to him, and behind her was a huddle of technicians and actors, all focused on the man himself. Vince had commissioned the work a year before, and although to most people the sickly pastel colours seemed the visual equivalent of airplane muzak, Vince had thought it a bargain at sixteen thousand dollars.

Alex had chosen to sit with his back to the work. To his annoyance, Vince had chosen to squeeze himself onto the same leather love seat, so that his painted image was only inches above his head.

Opposite them, Anne-Marie was balancing a herbal

fruit tea on her knee. 'The network has agreed to schedule a prime-time slot for *Unto the Skies* on March 9th,' she said. 'At eight.'

'That's fantastic,' Vince said. 'It's about time the network acknowledged me.' His eyes flickered around the room as quickly as a reptile's tongue. 'I meant us,' he said with a shrug. 'Us!'

'In actuality,' explained Anne-Marie, 'it was because of the strength of Alex's storyline that we felt we could take the risk.'

'Well, I'm going to make certain there are no weak links in that episode,' said Vince. 'The writing's got to be tight and we'll have a new director by then.'

'What's wrong with the ones we have now?' asked Alex.

'Howard Gains isn't renewing his contract for personal reasons, and I don't trust Ellen yet.'

'Because she's a woman?' Cathy suggested.

'No. Because she hasn't been directing long enough.'

Alex said, 'Why not hire someone high profile and make them a part of the new package?'

'Alex,' Vince said, clacking his new worry beads through his fingers, 'directing daytime is like being a traffic cop. It's what you do if you're never going to be high profile.'

'Let me find someone. I've got friends who . . .'

'Hoo-fucking-haa!' Vince hollered, swinging the beads as if they were a lasso. 'Alex to the rescue again.'

'We are somewhat short of time,' Paul reminded Alex in his own inimitable way.

'I know that, Paul,' Alex said. 'But let me try.'

'I hope this isn't another crazy Lubotsky plan, that's all. And talking of no time,' Vince added, 'what's holding us back from casting Dawn what's-her-name? Dawn Hope. You can't move in this city for actresses.'

'There's reluctance by the notable players to join the show right now,' said Cathy.

The general feeling was that *Unto the Skies* was on its last legs, and no reputable actors wanted to get involved with a dying show. In all her years in casting, Cathy had never experienced difficulties such as this.

'So tell them it's getting a kiss of life,' insisted Vince.

'How can I when it's a secret? Besides, agents are saying they've heard it from you before.'

'They are? Fine. Get someone new, then. That'll teach them. But get her fast. It's less than two months until taping.'

Paul Roberts turned to Alex. 'There's concern in our PR department over the feminist tone of your breakdowns, Alex,' he said, referring to the story outlines that the headwriter was required to provide for the producers, network and sponsors. 'I'm sure you're aware that we appeal to women in traditional roles.'

'Two Cs in a K, right?' Vince said with a laugh. He leant close to Alex and, in a whisper loud enough for them all to hear, explained, 'Two cunts in a kitchen.'

Alex made no acknowledgment of this information. The relationship between the two had warmed now that they were fighting the same war, but Alex did little to disguise his disapproval of the Executive Producer.

'Furthermore,' Paul continued, 'I don't think any of us want to turn the show into a commercial for the Democratic Party.'

'Nor do I,' Alex replied. 'That's why Dawn will be a Republican Senator and candidate.'

This idea had come to him the night before. What he was hoping to do with Senator Dawn Hope was to create a need among the American people for a female politician who would share Dawn's brand of compassion and understanding. It would then be left to him and Susan Grant to provide the product. The actual colour of Dawn's politics would not be of such importance, Alex believed, because most old ideologies were being swallowed up in the frothy compromise of feel-good politics. He knew that Susan's chances of making it to the White House would be considerably greater if she kept her ideals to herself.

'Also, Paul, I've spoken to many women on Grant's campaign trails, and I've read the letters my brother was sent, and I believe that viewers are craving strong women. I'm sure Anne-Marie and Cathy will agree. Personally, I think we can make Dawn as big as Roseanne.'

'God help us if she's *that* big,' said Vince. 'Which reminds me, Cathy. I don't want you finding a dog for this role. She shouldn't look too much like one of those real female politicians.'

'Susan Grant isn't unattractive,' suggested Alex.

'Yeah, but I guarantee she's an ice block in bed. That's why Grant plays the field. Am I right, or what?'

'Does Susan Grant have anything to do with this show?' asked Anne-Marie, unaware of the tremor her question caused in Alex's heart, 'or can we get back to what's important?'

'Shoot,' said Vince.

'I need to know what's been decided about the contracts of the actors due to die in the plane crash.'

Alex spoke up. 'No one's going to die straightaway. That'll mean we can keep the actors in their hospital beds until their contracts expire. I understand we'll have to pay them to lie there, but they won't be able to sue us.'

'Plus it'll soften the blow a little for the viewers,' said Cathy. 'They'll be able to prepare themselves for the losses.'

'What about the actors?' asked Paul Roberts. 'Are they going to be warned in advance?'

'They'll know when they get their scripts,' said Vince. 'Otherwise they'll talk to the press. You know what blabbermouths those faggots are.'

'So long as someone warns me when this is going to

happen,' said Cathy. 'I think I'll call in sick that day. There'll probably be a riot.'

'Never worry about the talent, sweetheart,' Vince assured her. 'It's the fans who'll eat you for lunch!'

Damn, it felt good! Miss Charlie Canon stood on the stage of New York's Public Theatre luxuriating in voluptuous applause. Was there, she wondered, anything better than this? She didn't believe there could be. She had found her personal heaven.

Towards the back of the auditorium a middle-aged woman was standing holding a placard, the word 'WONDER-WOMAN' emblazoned across the white paper. Wanting to be generous in acknowledgment, Charlie held out her hand and waved. As she did so, half the audience waved back as if she was something holy, someone who'd enrich their lives for years. Indeed, Charlie felt almost religious, spirituality surging through her and floating out over these disciples.

It was at moments such as this that she realised why she'd been born. It was to be a spokeswoman for the silent women of all ages, backgrounds, faiths and colours. Not for Charlie a life of coddled domesticity. Not for her the lazy defeat of motherhood. She had a vision, and no choice but to share it with the world. The challenge wasn't easy, but she was willing to sacrifice herself for the greater good of womankind.

She felt a hand at the small of her back. Dean, her publicist, whispered into her ear, 'They love you.'

'Did I look good?'

'Beautiful. Come on,' he added as the applause at last began to die down, 'you've got to get signing.'

A large trestle table, creaking under the weighty towers of Charlie's book, *Canon Fire: Women at War in a Masculine World*, had been set up in the foyer. A long line of admirers, some clutching two or three books under their arms, were waiting to meet Charlie, stand by Charlie, have their books touched and vandalised by the scrawl of blue ink that Charlie called her signature. She grinned and swept back her luscious, long hair. The book, a belligerent attack on male supremacy in the Western world, had climbed to number four on the *Times* bestseller list in its first week. A top spot now seemed inevitable, and it thrilled her to the core.

She asked an assistant to pour her a glass of mineral water ('San Pellegrino, or I won't sign,' she'd told them) and uncapped her pen. She loved this. It was like signing cheques to herself. A man, first in line, presented his copy. Charlie took it without lifting her eyes. She heard a voice. 'Sign it "To Alex, a man I once loved," will you?'

Charlie suddenly lifted her head, and then leapt to her feet. 'Alex Lubotsky. Wow!'

'Hi, Charlie. Long time no see.'

'Telling me. Did you hear my talk?'

'Of course.'

'And?' she asked, gripping his hand as if hoping to squeeze out a sweet answer.

'You'll make President yet,' he replied to her utter delight. Behind him a waiting woman, impatient to have her three copies signed, nudged at his ribs. 'Maybe we should talk later,' he said. 'Can you spare time for a drink?'

'For you, Alex?' she said, warmly rubbing his arm. 'Now what do you think?'

They met in a Japanese bar in the East Village. It was the perfect choice, a recently renovated haunt for liberals who wanted to be politically active in expensive and elitist surroundings. It was fairly intimate, but lit well enough for Charlie to be recognised, as she hoped she would be.

'I was very sorry you left the Administration,' she told him as the two sat at the small, round metal table. 'I liked having a friend there.'

'You still do. Jack has his faults but he's firmly on your side. Look at the Family Care Act.'

'I meant a real friend,' Charlie said, and as she did so she put a hand on his leg.

Immediately, Alex picked up her book. Although his love affair with Charlie had been passionate, it had also been ten years before and he didn't want to revive it from the dead.

'I was reading the chapter headed "Little Bo-Peep and Her Lost Penis Trauma",' he told her.

'Uh-huh?' Charlie said, lifting her hand from Alex's leg to sweep the hair off her forehead, as if to display her brain.

'I noticed how strongly you feel about the failure of television and film to portray women in a flattering or accurate light.'

'Absolutely, and that failure severely damages the psyches of young women which makes them unable to come to terms with their genital predispositions,' Charlie explained. 'It's a real problem when almost all the women on TV are either stay-at-home mothers or mindless bleached blonde bimbos. What we need, desperately, is to see more women on our screens for whom fulfilling employment and femininity are not mutually exclusive. Without that, there'll be another generation of girls growing up feeling guilty and ashamed of seizing the power they have a right to.'

'Exactly, and . . .'

'Can you be courteous enough to let me finish? What I'm trying to make women understand is that it's OK to be strong, it's OK to, as it were, *imagine* the penis so long as they remain grateful to, and for, their vaginas. I want to take away the shame of saying "Screw You!" to men, even though we are defined through our bodies as being the takers, the receptacles. I'm saying "Be assertive," I'm saying "Be those things that others have told you not to be." My generation is slowly becoming aware that it has to catalyse. The women of my generation need to be affirmative and create another that won't *need* to change, a generation,' she said, her voice raised, her fists clenched so tight that her manicured nails dented neighbouring smiles in the palms of her hands, 'made of women who already believe in themselves.'

Charlie relaxed her shoulders and turned her head, hopeful of an audience.

'Finished?' said Alex.

'Sure! Sorry.' She reached for Alex's hand and tickled her fingers against it. 'It's my life, you see. It's my whole life.'

'I don't think that's anything to apologise for. But what I wanted to say was that I can help you if you'll help me. Can I tell you something in strict confidence?'

'I've kept all our other secrets,' Charlie said with a wicked little smile. 'Haven't I?'

'Yes! Yes, you have. Well, Charlie, I have become the new headwriter of *Unto the Skies*.'

This knocked the wind from her sails. 'You've what?'

'Don't look like that. Not until you've heard what I think I can do for you. I believe, Charlie, that I can give you a voice on daytime television. There are millions of women waiting to hear your message. Together, we can make sure they hear it. But in return, there's something you can do for me.'

Crowded with astute, generous, liberal-minded people, many of whom would possess both the cash and the inclination to purchase copies of her book, San Francisco was Charlie Canon's kind of city. So when Alex provided her with an excuse to visit she was only too keen, and within a week of their meeting they were arriving on the West Coast, a hectic and lucrative schedule of appearances, signings and talks already lined up for Charlie by her publicist.

They arrived in the city in late afternoon, welcomed by the weighty, damp embrace of a fog that clung to them until they were behind closed doors, heading happily for their bedrooms and baths.

Warmed and relaxed, they met at eight in the impressive foyer and took a cab to a restaurant on Market that had been a garage before rental rates had pushed the mechanics into the suburbs. Cars, however, had remained much in evidence. The room was lit by dimmed headlights embedded in the walls and ceiling. The tables had been crafted from car hoods, flattened and repainted in a rainbow of bright colours. Rubber table mats kept the plates from sliding off and the chairs, perhaps inevitably, had all begun their lives as car seats.

Zoë Dunlop had arrived first and was sitting at the bar, which suited her fine.

'You haven't changed, have you?' said Charlie, giving her old friend a kiss.

'Unlike some of us,' Zoë said, gracelessly pushing her glasses up the bridge of her nose. 'You look much more famous than when I last saw you. Isn't it funny,' she added, turning to Alex and touching him on the arm though the two hadn't been introduced, 'how you can spot successful people a mile off. They're so together. I'm Zoë Dunlop, by the way. Sorry.'

Alex shook Zoë's hand and they were led to a table. As soon as they'd sat down, she said, 'Charlie, I'm dying to know what this big secret is.'

'Alex should explain. It's his idea.'

Alex proceeded to tell Zoë what he could about his involvement with *Unto the Skies* without mentioning Susan Grant's bid for the presidency. He made out, as he had to Charlie, that he was interested in nothing more than using Senator Hope for the advancement of women's rights. This being a motive that drove both of their lives, they felt no need to question it in another.

171

Once Alex had finished explaining what he hoped to do with Dawn, he asked the question Zoë had expected to hear. Would she consider a thirteen-week contract directing the show?

Zoë lit a Silk Cut and sucked in a lungful of smoke.

'I'm tempted,' she began.

'That's a wonderful start,' Alex said, turning on the charm.

'Actually, love, I was going to say that I'm tempted to get up and piss off before you trap me into this. I mean, let's be honest, directing soap operas is like crapping on a piece of paper and calling it art.'

'Are you working on something else?' asked Alex, knowing that she wasn't, because for the moment, Hollywood had turned its back on her. What's more, he suspected that because of the imminent lawsuit over *The Fur Bites Back*, she would be desperate for all the money she could get.

'I'm on the lookout for an interesting project,' she replied.

'Couldn't you go on looking in New York? Thirteen weeks wouldn't be a very long break.'

Zoë drew on her cigarette so hard that it seemed she was trying to inhale the tobacco itself. 'Who have you got for the woman?' She exhaled the smoke. 'For the Senator.'

'We're yet to cast the part.' Alex told her.

'If she's one of those flouncy blow-drys they usually wheel out for soap operas, then I can't see her having much effect on the advancement of women's rights. Can you, love?' she asked Charlie. 'Unless you make her come first in the love scenes.'

'I don't know about that,' said Charlie, 'but I've been terribly impressed with Alex's thinking so far.' She started to rub her foot against what she thought was Alex's leg. 'He's committed to giving this Senator a strong voice. I'm sure he won't allow the wrong actress to be cast.'

'She has to be convincing,' Alex said. 'Don't forget I have a reputation too.'

'I know you have. That's why I haven't said no yet. Also,' Zoë added, turning to Charlie and lifting her eyebrows suggestively, 'it's nice playing footsie-footsie with the trendiest feminist in America.'

Charlie looked as if she'd been slapped, but said nothing as she pulled her foot away.

With a smile on her face, Zoë continued, 'Nor, for that matter, is it every day that the most sexy politician in the country asks me to direct a soap opera for him. Maybe you Americans are even barmier than I'd thought.'

'Barmier, or smarter?' Alex asked.

'The jury's out on that one,' Zoë said. 'Let me think about it.'

'I'm here all tomorrow,' Alex said, 'but I have to catch the redeye home.'

'I'll let you know by then,' she promised. 'In the meantime, I need a drink to help me think. What do you two say to another bottle of this delicious Fumé Blanc?'

It was Annie's day off from the telephone lines, and she was lying in bed going slushy over *La Bohème* when the phone began to ring. For a while she just stared at it, but then she jumped naked from the covers and grabbed the receiver.

'Annie here!'

'Annie there, it's Sam. Are you dressed?'

'Sam! It's way too early to start talking dirty to you. Don't you have another 970 number to call?'

'Sugarplum, get dressed! You've got an audition.'

'Oh, shit, what for?'

'For Zoë Dunlop. Didn't I tell you this would happen?'

Now Annie was interested. Zoë believed in Annie's talent as an actress and had promised to call if a good part came along.

'Great. Tell me where.'

Sam told her to go to the Mark Hopkins Hotel and to dress naturally. Looking down at herself, Annie decided that this was as natural as she got but thought she should wear something, irrespective of what Zoë might prefer.

'What's the room number?'

'541.'

'541?'

'Yes, and hurry!' he said, but Annie had already run to the the kitchen where she was emptying onto the table the old keys and rubber bands and outdated stamps that she kept there in an old china mug. Soon, she found what she'd known was there.

'Yes!' she yelped. 'I knew it!' and then, clutching the paper fortune in her hand, she ran through to her bedroom to dress.

In the hotel elevator mirror, she checked her hair and smile and hoped there wouldn't be too long a wait. She kept seeing the same desperate faces at every casting. She was surprised, then, when Zoë opened the door herself, and said, 'Fantastic, you're here,' welcoming Annie into the lavish room.

'Alex, this is Annie.'

Alex turned from the window and held out his hand. Annie managed not to take a step back in shock, but she couldn't help clapping a hand to her mouth.

He stepped towards her. 'Alex Lubotsky.'

Annie shook his hand, and said, 'Annie Marin,' although she was almost too shocked to speak.

'Do you want some coffee?' asked Zoë.

'No thanks.'

'Take a seat,' said Alex, pulling out a chair at the table.

Annie's heart was galloping as she sat next to Alex and, although she could hardly believe what was happening, she felt as if she knew this man. Not only was he familiar from the television, he reminded her so strongly of Max. She stared at him as if he was a ghost from her past.

'Is something wrong?' asked Alex, waving his hand in front of Annie's eyes.

'Oh, no, sorry,' she said, blushing. 'It's just . . .'

'Yes?' he prompted, wondering whether anyone as jittery as this could possibly play Dawn Hope.

'I knew your brother,' she said quickly.

Alex looked astonished. 'Really? Where? You weren't on *Unto the Skies*, were you?'

'No. God no! Soap operas are definitely not my thing. No, I knew him before, at drama school.'

'You're Annie!'

Annie laughed and raised her eyebrows. 'I am called Annie, yes, I . . .'

'Of course, Annie Marin!'

'Do you two know each other?' said Zoë, joining them.

'No, we don't,' Alex said. 'But I know exactly who Annie is.'

Even now, fifteen years on, it thrilled her to learn that Max had told his brother of her. She didn't realise that he'd also written of her in his journals.

'You and Max were close, weren't you?' said Alex.

'We were, for a while,' she said. 'Yes.'

'But this is an incredible coincidence, isn't it?'

Annie agreed that it was, adding, 'Max used to talk about you a lot back then. I felt I knew you before . . . before we all knew you, with the President.'

'I kind of know you too. The way I remember it is that you and Max used to be best friends, and then something happened and he was always very sorry about that.'

'He never told me,' she said.

'Well, I'm telling you then. Second best!' he said and when he smiled she felt just as she had when they'd run into one another at Cornell Williams.

He's obviously forgotten that, Annie thought. And he
can have no idea that I once spent a night dreaming of
him and a morning hoping he'd return.

'I was very sorry to hear the news,' she said.

'Thank you. Actually, it's got something to do with why
I'm here.' Alex explained how he'd become involved
with *Unto the Skies*, and said that when he'd told Zoë
he was looking for a particular type of actress, she'd
recommended Annie. 'But from what you said,' he added,
'you wouldn't be interested in being in a soap.'

'I wouldn't, usually,' said Annie, 'but this doesn't sound
very usual.'

What she didn't add was that the idea of working with
Alex Lubotsky thrilled her. She thought she'd probably
act in a porn movie if he asked her – especially if they
could star together.

'Also,' said Zoë, 'we'd have to fly you to New York for
the audition.'

'Fine.'

'And, of course, you'd have to move there if you got
the job,' said Alex.

Annie said nothing. This was it then, this was the chance
she'd been waiting for. And yet now that it had come
it seemed so sudden. Could she really leave Jerry and
her friends in San Francisco for a part in, of all things,
a soap?

'Why don't you think about it?' said Alex, reading
Annie's mind.

'But quickly,' said Zoë.

By the door, Alex said, 'I don't know if you're a big
believer in Fate, Annie.'

'Sometimes I am,' she said.

'Well, I used not to be,' he said with a smile. 'Belief in
self-determination was probably rule number one in my
spin doctor's manual but, ah, a lot of things have been
happening recently that seem a little too ordered for real

life. Do you know what I mean? There aren't usually so many signposts.'

'I know exactly what you mean,' said Annie.

'Anyway, without getting too weird about it I wanted to say that I think Max would have liked this to happen.'

'That's not weird,' Annie said. 'I think he would too.' She took a step into the corridor and, as she looked at the number on the door, a sudden thought came to her. 'Do you mind my asking when Max had his accident?'

'It was on Thanksgiving.'

'Oh!' she said. 'Poor Max.'

As she walked away from the room, Annie looked again at the fortune she'd chosen as she sat alone on that Thanksgiving night. *541 is your lucky number*, it read. *Believe in it!* and at once she knew she was heading for New York.

As the headwriter of *Unto the Skies*, Alex had to decide which characters should live or die, marry or reproduce, suffer traumas or subdural haematomas, miscarriages or fits of anger, jealousy, passion, hatred or regret. However, because the show aired five days a week there was a huge amount of writing to be done and so five associate writers were responsible for the gritty business of setting dialogue to paper. Each writer had to churn out eighty-five pages a week, an episode per person. These drafts were then returned to the headwriter who did his best to iron out any inconsistencies of style or content before passing the scripts to the cast and crew. In doing this, Alex had the invaluable help of Bob Fein.

The first episode of *Unto the Skies* to feature ideas born in Alex's mind was due to be aired on March 9th, in an unusual prime-time slot. He had presented his story ideas to Vince, Shermer and the others in his first meeting at UBC, but before they began, those stories initiated by Max had to be wrapped up. It was on these that the two writers were concentrating now – Bob doing most of the work, Alex learning as fast as he could. Although he had spent hours studying Max's technique and style, he still had much to learn. He couldn't always rely on the signs!

It was because of his inexperience that Alex made the difficult choice to leave Titusville to move to the city and close to Bob. He was not looking forward to the delights of a Manhattan bachelorhood as he once thought he might. The life he'd been leading with Pam and the boys had, in a sense, been more contented than any he had known before.

Now, on his last night, he stealthily eased open the door to Matt's room and tiptoed to stand beside the bed. But for the rise and fall of Matt's chest, the body seemed lifeless, as if it had been carelessly dropped from above. The pillow had fallen to the floor and Matt had pushed the duvet off half of his body to reveal the rockets and stars of his astronaut pyjamas.

Alex wondered whether Matt would wake if he was covered back up. He stroked a hand across the child's fair hair. In a life spent fighting to save his own skin, the love that he felt for this sleeping child was a kind of emancipation. Until now he had never felt the need to change his view that children served primarily to interrupt the lives of their parents. Yet as he listened to Matt's soft breathing he felt a love so unselfish that it acted to dissolve all his concerns. The knowledge that nothing could matter more than this child calmed him. Never before had there been anyone for whom he'd be happy to give his own life.

Gently, he pulled the sheet up. It snagged on Matthew's foot, and the child took a sharp breath and opened his eyes. He lay motionless but stared up at Alex.

'Daddy?' he said inquisitively.

Alex smiled. 'It's me. Uncle Alex.'

'Daddy?'

'It's Uncle Alex. Go to sleep. There's a good boy,' Alex whispered. 'Night night.'

Like a butterfly first testing its wings, Matt opened and closed his eyelids a few times before drifting back to sleep.

Downstairs, Alex sat by Pam. She was gazing at TV commercials.

'All packed up?' she asked.

'Yeah.'

'Good.'

'What are you watching?' he asked.

She said, 'Ted Koppel.'

'Oh! Is it interesting?'

'Not really.'

'Is there anything else on, I . . .'

She spoke quickly, as if she'd been waiting to say this, 'You have to go, don't you?'

'I think so.'

There was a moment of silence before she said, 'It's going to feel very empty, here.'

'I know.'

'You don't think you could use the study? Max . . .'

'Pam, I . . .'

'OK.' She held up a hand. 'It was a thought. I'm sure you're right. It's only that since . . .'

Suddenly they heard a wail from a bedroom upstairs. They ran upstairs to find Matt sitting upright in bed, tears streaming down his face. Pam lifted him into her arms.

'What is it, Matty? What is it, baby?'

'I saw Daddy! I saw Daddy!'

'Did you have a horrible dream? Mm? Did you, baby? Did you have a horrible dream?'

'Uncle Alex said there weren't any ghosts but I saw Daddy.'

Alex stepped forward. 'You didn't see Daddy. You saw me. I came to see you.'

'Did you?' Pam asked sharply.

'I thought I saw Daddy,' Matt told his mother.

'I know you did, sweetheart. But it was Uncle Alex. You go to sleep now. We'll leave the door open, OK? And we'll be downstairs.'

She laid him flat and pulled the duvet up and waited for a moment before walking downstairs to rejoin Alex.

'I didn't tell him you were going, Al. In case you changed your mind.'

'I'll talk to him in the morning.'

She sighed. 'I think he was expecting you to stay for ever. I mean, he didn't question it. You came so soon after Max left us.'

'I'll talk to him,' Alex promised once more, and she nodded as if that would be enough, though she knew that to Matthew, losing Alex would feel like a death all over again.

And how was Pam so sure? Probably because she could feel the same cracks splitting her heart open too.

10

'**Y**ou just visiting, or what?' asked the driver of the car sent to pick Annie up.

'I'm not quite sure.'

She peered through the tint in the glass at snow ploughed into ugly, great banks by the airport.

'One of those, OK!' said the man. 'See how things turn out, then you decide. S'that it?'

'Yuh.'

The driver looked at Annie in his mirror. 'That's what you should do. See how things turn out, and if you don't like it you can go back again.'

'Yuh.'

She felt a kind of numbness now, not because of the freezing chill that had greeted her in New York, but because the previous ten days had passed in a kind of haze. Whether she'd been laughing or crying (and there'd been plenty of both) she'd felt somehow helpless, even though the decision to leave was hers.

Jerry's reaction had shocked her. She had expected him to take her leaving in his stride. She had expected him to roll a spliff and share a thought from his storehouse of Zen aphorisms. If it was meant to be, then so be it. Instead the words had hit his face like stones and he'd begun to cry at once. He'd cried, on and off, for days. This man of forty-four, who Annie had believed no longer loved her, had appeared broken, as if his world was ruined. And the only way that Annie had been able to cope was to be tough, so he accused her of a callousness she knew

181

she didn't possess. Only in the dark, after he'd made love to her with all the tenderness she'd once known from him, had she allowed herself to cry silent tears.

But today was worse than everything that had gone before. As Jerry had left for work (Annie had insisted, knowing she wouldn't be able to leave the apartment with him alone inside), he had looked at her, not with hatred on his face, but with an expression of such love that it was torturing her still. And when he had gone, her conviction had crumbled under the mental onslaught of vivid good times lived with him in those four walls, on their bed, in that air. She had stood with her fingers on the paint in the corner of the kitchen where his feet had scuffed the walls, and the last thing she had done was leave a note for him, on the floor where he'd see it, saying 'sorry' and 'I love you.'

'You been to Manhattan before, I take it.'

'What?'

'Manhattan,' the driver said. 'Have you been here before?'

'Yes, I have, but not for a long time.'

'It's a stinking pile of garbage,' he said. 'But you've got to love it.'

She smiled, because it was true. She did love New York. She had done from the second she'd first seen it. Now, as they rattled along squalid Van Wyck, she felt the churning excitement deep in her stomach. On the flight over, she had stared at her ticket thinking that even the words 'New York' held a glittering mystique, like a wrapped present waiting to be undone.

Suddenly the skyline came into view. This impossibly beautiful expanse of lights, torn like strips into the blue-black heaven, had never disappointed her. She wondered how many times she had longed to see a painting or a building or a canyon only to find that reality failed to live up to the postcard. Yet New York was always alive to her and to others because they saw in its lights their dreams. And when they arrived, from all corners of the world, they were happy to live with the crime and squalor, happy to forget their past and build a future, because here, amid the heart-wrenching beauty of its architecture, man could believe in himself.

When she had first arrived at Cornell Williams, Annie had thought that she could tap into the city's pulse and live off that. She was wiser this time. She knew that, more like an egg than the big apple it had become, the city's shell had to be cracked to find the richness inside. Cold and brazen, it was indifferent to the timid, to those who saw in it only noise and anger and shadow.

This time Annie had come to fight. She wasn't looking for world glory, for richness or fame. She was looking to win the part of Dawn Hope. That was all.

The car emerged from the Midtown Tunnel onto the island.

'So how does it feel to be back?' the driver asked.

'It feels great,' she said. 'It feels just great.'

'Zoë Dunlop?' repeated Vince Moscardini with despair.

'That's right,' said Alex. 'Quite a coup, huh?'

Vince and Alex were in a conference room of the advertising agency responsible for arranging the castings for *Unto the Skies*. Although Zoë had made her involvement conditional on Annie being given the part of Dawn Hope, Alex was keen to know the producer's reaction. When it came, it was something of a surprise.

'Tell me,' pleaded Vince, 'that there's two Zoë Dunlops in the world.'

'She's the only one I've heard of.'

'But she's a dyke!' He paused to light another cigarette. 'I mean, what a woman chooses to do in the privacy of her own disgusting bedroom's no business of mine, but it's not good for the show.'

Alex closed his eyes, leant back in his chair and rubbed a hand over his face. He spoke with noticeable tiredness in his voice, aware that however much he disliked Vince, the man was technically his boss.

'If she is or if she isn't,' he asked with a sigh, 'do you think that has any bearing on her abilities as a director?'

'I don't like her directing. Did you see that pile of shit about the hookers? It was so jerky I had to take a Dramamine while I was watching.'

This wasn't what Alex had wanted to hear. Zoë had received so much press coverage regarding her fight with AFM studios over *The Fur Bites Back* that Alex had been convinced the producer would enjoy the publicity she was sure to bring. Now he worried that he had approached Vince in the wrong way. The man would surely have loved the idea if he'd had it himself.

As Vince stood to pour himself another coffee, the door opened and Cathy came in with Anne-Marie, Paul, and the actor Walter Gregory who played top pilot Dale Irving on the show. Having been sworn to secrecy, he had been asked to read with Annie.

After they'd all greeted one another, Anne-Marie asked Cathy, 'Should I know this actress from anywhere?'

'I don't think so,' said the casting director, referring to the list of Annie's credits. 'She's had a pretty unexceptional career.'

'Sounds perfect,' Vince said as there was a knock at the door. 'My show's being invaded by amateurs.'

They all looked up as Annie was ushered inside by one of the agency employees. Despite having arrived only the night before, she was looking fresh and bright and had dressed in a sensible blue suit. She wore, too, a Wonderbra, having taken Alex's advice that Vince's judgment might swing on the size of her cleavage.

Though she shook hands with everyone, she reserved a special suggestive smile for Vince. Taking her mark in front of the camera, she ran through her name, agency and age, and then, with her judges in a semicircle, she began to read from her script.

Alex watched nervously. To win his war (both for Susan and for the soap ratings) he felt he had to be the victor in every battle, and the casting of Dawn Hope was perhaps the most important battle of all. In Annie he thought he had found the perfect actress. Although she seemed a little ditsy in real life, when acting she was totally at ease with herself and the part. He felt she had been born to act, for she was almost too expressive for everyday life. Once or twice he had found her wide-eyed enthusiasm off-putting, for he was accustomed to politicians who had learned to lie with their faces. Annie's, on the other hand, seemed a volatile barometer of every feeling. It could travel from concern through surprise to joy in the length of a sentence, and even when settled it seemed primed to react, like a house of cards in a strengthening wind.

She was younger than Susan, but that would only serve to add gravitas to the First Lady's challenge after the way had been paved by Annie. She was also more delicate and beautiful, with eyes as white as a porcelain doll's. Yet it was her evident feistiness that endeared her to Alex. In fact, she made him happy merely by her presence. He could imagine writing Dawn Hope's speeches with her in mind, for she radiated the same air of naiveté he hoped to impart in Dawn's vision. It was to be a package of enthusiasm and hope, and Alex could think of no one better to deliver it.

'*I think I'm falling in love with you,*' she said.

Alex, lost in thought for a moment, lifted his head in surprise. Annie was being held in Walter's arms. Their lips were two inches apart.

'*You are,*' Walter replied, '*the strongest woman I know, Dawn. I never thought I could love a woman like you.*'

'*Oh, Dale,*' said Annie. '*I'm no different.*'

'*But you are. When I'm with you I can't think. When I see you my eyes light up. When you touch me I feel like dancing.*'

Annie threw her head back in happiness. '*So dance with me, Dale. Dance with me until I drop and then carry me away in your arms.*'

'*May I have the pleasure?*'

Together they took a step, looked at one another, laughed and then relaxed and moved apart. Annie asked a question with her face and waited for a response.

Cathy spoke up. 'Thanks, both of you. Annie, we'll let you know.'

'You'll call me!' she said.

'By this afternoon.'

'Whenever. Thank you. Thanks, everyone.'

With a friendly wave, she left with Walter.

'I don't know,' said Alex to Vince. 'Did you think she was too young?'

'Not a problem,' Vince replied. 'We want someone mid-thirties to play someone early forties. It gives them that beauty edge.'

Alex risked the tactic again. 'It worries me that she doesn't look serious enough to be a politician.'

'If I had my way,' said Vince, 'I wouldn't let an unmarried career woman near my soap, but at least this one's got the right feminine attributes.'

'She reminded me of Maggie from *Northern Exposure*,' said Anne-Marie. 'I liked her.'

'Me too,' said Cathy.

'I'd appreciate a chance to see her on tape,' said the ever-cautious Paul Roberts.

Vince clicked his fingers and with a loud rattle the technician released the blinds and played back the video. They watched, were impressed and soon united. Annie would be the one.

Not before time, Annie had landed herself a job and Senator Dawn Hope had found a face.

Everything was fitting into place for Alex and his plan. As soon as Annie was cast in the role, he had called the UBC President to discuss Zoë Dunlop. Shermer had had none of Vince's reservations and within a day he forced the Executive Producer to hire the famed director. It was agreed that Zoë would direct Alex's first episode and be given a thirteen-week contract, as well as much publicity.

Alex's victories did not end there, for having learned that Curt Wallis had fired Rebecca Frear from the White House Communications team, Alex had contacted his protégée in DC to suggest she might like to join the First Lady's embryonic campaign team. He had taken the risk of revealing Susan's aspirations not only because he was keen to have someone as talented as Rebecca on his side, but because he suspected that she would resent the President for having let her go. Rebecca had jumped at the opportunity of working with Alex again and had been hired ostensibly to assist in the running of Susan's office. In truth she was to help formulate the campaign, acting as a vital go-between. Alex had already decided to keep his personal contact with Susan Grant to a minimum.

Today, on a bitterly cold January morning, Rebecca had flown up from the capital to Alex's sparsely furnished one-bedroom apartment on University Place. Despite the thump and slide of snowflakes dying on the windowpanes, the apartment was hot and besieged by hissing, clicking radiators filled with the steam that overheated rooms throughout the city. Alex was sitting on the floor in old Levis and a T-shirt. Rebecca was beside him, her skin still ruddy from the freezing winds. In her thick folder of notes was an outline of the issues that Susan Grant believed would form the heart of her 1996 presidential campaign.

'Where do you want me to start?' she asked.

'Anywhere. Just throw out some ideas.'

Rebecca flicked through the pages. 'Well – Susan's very keen to focus on children's issues. She thinks she'll be able to tap into concerns about teenage crime and truancy and so on. Specifically that means education, pregnancy programmes, college funding, looking at methods of making the streets and schools safer, that kind of thing. It's detailed here.'

'Great. Anything about kids or families is going to play well with soap fans.'

'And Susan's already proved herself over the Education Bill, as you know,' Rebecca reminded him. 'You'll see when you read this that there's a lot about safeguarding the country's future by investing in the citizens of tomorrow.'

'Perfect. What else?'

'Crime, of course. She's sure that's going to be the defining issue of the race.'

Alex, taking a swig of coffee, shook his head, and swallowed. 'I don't think so. Crime will dominate the midterms in November, but it's always the economy for presidential elections. I'm sure of it. Still, we can't touch that on the soap so there's not much point worrying now. What's her main thrust on crime?'

'That we need a softer approach.'

Alex looked concerned. 'Risky. She'd do better with public hangings these days.'

'Susan thought it would be the only way to distance herself from Jack's tough stance. After all, there's no point denying her gender. At least we can test out reaction, can't we?'

Alex nodded in agreement. He liked to witness Rebecca's mind at work. He had spent a lot of time teaching her his campaign philosophy when they'd been working for Grant, and there were few people he'd have preferred to have on his team.

'You're right,' he said. 'I can make Dawn maternal and nurturing towards criminals and wait for the feedback. We can do anything now so long as we know exactly where we stand when Susan goes public. I want her to be able to claim the moral high ground from day one. Is she going to church at the moment?'

'I don't think so.'

Alex tossed the pencil he'd been chewing to Rebecca. 'So make a note that she has to start going. No ifs or buts because if she doesn't, those Christian crazies are going to feed her to the lions. Tell her to make it once a month for now, then twice by the end of the year. Some church where she'll be seen.'

'That means any church anywhere,' Rebecca said.

'Right!' He stood to collect some cookies from the kitchen, took one and lobbed the packet at Rebecca. 'This is fun, isn't it? Trying to figure out what people want before they know it themselves.'

'Which isn't exactly easy seeing that there's another two and a half years before the election,' Rebecca said.

'Oh, I don't know. I'd say '96 is going to be about who can make us believe in ourselves again, that's all. Susan's going to have to pull people together again. And she'll have this advantage of knowing what people want better than anyone else. Now I think about it, this is going to be democracy at work. We'll be giving the voters what they really want.'

'God help us!' she said, leaning her head back on the seat of the couch and spreading out her arms like a crucifix. Was she flirting? Alex wondered. It was an obviously suppliant position. He remembered that when they'd made love before, in Rebecca's Washington apartment, it was after the excitement of a discussion not dissimilar to this. They hadn't made it to the bedroom that time, preferring a mattress of headed White House papers on the living-room floor. When had that been, he wondered.

Before Susan, anyway. That's how he dated his life now – before or after Susan had taken hold of his heart.

'But I've been thinking about your soap opera,' Rebecca said, lifting her head to look at him. 'Surely if we give Dawn Hope all of Susan's best ideas she won't be left with any herself.'

Alex shook his head. 'Nope. I don't see that at all. Dawn's going to be very different, which is fine, because if she says something's black and gets a million letters saying it should have been white, then we'll know where we stand.'

'What's the actress like?'

'Annie Marin? She'll be convincing,' said Alex, reaching across to snap a cookie in half.

'And what's she like as a person?'

He paused. 'Why are you asking?'

'Because you look embarrassed.'

'Don't be ridiculous.'

'I'm not,' said Rebecca, who wanted to hear nothing but a denial from Alex. 'Just tell me what she's like. Is she pretty?'

'Yeah!' Alex said, doing his best to sound offhand. 'If that's what you like.'

'And is it? What you like?'

'Rebecca, Annie is a very nice, attractive, talented actress who's here to help us get Susan elected to the presidency, and as far as I'm concerned, that's all there is to it.'

'OK,' said Rebecca, though with her smirk she made it known that she didn't believe him at all.

Coloured by exhaust fumes and street grime, most of the heavy snowfall had turned to black and grey. Manhattan had been held in a freezing grip in the weeks since Annie's arrival and great swathes of ice covered parts of the sidewalk close to her Upper West Side home. She

190

thought it gave the city a prehistoric look, as if nature was trying to claw back control in a place where it had been comprehensively conquered.

Annie had refused to join in with the communal grumbling about the weather. She welcomed the change from California, having not spent a winter on the East Coast since her mother had died, nine months after her father, in the autumn of 1989. Besides, she was far too content in her new life to be troubled by such seasonal inclemency.

She had found an apartment in an attractive Upper West Side brownstone, not far from the park and her favourite grocery store. Though lonely at times, she had missed San Francisco much less over the previous three weeks than she had expected. Jerry, on the other hand, had been suffering. He had called often, protesting that Annie had walked out without warning. She wondered how he dared say that. Men were so stupid at times, needing everything spelled out in black and white. Hadn't her moods been warning enough? How, as he was claiming, could he have thought that everything was fine just because she hadn't said aloud that something was wrong? She had kept quiet because she'd been hoping that things would sort themselves out, and she'd wanted everything to be as good as it could possibly be. Now Jerry was saying that *if only he'd known*, he would have made things right. The line he kept repeating every time he called was that he and Annie 'belonged' and that she owed him another chance. But Annie had moved on. She had a new job, a new home and a new life. She and Jerry were nothing but ex-lovers.

Annie did admit to herself, though, how lucky she had been with the job in New York. She had been handed this new life as the old one was collapsing. It had been a distraction filled with hope. In a sense, Jerry's pain had helped too. Annie knew that separated couples rarely felt simultaneous anguish, for when they did, they lost the resolve to stay apart. Knowing how sad Jerry was at his loss made her believe in herself.

There was only one disappointment, and he was Alex Lubotsky. As soon as Annie had seen him in San Francisco, she had begun to imagine them building a relationship in New York. It was uncanny that she should have experienced as strong an attraction for him as she had in the drama school fifteen years before. She felt no need to question if he was the one, feeling sure that he was. There was, too, the peculiar coincidence of the fortune cookie and of Alex finding her as well. Annie had felt secure falling back into the arms of Fate.

Yet Fate had allowed her to fall. Since arriving she had hardly seen Alex at all. She had called a couple of times, assuming that they were partners because of their mutual love for Max, but Alex had been nothing more than friendly. Over the previous ten days she had not spoken to him at all. Although she was disappointed, she had resolved not to chase him if he didn't want to be chased. Once before she had made that mistake with a Lubotsky. There was no way she was going to allow that to happen again.

If a jar of hornets, shaken up and angry, had been opened on the set of *Unto the Skies* during the taping of a love scene, it would probably have caused less alarm than the arrival of the script for episode number 11856 on the morning of February 16th. At first glance, the bright pink cover sheet that detailed the VTR date, air date, sets, producers, director, writers and cast looked innocuous enough. Yet on closer inspection it could be seen that two names had appeared for the very first time. They belonged to Zoë Dunlop and Alex Lubotsky.

Faith Valentine was in her dressing room when the script was brought to her. As usual, the first thing she did was to see which scenes she'd be in and when during the day they'd be taped. The days were usually scheduled so that the actors worked either in the morning or the afternoon, but for this day no fewer than fifteen characters were required for both sessions. Surprised, Faith turned to the next page to see that the majority of the afternoon scenes were set, not in one of the usual location, but on board a Brendan Air plane.

'What's going on?' she said out loud. The final scene, she saw, was set in the cockpit of the plane. Dale Irving, Brendan Air's most experienced pilot, was slumped over the controls. Beside him an air stewardess was screaming into the radio, 'Mayday, mayday, I think we're going to crash,' as ahead of the plane a mountain loomed . . .

'What's going on?' Faith said with almost as much panic as if she was on a plummeting plane herself.

There was a knock at her door and Johnson Bell entered with a script in his hand. 'Have you seen this?' he asked.

'Yes, I have,' Faith replied, tossing the pages aside, 'and I don't like it. Cliffhangers are cheap, Johnson. I thought Bob Fein was better than this.'

'He didn't write it, apparently. Alex Lubotsky did.'

'Who? I thought he was a political something or other.'

'He was. The President fired him.'

'Well, Johnson, I don't follow politics,' she said to excuse her ignorance. 'Still, I don't like the sound of . . . What are they doing? Bob Fein was . . . what are they doing?'

'As far as I can tell they're about to hospitalise us all. That's what. They're building the set in Studio C.'

'Hospital set? That's stupid! They're not going to save this show with gimmicks. They should trust the characters. Us, Johnson. You and me. We're all that's left of this show these days.'

'What I think,' Johnson began, but he was interrupted by a request coming through the PA system for everyone to gather in Studio A. 'Here we go again,' he said.

Studio A was where the majority of the show's scenes were taped. It was a large windowless room on the eighth floor. A tubular metal lighting grid covered most of the ceiling, and an array of spot and floodlights was angled from its bars. The sets, thought by many viewers to be real rooms, were constructed of wooden flats weighed down by sandbags. Cables snaked everywhere.

Wearing a natty grey Prince of Wales check suit and twisting an unlit cigarette between his fingers, Vince Moscardini was waiting for the cast to assemble. He had Alex on one side of him and Zoë Dunlop on the other. Most of the grips were carrying on unconcerned. The cast, on the other hand, were uppity in the extreme. They had seen the crash in the script and rumours were flying high that some of the longest-running characters were to be axed. Ally Springer, seeing Faith making her entrance, scuttled over to tease her with one of the juicier snippets of gossip. Faith made a face as Ally approached.

'Will these people stop at nothing?' she said, shaking her head in alarm. 'I mean, what *have* they done to your hair?'

'Nothing. This is me.'

'Oh!' Faith said, curling her mouth into a smile. 'Well, are *you* on the infamous airplane to hell?'

'No, I'm safe,' Ally said, enjoying her revenge. In fact, Ally's character, Carrie, was one of the few lead characters to have been left in Hill Way. 'More to the point,' she continued, 'nor is the new actress.'

'What new actress?' Faith asked, her eyes looking like they might pop from her skull.

'Oh, just someone wardrobe were discussing. They're spending a lot of money on her outfits, apparently.'

'But I haven't, I didn't . . . nobody told me!'

'I think they're just about to,' Ally said.

Vince was looking inordinately pleased with himself.

'Hey, hey, hey. If you don't mind! I'm a busy man.

Looking after you!' he seemed to be using his whole upper body when he pointed at his audience. 'And I'm doing that by getting some interesting people to work on this show. OK? You've probably seen the man on my right before. No, he's not Max raised from the dead, but in true soap-opera fashion . . .' Vince paused, and then, shouting as if he was announcing the winner of a boxing match, said, 'he's his identical twin brother come to fill his shoes! Mr Alex Lubotsky!'

There was an awkward pattering of hands as Alex held up his hand, not only because he seemed incensed by Vince's comments, but because the cast was clueless as to what was going on. They knew Alex as a politician, not a writer.

'But I didn't stop there. No. Over there,' he gestured towards Zoë Dunlop who, like Alex, was sporting the look of a murder suspect standing in the dock, 'is the girl who's about to replace Howie Gains as a director. Zoë Dunlop will be directing the plane crash script. Now,' he grinned, 'I can see a lot of worried little faces out there, so I want to say this. There'll be two fatalities on the flight,' he paused to relish the worry on the actors' faces, 'and they're both non-contract extras. No one's being written out in the crash. What happens with the survivors is Mr Lubotsky's department.'

There was a murmuring of voices among the cast members.

'I did want to introduce you to someone else, but I don't know . . .'

'Sorry, I'm here,' came a voice from the back of the studio.

Everyone turned around to see Annie being led towards the producer by his assistant. She felt uneasy under the scrutiny of so many eyes as she joined Vince.

'OK!' he said, putting his arm across Annie's shoulders. 'The party's complete now. This, ladies and gents, is Miss

Annie Marin, who'll be playing a new character called Dawn Hope. She'll be joining us in a couple of weeks.'

Annie smiled and as she looked about her, her eyes suddenly locked with Faith's. Faith was completely motionless, an expression of abject horror on her face. It was bad enough when any new character threatened to steal her limelight. But this was the bitterest of pills. Annie Marin? She hated Annie Marin. Worse still, Annie Marin hated her! She had expected their paths never to cross again. Why had the Lord been so cruel as to throw them together on the soap opera she had slaved and struggled to make her own?

Almost at once, she spun around to return to her dressing room, knowing that it wouldn't do for anyone to sense her distress. Back there she would compose herself, and make sure she was ready for the little bitch as soon as she put so much as a toe anywhere near the turf Faith Valentine had made her own.

11

Annie leant forward to finger a crumpled ten-dollar bill into the tray behind the driver's head as her cab parked outside the *Unto the Skies* studios. 'Keep the change,' she said, enjoying the chance to be generous.

The man peered at Annie in his rear-view mirror.

'You work here?' he asked.

'Yes. I'm an actress.'

'Oh, yeah? I watch the show sometimes with my wife. Like when I'm home. I never seen you.'

'Well, keep watching!'

She rode the elevator up to the production offices, and was pleased to see her picture had already been added to the wall by the receptionist's desk.

In his office, Vince was in a generous mood. He was holding a copy of *The New York Times* in his hand when Annie was led inside.

'Did you see this?' he asked. 'We got the front page. The front page! Can you believe it?' He read the headline out loud, '"With fitting drama, Grant's closest aide announces new position". How do you like that?'

'It sounds great.'

'It is. It is. And we got good coverage in the tabloids too. *Unto the Skies* is hot news, let me tell you.'

After a brief knock, Alex came in. Vince leapt to his feet to shake the headwriter's hand. 'This is good,' he said, holding the paper triumphantly in the air.

'I know,' Alex replied. 'They're making the right noises.'

Although it was nothing new for Alex to have master-minded the front page of a newspaper, he was genuinely pleased with the media's response to him. His experience at the White House had left him bruised and tender, and he had feared criticism from journalists over his new career. Instead, they'd chosen to reserve judgment until the show was aired.

Few of the serious journalists were accepting the appointment at face value. They were waiting to see what might be in it for Alex. The tabloids, on the other hand, were treating him with deference. He remained a seductive figure. Darkly handsome, single, obviously smart and with a greater knowledge of the President than almost anyone else alive, he was a political rock star and perfect grist to their mills. It could even have been suggested that by refusing to waste inches debating the peculiarity of his new career, the tabloids were acknowledging that the step Alex had taken was not so large after all.

Annie did her best to appear confident and relaxed when, after a quick kiss, Alex sat at her side on the long couch.

'*Entertainment Tonight* are doing a feature profile of me,' he told Vince. 'Which should help.'

'What I wouldn't give to be in Carol Stricknen's office right now,' Vince said in reference to the Executive Producer of *Forever a Family*, his closest rival in soapland. 'She probably wishes she had her hands on my new star.'

He winked at Annie, who winked back, disarming him. He held up a sheet of paper in his hand.

'*Soap Opera News* wants to feature you on their "Fresh Face" page. I told them about you, so you can thank me!'

'Thanks!' said Annie dutifully.

'I want to go through the Q and A sheet with you. Alex is here to help out with Dawn's image.'

'I thought the questionnaire was about me,' said Annie, 'not the character.'

'It is,' Vince told her, 'but you got to learn that these dweebs out there, they can't tell one from the other. You're going to be Dawn to them so we've got to make the right impression. OK? Now,' he looked down at the sheet. 'What's your height?'

'Five seven.'

'Five eight. Eyes?' He looked up.

'They're a mess,' Annie told him. 'They're blue, green, brown, I don't know. It depends what I wear.'

'What about when you're naked?' he asked, trying a seductive stare.

'Red,' she said, briefly glancing at Alex and wondering if he'd ever find out, or want to.

'Call them blue,' Vince said. 'What about birthday and star sign?'

'What's Dawn's?' asked Annie, smiling.

'This isn't a joke,' Vince said. 'This is the top-selling soap mag in the country.'

Annie's problem was that as far as she was concerned, that was precisely what made it a joke. She had always laughed at the magazines, at their haughty editorials, the desperate letters, the titillating glimpses of stars' private lives and the snippets of homely advice on such things as how to resist impulse buying or when to wear silk teddies to turn men on. How, simply because she was to be featured in one, could Annie take them seriously? Where was *Ms* magazine asking about the role of women in TV drama? Where were the serious issues that Alex had promised would define the new part? Who could possibly have such a vacant life that they'd care to know which day Annie had been born?

'May 18th,' she said. 'That's Taurus.'

'Any acting schools?'

'Yeah, Cornell Williams.'

'Didn't Faith Valentine study there?'

Annie paused. 'Mmm. We were in the same class.'

'So you two were best friends.'

'To be honest . . .'

Vince shook his head. 'Honest is not a good word. Trust me. You and Faith got on like a house on fire.'

'Can we add that I hoped she was sleeping upstairs when the fire started?'

She heard a snigger from Alex and turned to smile with him. She liked being appreciated by him, and it felt good to be partners. It was the right message – our lives are now intertwined, let's intertwine them some more.

'What,' Vince read on, 'was your most embarrassing acting job?'

'This one?' she hazarded.

Unamused, Vince tapped his pen on the side of the couch.

'Well, I guess there was the time when I was playing Isabella in *Measure For Measure* and I forgot . . .'

'How about when the catch broke and your skirt fell down when you were doing a charity performance for kids,' suggested Alex.

'I like that one better,' Vince said, beginning to write.

'But I never . . .' Annie began.

Vince interrupted her. 'Moving right along, how do you like to relax? And don't say a candlelit dinner with your Executive Producer!'

'I'll try hard not to,' she told him. 'I guess I meditate a lot. At least, I used to.'

'No good,' Alex said. 'Either she should go for something they'll love her for . . .'

'Like pigging out with a tub of ice-cream in front of a Saturday movie,' suggested Vince.

'I'm good at that!' said Annie.

'I'd prefer something wholesome,' said Alex.

'I went backpacking in Yosemite once,' Annie said.

'Good girl!' Vince said.

'Whenever I can,' she lied, 'I try to go on National

Park refuse collection walks. I love to feel that I'm doing something for the environment.'

Vince's pen hovered above the paper. 'Really?'

'Absolutely. You should come.'

He laughed nervously and scribbled down the answer as Annie and Alex once again shared a knowing look. She had begun to enjoy herself now. Vince asked her about her musical tastes.

'She has a wide taste,' claimed Alex. 'Everything from Mozart to Manilow.'

Vince repeated Alex's reply as he wrote it down. 'Now it says here, "Which is your favourite time of year?"'

'I like fall,' Annie said truthfully.

'She likes Christmas,' corrected Alex, 'because it's a time for families and . . .'

'And for Jesus. You're right, that's better,' Vince said.

Alex turned to Annie. 'Are you religious, in fact?'

'I'm sort of into Buddhism. Not as much as I was, but if I believe anything, it's that.'

Vince made a whistling noise as he inhaled. 'That's a no-no.'

'I thought Hollywood was big on Buddhism right now,' she said. 'What about Tom Sterling?'

'Oh, once you're a celeb you can get away with anything. Hamsters, boys, snakes, whatever. Because if you're not doing something kinky they're going to say you are anyway, so what the hell, you may as well have a good time. It's when you're climbing the ladder you've got to play it straight. Believe me, when the ratings hit ten you can be Mrs Dalai Lama for all I care. But not now. So,' he said, returning to the soap magazine questions, 'Warmest childhood memory?'

Again Alex answered without pause, 'Playing Mary in the junior high Nativity play.'

Annie shook her head in amazement. She had always done what she could to get out of the Nativity play. Now she rose from her seat and ambled towards the window. It was clear that she wasn't needed for these questions about herself.

'Weaknesses?' Vince asked.

'Shopping,' said Alex.

'Animals?'

'A cat called – Jackie. She's serene, like Jackie O.'

'Favourite dessert?'

'Choc Chip Cookie Dough ice-cream.'

My God! Annie thought. How did he know that? She spun around to ask, but Vince had moved on to the next question.

'Pet peeve?'

'Moaners.'

'But we love 'em moaning, don't we, Al?' said Vince.

Alex said nothing. He'd known that he would have to work closely with Vince, and he did his best to keep their working relationship warm, but he was far from forgiving the producer for the way he had treated Max.

'Favourite flowers?'

'Roses.'

'No,' interrupted Annie. 'Irises. They're much classier.'

'OK. Facial feature you'd most like to change?' Vince asked now.

Alex remained silent, and then he looked at Annie.

'Which is it, Alex?' she asked. 'Am I too perfect, or are you trying not to be impolite?'

'The former,' Alex replied, neither hesitating nor taking his eyes off her.

Is he flirting or making fun of me, Annie wondered. She locked into his stare, and said, 'My nose, then. Say my nose.'

Vince wrote it down.

'OK, last one. What's your best quality?'

'I don't know,' said Annie, coming to sit beside Alex again. 'Why don't we ask the spin doctor to answer that?'

'Her eyes?' he suggested, though he was no longer looking into them.

'Nah,' Vince said. 'They want a characteristic.'

'Then make it honesty. Say that Annie hates it when people don't tell the truth.'

'That's not true,' said Annie. 'I'm an actress. We like telling lies.'

'Thank Jesus,' said Vince. 'You're going to settle into this job like a fish to water.'

Miss Zoë Dunlop's first day as director on the set of *Unto the Skies* was hailed by all as a triumph. She'd endured a baptism of fire and had come out smiling. Many of the cast had been worried that a successful, upper-class British feminist movie director might be a little aloof on set, but that wasn't Zoë's style at all. In fact, with her bad language and chumminess, she fitted in rather well.

Zoë, too, had been fearful of what it would be like. She'd imagined that all these actors and actresses endlessly pining to the camera about their emotional traumas would be a self-conscious and tetchy bunch. Instead she found them much more like happy kids than irksome adults. Together with the crew with whom they spent five days a week, they behaved like a large, unruly family.

Most of the leading men were pranksters, alleviating the boredom of endless hours of overacting for the camera by spending endless hours overacting for each other. They pulled faces in attempts to distract those acting on set. They crept up behind the cameramen to make farting noises. They tied the hairstylist's shoelaces together and tried on his wigs as an excuse for more hilarious tomfoolery.

Few of the women were such show-offs. Instead, they had to be on their guard for the actors who'd usually be plotting some dastardly deed. On her first day on set, Zoë saw Stefano Benedetti, Johnson Bell and Walter Gregory in near hysterics as they sprinkled pepper into the oxygen mask that the show's air stewardess would soon be placing, with all the seriousness she could muster, over her nose.

Through all this, Zoë kept her calm and humour. It had been a challenging episode, the main story being the takeoff and imminent crash of Brendan Air's Flight 278 from Chicago to Los Angeles. In the studio, she had used the standard fuselage cross-section to capture shots of the characters in their seats, and these had been intercut with scenes in the pilot's cabin set before translights to give authenticity. Footage of an actual plane, decorated with Brendan Air's logo and filmed six years before, was used to lead into most of the aircraft scenes.

Zoë was successful because she'd realised that, in contrast to her deeply personal movie-making, her duty on the soap was simply to shoot the material handed to her in the most exciting and efficient way. For this dramatic scene she had decided to rely not on action, but on close-up reaction. When the plane began to shake, she had brought the camera tight in on a glass in William's hand to tug the audience into the tension. Next she showed the terror on the passengers' faces: on William and his wife, Mary; on their son, Jamie and his wife, Vanessa; and most especially on their grandson, Timmy. Timmy, the innocent little bundle of joy who didn't deserve to die, was granted a large amount of air time as he clutched his teddy in one hand and his mother's hand in the other.

As far as the audience was aware, debonair pilot Dale Irving had slumped over the controls with a heart attack, so endangering the lives of all the characters on board. It was this episode that was being aired at eight p.m., not at three, the hope being that enough people would be captivated by the cliffhanger to tune in the following day, when the show's new actress, Annie

Marin, was to make her much publicised and anticipated debut.

With her arms across the back of the salmon pink couch and her legs spread wide apart, Faith Valentine was staring out across Central Park wondering what would happen next. It had been a bad week. Although she was the undisputed star of *Unto the Skies*, the amount of press the show had been getting had brought her no pleasure. In all the articles, and during the many TV news reports, her name had been mentioned only twice. Twice! All that anyone seemed to care about was why the great Alex Lubotsky was turning to daytime drama and how feminist Zoë Dunlop could have sunk to such a level and what inspiration the Executive Producer had shown in bringing such talent together. And to make matters so much worse, there were rumours that it was through Dawn Hope, the show's new political character, that Alex was to show his true colours. The American public seemed to be holding its breath in anticipation of what Dawn would say, and Faith knew as well as everyone else that the lips through which those words would pass belonged to little Miss Annie Marin.

'Is something wrong?' asked Ned, lifting his head from between Faith's motionless legs. He'd been kneeling in front of her, doing things with his tongue that would usually have made her squeal with joy.

'It's as if they've forgotten, Ned, that I *am* that show,' she said.

'Do you want me to stop, then?' he asked.

'I think so.'

Faith leant forward and stroked the tight curls of her husband's thinning hair before bending double to hitch her panties back up her legs. Ned lifted himself onto the sofa beside her. She touched his thigh.

'Little Neddy can go diving in Mom-Moms later,' she promised, patting the senile insurgency in his pants.

'OK, my sweet,' he replied, kissing her long neck.

Ned had surprised Faith by arriving early from LA, and had wanted her the second he'd walked through the door. She had smelled so sexy and seemed so hot for it. If only he'd known that less than an hour before, her muffled, damp cavern had been entertaining a frequent Italian visitor, he would have skipped the snack altogether.

'I'm sure that whatever's good for the show will be good for you too,' Ned assured her. 'Won't it?'

'Not if they try to shovel me over the side of the ship, Ned. Like a dead coffin.'

'And are they trying to do that?'

'As good as. I'm all trussed up in a hospital bed after the crash. Who knows if I'll live?'

'Are you badly injured?' he asked, stroking her hair.

'I have terrible whiplash to my neck.' She touched it as if it was hurting now. 'And cuts.'

'That doesn't sound particularly life-threatening.'

Faith twisted her body to face him and, looking horrified, said, 'This is soap opera, Ned. A pin can be life-threatening.'

Ned kissed her on the forehead and, as he walked to the mirrored alcove that served as a bar, said, 'I still think that the writers and producers would have killed you in the plane crash if they'd wanted to.'

Faith leapt to her feet. 'But they *are* killing me. Inside! With these lavishments they're adorning on that bitch.'

'I don't see why you hate her so,' he said, pouring himself a long bourbon.

'We have a past, Ned. She resents me for being more appealing to men. It's a cross I've had to bear for many years. People can be so cruel,' she added in a trembling voice.

206

Although Faith rarely drank in the afternoon, Ned held up a heavy crystal glass as an offer. She wiped at her cheek, though she'd failed to produce any tears. 'Yeah, OK, give me a Stoli and 7Up. I need something.'

When he brought her the fizzing cocktail she was sitting on the edge of an armchair, reading an article in the newest edition of *Daytime*.

'Is there something in there about you, my sweet?'

'No, there damn well isn't,' she snapped. 'That's what I'm talking about. Look at this picture. Vince looks like he wants to eat her up. And listen!' She began to read the article in a voice leaden with pain and resentment.

'Executive Producer Vincent Moscardini and writer Alex Lubotsky welcome Annie Marin to *Unto the Skies* during a bustling press conference that was held at the Mayflower Hotel. Moscardini explained that Marin's arrival had nothing to do with the show's flagging fortunes but that "we wanted a new character, and we saw her great talent and chose to capitalize on both things at once."

'Marin arrived in New York three weeks ago after a spell working out of San Francisco. "I'd forgotten how cold it gets here," she said wisely. "But I love it!" She said she was happily anticipating her new role, but most of all she was looking forward to the shopping spree she was about to embark upon with *UTS* costume designer Terry Sheray. They were meeting after the press conference to pick out Dawn's wardrobe. "I hope we find something warm," joked the amiable new addition to the soap opera galaxy. A native of . . . Yugh!' Faith threw the magazine down. 'Tell me,' she snorted, 'can you be a galaxy, I mean, in a galaxy, Ned, if you're not a star?'

'There are planets, of course.'

'Oh! Don't you start too. I hate it.'

As she stared at her husband, her lip began to tremble and then her eyes bulged with tears. Slowly, she stood and turned to the wide glass doors that opened onto the apartment's balcony high up over Manhattan's East Side. She flattened a cheek against the glass, looking peculiarly doleful as if in an Ingmar Bergman movie.

'I may as well throw myself over,' she said.

Ned put a comforting arm on her shoulder.

Faith took a step or two away from him and, looking away, said, 'Sometimes life's a bowl of cherries on the sunny side of the street and sometimes it's like now – you feel that God's forgotten about you. Or that he's putting these obstacles in your way to test you. And when life's journey becomes an uphill struggle like this, you turn,' she turned, 'to the people you love to give you the strength to take another step. That's you, Ned. You'll help me, won't you?'

Ned moved to take her in his arms. He didn't care that, relaxing in his LA hotel room the week before, he'd heard Vanessa Sheridan give this same speech to her screen husband, because he believed the emotions behind the words. Haven't we all heard every line we've ever used at some time, somewhere before? he thought. And so he hugged his wife and told her he'd help every inch of the way, which, by chance, was almost the same response that Jamie Sheridan had given on the show.

Faith looked down at her husband, a trembling half-smile on her face.

'You do love me, don't you, Neddy? Don't you?'

'Of course.'

'You wouldn't just say it?'

'No.'

'How much do you love me?'

'I love you completely. I write songs when I think of you. I hear music when I see your face. I get wibbly-wobbly when you caress me. What more can I say?'

'Nothing,' she replied with a smile as she began to rub herself against his crotch. 'Don't say anything.'

And then, after a brazen wetting of her lips, she said, 'It's lollipop time,' and slowly slid to her knees to unzip Ned's flies with her teeth.

12

It was the day of Dawn Hope's birth into the fraught and wonderful world of soapland, and Annie was nervous as hell. She had been awake for most the night, her mind on the six a.m. alarm she'd booked with the telephone company. Though she had moved the phone unit close to the bed, and turned the volume up high, and put an alarm clock on a table just out of reach of her flailing, sleep-warmed arm, she had been troubled by the notion that something might happen and that she wouldn't wake in time. This had kept her in a state of jittery semiconsciousness. Also, she'd made the mistake of going to bed too early, so desperate had she been for a good night's rest. As the night had worn on she'd lain listening for a tick from her digital clock or for the ring of the phone. In a half-dream, she had pictured God's heavy fingers curled around the end of a black blanket, slowly lifting until dawn's light sneaked in around the edges to envelop her with a new day. Dawn's dawn! Something else to think about and keep her awake . . .

It was five forty now, but there was no way she was going to get up a minute before six. She had to look her best! Instead she tried to remember her first lines and the concentration sent her into a sudden deep sleep that could have lasted for hours had the phone not exploded with sound, jolting her heart and sending her shuffling towards the shower.

She made it to the studio on time. It felt a lot like going to a new school, the only difference being that she recognised the faces of all her classmates. It was odd being introduced to people she felt she knew. When she shook Stefano's hand, she wondered whether he would try to seduce her as he had all the girls on the show. Could Bobby *really* see, though he played a blind man? And were Johnson Bell and Olivia Rourke as affectionate off camera as the couple had been on screen, playing William and Mary, husband and wife, for almost twelve years straight?

Now, sitting on a cold metal folding chair like the ones they'd had at Cornell Williams, she glanced down at her script, checking her lines once again. Suddenly a shadow fell on the page. Lifting her eyes, Annie saw two red high-heeled shoes. She knew at once to whom they belonged.

'Hello, Faith,' she said, standing up. 'How are you?'

Faith, who hadn't given up her leaning, brushed her cheeks against Annie's in a lipless kiss.

'Welcome to our show,' she said.

'Thank you.'

Whatever physical features Annie had found laughable in the actress before – the lacquered, showy eyelashes like the thighs of an insect cancan troupe, heavy breasts like sweating balls of mozzarella in fishnets – seemed not lessened but exaggerated now. Faith was not Barbie, but Ken in drag, more woman than most women would ever want to be.

'Have you met the family?' she asked, her eyelashes kicking high.

'You mean the others? Yeah. Most, anyway.'

'If they're not friendly it's because we see so many of you. So many actresses coming, and then going. It's impossible to get personally involved with everyone.'

'I suppose so.'

'No, we can't, Annie!' Faith said as if contradicting her. 'They come and go.'

'Maybe I'll be here a while.'

'Get used to the early mornings then,' she said, 'or Make-up's going to hate you.'

Annie was going to reply but Zoë Dunlop had come into the room to start the rehearsal. If Annie worried that she herself looked awful, she knew Zoë looked worse. With a styrofoam cup of coffee in one hand, a cigarette in the other, her ginger hair sticking up in all directions and her thick, black glasses sloping across her face, Zoë looked as if she'd spent the night on the streets. Despite this, she seemed ready to start work. Putting down her breakfast, she began to pull the chairs into the centre of the space. Once they were in position, marking out the boundaries to be imposed on set, the actors could start blocking the first scene, beginning a day that would last twelve hours at least.

By lunch, Annie was wondering whether she'd made a mistake. This wasn't work, it was slave labour. She hadn't taped a single second yet, though she had done dry runs with the technical crews as well as being made-up and fussed over before running through the scenes again. In between rehearsing she hung around with the other actors on the sets. It felt as odd to sit on the Sheridans' marital bed as it had done meeting the couple. Having become so familiar with the room on TV, it almost felt as if it belonged to a friend. She recognised the fabric and furnishings, the bedside clock, even the glass of water that Mary kept by the neat pile of books on the bedside table.

It was almost three by the time the stage manager, Monty Prindle, came up to her, grinning. 'All ready for the big take-a-rooni, are we?'

'As ready as I'll ever be, Monty,' she replied.

Annie liked Monty, a large, gentle man in his late fifties with an avuncular grey beard. He reminded her of Lee Marvin, with a stomach that bulged out over his black jeans and strained the buttons of his brown check cowboy shirt. Monty seemed to be everyone's best friend, and it was from him that the cast and crew received their instructions on the set. While the taping was taking place, the director and line producers congregated in the production booth on the ninth floor. Monty, receiving instructions through his headphones, had to mastermind the operation on the eighth.

Annie's first scene was in the hospital ward where four of the crash victims were being tended. This was the storyline that Alex had imagined: the Brendan Air plane, carrying twelve of the soap's star characters, had come down soon after takeoff from Chicago. In need of urgent medical attention, they'd been brought to a hospital in the city, home to one of the Senators, the high-flying and beautiful Dawn Hope. Dawn, a compassionate woman running for the State Governor's seat, was visiting the hospital to see the injured characters, completely unaware that she was to reveal a past that would change their lives.

From within the production booth, Zoë Dunlop, headphones on and cigarettes by her side, told Monty that they were ready to tape. To Zoë's right sat her assistant director, who was following the taping with a stopwatch to ensure that it was running to time. To her left was the technical director responsible for switching between the three cameras on set when Zoë wanted a new angle. For soap operas, this was every few seconds. All of them, together with the line producer and the lighting engineer, followed the action on a wall of monitors in front and listened through speakers to the side. Each camera fed its picture onto a separate monitor and the one in use at any given time relayed its images to the larger preview monitor in the centre of the wall. Simultaneously, in the audio booth, sound effects and music were added.

On the studio floor Monty, sounding like a bingo compère, threw his booming voice over the hubbub.

'Here we go-go, gang. Opening places please.'

Annie stood on her spot, her heart thudding with nerves.

'We need some hush here,' said Monty.

Two of the male leads stopped their game of knuckles.

'Stand by. OK, and it's *Unto the Skies*, episode 11857, aaaaanda, take one.'

Joel, on camera two, moved in on the face of a nurse studying a clipboard at the end of William Sheridan's bed. She looked to her side.

In the booth, Zoë snapped her fingers. 'Three.'

The main monitor switched to camera three, a full-length shot of Dawn Hope and the doctor approaching the nurse.

Another snap of the fingers. 'One,' said Zoë.

Gormand's wrinkled, worried face appeared.

DR GORMAND
Nurse Mullholiland, this is Senator Hope. She's come to see the victims.

DAWN
How are they, Nurse?

NURSE
It was a horrible accident. It's a miracle there were so few casualties.

DAWN
A miracle and a credit to the emergency services. Nurse Mull – Mullholy – Mullyho – Oh shit!

Annie slapped her hands against her thighs with exasperation, and rolled her eyes. 'I'm sorry,' she said.

'Cut,' Zoë called out to the crew, then over the public address, 'Don't worry about it, Annie.'

'Do I have to say her name?' Annie asked, talking to Zoë through the camera.

'Jesus fuck,' the line producer said in thick Brooklynese, 'we've got an actress who talks back. What is this, *Tootsie Two*?'

'Hang on,' Zoë said over the PA. She turned to the producer. 'Mullholiland is a stupid name, Neil. Does she need it?'

'It's in there, so there's a reason for it.'

'What reason?'

'Don't ask me. Maybe her family built the hospital. But in soaps, sweetheart, there's a reason for everything.'

Zoë made a snap decision, assuming that she had more power than she did. She spoke again to the studio. 'Cut the name and let's take it from the top.'

The scene was repeated, and ran smoothly. Annie was soon standing by William Sheridan's bed. He was covered in bandages and bruises and had a crude scar on his face. Lou on camera three had silently rolled the podium for a close-up of the star's battered visage.

DAWN
Mr Sheridan, I'm Senator Hope, and you're a lucky man.

WILLIAM
Lucky, Senator Hope? My wife, she . . .

DR GORMAND
Don't give up. We're doing everything we can. Everything possible. And more. We know what a good woman Mary Sheridan is. She is a caring human being and we're going to care for her in return.

WILLIAM

Thank you, Doctor.

DAWN
(TAKING GORMAND ASIDE)

How is Mrs Sheridan?

'Go in very close on this one, Lou,' Zoë said.

DR GORMAND

Senator Hope, I'm going to be straight with you.
She's not good. She's suffering from bilateral acute
renal failure. If we can't get a donor soon, I'm afraid
she might die.

'Keep tight on William's face, Joel. And,' she clicked
her fingers, 'one, and three.'
The monitor showed the image from camera one, the
doctor's face, then to three, of Dawn.

DAWN

Is there nothing we can do?

DR GORMAND
(CROSSING HIS FINGERS)

We keep doing this until we find a compatible
organ.

Pauly, one of eleven members of the Lucci family who
worked as a grip on the show, whispered to his neighbour, 'My organ's compatible with that new actress's, no
question.'
'Your organ,' replied his cousin, 'is compatible with your
right hand, and that's the end of it.'
'You can talk!' said Pauly.
Monty turned around and held a finger to his mouth.

On set, Dr Gormand and the Senator were still in deep conversation.

DAWN
How long has she got?

DR GORMAND
How long? It's hard to say. She's a problem case. We need to find the perfect match for her tissue type, and that's not going to be easy.

While camera one had been trained on Dawn and the doctor, camera two had repositioned itself by Mary Sheridan's bed. Unconscious, she was surrounded by what looked like enough equipment to send the space shuttle to Mars. She had tubes in her nose and drips in her arms and an oxygen pump by her head. Her son, Jamie, played by the actor Philip Shaw, sat by her, a bandage round his own head.

JAMIE
(STROKING HIS MOTHER'S HAIR)
(TEARY)
Remember that time I fell off the horse, Mom-Mom, and the doctors said I wouldn't pull through and you came and sat by me, day after day you sat by me, and you stroked my hair just like this? You were the only one who believed I'd live, and it was because of your strength, your courage and your prayers that I survived. I want to repay that debt to you. You gave life to me twice over, Mom-Mom. The least I can do is help you hold on to yours.

NURSE
(TAKING JAMIE BY THE SHOULDERS)
Mr Sheridan, you have to come away now.

'Remember I want full-length of the curtain being drawn around her,' said Zoë. 'Then two on Jamie and Dawn.'

DAWN

Jamie? Jamie Sheridan?

JAMIE
(BAFFLED)

Yes?

DAWN

Hello. I'm Dawn Hope. I'm running for Governor in November.

JAMIE

Excuse me, Lady, but this isn't the time or the place for your campaigning.

DAWN

Wait! Please don't go!

JAMIE

Didn't you hear? This isn't the time. Or the place. There's been an accident, a terrible accident. My mother is suffering from acute renal failure, my wife could be dying in front of my eyes and here you are trying to get votes, I . . .

DAWN

I'm not campaigning, Mr Sheridan. I'm here because I think I can help.

JAMIE

Wait a minute. Do I know you?

'Keep in on Jamie's face, in, in, and three on Dawn and two . . . one . . . and we're up,' Zoë said. Then, over the PA, she said, 'Good work, everyone. Nice start, Annie.'

There was a moment when all the actors stayed in position before Monty said, 'Tapes are good.'

'Then let's go to Four A,' said Zoë.

The scenes were shot not in chronological sequence, but by set, to save money and time. One of the problems it gave the actors was that they had no time to brush up their lines on new scenes and, as endless repetition was an important part of every soap, it was often difficult to remember dialogue written for the start of a scene that varied only slightly from that spoken at the end of a scene taped five minutes before.

On the set, Monty had come to give Annie a kiss.

'Never easy on your first day, kid,' he said, patting his stomach. 'You were magnifico.'

'I didn't have much to do, Monty.'

'Try saying that to some of the Method boffins,' Monty said. 'Oh boy, oh boyo! The headcases we've had. Wait a mo,' he said, 'I've got the voice of God coming through my headphones.'

He listened to the instructions arriving from the production booth, gave the thumbs up to one of the cameras, and then said, 'Four A, from el toppo, gang. Joel, repo here.'

Joel repositioned his camera to its new starting place.

Monty spoke again. 'Ready, all?'

The house lights were dimmed once more. Jamie Sheridan and Dawn Hope were standing in the hospital set, as they had been at the end of the scene before, though when the show aired two other scenes and a commercial break would be separating this scene from the last.

'Very still now,' Monty said, holding out a clipboard. 'Give me some hush-a-rooni. And five . . . four . . .

three . . .' The last two digits were unspoken before the red light shone on camera two, indicating that taping had begun.

JAMIE

You said you think you can help?

DAWN

It's possible, Mr Sheridan.

JAMIE

I think I know you. I'm sure I've seen you somewhere before.

DAWN

I am quite well known. I'm the youngest female Senator in the Senate.

JAMIE

I'm very impressed, but there's something else . . .

In the audio booth the technicians were adding the bleeping and whirring of hospital machines in commotion. Two nurses ran past Jamie and Dawn, followed by a surgeon and Dr Gormand. Jamie extended an arm to stop him.

JAMIE

Doctor, what is it?

DR GORMAND

I wish I knew.

'Cut,' said Zoë, speaking over the PA system. 'The doctor's line is, "I wouldn't like to say, Jamie, but it sounds very serious." Not "I wish I knew."'

The actor playing the role replied, 'I meant I wish I knew what the line was!'

'Have you got it now?' Monty asked.

The actor had the line repeated, and they did a second take from the top. This time, it ran smoothly.

The next scene belonged to Annie, played beside the silent, comatose Mary Sheridan. Her husband William was seen to be listening from the neighbouring bed. Once the other actors had left for the day and Olivia Rourke had had the chance to breathe for a while without tubes rammed into her mouth, the crew settled down to tape. This was to be the last scene of the show when it was aired two weeks from now, and the most important in persuading viewers to tune in again. Alex had decided that Annie was good enough to carry it alone. Zoë, though she had decided to begin the scene with an establishing shot of Mary flat out in the hospital bed, was concentrating for the most part on Annie's face. The lighting engineer had given the scene a mood of mysteriousness by dimly lighting Annie's face from below.

'Yup,' Monty said in response to a question through his headphones, 'ready when you are, boss.'

He counted the scene in, and the cameras stealthily moved in towards Annie. She was sitting on the bed, holding Mary Sheridan's hand, talking softly so as not to be heard. The curtain was drawn about them.

DAWN

Please don't die, Mary. I've met your family and your friends today and never in my life have I known such warmth and love shown to someone. You must be a very, very special lady. I knew you would be. I've followed you in the papers whenever you and William were in the news. I saw the Society pictures

when Jamie and Vanessa were married and it made
me happy to see you happy. He sensed something
today, Jamie. He sensed something about me.

'Camera three on reaction shot of William. Aaand,'
Zoë snapped her fingers once more, 'back to two.'

DAWN

It's funny how things work out, isn't it? All these
long years I've been thinking of how to do this, and
whether you'd be proud of me.

As tears came to Annie's eyes, the line producer leant
forward in his chair and said to Zoë, 'Why's the stupid
bitch crying? She's meant to be strong.'

'I like it,' said Zoë. 'She's getting inside the character.'

'In my script,' he added, 'it says, "Dawn laughs self-
mockingly."'

'What's the difference, Neil?'

'The difference is that this isn't a movie. In soap you
play by the rules!'

Dawn's speech was coming to an end. The technicians on the floor had no such doubts about Annie's
performance.

DAWN

I don't know what I'd do if you never woke up, Mary.
I want you to be proud of me. I want you to look at
me and say, 'You did OK, Dawn! You did OK.' I
don't want you never to know who I am. Please
God, let this woman live so I can tell her who I am.

As the camera pulled back, the audience was left with the
final image of William Sheridan straining as he sat up in
his hospital bed and listening in amazement to what this
Senator was saying to his wife.

'Tapes are good,' said Monty. 'And it's a one hundred per cent wrap-a-roo.'

Almost as soon as Annie stepped away from the bed, the grips moved in to dismantle the set.

Zoë, looking exhausted after two straight days on the set, emerged from the booth to join Annie. 'I'm bloody knackered,' she said. 'Can you come for a quick drink?'

'Never in my life,' said Annie, rubbing her make-up off with a towel, 'have I needed one more. I'll be with you in five.'

13

Alex Lubotsky had this theory about executive producers that he was going to remember when he worked for President Susan Grant. The two jobs, he'd decided, were very similar. The most important task of any President throughout his term was to convince the American people to vote for him at the next election, while the executive producer's job was to persuade sponsors that what he had to offer was enjoyed by more people more of the time than anything produced by anyone else. Neither of the executives was ever called upon to *do* anything and this, Alex thought, was not healthy at all.

He came to his conclusion after a morning spent on the set. It was ten days after the team of Zoë Dunlop and Annie Marin had first made its appearance, and four prior to the airing of the infamous plane crash scene. The soap magazines were in a frenzy, the editors able, with their knowledge, to tease readers with hints and advise them to tune in to *Unto the Skies*. On the set the people who made the show, who spent twelve hours a day building sets and arranging lights and blocking cameras and taping footage and directing unruly show-offs being paid large sums of money to act like kids in front of a lens, *these* people, the people who relied on the show for the food on their tables and the shoes on their feet, were ecstatic about the changes, the publicity and the new spirit. They saw themselves climbing to number one and pocketing hefty bonuses before the season was out.

But what of Vince the Executive Producer? The captain

of the happy ship? On the day Alex visited him in his office he was chain-smoking a new brand of heavier, French cigarettes, pacing around his office like a bad actor trying to portray thought and jabbering about impending icebergs.

'It doesn't feel right,' were his first words. 'It's a screw-up. Something's not right. People do not like surprises. They do not want to see planes crashing out of the skies. It's too ugly. Would you like to see people you love in a plane crash?'

'No, I . . .'

'I didn't think so. And they love these characters. That's because they haven't met them, I know. It's because they haven't had to break their balls negotiating contracts with their agents, *I know*. But they love them. More than their own, sometimes. Did you know that?'

'Of course.'

'I know. Me too. But I should have listened to my head.' Vince tapped the side of his rather small skull. 'If it ain't broke, don't fix it.'

'It was broken, Vince. It was collapsing.'

'Whatever, it's not right.'

'Have you been on the set recently?' Alex asked.

'Where?'

'On the set. It's about two minutes from here.'

'No time. I'm busy. You want a coffee? It goes straight through me when I take a slash, but it's reassuring to know something's working right.'

'Please listen to me, Vince. Everything is looking fine.'

'Uh-uh. Not from up here it ain't.'

This was the moment when Alex's theory was born. Vince thought the show was falling apart because he was too far removed from it. His brief was to give the show its atmosphere and concept. In this he was like the President, only the President had a nation, maybe even the world, as his domain. Yet both talked a great deal about doing things, and they listened a great deal to other people explaining what *they* were doing and why, and they spent the rest of their time telling the people who were doing things what other things they thought they should be doing. What was needed to keep them sane and in touch and reasonable was some active involvement. The further away these executives were from the nuts and bolts of the worlds they were running, the more time they devoted to themes and impressions and packaging, the looser their grip on reality became. Hadn't George Bush been amazed by riots in LA?

'Vince,' Alex said, 'there's really nothing you can do now. Why don't you relax and wait for the response to the shows? If it's bad and if the ratings aren't kind, then we'll have to think again.'

'I can't do that,' said Vince. 'I can't relax.'

'Why not?'

'You don't seem to get it.' He leant over his desk, looking as if he was about to send a battalion of tears hurtling over the craggy terrain of his unshaven face. 'Because I have got a show to think about. Now please, go home, do some writing, and just leave me alone.'

The day before the crash scene was to air, Annie heard a knock on her dressing-room door and Faith Valentine came in, dolled-up as usual. Their relationship over the previous two weeks had been frosty, but as both had been doing their best to avoid one another, there'd been no major scenes. Over time, Annie thought, she would get used to Faith, just as she'd immunised herself against the sight of homelessness in Manhattan.

So this visit from her old enemy was as disquieting to Annie as finding a homeless man inside her building. It made the problem impossible to ignore.

Because Vanessa Sheridan remained hospitalised with a septic toe after the crash, Faith was wearing a nightdress

with a pink robe tied tight around her waist. Annie
wondered whether Faith's torso functioned in the same
way as a toothpaste tube, for the tighter her clothes were
to her waist, the more her breasts seemed to expand. Now
they seemed trained on Annie like the barrels of a sawn-off
shotgun.

'Am I wanted somewhere?' Annie asked.

'No, I came to see you,' replied Faith.

The dressing rooms at *Unto the Skies* were far from
palatial. As the new girl on the block, Annie had been
given one of the smallest. It had a tiny cupboard at one
end, a mirror along the wall surrounded by the obligatory
strips of white bulbs and a tatty beige armchair. The
shit-brown industrial carpet was patterned with cigarette
burns and coffee stains. Faith, without asking, lifted one
of Annie's towels from the open closet door and draped
it over the arm of the chair before sitting down.

'Is there something on your mind?' Annie asked.

Faith nodded. 'I'm here as a friend,' she said.

Annie brushed the crumbs of the pastry she'd been
eating off the desk.

'I don't think that's wholly possible, is it?'

'Well, even if you won't take me as your friend, I want
to give you some advice. Before others do. You see, I've
overheard things.'

'What things?' Annie wanted to know, suspicious already.
As far as she was concerned, everything was going as well
as it could be. The crew liked her, she got on well with
Zoë and the other director, and she was beginning to get
involved with her character.

'It's your face,' Faith said.

Annie turned to look at herself in the mirror. Faith,
behind her, studied the reflection as well.

'You move it too much,' she explained.

'What?' said Annie, suddenly conscious that her face
had screwed up in alarm. She relaxed it.

'Did you do just the tinsiest bit of theatre since you left school?' Faith asked.

'You could say that.'

Faith pressed her lips together to even out the lipstick. 'Well – this isn't theatre.'

'Really? Thanks for telling me. Because I've been wondering where the audience was every day.'

'There's no need . . . Look.' Faith lifted up her hands and, crossing the long nails like ceremonial swords over a wedding couple, she joined the thumbs at the bottom and held them within an inch of Annie's face in imitation of a TV screen. 'This is television. It's close up. If you move your features all the time, well, it looks like acting.'

'And I do that?'

Faith lifted her eyebrows and leant a fraction forward as if she wanted the question repeated, but then, almost in a whisper, as if she was offering secret information, she said, 'I've heard talk.'

'Oh yeah?' said Annie, unsure whether her indignation was directed at Faith or the invisible critics.

'Your movements too.'

'My movements?' Annie said, staying still and calm.

Faith, whose presence was bringing back all Annie's worst insecurities from Cornell Williams, nodded again and said, 'They're too jerky. On daytime you have to move slowly and gracefully otherwise you won't be in focus. I've been doing it so long they call me the swan.'

'And what am I? The ugly duckling?'

'No! But you're showing how new you are to acting.'

Annie let it pass. It was a common enough criticism. Nobody seemed to acknowledge you as an actress unless you were on TV and film. Annie could have been the greatest stage actress in the world and still the audience would search through the programme biographies to determine where on the screen they might have seen her. An actress away from a camera somehow didn't deserve to exist.

'Is that all?' Annie asked hesitantly.

She remained unsure whether Faith was telling the truth.

'Almost.'

'Almost!'

Faith splayed two fingers into a V and moved the tips towards Annie's eyes. Annie had a vision of the painted nails gouging out her eyeballs and winced.

'Your eyes move.'

'You want me to be like Bobby?' Annie asked.

Bobby was the blind character. The actor had trained his eyeballs so they rarely moved on set.

'No, but when you look into someone else's eyes, you should stare at one eye or the other. Never both. It makes your eyeballs move from side to side.'

'Is that so?'

'Yes.'

'Well, thanks for the tip,' Annie said, wondering now whether Faith, in her blundering, stupid way, was indeed being kind. 'I'll try it.'

'You should. It won't be easy getting another role if you haven't made a good impression in this one.'

Annie laughed. 'Do you think I'm going to need to look?'

'I shouldn't really say,' said Faith, standing up.

'But I suppose you've heard something.'

She leant in, and at once Annie knew what was coming next. 'Alex told me,' whispered Faith.

For a moment, Annie was speechless, but then the anger fired up inside her. Of course this was the whole purpose of the visit. To remind Annie of what had happened before, to let her know that it could happen again. Faith had already sunk her claws into Alex, tempting Fate to play the same hand of cards again. Annie rose to her feet, so incensed that she wanted to lash out at Faith.

Instead, it was the soap star who made the first move.

'This is my show, and it's going to stay my show. Even if I have to be stupid enough to sleep with the writer to keep it that way. Wasn't that what you said all those years ago?' Faith tightened the knot on her robe, held Annie's troubled stare for a moment or two more, and then added, 'Stupid, wasn't I?' before marching out of the room.

Sitting cross-legged and shoeless on his apartment floor, with notes and papers scattered around him and Herbie Hancock's 'One Finger Snap' bleating from the stereo, Alex Lubotsky looked more like an NYU student cramming for his final exams than a forty-two-year-old man plotting the campaign that he hoped would make Susan Grant the first female President in the history of the United States.

A couple of weeks had passed since the plane crash episode aired, and things were going wonderfully well. The reviews of the prime time show had been excellent, with Zoë's direction singled out for particular praise. Annie, too, had received acclaim rarely given a soap opera actress. *The New York Times* had credited her with a 'fresh and beguiling assurance' while the *Herald* suggested that the Dunlop–Marin partnership had given soap operas a good name.

The ratings were not yet in, but Alex was confident. He himself had received so much publicity that he felt curiosity alone would have persuaded enough viewers to tune in. All that he needed was one rating of 7.0 or above and he'd be paid the salary and bonus denied Max. At the moment, he was living off his own savings. If he was paid by Vince he would keep the substantial bonus for himself and give Max's $1,081,000 salary to Pam. It seemed the fairest arrangement.

Alex's intention was that, as soon as the arrears had been paid and he'd sucked all he could from Dawn's character, he would leave *Unto the Skies* to concentrate on the First Lady's campaign. For the moment, however, Dawn Hope was all that filled his mind, with Bob Fein taking responsibility for the rest of the headwriter's tasks. Had Bob not been so in awe of Alex, he would have probably resigned from the show, aggrieved at being headwriter in all but name and salary.

Now Alex was waiting for Charlie Canon to arrive. She had been promoting *Canon Fire* in Europe and had come back keen to discuss how Dawn might advance the New Feminist cause on *Unto the Skies*. She was unaware, of course, that Alex was giving Dawn her feminist credentials as a means of testing the water for Susan.

She arrived at the apartment in a taupe Armani trouser suit, with a sunbed tan and a bottle of Pinot Noir that she hoped to share with Alex alone. She was far from pleased, then, to find Bob Fein and Zoë Dunlop there as well.

'Did you get a chance to see the videos I sent you, Charlie?' Alex asked once they'd rattled off their comments about the endless freeze.

'Yes, I did. That's why I wanted to talk to you. I didn't realise,' she added tetchily, 'that I was being invited to a drinks party.'

She sat on the edge of the armchair so that her beautiful hair could hang down her straight back. She said, 'However, as you're here, Zoë, I want to say that I'm not happy with the differential framing I'm seeing.'

Zoë, cradling her gin as if it was an orphaned fledgling, confessed that she didn't know what Charlie was talking about. 'You speak a different language over here, darling.'

'Differential framing, Zoë, is the deeply sexist focusing of TV cameras on the faces of men but the bodies of women. I hoped that you, of all people, would do something to change that.'

'Quite frankly, I haven't been conscious of it.'

This seemed to upset Charlie. 'Could you *be* conscious?

It's only through consciousness that we can open eyes to discrimination like this.'

'I'll tell the cameras to pan down to the men's balls, and up to the women's faces then,' Zoë said. 'For equality's sake.'

'And that's another thing,' Charlie continued, adopting a Rodinesque pose. 'I find it hard to look at these women's faces. Why must there be so much make-up? Women need to be proud of their natural beauty.'

'It's just the way it is on soap,' Alex said with a shrug of his shoulders.

'"The way it is" happens to be my battle zone. Don't forget that.'

He held his hands up in defence. 'I'm just the writer.'

'That means you're responsible for Dawn, and in my opinion I see her as a step backwards for women. It's clear as daylight that the part is written by a man.'

'Charlie, I'm amazed. She's strong, she's intelligent, she's successful, she's breaking men's balls left, right and centre and . . .'

'Stop!' said Charlie with a loud clap of her hands. Sitting very still, remaining sculptural, she locked Alex's eyes in a hard stare. And then she stood and began to talk as she walked, as if she was practising a public speech in the privacy of her bedroom. 'Why, I ask myself, does Dawn have to be a ball-breaker? Why is she single? Why isn't she happily married to a man who can accept her strength and power as a fulfilled woman? Why doesn't she have children? Why has she given up everything for her career? What you're actually doing, Alex, is more demeaning to women than the blatant sexism of a show such as *Baywatch*. What you're doing is saying, "Look, here's a woman who's scaled the ladder of success, but the price she's paid is a life without family or friends." You shouldn't be equating success with misery. That's what's been taught for too long. Are you so blind to that, Alex, or is it just that you hate women?'

She had circled the room, like a wasp around food, and was now standing next to him.

He didn't bother to lift his eyes as he said, 'And how are the little ones, Charlie?'

'What little ones?'

'The little children that you and your husband had.'

She moved away. 'That's not fair. That is not fair! I have chosen not to get married and reproduce. It is my choice. I don't consider it the price of my success.'

'And nor does Dawn.'

'Well it would be refreshing, then, to see her with a lover, and one who'll treat her as an equal.'

'You should keep watching,' said Bob Fein. 'She may even wind up getting married.'

Charlie glanced at him as if she'd forgotten he was in the room. She once again took her seat. 'I'm not sure I want to encourage her entry into the limited state of a typical nuclear family. But what I thought I'd been promised was a role model who'd help women overcome their psychological fear of power.'

'We thought we were doing that. Didn't we, Bob? Dawn *is* a happy woman.'

'Come on! I've seen the script. She's about to mutilate herself in surgery. You've taken it to a physiological extreme by trying to display that she can only get in touch with her humanity through self-mutilation. I thought it was almost pornographic.'

No one said anything, though Zoë was tempted to accuse Charlie of talking out of her fanny. In the end, it was she who broke the silence. 'Darling,' she said to Alex as she rattled the ice in her glass, 'I'd love some more grandmother's poison.'

'Help yourself,' said Alex, pointing her in the direction of the gin bottle before turning back to Charlie. 'Is there anything you like about Dawn?'

'Yes,' said Charlie more softly, 'I like the fact of her

existence, and I'm encouraged by the unmasculine environment of the soap opera, though I can't understand why
she has to use such maternal terminology when discussing
her political ideas.'

Alex said, 'I've been trying to show the added dimension
she can bring to the political scene as a woman.'

'And you see women as non-aggressive and nurturing?'

'More so than men, of course. You can't argue with
nature.'

'Can't I?' shrieked Charlie. 'That's fucking bullshit!'

In the momentary silence, a large cube of ice chinked
into the base of Zoë's glass. Alex wondered whether he
should try to calm the nostril-flaring feminist, but he
couldn't think of anything to say that she wouldn't take
as offensive. He took a potato chip instead, and offered
the bowl to Charlie.

'Trying to fatten me up, are we?'

'No, I . . .'

'And while we're on the subject I'd like to say that
I've met plenty of women who are just as aggressive as
men. We're going round and round in circles, aren't we?
Men like you saying that because women are nurturing
and don't want responsibility in an aggressive world they
should be kept in their place where they won't have
to worry. That's what you're doing. You're denying
Dawn the voice of authority that is dormant within every
tough, competitive woman in the world. In fact, you're
castrating her.'

'Have we got our terminology a tiny bit jiggled up?'
asked Zoë, retaking her seat. She bit on the moon of
lime, dropped it back in the glass and added, 'Or do they
castrate women in this country?'

Charlie bounced to her feet again and advanced on Zoë.
'Did you know that the testosterone level of a woman rises
with age and that a man's declines?'

'No, that's news to me.'

235

'It's true, Zoë. Our testicles may be hidden, but no one can take them away from us.'

'Bob?' asked Alex. 'Is that a line we can use?'

Bob Fein tried not to laugh, but he couldn't keep the chortle down. Charlie pointed a manicured nail at him. 'I will not be laughed at. How dare you? My book has been in the best-seller chart for six weeks! How dare you?'

'I'm sorry,' Bob said. 'I didn't mean . . .'

'Men never *mean anything*, do they? It's always just the way it is. Fine. I'm prepared to sacrifice.' She held out her hand to Alex. 'I'm sure we'll speak,' she said.

He stood, casually, a hand in his pocket.

'Charlie, that was my fault. But Dawn's a soap character. We can't start frightening the viewers away.'

'Well, there's courage for you!' she said, sneering at him as she grabbed her coat and left the room.

'Jesus,' said Bob. 'What's got into her?'

'No one,' said Zoë. 'I'd say that was the problem.'

'I think I may have promised too much when we first talked,' said Alex, running a hand through his hair. 'I think she thought I was going to base Dawn on her.'

'Can you imagine Vince's reaction if we did?' Bob said.

The three of them began a discussion on how funny it would be to leave Vince and Charlie alone on an island together, and an hour or so later Bob and Zoë left. Almost immediately, the door buzzer rang again. Alex glanced about the room to see if one of them had left something behind. He spoke into the box.

'It's a Charlie Canon,' said the doorman.

'Hello again,' he said, leaning on the door as she walked briskly from the elevator.

'Can I come in?' she asked, angling her head to look into the room.

He stepped back for her to sweep by. She stood in the centre of the room like someone waiting to leave.

'Would you like another glass of your wine?' he asked.

'So you've forgiven me!' she said, her shoulders visibly relaxing.

'Aaah . . . yuh! I think we can safely say that.'

'Good!' she strode to him and then, putting her lips against his ear, she whispered, 'I've got nothing on under my clothes.'

Alex rewound the sentence and played it again in his mind. Then he said, 'Nor have I.'

'I mean, dummy, no underwear. Feel.'

She took his hand and slid it beneath the waistband of her silk trousers to flatten it against her vagina, like a picnic rug on a mossy knoll. It was spongy to his touch, and more than a little damp as if whispering its desperate invitation. For a moment, Alex, a man who'd seduced scores of women in his lifetime, felt like a virgin with a prostitute. He didn't move his hand. It was Charlie who pushed her body against him.

'I hate you for still doing this to me,' she said.

'What am I doing?' he asked, his hand shell-like over its restless pearl.

'You make me want you. You still make me want to give myself to you.'

Although it had been over ten years since he had last considered sleeping with Charlie Canon, it was with some relief that he felt his body responding to her touch. Together, his heartbeat and prick twitched from their slumber. Surprising her, Alex pressed his finger against the slick fold, and then forced it deep inside.

The nation's most famous feminist breathed in sharply, smiled, and then turned her face to Alex, eager to meet his adorable lips as she felt for his hardness with an impatient hand.

*   *   *

No doubt Ivan Petrovich Pavlov would have been intrigued to learn that the dramatic, racing strings of *Unto the Skies'* theme tune always brought Barbara's dog scampering to the television set. When Barbara had first turned on the show to see her oldest friend, she had not expected to get hooked. Now it was a vital part of her day, and when she couldn't watch at three, she would see it last thing at night, when Michael and the children were in bed. She was usually accompanied by a bag of cookies and the dog, who would take scraps from her hand as she was distracted by the turmoil and torment on screen.

Today it was almost midnight when she turned the video on. At once Dobby (so named by Barbara's youngest, Ken) ran in and sat close to the screen, apparently staring at the pictures. Today, the show began with Annie, as Dawn, talking to Dr Gormand in his office. The two of them had never looked so troubled.

> DAWN
>
> You say you've got the results, Doctor?

> DR GORMAND
> (WITH OPEN FILES IN HIS HAND)
> Yes. They came in this morning.

> DAWN
>
> And?

> DR GORMAND
>
> The results seem to support your theory. If you want to go through with this operation, if you are willing to offer your kidney to Mrs Sheridan, then I can have no medical objections.

The dog suddenly barked, making Barbara laugh. 'Hey, Dobby, you enjoying yourself?'

Although Dobby had watched the show almost every day since Annie had made her first appearance, he was a dog and so failed to comprehend fully what was going on. He didn't know, for example, that Mary Sheridan had been born with only one kidney and that the second had been damaged in the crash. He wouldn't have had a chance of remembering that there'd been a frenetic search for a donor and that Senator Hope had taken the issue all the way to Washington. And his chances of accurately reading the concern on the doctor's face and of understanding that Mary Sheridan had only a few days left to live unless a kidney was found to match her rare tissue type, were almost nil.

DAWN
But personally, Dr Gormand, what do you think?

DR GORMAND
You can survive as well on one kidney as on two. I'm not worried about your physical condition. But I wonder . . .

DAWN
If you wonder if I'm strong enough, let me tell you, Doctor, I am. Women can be tough when we need to be and I need to be now. Mary Sheridan is dying and I have the chance to save her life. I want to give her one of my kidneys.

DR GORMAND
I hope this has nothing to do with your candidacy for the State House. I hope you don't believe you can buy votes with this magnanimous gesture of yours.

DAWN
(ANGRY)

Let me tell you something, Dr Gormand! I became a politician because I care about people. I look out of my window and I see homeless people, children born with AIDS because their mothers are prostitutes, children without daddies, wives without husbands, and I want to open my arms and hold them all. I'm not a mother myself, no I'm not, but I feel like a mother. Can you understand that? A mother to the people of this city and this state. I was born to care, and I care about this brave and wonderful woman. I wouldn't be able to look myself in the eye ever again knowing that I could have saved her life but chose to do nothing instead. Do you understand me now?

DR GORMAND

Yes. My apologies. I admire your honesty, Miss Hope. And your strength. I'm going to recommend that the operation take place as soon as it possibly can.

DAWN

When will that be?

DR GORMAND

I see no reason not to go ahead soon. Mary Sheridan is a very sick lady, and the sooner we can operate the better it will be for all of us.

DAWN

I hope so, Doctor. I hope so.

The camera moved in on Dawn's face as she contemplated her decision, and then there was a cut to Paolo Lunardi sitting sullen in jail, waiting for his wife to arrive.

Suddenly, as if only Annie held his interest, Dobby rose to his feet, stretched, released an almost silent fart and scuffled away, leaving Barbara alone in the stench to watch the rest of the show.

14

It had become like the end of a James Bond film, for today was not only the day on which Vince Moscardini's contract with the Lubotsky brothers was to expire, but also when the rating for Alex's first show was due to arrive. When he had first hatched his plan, Alex had never dreamt that it would go down to the wire like this, but the whole process had taken so long that now he considered himself lucky that the ratings were to be declared in time. At least the calculations had become simple. If the show had not received a rating of 7.0 by midnight tonight, then Max's salary would be for ever lost.

The cast and crew of *Unto the Skies* knew nothing of these shenanigans between headwriter and Executive Producer. They all had their personal reasons for wanting high ratings, their own hopes and plans – for houses, cars, kids, lovers, bonuses. There was a considerable sense of optimism. The response in the press to the first weeks with Alex, Annie and Zoë had been positive, and most felt that the storyline had strengthened with the deaths in hospital of a couple more characters from the crash. Publicly, Alex's reasons for killing off two stars – Jim Brenner's wife, Eleanor, and their longtime friend Clayton Whelk – were that they'd been on the show too long and that the audience needed some fresh blood. In truth he'd wanted revenge, for in his journals Max had written of the misery these actors had given him. They had complained endlessly, refusing on set to speak the lines written for them and together trying to persuade first Bernie then Vince to fire Max for failing to develop their parts. It gave Alex considerable pleasure to be able to do Max's dirty work for him, and his one hope was that, wherever he was, Max had tuned in to the episode in which the characters died.

He was working now in his living room. He and Bob Fein had spent most of the day editing scripts. By now, the action had shifted out of the hospital. Only Mary Sheridan remained inside, having received a life-saving kidney from Dawn Hope. The reason behind Dawn's sacrifice had still not been revealed. Back in Hill Way, the Vanessa–William love story was being expanded while Mary remained bedridden. Bob was keen to expand the role played by Faith, arguing that she remained the soap's main star, however much attention Annie was getting. Alex was less sure. He didn't like the way Faith kept calling him with compliments. He'd spent too long in politics to take candy from such a stranger.

The phone rang. Alex and Bob looked at one another. It rang again. Alex pulled up the aerial and walked away. Two minutes later he reappeared.

'Vince wants a word with you,' he said.

'Has he heard?'

'Can you manage here on your own for a while?'

'Yeah, sure,' said Bob, the phone in his hand now. 'Have they heard?'

'Just close the door behind you, will you? I'll see you tomorrow.'

'Are you OK, Al? You look kind of weird.'

'I'm OK, but there's somewhere I have to go.'

At her beautiful Titusville home, bought when things had been good with Max, Pam Lubotsky listened to Alex's news with tears streaming down her face.

'I'm sorry,' she said, 'I shouldn't.'

'It's OK. It'll make you feel better.'

Though she knew he was being kind, she wanted to scream that no amount of crying made anything better. How could Alex think that merely by letting grief show its face, it would release its grip on her? She felt it clenching the blackness inside so that she carried Max's death wherever she went as consciously as she had her growing, kicking sons. How could anything help when nothing existed but this hunger to touch Max, to see Max, to have Max sleep by her side?

Alex brought her some coffee in a cup he'd found unwashed in the cupboard. She looked at him with a face that seemed bereft of life.

'It'll get better. I promise,' he said, squeezing her fist.

He felt ashamed of his neglect of her since he'd become involved with *Unto the Skies*. As if to justify himself, he told her that she'd seemed stronger when he'd left, that he had not expected her pain to sharpen.

'Max hadn't really left us when you were here,' she explained.

'How are the boys?' Alex asked, not wanting to be led down a path that had no ending.

'I don't know,' she said. She was picking the sulphur off a matchstick, needing to concentrate on doing something, anything, to keep the tears away. 'I got them fixed up with some counselling.' She said this quickly, as if ashamed.

'Are they . . .?'

'Don't judge me, Al!' She looked at him sternly. 'I didn't want to. But I can't be the mother they need. Sometimes I catch myself resenting them for not understanding what I'm going through. Can you believe that? It makes me feel like a stranger to them. This is the only childhood they've got, and I'm ruining it for them.'

'Why don't they come to New York for a few days? I'll get tickets for the Knicks, or something,' Alex said, wanting to cheer her.

She nodded and tried to smile. There was a silence

245

between them, during which Alex raised his eyes to see that four or five spotlight bulbs had blown and not been replaced.

Pam spoke. 'I'm sorry about this . . .'

'Don't be silly, I . . .'

'I mean it's fantastic! It really is. You're so clever. And the money . . .' She blew her nose into a tissue, and tried another smile. 'I honestly can't believe it. How much am I getting again?'

'More than a million,' said Alex. 'It should help.'

'I think it might!' she said with a sound that was as much a sob as a laugh. 'We'll be able to keep the house. What did you say the rating was? I forget.'

'Eleven point six,' he replied, truly proud. 'We're number one, for the moment at least.'

'God, that's phenomenal. What is it about you, Al? What's the secret?'

'I don't know. Arrogance, I suppose. I never do anything unless I think I can do it better than everyone else.'

'Rob could use some of that confidence. Really, he could. I see so much of Max in him.'

'I'll sort him out. I promise.'

'He got some A grades last week. Did he tell you?'

'Yeah,' Alex said, relieved that they'd moved on to good news, away from Max. 'It's fantastic.'

'And you know what I did to the poor guy?' Pam said. 'He ran in and told me like it was something that would snap me out of this and, you know, put some humour back in the place. And guess what I did? I just burst into tears.' She tilted her head back slightly and widened her eyes, as if to encourage the tears to seep back inside. 'Nobody warned me how much the happy moments would hurt. You should put that in your soap opera. I mean I *knew* that I'd miss Max like crazy at night or, or when I wanted someone around who really understood me. I knew I'd miss him then. But it's when something good has happened, when everyone else is happy, that it kicks the hardest. I couldn't help thinking how happy those grades would have made Max. Or what about this soap rating? He wasted his life trying to get back to number one.'

'No, he didn't waste that,' Alex said. 'Almost everything I wrote and every idea I had came out of Max's journals. They're rating *him* number one. I couldn't have got close without him. And you know something?'

There seemed to be some glimmer of hope in her tired, red eyes when she looked at him, as if he was going to tell her something that really would make things better.

'I think he knows it. I never believed any of those stories about twins until now. I never felt simultaneous pain or danger, nothing like that. But now . . .' Alex shook his head, because here was a universe he knew he couldn't control. 'Now I feel him all the time and I think he's happy with what we've done. I believe that. The only thing left is to make you smile, and, I don't know how, but *somehow*, we're going to make that happen too.'

The episodes of *Unto the Skies* featuring Annie Marin as the tough but tender Senator, Dawn, had been on air for three weeks when the letters began to arrive. Some were resentful. These fans of the show found fault with her hair or her wardrobe or her teeth or the way she allowed the outline of her nipples occasionally to be visible. They blamed her for the deaths of Eleanor and Clayton, saying that her spite and selfishness had cost good people their lives. She was accused of mumbling by some and speaking too crisply by others. There were letters questioning her devotion to God while others hinted that she was trying to plant a piece of the devil in Mary Sheridan by donating a kidney.

However, these letters were greatly outnumbered by those in her praise. To most she was a 'ray of sunlight', an 'inspiration to all', and a 'sweet girl who deserved everything she could get'. In a surprisingly short space of time, Dawn was accepted as a rightful member of the Sheridan clan.

Alex, taking a break from editing, picked up a letter written to him by a woman in Oklahoma, and read,

> *Dear Mr Lubotsky and other writers of <u>Unto the Skies</u>,*
> *I'm writing to say that I was what I'd call an on-off watcher of your show for many years. If there was a story I was enjoying – Jamie Sheridan's terribel horseback riding accident is one leaping to mind – then wild Horses couldn't keep me away.*
> *But for a long while I have been <u>off</u> the show. I understand that your Brother was the head-writer and so must temper my words while also sending my condolences (does he have family as my Son-in-law works in a porcelain studio and I would be glad to send Mrs Lubotsky a figurine?) but things were getting very monotonous in Hill Way so that you could turn off and turn on one month later and not miss a thing.*
> *I am very pleased to say this has changed. The airplane crash was of the first water although I was worried about William knowing the problems he's had with his heart, excetra. In fact, my Husband Billy-Bob died of a heart attack coming on for three years ago now and so I worry almost constantly about William's exertions. He is a good Father but there comes a time when everyone has to slow down. But what I wanted to ask was if the Director of the program did in fact steer a real plane into the field or was this done in another manner? I am greatly concerned about the countryside and don't like to think of debree and other filth spreading out on it. My Sister Debra lives in Chicago and she loves the animals, as I do as well.*
> *The reason I am writing to you now is by way of*

*congratulating you for turning me on to Unto the Skies
on an everyday basis. Like flour and water I'm stuck
on the show because of the exciting and moving stories.
I think that Dawn is a wonderful Woman and if only
we had some more politicians in the country like her
we wouldn't be going to the dogs like we are with that
Hillbilly Grant. He should be locked away is what I
say, what with His adulterys and Hollywood friends.
But I would most definitely like to see Dawn Hope as
the President of the United States. Can You imagine how
many other people would let themselves be operated on
and give up a Kidney to another person? The good Lord
JESUS gave us His example by laying down His life for
Man (and Women) so Dawn gave her kidney. Though
these stories are of course not the same they are similar,
and show us how God's teaching can be used in this
world even with the changes going on with the ozown
layers, excetra.*

*At first I thought Dawn gave so generously of herself
because she is a kind and wonderful Woman but when
it was revealed that <u>she was in fact Mary Sheridan's long
lost daughter</u> I tell you I could hardly believe my eyes and
ears. It does not surprise me that Mary had to give away
her beautiful baby girl because I remember that times
were more strict in the 1950s, but I do want to make
very sure that she does not suffer undue heartache over
the decision she made to have the baby Dawn adopted.
There are some things we all wish in our hearts that we
had never done, but at the time we had no choice. (I'm
thinking about my Cousin Joleen, of course.)*

*What I believe is that the young couple who did
take Dawn when she was a child were definitely good
although I am led to wonder why they couldn't have
children of their own. Will this be made clear? I know
that the man who adopted her was a Priest or some
such thing, but does that make it ok to adopt but not go*

*through the physical process of making children which I
think, because God made it pleasurable, must be a holy
thing? There are times I get confused by what's on the
show and want to say, STOP! or WHAT'S GOING ON?
but usually if I keep watching things make themselves
clear in the end.*

*I don't know if we will meet the adoptive parents but
I feel they should be <u>Congratulated</u> on rearing such a
wonderful Woman. She is most attractive as well as
being what I call ZAPPY, which is my word for 'very
with-it'. So many times the people who are ZAPPY are
mean-spirited, and their eyes are too close together. You
will notice that Paolo's eyes are very close together, as
are Bobby's. He was evil, and God punished him with
blindness.*

*I want to mention that you will burn in Hell if William
lays so much as one single hand on Vanessa. Man is
too often misled by sexual urges, it is his condition,
but you have the power to prevent this terribel thing
from happening. Also, Paolo should be released from
jail. He is a reformed man with nice legs.*

*Mandy Cranborne is a Hussy of the first water. The
sooner we see the back of her, the better I say. Marriage
to her would ruin Raymond. She uses people, like Alice,
Pierce, John-David and Petal.*

*But in finishing I want to send my warmest thanks
to you for making my world a better, richer place with
Dawn Hope. She is a new Friend to me. Already I
am hoping that she will win the Governor's seat in
November. I would vote for her if only I lived in Hill
Way, Illinois. But please make sure she lets the world
know her feelings about the issue of abortion. I know
she would do the right thing, as it is written in the Good
Book, and also in the Oklahoma Fellowship of Christ
Newsletter which copy I am sending to you with my
genuine thanks.*

*You are a good Man, Mr Lubotsky, and from next
Tuesday (17th) you will feature prominently in my
prayers.*
    Charlene Dufford.

Grinning, Alex folded the pages carefully back into
their envelope. Charlene's was by no means the only letter
extolling the virtues of Dawn's political philosophy. He
could see he was doing something right. And if he could go
on doing something right, could anybody stop him helping
Susan Grant all the way to the highest office in the land?

Unto the Skies had become Annie's life. As the new girl
in the fictional suburb of Hill Way she was being written
into more scenes than any of the other actors (much
to Faith's distress) and so was compelled to work the
hardest. During the six weeks since she'd begun, she had
frequently endured twelve-hour days, from seven to seven,
so her nights were spent recovering from the days and her
weekends from the weeks.

Given this, it was little wonder that her private life had
as much chance of flourishing as an igloo in Death Valley.
Although being back in New York was as gratifying as
returning to the arms of an old lover, she'd had too
little time to build a fulfilling private life. Most nights,
she ordered a take-out meal when she left the studio so
that her food would arrive at the same time as she. Then
she would scrape the make-up off and grimace at skin
that, without foundation or California's sun, was looking
increasingly imperfect. After a shower she would settle
down to learn yet more lines and then go to bed.

Today, tired out, she'd closed her eyes for a nap on the
Sheridans' bed and was about to fall asleep when the stage
manager called out, 'Dawn, my darling, you're on.'

They were rehearsing a scene in the Sheridan living
room, its three flimsy wooden walls standing illuminated

251

in the wide blackness of the studio. Acting with her in this scene were Olivia Rourke and the brattish ten-year-old Jude Gurkin, who played Timmy Lunardi, Mary's grandson.

'I need powder,' he said.

'This isn't a take,' Monty told him.

'I feel shiny,' Jude squawked. 'I don't like that.'

Timmy was powdered, to shut him up, and then Monty said, 'A little quieter now, folks, and let's go-go.'

TIMMY
Davey's waiting for me, Granma. Can I go?

MARY
You run along then.

DAWN
He's an adorable little boy, Mary. You must be very proud.

MARY
I am. But I worry he'll inherit his father's restlessness. Paolo's been in and out of jail more times than I can remember.

DAWN
It's hard to imagine how such an innocent young boy would ever grow into a criminal.

MARY
You love children. I can see that.

DAWN
I know.

MARY
Come here. Do you hear what I hear?

DAWN
I can't hear anything.

MARY
Yes, you can hear the clock, can't you? I don't want
time to run like sand through your precious fingers,
Dawn. I don't want you to run after this career of
yours and leave it too late to have children of your
own. A woman is not whole without a child.

There was a long silence before Monty said, 'And cut.
Annie, m'dear, is something wrong?'
Annie knocked at the side of her head with the ball of
her palm, to show she was just being dozy. In truth, she
had forgotten her cue because she'd been listening to Mary
as if Mary had been speaking to her, as Annie. Sometimes
that happened. Sometimes she'd even found herself giving
her own answers instead of those in the script.
What Mary Sheridan had said struck a chord in Annie.
Now that she had left Jerry, she feared it would be years
before she could take the plunge again with another, and
then how long would it take to decide if her lover was a
suitable father? Although she'd always wanted a career
as an actress, and although she intended to pursue one
however many children she might have, still Mary's words
cut deep.
'OK, Annie?' asked Monty.
Annie nodded.
'So take it from the last line.'

MARY
A woman is not whole without a child.

DAWN
Listen to you! I've only been around a month and
already you're nagging me!

MARY

I am your mother.

DAWN

So you should trust that I'm doing what's best. Besides, I have a child.

MARY
(SHOCKED)

You do?

DAWN

Yes, Mary. In a funny sort of way I think of America as my child. I think of the innocent, blue-eyed thing it once was and the monster it has become. I want to embrace it and say I know you have done wrong but I still love you. Because you are a part of me. We need to do what we can to rediscover the innocence we've lost.

MARY

You're a special lady, Dawn Hope.

DAWN

Oh, I'm not special. What's special about dreaming of schools where the students aren't afraid of guns, or wishing you could give your child a new bicycle without being scared he'll be mugged for it? What's special about trying to protect the little children from the horrors of the adult world? That's all I'm doing, Mom. I'm trying to put this country back on its feet.

TIMMY
(RUNNING BACK IN)

Auntie Dawn, do you want to come and see my rabbit?

DAWN

Of course. I'd love to. Are you all right here, Mary?
It's not too painful?

MARY

Oh, no. You two run along.

TIMMY AND DAWN EXIT. CLOSE-UP ON
AWFUL PAIN ON MARY'S FACE AS SHE
CLUTCHES AT HER OPERATION SCAR.

'Great,' said Ellen. 'Let's go straight to tape.'

They soon finished, and Annie changed and left as fast
as she could. Outside the studio were a few autograph
hunters. Over the past two weeks, most had come to wait
for Dawn. One, a tall, nervous woman in her thirties with
gangly arms and jumpy eyes, had been waiting every day
for a week, leaning against the wall of the building. She still
hadn't stepped forward to ask for an autograph. Tonight,
Annie smiled at her, but the woman turned her head away.
Annie shrugged her shoulders and twisted back to sign a
couple of publicity shots distributed by her fan club.

'Can I ask you something personal,' a middle-aged
woman asked. 'Are you going to start seeing Dale Irving?
Is there an attraction there?'

As usual, the question was about Dawn's personal life,
not Annie's. 'It's not for me to decide, I'm afraid,' she
said. 'You'll have to wait and see.'

Annie held her hand up at a cab, which stopped. She
had a hand on the door when one of the waiting fans thrust
an envelope towards her. It was addressed to Senator
Dawn Hope.

'Thanks,' said Annie, ducking in.

As the cab pulled away, Annie saw the strange, gangly
woman step from the wall and hail a cab herself, but
she thought nothing more of it as she ripped open the

envelope. To her amazement, clipped to a simple note reading *This is to help you with the election campaign. I love and respect you, Nancy Morray*, was two hundred dollars in cash.

Annie held it up as if to see if it was real.

'Hmm,' she hummed with amusement. 'What a joke!'

She turned around, thinking she might see the fan even though the car had travelled two blocks. But there was only another yellow cab behind them, carrying a lone female passenger, just like herself.

15

Weeks passed and Manhattan lurched through a draining, sidewalk-softening summer. All but the city's poorest and richest settled on a uniform of T-shirts and shades and did what they could to escape from the heat. Air-conditioners struggled and cried, dripping stains on building faces from Harlem to the Battery. Ben and Jerry boomed but condom sales drooped as couples skipped copulation and lay, itchy and restless, on dampening backs with only their fingers touching at the tips.

As the months raged, much of America distracted itself with the gossip and scandal of two families – the Grants of Pennsylvania Avenue, Washington DC, and the Sheridans of Hill Way, near Chicago. And it was upon the starring women of these families, Jack Grant's wife, Susan, and Mary Sheridan's daughter, Dawn, that the keenest focus landed.

In Washington, the unremitting summer rays hitting Susan Grant were much less welcome than those in which Dawn was basking. In fact, they seemed to scorch the entire Administration's skin, making it red and sore as complaints about personnel, accusations over the Cochabamba scandal and failures on the Hill sapped the spirit from staff for whom two years now felt too long. Since Alex had left, Jack Grant seemed to have lost faith even in himself, and what had once been a fiery, hopeful team appeared defeated and sad, resigned to watching the evaporation and collapse of its legislative agenda.

As the pendulum swung against him, so Grant's press team did nothing to deflect the blame being levelled at his unelected adviser, the First Lady. During the campaign for the presidency she had been sold as a crucial part of a winning partnership, a Bobby Kennedy to Jack's Jack, but since the Administration's policies had begun to splutter, her role was increasingly called into question. Now, with the unexpected defeat in Congress of an Education Bill into which she had invested her time and, more importantly, her heart, the hard-line Washington men recently employed by Grant decided it was time for Susan to take a back seat. FLOTUS, it was decided, had become an awkward embarrassment.

By contrast, with *Unto the Skies* holding the number one position for almost four months, Dawn Hope had become the most popular character on daytime television, and so Annie's face was appearing on magazines from coast to coast. Suddenly, as a TV personality in a nation where TV was the community, she meant something to millions of strangers, and became someone who was discussed, criticised and loved. Throughout the land people began to claim an affinity with the actress, whether from schooldays or more recently, having been in the same restaurant, or shop, or street.

As Annie spent most of her days acting into the black hollow of a TV camera lens, she hardly noticed this extraordinary fame creeping up on her. Interviews in magazines and papers would come out without her knowledge, silently adding another few hundred thousand names to the list of people who were aware of who she was. She hadn't travelled out of New York for months, so had not experienced the thrill of being recognised on almost any street in any town in the country. It was only when she started to see her face on the covers of magazines and in the pages of newspapers that it struck her that she had become truly famous throughout the States.

She enjoyed it at first. It made her feel more complete. She liked being recognised and complimented. She liked walking into a room full of strangers informed of her accomplishments. She liked believing that young actresses were using her as a role model as once she'd admired others. And although her daily routine – up at six, in the studio by seven, out twelve hours later to eat Chinese while learning her lines – had not changed, her weekends and days off began to be filled with appearances and events organised by her new publicity manager, Tamara Row. Effervescent and persuasive, Tamara had established Annie over the summer months as a 'must-have' at many of New York's celebrity gatherings. This exposure lent so much momentum to Annie's fame that many observers were not aware of the reasons for it beyond the fame itself.

During the season Tamara placed Annie on cable TV shows, network shows, talk radio shows, at live fashion shows and first nights on Broadway. In June and July, when it was all exciting and new, when Annie was dazzled by the money she was earning, the clothes she could afford and the company she was keeping, she could not understand why the famous spent so much time complaining about their fate. Although she had expected a different route to such stardom, her dream was at last coming true. How could she not be happy? Those things that had once been out of reach were now in her hands – large figures in her bank statements, champagne dinners, opened doors and endless smiles.

But it was not until one afternoon in early September that Annie realised quite how famous she had become. Hurriedly summoned from the set of *Unto the Skies*, she joined a few of the other actors and crew in the production booth to watch the top story on UBC's *Early Evening News*.

In a box at the top of the screen was a split image

showing the First Lady beside Annie in her role as Dawn Hope. The austere, wrinkled newscaster, Daniel Cramer, was speaking. 'First Lady Susan Grant found herself at the centre of yet another embarrassing storm today after an appearance at a high school in Birmingham, Alabama. Clara Schnachfeldt is there, and has this story.'

Clara was standing in an empty school auditorium. Behind her was a circle of chairs.

'Only three days into her national "Eyes and Ears" tour, described by the White House as an informal information-gathering exercise, the First Lady has run into trouble over replies she gave to students of this Birmingham high school.'

The picture changed to one of Susan wearing a pale green sweater, a string of pearls and a new, more natural hairstyle. She was waving as she stepped out of her heli-copter. The grain and shake of the school's home-video image added immeasurably to the urgency of the story.

'Seeming noticeably more relaxed and open in her manner than she has been of late, Mrs Grant began by saying she'd come to listen, not to talk. In retrospect, perhaps she wishes she'd done just that.'

Now, with the school's video obviously settled on a tripod towards the rear of the hall, the news viewers saw Susan Grant sitting in the middle of a circle of students earlier that day.

'The First Lady began by answering questions on sub-jects as diverse as family planning and home cooking. She even made a joke about her husband's addiction to junk food, all the time steering well clear of politi-cally sensitive issues. But it was when fourteen-year-old Chantelle Francis asked what she should do to make the world a better place that Mrs Grant talked herself into shark-infested waters.'

Now it was Susan's voice that was heard, concluding her answer to the child. 'What I believe, Chantelle, is that if all of us treated America as our own home, and strangers as if they were members of our family, then the land would be cleaner and safer and more pleasant. We owe it to each other and to our founding fathers not to betray the sacrifices they made. We need to understand that it's just not good enough to pay our taxes and leave government to take care of the rest. We should remember that duty is a two-way street. We have to help others to help ourselves.'

Clara returned to the screen. 'On the face of it,' she said, 'Mrs Grant's words seem like the sensible response of a conscientious First Lady. But among this morning's audience was a local newspaper reporter, Kathy Pewlis.'

Kathy, a chirpy young thing in her early twenties, was shown sitting at her desk at the *Birmingham Recorder*. She spoke, saying, 'I knew I'd heard those words before. It was then I made the connection with Dawn Hope.'

Annie felt her heart jumping. She was the top story on the nightly news! A few of the actors turned to share their surprise before returning to the report.

'Dawn Hope,' Clara explained, 'is the core character of UBC's *Unto the Skies*. Played by actress Annie Marin, Dawn is a Senator whose popularity must be envied by those politicians in the Democratic Party soon to be contesting the Congressional midterm elections.'

Kathy again: 'I could hardly believe my ears when I played back an old tape of the show. Mrs Grant's words were almost identical.'

As she spoke, a segment from the soap began to play. A little cheer went up in the production booth.

The clip showed Dawn, off on one of her lectures, saying, 'Wouldn't it be great, Vanessa, if we could all treat America as well as we treat our own homes? I think the land would become safer and cleaner and happier for us all. Our founding fathers made sacrifices that we have to remember. We have a duty to help others, and all of us have to work at putting something back.'

Clara returned, the muted soap playing on a screen behind her. 'Had Mrs Grant been reciting from a prepared speech the blame could have been shifted to a lowly speechwriter. Instead, she was speaking without notes and has revealed herself to be one of the fans of this popular soap opera character. Nerves will surely be raw in the First Lady's office. This incident is certain to cast doubts on Susan Grant's credibility as an original thinker. And while it is hardly uncommon for politicians to read from scripts, it is perhaps a portent for the future that in this case, the beleaguered First Lady of the United States was reciting from the script of the nation's most popular daytime star. This is Clara Schnachfeldt, reporting for the *Early Evening News* from Birmingham, Alabama.'

While word of the First Lady's apparent plagiarism was producing an atmosphere of near-euphoric excitement in the studios, elsewhere it was causing great distress. In his apartment, Alex had been warned of the story by Rebecca Frear. Now he was waiting for her call, wondering whether his cover would be blown. He picked up on the first ring.

'Jesus, Becca,' he said. 'That was terrible.'

There was a brief silence, and then the First Lady spoke. Her anger was evident. 'You have completely and totally humiliated me,' she said. 'Didn't I warn you that something like this could happen? I cannot believe how far you took this.'

'I took it as far as we'd planned . . .' he stuttered.

'No!' she shouted. 'As far as *you'd* planned. You, Al. This was always your idea.'

As ever, Alex fought the hardest when trapped in a corner. 'My idea was to get people more used to the notion of a dynamic female politician. That's worked.'

'There are over fifty dynamic female politicians in Congress, Alex. Or haven't you noticed?'

'What I meant was a woman with dynamic ideas. How was I to know that you were going to steal her words? That's the reason we've got a problem here, Susan. You should not have been repeating Dawn's lines.'

'They're not her lines!' yelled the First Lady. 'They're my lines! You were the one who stole them and put them on TV. Why didn't you warn me that you'd done that? Did you *want* me to look like a complete fool?'

Alex hesitated. He had genuinely not heard the First Lady use that speech before. He'd assumed the mistake was hers. 'Where did you say them?' he asked, more softly.

'I told Rebecca. Your Miss Marvel.'

Alex sighed and snapped in half a pencil with which he'd been toying. 'So it's her fault.'

'Oh, how unlike you to blame someone else!' she said, real venom spiking her tone.

'I meant that Rebecca has been writing some of Dawn's lines recently and she must have borrowed your quotes. She should have warned us. I'm in trouble too, don't forget.'

'Don't give me that, Alex. They're calling you some kind of fucking hero for creating a character so true to life. I'm the one who's being laughed at.'

'What I meant is, I'm in trouble because I'm on your side. I don't want to see my future candidate get in trouble like this.'

'It's good to know I've got friends like you. Now I see how Jack felt having you work for him.'

'So go ahead, Susan, fire me too.'

There was a silence before she said, more calmly, 'I don't want that. All I'm asking you to do is get me out of this hole. Go public with the fact that you used my lines for Dawn Hope's speech.'

'I can't yet afford to do that. For one thing, I promised Barry Shermer that I wouldn't be using *Unto the Skies* as a platform for political ideas and secondly, you've already told me that you never said any of this in public. If I say that I've been quoting from your private notes, there are going to be a lot of questions asked. Everyone will see the link between us.'

'The alternative isn't very pretty, Al. The alternative is me being totally discredited and humiliated.'

'It'll blow over.'

'You mean like Cochabamba? Of course it won't. Can you imagine any of those upstart little journalists letting this one die? Finally Lady Macbeth has got her comeuppance. They already think it's a big joke that I didn't say the lines as well as that actress did. Imagine that, Alex! Alex?'

Alex did not reply because, for once, he didn't know what to say. He was as surprised as everyone else by the success of Dawn Hope. The impossible seemed to be happening, that from his mind had come the perfect politician, and it was to her, to Dawn, that Susan and the rest were now being compared. As far as he could see, the only way out was to kill Dawn off as soon as possible in time for the public to forget her before Susan's campaign began. And yet he couldn't conceive of the network sanctioning that, nor did he want to throw away this brilliant means of gauging public opinion. In short, he feared he'd dived from the high board without checking for water in the pool.

'Alex?' Susan said. 'Are you still there?'

'Let me think about it,' he said.

'Meanwhile I get screwed by the world's press.'

'So lie low,' he advised. 'Refuse to talk to them.'

'Which you always said was a sure sign of guilt.'

'Listen, I promise that I'll think as quickly as I can, and I'll reach you through Rebecca. The last thing we want is for anyone to know we're talking. OK?'

'Yes, OK! But it's not OK, Al. It's a very, very, very long way from being OK.'

You don't have to tell me, Alex thought to himself as he hung up the phone. You don't have to tell me that.

As far as Faith was concerned, this whole First Lady farrago was the final straw. Annie Marin was now not only getting the most scenes, the most airtime, the most everything, she was becoming a feminist icon as well, as if Annie herself had something to do with Dawn's popularity. Faith couldn't believe it. She'd even read this poll in the *Herald* saying that Dawn was rivalling Cindy Crawford as a role model. And that coming right after Annie was voted soap's favourite actress in the most recent issue of *Daytime*. How can this be happening, worried Faith, when she's got none of my curves, not a drop of my feminine maturity? Were the fans so easily duped into liking Annie just because it was big news that Alex Lubotsky and that lesbian bitch Zoë Dunlop were working on a soap opera? It just didn't make sense. Couldn't the whole world see that Faith was by far the sexier of the two?

Clearly, something had to be done; only what? Faith had tried, God how she'd tried, to get into Alex's bed, but he wasn't the pushover his brother had been. And she'd fucked Bob Fein a couple of times, but that hadn't got her very far. So what was there left to do? Sure it was nice to be on the number one daytime show, with *Unto the Skies* pushing a record 11.9 in the ratings chart, but all the fun had been taken away by someone else stealing the limelight. Faith Valentine had not sweated under the bright studio glare for fifteen years to be pushed aside by a woman with revenge on her mind. Revenge! It was so childish of Annie. I'll have to get my own back, Faith decided, and get her off the show.

Her husband Ned interrupted her thoughts.

'Feeling good?' he asked.

Sometimes Faith wondered whether her husband guessed that she used the time of their lovemaking to unscramble pressing concerns.

'Oh yes, Daddy,' she said, though her mind had been a million miles away from Ned's monotonous, breathy exertions.

Ned was a sex fiend, which was a shame, because sex with him reminded her of being forced when a child to eat too large a plate of food. Halfway through and the end seemed a terrifying distance away. And just as her large servings had been given out of generosity, so Ned assumed that his ability to pump away for hours (or what seemed like hours) was a blessing to his wife. Instead, she was always looking for a way out, an equivalent to sneaking a handful of food under the table to the dog.

'Oh, yes, Daddy,' she moaned. 'Oh, God, yes.'

She knew this flawless old trick would always do it, so she began to scream in a crescendo of satisfaction while gyrating her hips and digging her fingers into his back. 'Oh, God, yes,' she screamed through gritted teeth. 'Yes! You're so great, Neddy. You're making me come. Now, now . . .'

With a final squeal and a juddering of her body, Faith faked with all her might. As she did so she felt the flattered twitch and swell of her husband's prick and knew that it was over.

'That,' said Ned, flopping on his back, 'was sensational. Inspirational. Fantastical. In fact,' he added, breathing so heavily she thought for a second he might croak and leave her all those lovely royalties, 'you, my sweet, have inspired a song in me. That's good, isn't it?'

'Mm,' she said, sitting up. 'What?'

'You've inspired a song.'

'Oh, good.'

She trudged to the bathroom, thinking that if anyone

needed inspiration it was she. She needed a way to get shot of Annie Marin once and for all.

'Did you see this article about Alex in *The Times*?' asked Annie's publicity agent as the two of them sat in the back of the limousine taking them to Costelloe's, the legendary bookstore on Fifth.

Annie yawned and shook her head. Really, this constant loop of performance was getting too tiring. Last night had been horrendous, she acting as the celebrity judge at a Madison Square Garden cat show. She had returned home at midnight to learn some lines and had fallen asleep with the script in her hand and the sound of preened cats meowing in her ears.

'Alex made a statement about the Birmingham high school incident,' said Tamara as she read. 'He's claiming that it wasn't the First Lady who used Dawn Hope's lines, but that Dawn used hers.'

'What?' asked an amazed Annie.

'Apparently he and Susan Grant discussed this whole issue of citizen's duties before he left the White House. He says he must have "inadvertently borrowed some of the First Lady's perceptive concepts", and that he offers his "fullest apologies for any embarrassment caused".'

Annie laughed. 'She probably threatened to chew his balls off. I hear she's a complete bitch.'

'Successful women always are,' said Tamara with a mocking glance at Annie. 'Aren't you?'

Annie didn't reply. Her success had come so fast and with so little effort on her part, that she felt it didn't really belong to her. In a strange way, it belonged to Dawn instead. When she was playing Dawn she felt more confident and proud herself. She wasn't sure how much she liked the sensation. When she was at Cornell Williams she had firmly rejected the method of worming so deeply into a character that one became, to all intents, that person.

Having always found it easy to step away from her roles, it was alarming that the boundaries between her character and herself were becoming so hazy.

This confusion was hardly surprising. Today, Annie was being driven to a promotional appearance for a book of Dawn Hope's speeches from *Unto the Skies*. Annie had written not one word of *Selected Speeches* and yet it was she whose face appeared on the cover, it was she who signed the books (and collected some of the royalties) and it was she who was being celebrated and damned for the words inside. It made her feel something of a cheat. Only recently she'd had a dream in which she'd been accused by the real Dawn Hope of impersonation. On waking the next day, Annie had found the notion hard to shake off.

'Hey look,' Tamara said, turning the paper towards Annie. 'There's you!'

There was a photograph of Annie, as Dawn, on the books page above a review of *Selected Speeches*.

'What does it say?'

Tamara folded out the article. 'No doubt,' she began, speaking as quickly as always, 'to the dismay of John Grisham, Stephen King, Gary Time and those other writers accustomed to setting up camp on the top of the bestseller lists, the *Selected Speeches* of Dawn Hope has shot to number one within a week of its publication. There is much debate as to whether the book, penned by former White House Communications Director Alex Lubotsky, should have been classified as fiction at all. Had the same motley collection . . .'

'Motley!' complained Annie, who didn't really care. 'How dare he?'

Tamara carried on. 'Had the same motley collection of essays been published under Mr Lubotsky's own name, *Selected Speeches* would have been labelled as non-fiction. However, Lubotsky claims that Dawn Hope is a fictional character and that her opinions should be judged in the context of her position as a Senator on the number one-rated daytime soap opera *Unto the Skies*.

'That Mr Lubotsky, once a man admired for his political astuteness, should have wished to distance himself from the populist banalities contained in *Selected Speeches* comes as no surprise. His character has a particular predilection . . .'

'Predilection?' said Annie. 'What an asshole!'

'For constructing speeches around such glib notions as *It's time to look out of the window, Let's make some sacrifices, Whose country is this, people?, Don't be scared of tomorrow* and *Let's get back to where we came from*.

'UBC's decision to publish comes as little surprise given the immense following that the character enjoys. What is more intriguing is why these political sentiments should have caught the nation's imagination. Laura Larsfeldt, author of *Pork, Media and Politics for the New Millennium . . .*'

'They made her up,' said Annie, 'they must have done.'

'They didn't. I saw her on Charlie Rose. Anyway, she thinks that Dawn Hope's simplistic appeals are more sophisticated than those populist platitudes espoused by previous fictional politicians, such as Chauncey Gardner or Jimmy Stewart's Mr Smith. "Instead of focusing on the calumny and corruption of Washington politics," says Larsfeldt, "Dawn Hope's vision is both upbeat and enthusiastic." Larsfeldt believes there is a strong link between the unease people are feeling with the approach of a new millennium and their desire to embrace a more spiritual, humanist kind of politics.

'Though a dip into the soapy latherings of *Selected Speeches* is designed to leave one feeling clean and fresh, it's more like swimming in a dirty pond. In speeches given such titles as "Time to talk about our kids", "Taking Care of God's Garden (the litter problem)", and "Crime:

"Tough Love, Tender Care", we are bombarded with statistics about the nation's malaise. But Dawn Hope offers no solutions. Her appeals for a rediscovered morality may strike a chord in the ears of many, especially those on the political right, but while it remains impossible to legislate morality, so her answers remain redundant. It is naïve to suggest that neighbourly love and community spirit will bring a halt to the spiral of violent crime and social breakdown. And her constant references to a golden past and to the founding fathers are surely insulting to those more recent immigrants with a history and cultural identity of their own.

'Dawn Hope may be a fictional character, but it seems to be Mr Lubotsky's intention to fashion a society in her image. Might it not have been better to have understood that the vanity, implicit racism and vacuousness contained in the daytime dramas and their female stars are the very same characteristics that are damaging to present society? Isn't it time for Dawn Hope, and the rest of us, to start looking into a different kind of mirror?'

'God!' said Annie, 'why do they take it so seriously?'

'Why?' Tamara said. 'That's why!'

She pointed through the window to a line of people queuing along 45th Street up to the junction with Fifth Avenue. Annie slid to the edge of the seat. She rubbed at the window and peered out through the limousine's blackened windows. 'You don't think . . .'

'Yes, I do.'

'Oh my God,' whispered Annie, more scared than excited. 'There are hundreds.'

Annie was aware that in the few days since the book had come out, her fan club (based in New Jersey, the company handled the clubs and newsletters of a number of soap superstars) had been deluged with admiring letters and, as ever, campaign donations. But this was like something out of a dream, or a nightmare. She saw the police had

been forced to erect barriers and there was more than one
TV van parked by the corner.

'This is like being a rock star,' said Annie as the limo
crawled to a stop. She could see the excited, expectant
faces of the fans as they waited. Why me? she wondered.
What have I done but speak the lines written for Dawn?
What if I disappoint them?

Seeing the fear on Annie's face, Tamara took her hand
and said, 'Imagine that none of this is real. Imagine they're
all extras and you're filming a movie. You're Dawn Hope,
you're used to this and they love you, whatever you do.
All right?'

'No,' said Annie.

She was beginning to feel sick, but suddenly the passenger door was opened and there was no turning back.
Annie took a very deep breath and then, as if stepping
out on stage, she began her performance, toe first out of
the limousine.

There was a cheer from the crowd as, dressed in a
bright red suit with gold buttons down the front that she
would never have chosen to wear if the choice had been
hers, Annie stepped into the late September sunshine
and waved. The cameras began to flash and there was
a spontaneous round of applause.

Keep smiling, Annie was telling herself. Be brave! Be
Dawn! They're all on your side!

A few of the fans behind the velvet rope barrier pushed
forward and held out their arms, hoping to touch her.

'Thank you for coming,' she said to them. 'It's good to
see you all.'

She was led inside by the store manager and followed
by a TV crew that had its lights facing a heavy wooden
table in the centre of the tiled floor. A grand winged chair
awaited Annie's backside. Behind it was a semicircle of
shelves filled with copies of *Selected Speeches*, the cover
of which showed Dawn smiling with confidence. Annie had

feared from the start that it looked like an advertisement for dentures.

As she made her way to the table a curious stillness fell on the room, as if they were all in the presence of royalty. Annie made herself comfortable in the chair, with Tamara standing to her left and the manager to her right, holding a copy of the book open for Annie to sign.

'We haven't seen anything like this since Howard Stern,' he told her. 'You must be happy.'

'I'm very pleased,' said Annie. 'Obviously we've struck a nerve.'

'We've reordered another five thousand.'

Five, fifty, five hundred thousand? These numbers meant nothing to Annie any more. She kept being presented with statistics that proved her popularity, and each one seemed more surreal than the last. Four mailbags of letters per day, nine thousand dollars in Hope campaign funds, 230,000 new members of her fan club, a half-million copies of *Selected Speeches* printed. A part of her wouldn't have been surprised to learn of a movement supporting her canonisation.

Now the deputy manager returned with a pen, and the first fan, who'd been waiting almost four hours, jogged forward from the rope, clutching a copy to her breast.

'Hello,' Annie said with her best smile.

The woman, who was fat, was wearing a shiny purple running suit and a frizzy perm as glamorous as a broccoli floret neglected in the fridge. 'I'm so excited meeting you at last,' she said. 'We're here on holiday, from Nebraska. Twelve of us. We're all here.'

'How nice. Who shall I sign it for?'

'Dawn!' the woman said with considerable pride.

'Really? There's a coincidence.'

'I know. I'm so proud.'

Annie wrote, *For Dawn, Best Wishes! Dawn*, which was

all she could think of, but it seemed to bring an inordinate amount of pleasure to the woman, who left, after a further outpouring of gratitude, fingering the inscription like a child writing in air.

Next came the gangly fan Annie had often seen waiting outside the studio, but who had never before dared step forward.

'Hello again,' Annie said. 'I've seen you before! What name shall I write?'

'To my number one fan,' the woman said.

'That sounds like . . .'

'*Misery*,' the woman interrupted. 'I know.'

Remembering the movie, Annie hesitated, but then wrote the words, thanked the woman and welcomed the next in line.

More than three hours later, the last of the patient customers approached the desk and Annie wearily signed Dawn's name across the page. Behind her, Tamara was on her mobile. She hung up as Annie stood, stretching the fingers in her right hand.

'Thank God I didn't have to write the book too,' she whispered to her manager.

'Don't complain, darling. You're getting rich and famous. You know who that was on the line?'

'God?' Annie guessed.

'No. Better. Carl Conrad.'

'So?'

Tamara smiled but, realising they still had an audience, she said, 'Why don't we get in the car and I'll tell you all about it then?'

The following day, Annie arrived at *Unto the Skies* feeling on top of the world. She was still intoxicated by Tamara's heady news the day before. She had called Barbara in Pittsburgh the minute she'd got home, and now she was looking forward to telling her colleagues on the show.

It was, then, with particular glee that she noticed Faith in a darkened corner of Studio B, running through her morning routine. The practice involved exercise of the voice, body and mind, those very things upon which almost no demands were made of the soap opera actress. Annie crept over and, leaning low to the chair, loudly chirped, 'Hi Faith!' into her co-star's ear.

Faith jumped in shock and opened her eyes. 'Dawn!'

'My name's Annie.'

Briskly slapping her fingers against her cheeks, Faith replied, 'Your name's mud as far as I'm concerned. For disturbing me!'

Sitting upright in the chair, Faith wrapped one hand around her chin, and with the other on the back of her head, she twisted her head sharply to the side. There was a click.

'Ow!' said Annie.

'Do you mind?' Faith said, looking indignant.

'Not really.'

'I mean do you mind clearing a space? I'm relaxing.'

'Oh, is that what it is? Can I suggest something, you know, just off the top of my head?'

'If you must.'

'Marshmallows! Take a pack, a long, comfortable couch, and a great movie – especially one with Andy Garcia or Tom Sterling – and you'll get all the relaxation you want.'

'I was professionally trained,' Faith haughtily replied, 'to do this.'

Annie folded her arms and shook her head as if she was both amazed and impressed. 'I know, I was there. What I can't believe is that you're still doing it.'

'Can't you? Perhaps that's a signal of your underdevel-opmentation as a mature actress. You can't stop training just because you found a job.'

'No, you're right. I'll bounce over there and imagine

I'm a jealous kangaroo lost in the Antarctic, shall I? That should tune up a few emotions.'

Faith rolled her eyeballs like a twelve-year-old girl. 'Are you standing there just to torment me?' she griped.

'No, not at all. I came to ask if you had any messages for Tom,' said Annie matter-of-factly. 'Tom Sterling.'

'Is he here?' Faith squealed, desperately peeking around Annie.

Tom Sterling was arguably America's most famous movie star, and certainly one of its most bankable. Annie had been in love with him for years.

'No. Tom won't be in town until next week,' she said as if she alone knew this.

'You know him?' Faith asked with mounting suspicion.

'Not really, but we're both going on Paddy Darwin together. It should be a lot of fun.'

'You? On Paddy Darwin? You can't be!'

'I can, actually. Next Wednesday, so remember to set the video.'

This was Tamara's great news. Carl Conrad, Darwin's producer, had invited Annie onto the chat show to discuss *Selected Speeches*, as well as her 'run-in' (his words) with the First Lady. As far as Annie was concerned, every publicity item she'd done was small fry compared with an appearance on the Paddy Darwin show. So what if he was an arrogant chauvinist? He was the host of the most popular late-night talk show in the country. Watched by millions, he was accustomed to playing host to the world's superstars. When things had been tough in San Francisco, Annie had enjoyed absurd dreams of charming Paddy and the nation with her good humour and wit. Now she was being given a chance and, more than that, she was to be appearing with the sexiest, most fantastic actor in the world. In fact, as she'd lain in bed the night before, she decided that, given the choice of all the men in the world, she would choose Tom Sterling as her fellow guest.

'You shouldn't look so worried,' she said now, patting Faith's shoulder. 'I know it'll clash with a taping but I've been to see Vince and he's said not to worry, he'll shift things around. So I won't be screwing anything up.'

'Isn't it a little late for that?' said Faith, stretching her arms in front of her.

'Ow! Am I trespassing on your territory? I'd better not keep you, then. Don't forget to exercise the lungs,' said Annie, clumping her fist against her chest. 'Yaa-ga-ga-ga-ga-gaa. Like that, remember?'

Faith stared at Annie as if she wanted to pull her eyeballs out with hairpins. Annie smiled in return. 'You know,' she added, 'you could always leave and become an extra in Shakespeare in the Park.'

Then she spun around and pranced off, wondering what had come over her, but amazed at how cathartic such bitchery was.

This was too much for Faith, so taking the stairs down a flight, she knocked on Vince's office door.

'Is there a problem?' he asked once she was inside. 'Because I'm snowed under today.'

'Um, no, there isn't, Vince. Not at all. But I haven't seen you recently, and I wanted to say that I'm proud of what you've done to *Unto the Skies*. I haven't had a chance to say that before.'

Vince lit a cigarette and sat on the edge of the couch. 'What the fuck's this about?' He coughed the smoke out. 'More money?'

Faith looked convincingly offended. She turned to leave, and when she looked back at him, her eyes seemed to be promising a flood of tears as their forthcoming attraction. 'I have never . . .' she stopped, swallowing a sob before a snippet of one of Vanessa's speeches presented itself to her. 'I mean, what is wrong with the world these days? I was being kind. I know we've had our differences, I know that, but they were only to be expected with the pressures this job brings. But now I want to put them behind us. I've come to realise that you have been good to me, and I haven't shown you the respect you've deserved.'

Jesus, Vince thought to himself, is the bitch being serious? He decided to give her the benefit of the doubt.

Faith was coming to her climax. 'And I don't think the hard work you put in is appreciated enough. That's why I came here. To show you that someone understands and admires you and the things you've achieved.'

Vince was so surprised that he stubbed out his cigarette instead of smoking it until the filter burned, as he usually did. 'Faith, I'm glad someone's noticed because . . .'

'Because it's all Alex Lubotsky, isn't it?' she declared, stepping back into the room and leaning a little.

'Now you're talking my language,' Vince enthused.

'I imagine I am. Alex this, Annie that. It's all them, them, them. Only today I heard her – I shouldn't say.'

Vince stood. 'This is a family, Faith, and as an Italian man and the head of the family, I need to know everything or else mistakes will be made.'

Faith wiped at the tears that she hadn't quite managed to squeeze out. 'I don't think I should.'

'Believe me, you should. For the sake of *Unto the Skies*, and for the sake of our continued friendship.'

'Very well. Annie said that she and Alex saved this show from the gutter where you'd put it.'

'Did she now?'

'Yes. And she said that she and Alex were going to persuade Mr Shermer to give them a show of their own like *I Love Lucy*, only with Dawn instead of Lucy. And she said other things. Things like that.'

'I'm glad you told me.'

Faith walked to the producer's side to touch his arm. 'You won't tell her what I said, will you? I value my friendship with Annie, and I don't want Alex writing me out of the action.'

'Of course not. Besides, you've got the producer on your side, haven't you?'

'You won't do anything, will you?' asked Faith hopefully.

'I'll do nothing that doesn't have to be done,' he said, and then he kissed her on both cheeks as if suddenly transformed into Don Corleone himself.

16

'**B**ra, I gotta go. He's going to be here any minute,' said Annie, glancing at her watch.

'Sweetie, will you calm down? God! Anyone would have thought you were going on a date with the President.'

'I am, practically. Except Grant would be easier.' Annie took the phone to the window and looked onto the street. Alex wasn't there, but she did see a strange-looking woman loitering in a doorway on the other side of the street. The block was an unlikely haunt for a streetwalker.

'You're creating problems where there aren't any!' Barbara complained. 'Alex called you, didn't he?'

'Mm,' Annie replied distractedly.

'And then he asked you out to dinner. Yes or no?'

'Yes, yes he did.'

'And now he's coming to your apartment for a drink?'

'So?' Annie asked.

She was getting impatient with Bra now. Alex could arrive any moment and she had to check her hair in the mirror again.

'So these are the moves a man makes when he needs to get laid. Believe me, I've been there. Not for a long time, but I was there.'

'Please don't make me sink to your level, Bra.'

'Annie, if you want a man then you have to imagine the lowest, filthiest level you can, and sink below it. It's where they're happy.'

'I'm going to hang up before you talk me into answering the door in a lacy G-string.'

'There you go!' Bra said with her throaty laugh. 'Make the kill straight out.'

'Bye, Bra. I'll . . .'

'Hey, Annie! Remember. Never be scared of asking them in for a coffee. The worst they can do is say no.'

'OK, Bra. I'll call you!'

Annie had rung Barbara to calm herself down, but it hadn't worked. She felt as nervous and excited as she had all day, since Alex rang the studio to ask her out. She had been so disappointed by his apparent indifference over the past few months that she'd as good as given up hope. Now it seemed as if she might have been too impatient.

She decided to go to the bathroom to splash cold water on her red cheeks. She'd not only been feeling nervous all day, she'd been feeling horny. It was as if her body was preparing itself for a man, trying to display its fertile willingness. Or else, she thought, it was rebelling against months of hollow starvation: six now, since the last time; since Jerry. She almost couldn't bear to think how she'd behave if she and Alex ended up in bed. She'd be like a jellyfish on heat. But it would be fantastic, she thought, as she stood before the bathroom mirror. It really would.

She lowered her hand and slipped it under the elastic of her knickers to touch herself. She shivered at the lively, raw welcome given her fingers. What would his tongue feel like here? His tongue and his fingers and his co—

'Oh, my God!' she said, hearing the buzzer sound.

Outside, Alex was thinking how much he was looking forward to dinner. He had not seen enough of Annie since she had arrived in New York. And now? Well, now it was too late. The incident in Birmingham had changed everything.

It had not taken him long after his discussion with the First Lady to realise that he had no option but to accept blame for her apparent plagiarism. For one thing, it was true that his character *had* used the First Lady's lines.

But of greater concern than the truth was the thought of leading Susan through the presidential race with this incident hanging over her head. Already great damage had been done by the many editorials, cartoons and TV jokes, and even the President had suffered, since many commentators had claimed that the scandals, intrigues and adulteries on *Unto the Skies* were as nothing compared with those in the White House itself.

The problem was that Dawn had become too popular for Susan's good. Although Alex felt a great pride in having read the nation's mind, he foresaw the danger in having Susan run for President with her contradictory, liberal ideals. He feared that he had created in Dawn a formidable enemy for the First Lady, because now Susan would be fighting not only the reality of an invigorated Republican Party but the image of a perfect female politician as well. It wouldn't matter to the voters that Dawn was too good to be true. What would concern them was the extent to which Susan Grant's candidacy failed to match up to Dawn's promise.

There was, then, nothing for it but to kill Dawn Hope. His only concern was Annie. He knew she would be hurt by his politics, but he couldn't allow feelings to get in the way of the First Lady's presidential bid.

Now he heard Annie's voice, and she buzzed him in and told him to come up to the third floor where he found her waiting with a smile. He kissed her and stepped inside, saying, 'This is a very nice place.'

It was indeed pleasant, a three-room apartment with hardwood floors, a working fireplace and an attractive cornice, decorative as birthday ribbon on the cream-coloured walls. The furniture was to Annie's taste with a lot of pine, many earthy, warm-coloured rugs and cushions, a large blue glass vase holding an enthusiastic display of dried flowers and a Mexican-patterned sofa bed that had never been used. Mexico made it to the walls too, with four large Diego Rivera prints. The windows were original and extended down to the floor, indulging the room with light.

'I've just opened a bottle of white wine. Would you like some? It's not bad,' said Annie, meaning that she'd spent twenty-five dollars on it, which was about twenty-one more than usual.

'I'd love some.'

Standing by the unlit fire, Alex thought how much he'd like to live in a place such as this. His apartments were always bare and utilitarian. He'd thought of spending some time and money at University Place, especially as he'd enjoyed the cluttered charm of Pam's Titusville house, but he had stopped himself. Somehow, he didn't think it worth the effort while he was alone. He wondered how many years it would be before he stopped living like a young bachelor. He was forty-three now, some little way into the latter half of his life. He didn't want to reach old age without having owned a comfortable home.

'Here you go,' Annie said, handing Alex the wine.

'Thanks.' He took a sip. 'This is nice.'

'Isn't it!'

'I meant being here. I never seem to take an evening off these days.'

'Join the club,' she said, chinking her glass against his. 'If you weren't here I'd probably be eating Chinese and learning my lines, or else,' she paused for a second as the phone began to ring, but then continued, 'or else I'd be making an idiot of myself at one of Tamara's events.'

The answering machine clicked on, but no voice was heard. They both looked at it.

'How can you screen your calls when you can't hear the message?' asked Alex.

'You obviously don't know me very well. I'm a phonaholic. If I let myself hear who it is then nine times out of ten I'll pick up. This way I can listen to all the messages at once.

282

Usually the phone's turned down too, but I had it on in case you called.'

'So I get special treatment, do I?'

'Only tonight.'

'Sounds interesting,' he said, laughing so that she didn't know whether he was being serious in his flirtation. But then, as if to settle the issue, he said, 'I spoke to Zoë Dunlop today.'

'Did you? I like Zoë a lot,' Annie told him.

'I'm glad, because I invited her to join us for dinner. I hope that's OK.'

Annie called on all her training to keep the dejection from her face. 'Sure,' she said, though it had been the prospect of dinner alone with Alex that had excited her, as if they were a couple already, their legs under the table touching as the wine loosened their minds and limbs.

'I said we'd meet her at this Japanese restaurant close by, if that's all right.'

'Whatever,' Annie said, because already she could see this evening, this man, slipping through her fingers before she had a chance to close them upon him. 'Japanese sounds good.'

And yet by the time they left Annie had regained much of her good humour. Zoë was great company at any time, and she was hardly a challenger for Alex's affections. Besides, Annie couldn't be upset with the world on such a beautiful evening in such a beautiful city and with such a beautiful man. Here and now, as the subtle September breeze sent the leaves gossiping ahead of them along the cracked sidewalk, she felt happier than she had in years. She thought she would like to freeze this moment so that Alex would never leave her side.

They rounded the corner onto Amsterdam Avenue. A woman perusing a stall of second-hand books glanced at them both, looked down and then jerked her head back up again.

'Uh-oh,' said Annie. 'I see trouble!'

'Where?'

'That woman! Look at her. She's got that limpet look – the way she's tucking her chin into her neck.'

'You think?'

'I know,' Annie said, then, wickedly, 'Let's have some fun.'

As they neared, the lady tossed aside the book and took a step towards them, blocking their path. 'Excuse me,' she said, 'but you're Dawn Hope, aren't you?'

Annie smiled broadly. 'Yes. Yes I am.'

At the beginning, when the groups had started to cluster outside the studio doors, Annie had insisted on calling herself by her real name, but soon she had discovered that no one wanted to meet or know Annie Marin. It was Dawn who fascinated, inspired and excited them.

The woman reached out and touched Annie's hand. 'I feel so embarrassed bothering you like this but I just had to come over and say that I love what you're doing and I love the way you say things and I think if there's any justice in the world then you'll make it to Governor.'

'Thank you,' said Annie, looking genuinely pleased. 'It's a tight race, but I'm hoping that common sense will win the day. And that our funds last, of course,' she added with a self-deprecating little laugh.

'So do I.' Fearing that Dawn would leave, the woman quickly said, 'Do you mind if I ask what you were planning on doing about the overfeeding of animals in our national parks? I know how much you like to walk in the countryside and I've been just sitting there hoping for you to say something about the issue.'

Annie replied without hesitation. 'I agree it's a problem. I know that in my own state there are areas of natural beauty where the animals are fed so much that they multiply and die in winter from overpopulation.'

'Oh, yes, exactly and . . .'

Annie held up a hand. 'Also,' she continued, 'these creatures lose their survival and hunting instincts. People are killing wildlife with kindness and I'm certainly going to look at ways to educate and so eradicate all such irresponsible attitudes in, in – God's gardens.'

The woman closed her eyes and then a look of great relief spread across her face. 'Oh, thank you,' she said as she delved into her bag and produced a twenty-dollar bill. 'I knew you'd see it my way.'

She handed the money to Annie, who took it. 'Thank you too. I'll put this to good use.'

'I know that.'

Annie shook the woman's hand and, with Alex, moved on.

When they were half a block away, he turned to her and, almost under his breath, said, 'What was that all about?'

'Dinner funds,' said Annie, laughing as she shook the bill in front of his face.

Alex had lost his sense of humour. 'But you can't do that?'

'Don't panic. I give it to charity in the end.'

'I mean,' he looked nervously behind him, as if they had just robbed the woman, 'you can't go around impersonating political candidates for money!'

'Who am I impersonating? I'm me.'

'Besides,' he complained, 'I've never written anything about animal overpopulation.'

Now Annie stopped walking. 'I do have a brain, thank you. I am able to think for myself.'

'But that's my point! You're not thinking for yourself. You're thinking for Dawn and she can't walk around the Upper West Side. It's not possible.'

'Ah-ha,' said Annie. 'Maybe you've created a monster, Dr Frankenstein. Spooky. I've got a life all of my own. Oh look, there's Zoë.'

The director was at a thickly varnished table by the

window, drinking sake. Inside, Alex and Annie passed a tiny Japanese waterfall to join her.

Alex was still troubled as he sat on the small wooden chair. 'You're not going to believe what just happened to us,' he said to Zoë. 'We were walking down the street when some nut-head came up to Annie and started talking politics with her.'

'And? It happens every time I'm with her,' Zoë told him. 'She's a TV star! It's hardly surprising, darling.'

'It's surprising when she starts discussing state issues that haven't even come up in the script. It was like she was actually trying to win votes!'

'I already had that one,' Annie said earnestly. 'Don't you think?'

Alex shook his head as if he felt he was the only sane man alive in the world. 'But you're not running in any screwing gubernatorial election. You're an actress.'

'Why don't you have some sake, Al,' suggested Zoë, 'and calm down a bit.'

'I just think it's a little odd to get your kicks by duping people, that's all.'

Annie split apart her wooden chopsticks and slashed them against one another to smooth away the splinters.

'Alex,' she said, 'what do you want me to do? Hu? If I say that I'm not Dawn they start to argue with me, and if I say I am, then they want an opinion about something. So where's the harm? I know what Dawn's like by now.'

'All I'm saying,' he said in a conciliatory tone, 'is that it's strange pretending to be someone you're not.'

Annie slapped her hand onto the table in genuine frustration. 'I spend all day pretending to be someone I'm not. You can't expect me just to switch off. You know, this whole thing has happened so fast that, to tell the truth, I find it easier pretending to be Dawn when I'm out. I can imagine *her* being famous. *She* likes it! But Annie isn't used to it yet. You see what I mean? I'm not used to being followed down the street. I'm not used to being invited onto the Paddy Darwin show. It wasn't very long ago that you two first showed up in San Francisco. Remember?'

'I know what it's like being famous, but . . .'

'No, Al, sorry but you don't. When people recognise you they're seeing the guy who got Jack Grant to the White House. The real you. But with me they're not looking at Annie Marin. They're looking at Dawn, and the only way I can keep a grip on things is if I keep it like that. So at least do me the favour of letting me cope with this mess you've got me into in my own way, will you? It's my freedom that's disappeared. You can do what you like with Dawn on the show, but I'd appreciate it if you wouldn't try to pull the strings in real life. Is that a deal?'

Alex said nothing, though he wished he could explain to Annie that real life was precisely what Dawn was all about. He wished he could explain that unless she slowed down she would screw up the real life he'd been trying to direct.

Yet she had a point. Ever since he had first imagined Dawn, he'd seen her as nothing more than a stepping stone to Susan's presidency. He had not given much thought to the character's own popularity, nor to the actress bringing her to life. Annie had forced him to think again. He was surprised by this. Although he'd been physically attracted to her from the moment they'd first met, he had refused to take her very seriously. Aside from the fact that she frequently seemed giggly and nervous around him, he had assumed she was merely another actress, and they were a breed of which he had never been fond. In wanting to be loved so badly, and by so many people, they tried too hard; and in trying, they would borrow mannerisms and emotions from performances that had been successful in the past, so making it almost impossible to discover the genuine person beneath.

Suddenly, however, Annie had shown there was more to her than that. She was obviously smart and sensitive and, most remarkably, she didn't seem to crave love and fame. By wanting fans to recognise Dawn instead of Annie she had revealed a rare modesty. He smiled at her and she smiled back and said, 'Well, now that's out of my system, we can have a nice time.'

'I'll drink to that,' said Zoë.

'You'll drink to anything,' said Annie. They all laughed and this encouraged her to say, 'We should get together every week, don't you think? Since we're the only sane people on the show.'

Alex and Zoë glanced at one another and their expressions became serious.

'Annie,' he said, 'Zoë and I are leaving the show.'

Annie felt as if he'd punched her. She couldn't believe this. The dinner was meant to have been the start of something, not the end. He couldn't be leaving! He couldn't! 'Have I missed something?' she asked, trying to appear relaxed. 'Because I thought things were going, you know, kind of well.'

They certainly were for her. She was getting over five thousand dollars a week. A year or two more and she'd be richer than she'd ever thought of dreaming.

'They are,' said Alex, 'but I've got something important about to happen in Washington.'

In fact, he had convinced himself that as soon as he stopped writing for *Unto the Skies*, Dawn would sink into soapland's quagmire, thus becoming politically insignificant.

'And I'm going back to the real world,' said Zoë.

'Leaving me in the fake one,' Annie said. 'Thanks!'

'You could leave too,' said Zoë. 'I'm sure you'd get hundreds of offers.'

'You think?' said Annie. 'What I think is that every casting director is going to see me as Dawn Hope. I'll end up getting offered guest appearances as a soap actress on *Murder, She Wrote*. Like some kind of female Lanny Mason.'

'So stay on the show and make some real cash,' Zoe suggested. 'You probably won't even notice we're gone.'

Annie knew that she would. Even though Alex rarely came on set she would feel his absence. She liked knowing that he was writing the scripts for her. She liked feeling part of a team with him and Zoë. It had made her believe she was a part of something special. Now she would have to accept her place as merely another actress who couldn't make it anywhere but on a lousy fucking soap.

'And you'll still have Faith and Vince for company,' said Zoë.

Annie scowled and took a sip from her sake, as if drunk was the only state in which she could face those two. 'My idea of complete hell would be being stuck in a room with those two for ever,' she said.

'Now I really will drink to that,' said Zoë, laughing, and she knocked back another little cup of sake, as did Annie and Alex, and before long, like the tide at dusk, the devious drink had soaked them unsober until they were laughing loudly at jokes without punchlines and the blood was burning in their cheeks and Annie's hands were touching Alex much more than she'd have dared before. Not that Alex seemed to mind. He even took Annie's hand in his own and squeezed as a lover would, as her lovers had in the too-distant past when she'd known such love.

They slowed the drinking during the meal and stayed for a few hours enjoying the kind of evening that Annie had hoped, when first they'd met, to enjoy often.

After the meal, Zoë told Alex she was going to see 'you know who' and jumped in a cab.

'Who's "who"?' Annie wanted to know.

'Just someone she's having a fling with,' he said, taking Annie's arm and walking towards her apartment as if this was the most ordinary event in the world.

Annie couldn't believe her luck.

'Is she famous, this lover?'

'He,' said Alex. 'But don't say I told you.'

'But I . . .'

'Our lesbian friend isn't all she seems, Annie,' he said. 'I don't think she's ever had an affair with a woman. She told me that she'd "stepped into the closet" as a career move, and now the label's sort of stuck.'

'So that's why she never hit on me!'

'Oh,' laughed Alex as they quickened their pace across the road to beat the DON'T WALK sign, 'you think you're that irresistible, do you?'

'Aren't I?'

She risked a look to her side to find that he was smiling. He said, 'Perhaps.'

Now they were silent for a while, ambling arm-in-arm on this balmy evening. The Upper West Side had changed much since Annie had moved from the city. It had become gentrified, splashed with cafés and boutiques and shops designed for rich browsers. There were plenty of ice-cream parlours too. It was definitely the plumper side of the city. Here, the women were rounder and healthier (not least, Annie hated to see, because so many were pregnant) than anywhere else. A short trip to the east was like a journey into a foreign land where brittle grandmothers, wearing jewellery enough to double their body weight, taught their loved ones to suck in their cheeks and sick up their meals to achieve a divine physique.

'You want some Ben and Jerry's?' asked Annie as they neared one of her favourite spots.

'I shouldn't, but I will,' he said. 'Or did I mean, I would! Look, they're closed.'

'Oh! Never mind,' said Annie happily. 'I've got some

we can have back home.' She stopped, realising what she'd done. 'I mean if – if you'd like to come in.'

She looked into his eyes. It was a kind of torture to be as close as this without touching him, without possessing him. She longed to know what he was thinking.

'That would be very nice,' he said.

Nice, thought Annie, as she started to walk, faster now, towards her block. How can he call the idea nice? It was heaven, better than heaven. Heaven without Christians, maybe; something like that.

'At least I'm not asking you in for coffee,' she said.

'I think I'd come in even if you were offering plain water,' he said, and then he stopped and turned to face her and, even though there was a stream of people on the streets, she felt they were alone in the world. Alex Lubotsky was going to kiss her, she knew it, and she couldn't imagine anything she'd want more.

Suddenly, something in the background caught his eye. He let go Annie's arms and saying, 'I won't be a second,' ran to the news-vendor on the corner of her block.

She strolled towards him but, as she approached, it was as if he hid the front page of the following day's paper from her. He threw the copy down, and stepped from under the awning.

'Annie,' he began, and she didn't like the tone of his voice. 'I'm sorry, I have to go.'

'What? Why?' she said, feeling as if she could burst into tears right there on the street.

'There's someone I have to call. I completely forgot. And, ah, it's long distance.'

Annie relaxed. 'Well come on then,' she said, smiling as she pulled on his arm. 'I've got a phone, even if it is turned off. And I'll make myself scarce.'

She imagined herself waiting for him in the bedroom, skipping the tricky transition from kitchen to comforter.

Alex took a few steps with her, and then said, 'I don't have the number. I'd better go.'

'Oh!' she said, doing nothing to hide her regret.

'I'm sorry. Let's do this again soon, yeah?' he said, stroking her upper arm as if her pain was physical.

'Yuh,' she said solemnly, trying to be strong, trying to hide the shame and the hurt.

His eyes weren't even on her any more, but fixed on an approaching cab instead.

'You get that,' she told him. 'I'm fine from here.'

'OK,' he said, and after a hurried peck on her cheek, he was gone.

She stared at the cab's taillights in disbelief. He'd seemed so keen, hadn't he? They'd been having a good time together. With a heavy, heavy heart, she trudged to her building and shuffled up the steps.

Behind her, the news-vendor flicked open his knife and cut at the tape binding the next batch of papers. He glanced again at the *Herald*'s headline, 'PREZ GRANT CLEARED OF COCHABAMBA', beneath which were the words 'LA journalist admits fabricating story', before returning to his stall where an edgy teenager was waiting to buy a porn magazine from Poland for men who liked oversized breasts.

Though it was past midnight when he arrived home, Alex called Rebecca at once. She answered on the first ring.

'Where have you been?' she asked. 'I've left a thousand messages.'

Alex noticed the blinking red light on his answering machine. It seemed an appropriate symbol for how he felt.

'For once in my life I had an evening out,' he said. 'When did all this happen?'

'Around five Pacific.'

'And we believe Draker?' asked Alex. 'This isn't some trick that Wallis has pulled?'

'No. I asked, but they were as surprised as me. It seems authentic.'

'I can't believe this,' he mumbled. 'This can't be happening.'

His mind, usually so capable of clarity however deeply mired in the shit, couldn't come to terms with what he'd read. Out of the blue, Jason Draker, the Californian journalist who'd broken the Cochabamba story months before, had appeared on television to confess that he'd been paid by a right-wing group to fabricate the entire scandal. The President, Jason admitted, had never, to his knowledge, accepted laundered drug money. What clues there were (and despite the legions of reporters sent to investigate, they had remained scarce) were planted by him. Officials in South America had been paid to lie. The whole episode, Draker claimed, had been manufactured for the media to discredit President Grant and his Administration.

Alex flicked the TV on to CNN, with the volume off. There was a feature on rehearsals for the Radio City Christmas show.

'Have you talked to the First Lady?' he asked.

'Yes.'

'And what's she saying?'

'I'm not really sure,' Rebecca answered. 'Why don't you get a good night's sleep and talk to her yourself in the morning?'

'Don't patronise me, Rebecca! I don't need sleep, I need answers. Tell me what Susan said.'

Rebecca remained silent.

'He's telling the truth, isn't he?' guessed Alex. 'Draker's telling the fucking truth and Susan knows it. She hasn't got anything on Jack, has she?'

Only a week before, Rebecca had pressed Alex on why he wasn't concerned about the President running for re-election. At last, he had revealed the First Lady's claims about Cochabamba.

'Alex,' said Rebecca, 'I don't think it's my place to repeat what the First Lady told me. Please, can you talk to her tomorrow?'

'What's her day like?'

'Relatively clear.'

He flicked open his diary. Damn, he'd forgotten that Pam was coming to stay the night tomorrow. Still, he could be back easily enough. 'Can you arrange for Susan to come to your house?' he asked.

'I don't know how secure the line will be, Al.'

'Doesn't matter – I'm coming to see her.'

'How can you? The Secret Service will know you're here.'

'That's not a problem. I'll arrive first, and you can tell them I'm staying with you. Besides, I've never been considered a security risk before.'

'Can't it be elsewhere?'

'How? She's got a perfectly legitimate reason to visit you, and it won't involve much protection clearance. Please.'

'Do you want me to change the sheets?'

Alex was stunned. He'd told Rebecca everything about Susan's bid for power but never, ever, anything about their relationship. Nobody else knew about that. Yet he managed to sound calm enough when he asked, 'What are you talking about?'

'Forget it,' Rebecca said lightly. 'Dumb joke!'

'No, that's not good enough. Tell me what you're talking about.'

After a moment's pause, Rebecca said, 'You really don't know?'

'Know what? Come on,' he said, blankly staring at the television, on which the Rockettes were going through their paces. 'It's clearly a night of surprises.'

'We know about it,' she said. 'Some of us.'

'Know what?' he said, his heart beating wildly.

'Alex!' she protested, 'I can't believe I'm being made to do this!'

'Tell me,' he shouted. 'Tell me what I should know.'

He couldn't remember his nerves ever being so raw.

'About you and the First Lady,' Rebecca quickly said. 'About what has happened in her office and other places. About your relations.'

Although Alex was shocked by the words, he managed to laugh. 'My relationship with Susan has always been professional,' he told her.

'Even in her bathroom? Alex, this is something Susan's staff know.'

Alex could hardly believe this. He felt physically weak. If the staff knew, it would only be a matter of time before the rest of the world found out as well. 'I don't think this is getting us anywhere, Rebecca,' he said. 'Expect a call early tomorrow in the morning. I should be there by eleven.'

'OK,' she said, sounding unsure.

'Goodbye.'

'Alex,' she began, but he'd already hung up the phone.

He stared for minutes at the silent TV before rising in a kind of daze to go into the bedroom. There he sat on the bed's edge and looked at his reflection in the glass of the curtainless window. In the distorted image, it seemed that there were two of him. As he stared, horrified about the knowledge of his affair, shocked about Cochabamba, he thought he saw one of the reflected images move in the glass. He continued to stare, and said, 'I know, Max. You're right. It's probably what I deserve.'

He stood, and turned out the light in the living room. On his way past the phone, he decided to give Annie a call. Maybe here was a chance to do something right. If President Grant ran for re-election, and if he himself stayed in New York, then maybe he and Annie would have a real chance together. He had hated leaving her tonight, though he'd had no choice.

He dialled the number, but the line was engaged. Twenty minutes later, he tried again, decided she'd taken the phone off the hook, and, feeling more depressed than he had since Max's death, he slid into bed, wondering what tomorrow would bring when he came face to face with the woman who'd last filled his heart.

17

Tic-tic-tic-tic-tictictictic-tic-tic. Tic.

Knock.

Vince Moscardini stopped rattling his fingernails against the base of his front teeth and shouted out, 'Yeah!'

Zoë strode into his office, smoking a cigarette.

'Do you mind not smoking?' Vince said, rubbing at the stubble on his chin. 'I gave up. It's not good for the nerves. Anyway, what do you want?'

'I've got something to tell you. Can I sit down?'

'Sit! Sit!' Vince said, hopping up from behind the desk to perch on its front edge. 'What?'

'I'm leaving the show when my contract expires.'

'You what? When is that? Three months?'

He pinched the bottom of his nose and sniffed. Zoë wondered if he'd been at the cocaine.

'No, three weeks.'

'I dreamt this. I dreamt it. The day we got to the top I said, Vince, this time it's really going to hurt when you crash. I said that.'

Vince picked up the ashtray containing Zoë's cigarette and threw the whole thing into the bin.

'I'm very flattered that you think *Unto the Skies* is going to collapse when I leave,' Zoë said, 'but I'm sure you'll find plenty of other directors.'

Vince was walking around the edge of his office now, not unlike a madman in his cell. 'Why are you doing this?' he asked in an unusually high-pitched tone.

297

'There are a number of film projects I'm interested in developing.'

'Oh, so we're not good enough for Zoë Dunlop! Fine. Go. GO. But don't expect glowing references.' He pointed a finger at her. 'Don't expect me to, you know, to, to help you. Not after you've treated me like this.'

'Poor me!' Zoë said, taking a fresh cigarette out of the box and lighting up. She got to her feet. 'No doubt I'll be seeing you around.'

'Mm,' grumbled Vince.

At the door, she turned. 'It's probably quite lucky these windows don't open, isn't it?'

'What?' Vince said. 'Why?'

He ran a hand through his hair and returned to the revolving chair at his desk, scratching his elbow as he went. 'Stupid dyking bitch, anyway,' he muttered. 'She was a lousy director. We're fine. We're number one. We're staying put. Definitely.'

Recently, Vince had not taken his success well. Although the ratings for *Unto the Skies* continued to cruise at a higher altitude than those for any rival show, and although it had been breaking revenue records from sponsors who'd discovered that many AB consumers were taping the programme to watch after work, Vince was convinced that he was destined for a fall. His greatest terror was that, because he didn't know what had taken the soap to the top, he wouldn't know how to keep it there. Still, he'd become convinced since his little chat with Faith that the show had seen quite enough of Alex Lubotsky and his politics. The time had come for the Executive Producer to assert himself and bring some spice back to the storylines. He'd had it with the show being run by writers and sponsors and network officials who knew nothing about real drama. Drama was in his blood!

He decided to waste no more time and dialled Alex

Lubotsky's number. 'Sexual harassment,' he said when the phone was answered. 'Can you handle it?'

'Hello, Vince, it's Bob here.'

'Oh! Where's Lobotomy?'

'He's had to go out of town on some emergency.'

'Just like his screwing brother, huh? Well, maybe he'll meet a sticky end too. Maybe I'll get my show back.'

There was a pause before Bob asked, 'Do you need something, Vince? What's this about harassment?'

'Dawn! I want her tickled up, put in her place a little. We've had a lot of complaints that she's not acting womanly.'

'And you're thinking a hand up her skirt will redress the balance? It's a very sensitive issue, Vince.'

'So's your salary, dick-face. And another thing – I don't need my ideas questioned every minute of the day. In case you hadn't noticed, I'm Executive Producer of this heap of shit, and what I say goes. And what I say now is that I want a story that puts across the man's case for once.'

'Which is?'

'Christ, Bob, are you a faggot or something? Haven't you noticed that we're being taken over by whingeing little dykes? Jesus. You can't move these days without being accused of something.'

'Doesn't that depend on what kind of movement you're making, Vince?'

'You see?' Vince shouted. 'They've even got to *you*. Maybe you're too limp-wristed to write this.'

'No! I'll see what we can come up with.'

'Good. Get back to me,' the producer said, hanging up the phone and swinging his chair around to look onto the street where a vendor was selling hot dogs from his cart.

'What a beautiful job,' Vince said to himself. 'What a great no-worries kind of job.' He sighed, swung back and picked up the receiver. He dialled an internal number. 'Dave, I need to see you.'

'What for, boss?'

'I don't know yet, but by the time you've walked to my office, there's sure to be something on my mind.'

He tossed the receiver back into its cradle and began to clack a pencil between his teeth. Tic-tic-tictictic-tic.

Tic.

Unlike many members of Jack Grant's Administration, Rebecca Frear had chosen not to live near the White House but in Georgetown, on a peaceful street close to the University that was so clean that even the bricks looked as if they received a weekly wash. Rebecca's early nineteenth-century house was sheltered by trees and a tall fence of living bamboo. It was hidden from the street down a narrow driveway. With its untypical white clapboarding, mossy green shutters and balcony wrapping the entire first floor, it was strongly evocative of a swampy America further south and, as such, had always possessed a romantic air in Alex's mind.

For a while he had thought of moving to the quiet neighbourhood himself, but too often he had been called to the Oval Office late at night by a President struggling with the opinions he insisted on hearing from all sides. Alex would sit with Grant, a beer in hand, maybe some Webster or Coltrane on the machine, until three or four in the morning, listening to the mental wrestling of a man hoping to save the nation from itself. With so much promise and hope, they hadn't needed much sleep. Most of all, though, there had been their friendship and trust in one another, the same belief in themselves that had taken them all the way to the top.

As the cab proceeded further from the White House, Alex felt a sudden shame at abandoning that friendship. He had known in his heart that Jack had been innocent of Cochabamba. He'd known it. And yet he had swallowed Susan's story like an addict needing a narcotic to bring his particular world into focus. Now his sight was bleary again, and it made him nervous of stepping where he couldn't see.

Rebecca met him at the gate with the news that Susan was due at twelve. A few security guards were going to check over the building in half an hour, but she had time enough to make him some coffee, she said, her smile a white flag for the unpleasantness of the previous night.

'I'm sorry I said those things,' she told him as the front door snapped behind them. 'I shouldn't have.'

'Or maybe you should,' he said. 'Maybe someone should have said them a long time ago.'

The house smelled of beeswax polish and toast, and its stillness reminded him of Pam and Titusville before the noise and calamity of New York City. He would have liked to have heard the sound of Robbie or Matt running down the steps, taking two at a time as he and Max used to do.

'I've been watching the news,' Rebecca said. 'You were on.'

'I was? Why?'

'You're being cast as one of the Cochabamba casualties.'

'As a good guy? There's a change.'

She poured coffee from a chipped enamel jug and whisked the hot milk before adding it to the wide blue-and-white-striped cup. 'The media's feeling more than a touch of collective guilt over the scandal. So now they're giving Jack great press, of course.' She handed Alex the drink. 'The pendulum's swinging right back.'

'You know it was me who advised him not to rise to the bait, don't you? I told him to sit tight.'

Rebecca patted Alex on the shoulder as she passed.

'You're a saint, Al. I'll alert the media.'

'Yeah, well.' He called to her out in the hallway. 'By the way, we're telling Susan's protection that I'm staying here, yeah?'

301

'Al,' she replied, her footsteps loud on the old floor-boards, 'it's your game.'

As he'd predicted, the guards took little notice of him when they arrived to give the building a once-over. They didn't stay long, though an officer was posted outside the front door to wait for the First Lady.

She arrived with the Secret Service soon after, riding shotgun in a chunky black Chevy Suburban with windows black as night. She looked unusually diminutive beside it when she stepped from the seat and walked unaccompanied to meet Rebecca. Alex was waiting in a room up stairs that creaked and cracked as Susan climbed them.

He was sitting on the edge of a single bed when she came in, tidy in her charcoal Donna Karan.

'Hello, Alex.'

Under his watchful eye, she pulled an unsteady wicker chair from beside the dresser. She sat on it and neatly crossed her legs. Motionless in the cold room, they were an unlikely couple, like travellers from a Vermeer.

She said, 'It seems you've summoned me.'

Alex nodded, and was silent for some time before asking, 'Did you lie to me?'

'Yes,' she said. 'I did.'

Alex couldn't help but admire this audacity. Hadn't it been what he'd fallen in love with at first?

'You needed some persuading,' she said in explanation.

'To do what?' he asked, his eyebrows raised. 'To waste my time on a pointless campaign?'

'I thought Jack wouldn't run,' she said, only now looking away. 'Believe me.'

Alex's laugh was filled with contempt. 'Did you think something better than the presidency might come along for him?'

'God, you always have to act smarter than the rest of us, don't you? You always think you know everything.'

'Fuck you, Susan!' he said very quietly. 'You've wasted months of my life. You promised me that Jack wasn't going to run.'

'And I believed it. There were things that he said to me, privately to me, his *wife*, Alex, that convinced me that he was not going to seek re-election. I tried to tell you – remember? – but my word wasn't good enough for you. You insisted on something concrete.'

'And so you made up something that couldn't have been less concrete. In fact, Susan, it was because I believed you that I walked out of the White House.'

'You were fired,' said Susan, walking to the window. 'Or did you choose to forget that detail?'

Outside, the Secret Service men were huddled together, smoking cigarettes by the front gate. They looked shifty, as if appearing criminal was part of the protector's job. After a minute or so, the First Lady returned to Alex, sitting by him on the bed. He tensed at her touch.

'Listen, Al, I don't want to argue. You were right, I admit that. But what if I'd been right and Jack *had* decided not to run? I couldn't afford to wait until I was sure. It might have been too late by then. I might have lost you altogether and I didn't want that. Do you see? Mmm, Ali? I didn't want that. I still don't.' She stroked his hand and he jerked it away and jumped to his feet. She followed him and held him at the waist. 'Look at me, Al! Don't you dare tell me you don't want to be with me too.'

He wouldn't look at her.

'Can you tell me that?' she repeated. 'Can you look at me and tell me that you don't want to be with me too?'

He closed his eyes and felt her soft lips press against his. And then he whispered, 'Get undressed.'

She kissed him again, with passion this time, and then she unhooked her dress and let it fall to the floor.

'Keep going,' he said. 'I want to see you naked.'

He watched her thumb her underwear and tights off

her legs. Then she lifted her arms and released her bra. Naked, she did as he asked and lay on the bed.

'Come here,' she said, holding out her arms.

Fully clothed, he sat on the bed and slowly stroked his hand down Susan's body, from her neck to her thighs. Then he bent to whisper in her ear. 'The answer's yes, Susan,' he said. 'I *can* say it.'

She opened her eyes, alarmed by his tone.

He said, 'I'm looking at you and I'm saying that I don't want to be with you.'

Now she sat up, bringing up her knees to cover her nudity. 'Alex, I'm sorry if . . .'

'I don't want to be with you now, or tomorrow, or ever.' He stood, and took a step towards the door. 'And one more thing,' he said. 'I never did think you'd become President. You've got the wrong kind of balls.'

'Alex!' she exclaimed, rising quickly to her feet.

She ran to him, but by the time she reached the door her lover had gone and was clumping noisily away down the old wooden stairs.

Promising to call later, Alex quickly left Rebecca's house, ignoring the Secret Service men as he strode away. Though in a hurry to leave the First Lady, he wasn't sure where to go. The encounter with her had left him feeling numb and directionless.

On the way to Washington he had worried that he wouldn't have the courage to turn his back on Susan, but when he'd seen her he'd been surprised by an unusually deep coldness. It had always been a failing of his that he could not forgive those who stood in the way of his career and now he blamed the First Lady for planting in his mind unjustifiable doubts about the President's conduct. He believed that all his mistakes flowed from Susan's lie about Cochabamba – his dismissal, his commitment to a campaign that now lay in ruins and his flight from the city he loved above all others. He wondered if he was being punished for the crime of his affair. If so, now that it was over, might there be a way back into the President's heart?

For a moment, he stood on the junction at Wisconsin wondering what to do but then, deciding he had nothing to lose and everything to gain, he hailed a cab and climbed into the back seat.

'The White House,' he said.

It was time to make amends.

18

'If you look like a whore,' Bra had said, 'they'll love you,' so Annie had settled on her little red sheath dress to wear on the Paddy Darwin show. She wanted to get some attention.

When Annie had called Barbara with details of Alex's escape, she had complained that becoming famous had ruined her chance of a decent love life. There was more than enough opportunity for an indecent one, her mailbag being as loaded as a Chippendale's jockstrap with lurid proposals and photographs of enthusiastic genitalia, but she never seemed to meet any decent, ordinary men any more. Like everyone else, Annie had assumed that fame would bring with it endless sexual and romantic opportunities. Now she was beginning to wonder if the reverse wasn't true. People were scared of her, and she too had developed a guardedness to protect herself from the unwelcome millions who claimed her love. It was a curse similar to that of immense wealth, for it became increasingly difficult to determine who wanted what, and why.

Yet as she climbed into the monstrous white limo sent by Paddy Darwin, she thought there might be one man watching who'd like her for the person she was and the legs she had. One was all she would need. Perhaps it would be Tom Sterling. His brief marriage to supermodel Wendy Radcliff was definitely over, and there would be no fears that he was after any reflected glory.

Paddy Darwin's show was taped on the sixth floor of

307

UBC Tower in mid-Manhattan. In a radical break from
the past, and from its rivals, it was no longer taped in the
afternoon, but was shown live at ten p.m. Annie was met
by a production assistant wearing headphones and carrying
a clipboard. She had sometimes wondered whether these
TV researchers had clipboards glued to their hands on
being employed, for they were never without them.

'Paddy will take ten minutes at the top of the show for his
intro,' the girl explained as they set off down a seemingly
endless corridor, 'and there's one guest before you.'

'How long am I on for?' Annie wanted to know.

'About six minutes.'

'Great! Has Tom Sterling arrived yet?'

Annie hoped that sounded casual enough, as if she was
looking forward to seeing him again.

'He's right in here,' the girl said, stopping at a door.
'Help yourself to whatever you like and someone will be
along in a minute to mike you up and see about hair and
make-up. OK?'

The girl swung open the door with one arm and Annie
stepped past her into the hospitality lounge. Low armchairs hugged the walls, all but two of which were empty.
On the edge of one a woman sat talking into a mobile
phone, her Filofax sprawled over her lap. Beside her sat
a man. Though his head was buried in a book, there was
no mistaking the flowing grey locks of movie star Tom
Sterling.

'Hello,' Annie said.

She was fifteen feet away, standing nervously by the
door.

The woman raised and lowered her eyes. Tom Sterling
fanned open the fingers of his right hand as he held the
book, but didn't bother to look up. Feeling uncomfortable,
Annie poured herself a glass of wine, but it came out
too quickly so an embarrassing splotch spread like blood
across the virginal white cloth. Furtively, she slid a plate

of sandwiches over the stain and wondered if Tom had looked up yet, and if so whether he'd know who she was. Sometimes she would amuse herself by marvelling at which celebrities were aware of her existence. President Grant probably was, she thought, Princess Diana probably wasn't, even though she had recently holidayed in Martha's Vineyard. But what about Oprah Winfrey, Richard Gere, Lorena Bobbitt, Meg Ryan, Meatloaf? Would they think anything if they saw her face? She liked to think they would.

As she picked up a copy of *The New York Times* (it led, as they all did, with the Cochabamba incident) and took a seat as close as she dared to Tom, Annie decided that an appearance on the Paddy Darwin show would act like a seal of approval on her fame. She was certainly mixing in the right company, and she was certainly being handled like a star. This meant, of course, being coddled like a helpless child.

Annie made a lot of noise turning the paper's page, but neither Tom nor his assistant looked up. Instead, the PA was reeling off names of celebrities to invite to the première of Tom's latest movie, *A Beggar's Life*. It had been filmed in Tibet and Nepal, a semiautobiographical version of one actor's spiritual awakening in the Himalayan foothills. Tom Sterling was Hollywood's answer to the Dalai Lama, his Buddhist beliefs widely known. Now, at forty, as he'd said in the last interview Annie had read, he was a man defined by 'a great need to share'.

The door opened and Paddy Darwin bounced in. A tubby Irish American, his success had surprised most TV executives and commentators. Only Barry Shermer had been willing to take a risk with the host and with the live-time slot, and now no star could afford to refuse an invitation to appear.

'Thomas Sterling!' Paddy said. 'Thanks so much for coming on.'

Annie caught her breath as Tom Sterling lowered his book. It was such a relief to find him as compelling in real life as he was on film, although whether his magnetism was born of his absolute fame or some innate charisma, it was hard to tell. All that Annie knew was that being with him made her feel more alive.

'I do what I have to do,' Tom said.

'We're lucky to have you doing it to us, Tom. Very lucky.'

Paddy moved to Annie and held out his hand. He introduced himself and thanked her without seeming to know who she was and then he was gone.

'He's an asshole,' Tom said.

Annie paused a moment to see if the actor was talking to her. He was.

'Oh, I, I don't really know him,' she replied, hoping to sound relaxed.

'He's an asshole.'

'Probably,' she said, though she had always quite liked the chat show host.

She was about to say something else when Tom returned to his book. Suddenly Annie saw he was reading a work of Buddhist teachings, *The Gateless Gate*. It was a favourite of Jerry's and she herself had brought an old copy to New York, as much for its romantic dedication as its content. Though Annie could hardly believe her good fortune, it was at least twenty minutes before she mustered up the courage to speak. 'Mumon was a wonderful teacher, wasn't he?' she said, leaning forward, her hands pressed together and held between her knees, as if praying for a response.

'Are you familiar with him?' Tom asked, lifting his eyes straightaway.

'Oh, yeah. I found him . . .' Suddenly Annie's mind was as ordered as a collapsing bookshelf. 'Good. I found him good.'

'I find him good too,' said Tom, and then Annie saw

him standing and walking over to sit beside her. She was filled with a mixture of terror and delight.

He held out a hand. 'Tom Sterling.'

'Yes, hi! Um, hi!'

There was silence. Tom, his eyebrows raised, seemed to be waiting for something.

'And you are?' he asked.

'Oh, right! Sorry. I'm Dawn. No! What am I thinking of? I'm not Dawn! I'm Annie. Annie Marin.'

'Now, you're sure about that,' said Tom, leaning close and coming out with an effortless actor's laugh.

Annie laughed too, and blushed. 'Yes. I don't know why I said that. Dawn's my character. I'm on a soap opera.'

'You said her name because being in touch with who we are is not easy for anyone. But for those of us who spend more time in character than out of it, the struggle is much more difficult.'

'That's most likely what it is,' she said, though she was thinking that the real struggle was to be found in attempting to form and utter a complete sentence while staring at a man she'd met before only in sexual fantasy.

'What is it about Mumon that you like?' Tom asked.

'I can't talk about Buddhism right now,' Annie said.

'Excuse me?'

'Did I say that?' Fidgeting, she pulled down the hem of her little red dress. 'I, I didn't mean to say that. I meant to say that I like the way that when you're reading a Buddhist teacher, especially one like Mumon, you have to, you know, you have to, to . . .' Suddenly a phrase of Jerry's was spinning through the black hole of her head. 'You have to totally suspend logical thought and free your mind of all obstacles to pure meditation.'

She was impressed with herself. Tom seemed impressed with her too. He leant in closer, knowing that there wasn't a woman in the world who'd object to having her personal space invaded by him. 'Well said.'

'Of course, if . . .'

The researcher had come in and now stood in front of Annie and Tom. 'Excuse me interrupting, but you're almost on, Miss Marin.'

Annie felt like grabbing the cheese knife and putting it through the researcher's heart.

'We need to mike you up and give you some powder,' the girl added. 'OK?'

'OK,' said Annie, disappointed. 'Tom, I hope to talk to you later, maybe.'

She shook his hand, savouring its smooth warmth.

'I hope so too,' he said.

Of course, now she was leaving she wished she'd had the courage to speak up sooner. She didn't think she had spent long enough talking to the movie star for him to remember her.

From Alex Lubotsky's kitchen, Pam called out, 'How long before Annie Marin's on?'

Alex called over his shoulder, 'Soon, I think. After this guest.'

She returned with two cups of coffee. In the city to meet a financial adviser, she was staying the night for an appointment the following day. Alex had welcomed the opportunity to see her and was even happier to find her in such an improved frame of mind. A little while before, he had pressed her for an explanation and she admitted having met a man, a widower himself.

'So what does he do, this mystery man?' Alex asked now.

'He's an accountant of sorts,' said Pam, easing off her shoes. 'He couldn't be more different from Max, really. His mind is very ordered.'

'And do you think it's serious between you?'

'It's hard to say. I've spent so much of this year dreading even waking up in the morning that when I met Richard it was like having, I don't know how to describe it, like opening the windows in my head and letting the fresh air blow through. I thought I'd feel incredibly guilty, but I don't. I'd bring Max back if I could, Al. You know that. But I can't. Do you think I'm bad?'

After a quick glance at the muted TV, Alex said, 'I think you don't want to be drinking this.' He took Pam's cup of coffee into the kitchen and emerged with a bottle of wine and two glasses. 'I think we should be celebrating the future!'

The gesture was partly for Pam and partly for himself, because he needed a drink, not to celebrate his future, but to try to put it out of his mind.

His day in Washington had been a disaster. After leaving the First Lady at Rebecca's home he'd taken a cab to the White House and tried to make an appointment to see the President, to congratulate him, he'd said, for his victory over the press. After an hour of waiting like some nobody in the press office he'd once ruled, his request had been denied. Curt Wallis, as smug a bastard as Alex had ever met, had assumed an unasked-for chumminess in recommending that Alex give Jack 'about a decade to cool off' before calling him again.

After that, he spent the afternoon wandering around his beloved city, knowing that he belonged there, in DC, but not sure of what he might do. Running for any kind of office would seem a climb-down from his previous position dictating policy within the Administration, yet with Susan no longer in the presidential race, what hope did he have of working in the White House again?

So, with a tired heart, he'd returned to New York grateful for Pam's company. She, of all people, had helped him put his problems in perspective. She'd climbed a much more arduous slope and seemed to have ended up smiling.

Alex raised his glass. 'Let's drink to tomorrow, because

it'll be better than today. I think . . .' He was interrupted by the phone ringing. 'Excuse me.'

Pam could hear Alex asking the person to call back after Paddy Darwin's show. He came back shaking his head.

'That was Charlie Canon,' he said.

'The feminist?'

'Yes. She's driving me insane.'

'Why?'

He sat on the floor and groaned when he leant back against the sofa. 'Let's just say she read more into something that happened than she should have. And she's not getting the message. Or else she's refusing to listen.'

'Why don't I answer the phone next time?' said Pam. 'She won't like hearing a strange woman in your apartment.'

'Now that's a fantastic idea,' he said, fondly patting her leg. 'Would you do that? Say I'm in the shower, or something.' Suddenly he noticed that the commercials had ended, so he turned up the sound on the TV.

Paddy Darwin was talking. 'My next guest, ladies and gentlemen, my next guest is an actress who's threatening to take over America with her portrayal of Dawn Hope, a ballsy, peace-loving Senator on the soap opera *Unto the Skies*. Please welcome Miss Annie Marin.' He stood. 'Annie Marin, ladies and gentlemen.'

Much like the arrival of Annie's fame, it happened very quickly. One minute she was listening to the intro from behind the painted screens (the image of a fictional cityscape uniting the most celebrated skyscrapers in the land was familiar to almost every American with a television set) and the next she was hearing the word go being whispered in her ear by a producer with a clipboard glued to her hand.

Annie moved into the glare and counted the steps down, three, two, one, as she smiled and waved at the applauding audience. She shook Paddy's hand and sat, a gash of red in the boxy blue armchair. She paid no attention to the hulking podium cameras that had become her companions every working day.

'Welcome to the show,' said Paddy. 'Good to have you here.'

'It's good to be here,' Annie replied, crossing her legs in defence against one lens that she feared might see too much.

She'd been so worried about tripping over the cables, or coming on at the wrong moment, that she felt she'd crossed a great hurdle already. And this chair, and set, and man, were so familiar that she found she'd forgotten that millions of viewers were listening to every word.

'Now!' Paddy reached over to pat the side of Annie's chair, presumably to make her feel at home. 'When you got this role – when was it – eight months ago?'

'Yes,' said Annie.

'Did you have any idea at all that it would cause the sensation that it has?'

'Not at all! I was just happy to get the part. I mean, if you're lost in the desert and you see food, you don't stop to think whether it's a gourmet meal.'

The audience, easy to please because Tom Sterling was in the building, liked that and laughed.

'So you were *resting*,' joked Paddy. 'That's what actors do, isn't it? They *rest*.'

'I think I was sleeping, to be honest.'

As the audience tittered, Annie leant forward and took a sip of water. It was warm and unpleasantly metallic. She hadn't even wanted it, and yet, like countless guests before, she had been keen to impress the viewers with her calmness despite the adrenalin-heavy high of her entrance.

'OK, very good. So you're asleep in, where was it?'

'In San Francisco.'

'So you're in San Francisco one minute and the next

you're one of the most famous people on TV. Now, what I want to know is when you first realised that this was happening. This whole, this whole, ah, Dawn Hope thingummy?'

'When did I know? I guess soon after my first show was aired. A lot of fans began to gather at the studio and we, we started getting letters.'

'Saying?'

'Basically that Dawn was their idea of what a politician should be.'

'So it was Dawn they were crazy about, and not you.'

'That's right, Paddy,' she said, glad to have found an opportunity to slip in his name. It was something she'd practised in the shower the night before.

'Wasn't that a problem for you?'

'No, not at all. An actress has to make her character come alive. It's not about me. It's about making the people out there believe that Dawn is real, and they do. I think.'

'They certainly do,' said Paddy. He leant forward again in his chair. 'Now you don't know this . . .'

'Don't tell me you've got a picture of me at school,' said Annie, looking out and beyond the cameraman.

'No, but what we *have* done is send out some researchers onto the windy streets of Chicago, Illinois, to ask the good people of that city who they're planning to vote for in the midterm election.' Paddy picked up a sheet of paper and snapped it in the air. 'Now, what we did is we added the name of Dawn Hope to the list of candidates.'

'Oh, no,' laughed Annie.

'Oh, yes, oh yes indeed, and this is what we found,' he said, studying the page. 'Twenty-two per cent said they'd vote for Simon Owen, who's the Democratic candidate, forty-eight per cent said they'd like Republican Ed Lyndon to hang onto his job, ten per cent said don't know and don't care, but – listen to this – twenty per cent, two-o per cent of the voters of Chicago, said they'd vote for Dawn Hope as Governor.'

'You're kidding,' said Annie.

'I kid you not. Carl,' he said to the producer who was standing beside camera one, 'is this or is it not a genuine survey?'

'It is,' Carl said.

'You see? And Carl never lies. Carl could be God if the position was open.'

'You actually did this?' Annie asked again.

'We actually did this. We thought that since the First Lady was using your lines for herself then you must be making some sense to the American people.'

There was a spontaneous round of applause.

'That's incredible,' Annie said.

'That's incredible,' said Alex, turning to Pam. 'Did you hear that?' He was evidently excited by the poll, as if Annie was his actual candidate. 'If that's true, Pam, if that's true it means Dawn got a fifth of the vote in a place she's never been to. Jack made it to the White House on forty-three per cent.'

'Maybe Annie should run for President, then.'

'Right,' said Alex, laughing. 'Maybe she should!'

As if he could hear this conversation, Paddy Darwin had wandered to the front row of the audience to ask, 'How many of you people would rather have Dawn Hope as President than Jack Grant?'

A third of the audience, giggly with the thrill of their television appearance, held their arms in the air.

'See? It must be your legs, Annie!' said Paddy. 'And you heard it here first, folks! Now we've got to take a short break, and when we return not only do we have more from the delicious Annie Marin, but Tom Sterling will be joining us. So don't-you-go-anywhere. And I mean it!'

Paddy ambled back to his seat amid cheering applause.

317

Alex hit the mute button. 'Twenty per cent,' he said again.

'Dawn Hope is big news, Alex. Haven't you figured that out by now?'

'There's a difference between a soap character being big news and twenty per cent of Chicago's electorate saying they'd vote for her.'

'Is there? There was an article in Princeton the other day saying Annie Marin had been invited to the campus to speak. I'm afraid I don't watch the show enough to know what Dawn says, but whatever it is, people are listening.'

'I know,' said Alex, looking down into his glass. 'And all for nothing.'

'What do you mean?'

'Forget it,' he said as, once again, he turned the television volume up.

'Welcome back,' said Darwin. 'Movie superstar and sex god Tom Sterling is here, I kid you not, but for the moment I have Annie Marin with me, famous to us all as Dawn Hope. Now you've got a book out, haven't you?' he said, picking up a copy from his desk.

'Yes, *Selected Speeches*.'

Paddy knocked on the book's hard cover. 'How's it doing?'

'I think very well. I mean, it's number one.'

'Really? Wow! I think "very well" too, then. Like hot cakes, even. Have you ever had a hot cake?'

'I don't know what they are, to be honest.'

Paddy looked out to his producer. 'Carl, what are hot cakes?'

Clipboard in hand, Carl shrugged and said, 'I don't know, but I hear they're selling as fast as Dawn's book.'

'The book!' yapped Paddy. 'Of course, we have to plug the book. So, what's so hot about the book, do you think?'

'I think it's because most of the speeches focus on the positive things about America. We're reminded that this is still the greatest country in the world.'

'This is an interesting question, isn't it?'

'Did you just ask one?' Annie wanted to know, playing for a laugh.

'Well spotted, I didn't, but I'm about to because it's my job. Isn't it, Carl? To ask questions.' The camera cut to the smiling producer, then back to Paddy. 'OK, what I want to know is how much of you is in this book, or are you just spouting someone else's lines?'

'Uh-oh,' said Alex in the apartment.

But Annie didn't seem bothered by the question. 'I agree with Dawn on a lot of the things she says. She's a good role model. I mean, if all we had on TV was housewives or whores – which is the way most women are seen – then girls would be growing up thinking that's all they can be. But Dawn is showing that it's very possible to make it to the top as a real woman.'

There was applause from the audience.

'Is that important to you? You don't look like a feminist,' said Paddy, his eyes clearly travelling down to her bare legs.

'I don't know what feminists look like,' Annie instantly replied, 'other than that they don't have balls and a thick skull.' This drew great applause and a few cheers. Annie was encouraged. 'What Dawn is saying is vote for me because I care about this country and I want to put it right instead of playing political games. She's saying that it doesn't make any difference that she's a woman because she's the best suited for the job. I don't think that's feminism, Paddy. That's, I don't know, that's good manners! Treating women as something other than doormats.'

Alex clapped his hands and whooped with laughter. 'You tell him, Annie.' He looked at Pam. 'That was perfect for a chauvinist shithead like Paddy Darwin, wasn't it? "That's not feminism, that's good manners." Hah!'

Paddy was making much of wiping his brow. 'OK, let's get back to Planet Earth here,' he said, tossing the book aside. 'There's something I have to ask you or the audience will kill me: Faith Valentine's breasts.'

'Yes?' said Annie, a little unsurely.

'Are they for real?'

'As far as I know, yes.'

'As far as you know,' Darwin repeated, making a face to suggest he didn't believe her. 'But you haven't been in an airplane at thirty-five thousand feet with her?'

'Not in real life, no! But they seemed OK when we shot a flight scene on the show.'

'You didn't hear any popping sounds?'

'No,' said Annie, genuinely laughing now.

'Well, that's good. Very good. There's something else I need to know – why is it that these men on soap operas keep getting body rubs and I never get any? Can you help me out on this?'

'Is that a request?'

'Are you offering?' Paddy said.

'I think I'll wait for Tom Sterling.'

There was a squeal of delight from someone in the audience.

'Calm yourself, woman!' Paddy said. 'Calm yourself!' He twisted back to Annie and held out his hand. 'Annie, thank you very much for coming in. I wish you continued success on the show and with your book . . .'

'*Selected Speeches*.'

'Exactly. And I hope Dawn Hope wins by a landslide. I'm sure she will.'

'Thanks. Fingers crossed.'

'Annie Marin, ladies and gentlemen. A very special lady. Annie Marin.'

Annie left the set as the band took the show into another commercial break.

'You were great,' said one of the producers. 'Paddy liked you.'

'She was great, wasn't she?' said Alex, hitting the mute button, though Pam wanted to see Tom Sterling.

'She came across better than I expected,' said Pam. 'She doesn't come across as a typical soap actress.'

'Oh, Annie's in a completely different league.'

'You seem pretty fond of her,' said Pam, nudging him with her foot. 'Are you?'

'Did you know she knew Max at Cornell Williams?' said Alex.

He wanted to change the subject because he'd been thinking about Annie all the way home from Washington, thinking how he wished he hadn't had to run from her apartment the night before. The last person to have affected him so was Susan Grant, but when he'd seen her in Washington he'd felt nothing but contempt that she should have tried to use him. Annie was different. He couldn't imagine her trying to use anyone at all.

'I think he did mention her a couple of times,' said Pam. 'I sort of remember him trying to reach her but he didn't know where she was. He called her one of his loose ends. There's obviously something about her that appeals to the Lubotsky genes.'

'I didn't say I liked her.'

'You didn't have to.'

Alex refilled his glass of wine and shook his head. 'I can't believe she got twenty per cent! She could probably go to Illinois and win.'

The midterm elections for Governors and Congressmen were taking place in a little under two weeks, on November 8th. Jack Grant's Democrats were trailing badly in the polls, and it was the candidates who shared many of

Dawn's jingoistic beliefs in American family values who were faring the best.

'I think people are going to vote against the Democrats just because they don't like Grant,' said Pam. 'I don't give him a hope in 1996, do you? Unless you run his campaign, of course. Al?'

'Mm?'

'Were you listening?'

'No,' he said, standing and looking almost as if he was in a trance. 'Sorry. I have to make a call.'

'Who to?'

'Annie,' he said, dialling her number.

He knew she wouldn't be back but left a message asking her to call. Half an hour later, after they'd watched Tom Sterling on the show, he tried again.

'She's probably not back,' said Pam.

'She should be. She's only ten minutes from the studio and she has to get up at six. I bet you she's home but not listening to the phone. She does that.'

'So speak to her at the studio tomorrow,' Pam said. 'It can't be that important.'

'Can't it?' he said. He didn't want this to wait. Besides, he was excited about seeing Annie. He was wondering if there was any way they could start off where the previous evening had ended.

'Pam, are you OK on your own for a while?'

'I think I'll probably manage! I'm going to take a bath. But where are you going, more to the point?'

'To tie up some loose Lubotsky ends,' he said.

Almost as soon as he'd left, Pam opened the door and called after him. 'What shall I say if she rings?'

'She won't, unless it's in the next ten minutes in which case say I'm on my way. And you know what to do with Charlie!' he said with a laugh.

Pam smiled at the thought. Although she'd been a fairly radical feminist in her youth, she hadn't taken to Charlie Canon as the rest of the country seemed to have done.

At UBC studios, Annie had been about to leave when Tom Sterling, having watched her interview, asked if she could wait until after the show so that he could give her a lift home. So of course she had waited, hardly able to contain her excitement, wishing Alex was there to see her. This would show him for leading her on and then dumping her as he had! There was hardly a woman in the land who wouldn't envy Annie now, and still the night was quite young. Annie was too proud to give herself to Tom in the back of a limousine, but not by much. Perhaps by the second drive . . .

When leaving, Tom had insisted on taking the front entrance, and he led her past the fans and the photographers and she felt as if she was flying though air as she gripped his arm and gloated (she couldn't help it) in the envious screams of the throng of fans. And although Tom's assistant Laurel was waiting for them in the limo, Annie was too excited to let anything spoil her mood.

As they were driven towards the West Side, Tom thrilled Annie by inviting her for dinner. He had Laurel check his diary, and they chose a day ten days from now, November 7th. Annie saw it written in black and white as the car came to a halt outside her home.

'I don't suppose you've got a copy of *Selected Speeches* at hand, do you?' asked Tom.

'Sure. I'll run up and get it, unless you – you both, that is – unless you want to come up.'

'I can't,' said Tom, though he did step out of the limo with her. He tapped on the chauffeur's window. 'Drive to that deli and get me a Diet Coke, will you?'

He waited outside as Annie ran up for the book, which she signed with her own name, not Dawn's, and brought down to him, breathless from the excitement, and the stairs. She handed it to him.

'Thank you, I look forward to reading it,' he said, and then he embraced Annie as behind them a cab was slowing almost to a halt.

'Here?' asked the driver.

'No,' said Alex, staring at Annie in Tom's arms. 'She's not home. Take me back downtown.'

The cab accelerated away. Alex didn't turn to see Tom step into his limo because he hadn't liked what he'd seen the first time. The only thing of which he was sure was that he'd been a fool to deny his feelings for Annie. What had scared him? he wondered. And why had he been so arrogant as to believe she would wait for him? She was a famous actress, now being chased by a Hollywood star. He felt a sudden anger and disappointment that he'd not tried to win her before.

Back in her apartment, Annie headed straight for the phone to call Barbara. Tom Sterling was a dream come true.

Tom Sterling had asked her out on a date! She pressed the play button on the answering machine and poured herself a cranberry apple as she listened to messages from Tamara, Dave, Maurice and then one from Alex saying that he was sorry, and would she call him when she got in.

The machine clicked off. Annie was amazed how the sound of his voice affected her, even while she was excited about Tom. She decided to ring back. So what if it was a quarter of twelve? Alex would be up, and she could tell him about Tom. That'd show him!

She dialled the number, her heart thumping. A woman answered. 'Yes?'

Annie thought of hanging up to redial, but then said, 'Um, I was trying to reach Alex Lubotsky.'

'Hang on.' Pam put her hand over the phone and pretended to call out. 'He must be in the shower. Do you want to leave a message?'

'No,' said Annie. 'No message at all.'

She slammed down the phone, and dialled her best friend's line. It rang and rang but there was no answer, so feeling upset and alone, she shuffled into her bedroom and flopped onto her bed. Damn Alex! Damn him! How was it possible that he could spoil even an evening such as this?

In his limousine, Tom Sterling was flicking through the *Selected Speeches* of Senator Dawn Hope. 'You know,' he said to Laurel who was sitting on the seat opposite, 'I think she might be the one. I really do.'

'I think she might too. She's got it all. Why don't you ask her?'

'I will. When we have dinner, I definitely will.' He smiled. 'That's made me feel just great. In fact,' he added, 'it's made me feel like this.'

Stepping across to Laurel's seat, Tom slid his hand between her legs. Sighing inside, Laurel folded shut her Filofax, depressed the aerial of her mobile phone and dutifully unzipped the fly of Tom Sterling's trousers.

19

It was six thirty and already Annie was late. She had taken to walking to the studios recently, not only because in the autumn a blissful postcoital calm wrapped Manhattan after the ravishment of spring by summer, but because the ceaseless diet of heated, stale air in the studios of *Unto the Skies* had begun to make her feel ill. She needed this walk before the madness began, before she checked in her personality to assume another. She needed this walk on streets empty of gawping strangers; and she needed this walk today, more than ever, to clear her mind after a restless night.

Hearing Alex's voice had brought her back to the real world after the excitement of Tom Sterling's attention. She was not so fickle that she could dismiss Alex from her heart after a single invitation from another man. And much as Alex had upset her the night before, she had wanted to forgive him, and for him to explain. So when his lover had answered the phone with such glee in her voice it had felt to Annie that Alex was laughing at her, as Max had done all those years before. The Lubotsky twins obviously carried a bad gene, she thought. They needed to be loved but refused to give anything in return. She had been willing to give him one final chance, but he'd as good as spat in her face. She would never be so stupid again. Never. She was glad he was leaving the show now. It was only a shame that Washington wasn't further away.

Juggling her possessions in her hands, Annie skipped down the stairs of her building. She pushed open the heavy wooden door and almost collided with a woman who seemed to be coming in.

'Sorry,' she said, continuing down the front steps.

Then she heard a voice behind her.

'Do you like my hair?'

Annie glanced back over her shoulder, doubting that it was she being addressed. Yet, so early in the morning, there was no one else on the block.

'Excuse me?'

'I said I hope you like my hair.'

The woman took a step nearer. Suddenly, a wave of fear ran through Annie. She knew her! She was the gangly fan who waited outside the studio, the one who'd called herself Annie's biggest fan at the Costelloe's book signing. She had been hard to identify at first, because her hair had been cut and dyed until it looked exactly like the bob that distinguished Annie herself.

'It's very nice,' she said, walking away.

'I did it for you,' the woman said.

She had a thin, high-pitched voice that might usually have been considered unthreatening, perhaps even comic, but in Annie produced a sense of unease, adding, as it did, to the fan's peculiarity. Now the woman joined Annie, who held her ground.

'I came to show you my hair.'

'Thank you. But I have to go, to the studio.'

'I'll walk with you.'

'No, you can't,' Annie said, trying to be as forceful as she could, though she didn't know how she would stop the woman.

The fan seemed unperturbed. 'I wouldn't have dared ask before, but you gave me my voice. You empowered me.'

She smiled, making Annie feel she was being unreasonable. After all, this woman with her thin, white skin and delicate arms wasn't about to kill or rape her. Annie relented, thinking it would be safer to learn all she could about who the woman was.

'You can walk with me for a block.'

They set off side by side. The woman seemed unable, or unwilling, to walk in a straight line, so her shoulders kept colliding with Annie's. Looking down to check it wasn't she who was walking at a peculiar angle, Annie was shocked to see the fan struggling in high-heeled shoes identical to those worn by Dawn on the set.

'I usually like to be alone in the morning,' Annie said. 'To think.'

'You're such a sharp thinker, Dawn.'

'Please don't call me that,' Annie said. 'My name's Annie.'

'I know your stupid name,' the woman retorted sharply.

Annie was taken aback. 'Well, then, that's settled.'

They'd reached the junction at Central Park West, busy with cabs. Annie thought of hailing one, but realised she still knew nothing about her stalker. As it stood now, the woman held an unpleasant advantage.

'You haven't told me your name,' Annie said.

'I don't have to.'

'It's only fair, isn't it?' said Annie, acting sisterly. 'You obviously know a lot about me.'

'Yes, I do. I know everything.'

Annie shivered at the thought.

'You shouldn't have been with that man the other night,' the woman added quickly.

'What man?' Annie asked, stopping to glare at her.

'Mr Lubotsky. The writer. He's a snake and he wants you.'

'What? God! How did you know about him anyway?'

The woman made a stupid face to suggest that Annie was asking a childish question. 'I saw you, didn't I!' she said. 'I saw him and I saw you and I saw him leave.'

'Where were you?' Annie asked sternly.

The woman lifted both hands in front of her eyes, and wiggled her index fingers. She said nothing.

'I could have you arrested. Do you know that?' Annie looked about her on the street, as if searching out a cop. 'For harassment.'

Suddenly, the woman reached into her bag. Annie leapt back, terrified, but all she was being offered was a slice of carrot cake. The icing was thick and soft and dented by the woman's firm grip. She held it out to Annie.

'It's for your birthday,' she said.

'But it's not . . .' she began, before remembering that Dawn Hope's birthday party had been taped two weeks earlier, and would be transmitted that day.

'That's kind of you,' said Annie. 'I'd like to write and thank you. What's your address?'

The woman smiled. 'No need. We'll be seeing each other often.'

'No,' Annie replied. 'I don't think we will.'

'But I love being with you.'

'I'll be with you every day at three in the afternoon. On *Unto the Skies*.'

Annie felt that was the right kind of thing to say.

'That isn't enough,' the woman said.

Annie decided to change tack. 'Look, I don't care. I'm busy. And I'm late for work. I'm sorry, but that's the way it is. And if you appear at my door again, I'll call the police. Do you understand that?'

'Temper, temper,' the woman replied.

Why this should have annoyed Annie more than any-thing else, she didn't know, but in response she flung the cake into the street and ran towards a cab just dropping off a fare.

'Where to?' the driver asked.

'53rd, East Side.'

As the cab pulled away, Annie turned to see the woman

in the road, on her knees, as she tried to scoop the cake back into her hands.

Once on set, Annie found it hard to concentrate. She told Johnson Bell, one of the show's most experienced actors, how her stalker had followed her from the apartment.

'You'll be fine,' he said to calm her. 'So long as you never get trapped into a conversation. It'll make her think you want to be her friend.'

'Too late!' said Annie, biting on her lower lip. 'Should I call the police?'

'Nothing they can do. Not unless she hurts you.'

This frightened Annie. 'Does that happen?'

'No,' he said, giving her a hug. 'It's only us men you need to be scared of,' and he squeezed her and swung her around.

'Have you two lovebirds finished?' asked Monty Prindle, 'because we're going to tape.'

Annie and Johnson were powdered and brushed and then they took their places on set. Quiet reigned.

'Stand by aaand it's *Unto the Skies*, episode 12069, taaaake one.'

DAWN

And thank the Lord the Cold War *is* over, William. The world's a much safer place for us all.

WILLIAM

If you ask me, we should keep the big guns aimed that way for a few years yet.

DAWN

I know you're a veteran, William, I know that. But don't you think we should show a little understanding?

WILLIAM
It's easy for you to say. You're a woman.

DAWN
That's right, I am. And I'm proud of being a woman if it means showing a little understanding. You men are so belligerent! You rush headlong into everything and then you get surprised when there's a fight. Well, just maybe there's a better way. If we all looked into our hearts, then fewer people would be looking down gun barrels.

WILLIAM
You sound like Mary.

DAWN
She is my mother, and I can see her hurting. Why don't you explain what happened between you and Vanessa?

WILLIAM
You think so?

DAWN
Yes. Compromise a little. Try to see it both ways. Get rid of the big guns!

WILLIAM
(EMBRACING DAWN)
You've an answer for everything, don't you, my dear?

DAWN
Call it womanly intuition.

WILLIAM
I hope you're right. Thank you, Dawn. I love Mary,
and I don't know what I'd do without her. I hope it's
not too late.

DAWN
It's never too late to give love the chance it deserves,
William. Never.

WILLIAM
Never? Let's wait and see . . .

Annie and Johnson held the embrace till Monty shouted out
that the tapes were good, and that the crew should move
onto the next scene. Annie looked up and, to her surprise,
saw Alex standing by the set. He rarely came by any more,
knowing that he would be pestered by fawning actors urging
more, and better, attention for their characters.

Annie stepped out of the set's bright light.

'You're very convincing,' he told her.

'It's your wonderful writing,' she said with undisguised
sarcasm as she skipped out of the way of a thick camera
cable snaking under her feet.

'Annie, I hope you're not angry about the other night.
There was nothing I could do.'

She felt a knot tighten in her stomach. To make matters
worse, Faith was walking towards them. Annie had always
marvelled at Faith's ability to sniff out brewing trouble.

'I called you last night,' continued Alex. 'Did you hear
my message?'

'No. Anyway, I was busy.'

Pam had told Alex that a woman had called. He was glad
to find that Annie hadn't been mistaken for the pestering
Charlie.

'I watched you on Paddy Darwin,' he said. 'You were
wonderful.'

'Thank you.'

'I saw it too,' said Faith, arriving to lean aggressively. 'It was disgusting the way Darwin referred to my bust.'

Briefly lowering his eyes, Alex couldn't help thinking that Darwin's namesake, Charles, would have been quite impressed with the evolutionary sophistication of Faith's cleavage in a city suffering such a paucity of single, straight men.

'Faith, I'm sorry about that,' said Annie, who really didn't feel like having this argument now. 'There was nothing I could do.'

'You didn't have to laugh!'

'No,' said Annie with resignation. 'I didn't.'

'I don't even remember it,' lied Alex. 'I wouldn't worry.'

'Huh,' grunted Faith, then, almost under her breath, she told Alex, 'She'll try anything to knock me down,' before clicking her heels onto the set, where she was required.

'I'm going to my dressing room,' Annie said. 'Bye.'

'Annie, it was you I came to see.'

She stared at him for some time, but now he was with her she couldn't hate him as she had this morning, nor could she find the courage to turn him away. Yet again, he was melting the ice around her heart. 'Come on, then.'

Once they were inside the tiny room, Alex knocked against the walls. 'Can you hear through these?' he asked.

'I don't think so,' she said, sitting in front of the mirror.

'Good. Can you promise to keep a secret?'

'Absolutely,' said Annie, knowing that there had never been anything she'd kept hidden from Barbara.

'Then listen to this.' Although he changed many details, and although he kept secret his love affair with Susan Grant, Alex proceeded to tell Annie that he'd been writing Dawn's lines as a way of testing the public's mood for a possible election bid by the First Lady.

'Are you serious?' said Annie.

Alex nodded, evidently pleased with himself.

'So when she said those things at the high school in Birmingham . . .'

'Exactly!'

Annie could hardly believe it. True, there'd been plenty of speculation about Alex's hidden agenda, but she had always assumed that he had taken the job for Max. 'And that's why you're leaving, is it?' she asked. 'Because I'm no use to your plan any more?'

The way he was grinning annoyed Annie. She wanted to scream at him that he'd broken her heart by walking away, by keeping some slut in his apartment to scrub his back in the shower, by making her love him when he had no intention of loving her back. But she wasn't about to give him that pleasure. 'Are you just telling me this so I can know how clever you are?'

'I'm telling you because I've changed my mind,' he said.

'About leaving?' she asked, surprised, after all that had happened, how the news pleased her.

'Yes. About leaving and about the First Lady. I went to Washington yesterday and when I came back I sat down and I watched you on the Paddy Darwin show and I realised what I'd been missing all along. Annie, you're the one who should be running. You've got everything it takes.'

Annie was motionless and silent. She didn't know whether Alex was being serious or whether this was another of his games. Surely it had to be! It was insane to think she could be a candidate for President. Turning from him, she reached for a packet of Camel Lights forgotten by Ally Springer. She took one and lit up.

'I didn't know you smoked,' Alex said.

'I don't usually,' she said, staring at him with suspicion. 'But I don't usually get accosted by insane soap writers either.'

She puffed on the cigarette.

'See? You're a natural,' laughed Alex. 'You don't even inhale!'

'Have you come here just to make fun of me?' she said, twisting to sit in front of the mirror with her feet on the chair.

'God, no! I can't begin to tell you how excited I was watching you last night. You were perfect. And you've proved you can do it by getting twenty per cent in Chicago. We're already more than halfway there.'

'One little thing, Al,' said Annie, killing the cigarette in a cup. 'I'm an actress, not a politician.'

Alex grinned again. Only once before had Annie seen him like this, and that in a documentary about the Grant presidential campaign that had been another world to her. Now, like an Alice in Wonderland, it appeared that she'd magically stepped into that world herself.

'It's precisely *because* you're an actress that you're going to win. Don't you see? This,' he said, almost lovingly stroking the screen of Annie's TV, 'is the battlefield nowadays. This is where it's won, and you're going to be so much stronger than everyone else because you know how to use it. You've got an exceptional talent to make people feel what you want them to feel. You affect people here,' he said, pushing his fist into his stomach.

Annie looked at him as if he was mad. 'Um, I don't want to quibble about minor details, Al, but don't you think that voters should be made to think *here* instead?' She tapped her head. 'I don't happen to have a list of domestic policy ideas in my back pocket. My lists stop at toilet paper and melons and ice-cream. They never get to balanced budget amendments and civil rights. You know what I'm saying?'

'Do you know how many times I've wished I could have heard that from a politician?' said Alex excitedly. 'These guys get so carried away with ideals they forget that people don't want to think.' Now he surprised her by taking her hand in his. 'Besides, it's no longer possible to have ideas that'll appeal to the majority of Americans. There isn't a majority any more. We're just so many minorities wanting what's best for each of us. That means the *only* place we're united is in our hearts. Ideas should be like . . . like the wrapping on candy. We only need them to give the TV pundits something to argue about.'

Annie continued to stare at Alex in utter amazement.

'OK!' He walked to the door and leant against it. 'Think of it like this,' he said, speaking very fast. 'Imagine you've got a crowd of people on Broadway and they see some black kid running out and getting killed by a speeding car that's driven by a white guy. OK? Now I guarantee that everyone there would have a different idea about, say, what should happen to the driver, or whether the driving exam was too simple, or if the boy was undisciplined because he was black, those kinds of things. But they would all feel sorry for him. *That's* the bond, and it's your territory. People's hearts and souls. Their basic humanity.'

'I'd be the kid!'

'You'd be the person exciting those emotions, yes,' he said, sure that she could affect others as she'd affected him.

Suddenly, they heard a knock on the door. 'Shit!' whispered Alex. 'Do you think they heard?'

The knock came again.

'Just sit there,' said Annie. 'It's probably wardrobe.' Annie opened the door. 'Vince!'

'Faith said you wanted to see me abo—' Vince stopped dead when he saw Alex sitting in the dressing room. 'Well, what a fucking surprise!'

'Alex dropped by to talk about something,' said Annie.

'I bet he did! Something about going it alone, perhaps?'

said the Executive Producer in the tone of someone proud to have foiled their plot.

Alex stood to shake Vince's hand. He hoped the producer hadn't heard him talking with Annie. 'I wanted to know how Annie felt about your sexual harassment idea.'

'Yeah!' said Vince sarcastically. 'Sure you did!'

'It's true,' said Annie.

One of the benefits of being an actress, Annie knew, was that deceit became second nature.

Vince, however, didn't seem convinced. He thrust his hands into his pocket, and said, 'Let me tell you, I am no noodle-head. OK? I am not some dumb fuck who can be walked over. I have been the captain of this ship for too long to have you two try and sink it. Are you with me? So, Mr Lubotsky, when you've finished your scheming I'd like to see you in my office. And Annie, you and I need to talk about your contract. That's *if* I renew, of course. OK? Alex, I'll be waiting.'

Vince scurried off. Annie closed the door behind him.

'What was all that about?' she said.

'I don't know, but I don't think he heard. Obviously Faith sent him down for some reason.'

'That woman doesn't need reasons,' she said, pouring herself a glass of grapefruit juice. She offered some to Alex, who said no. Swilling the drink around in her glass, she spoke with her eyes fixed on the spinning liquid. 'Tell me one thing, Al. If I did this, would it be as Annie or as Dawn?'

'I see *you* doing this and I see *you* being able to carry it off because of your skills. Now, maybe you'd need to change your name to Dawn to make it simpler to . . .'

'Stop it,' Annie said, holding up a hand. 'You're actually being serious, aren't you?'

'Yes, because I know we could win. You've already got *Selected Speeches* as your manifesto, you've got national recognition, you've got ten million loyal fans who'll vote for you without thinking, and you've got a better chance than anyone I can think of.'

Annie nodded as if persuaded, but then, speaking gently, she said, 'And can you tell me why would I want to do this?'

'Why?' Alex said, laughing. 'Why? Because everybody wants to be President!'

'Uh-uh,' Annie said, shaking her head. 'Not me. I don't.'

Alex's laugh spluttered like a scooter running out of petrol. 'You're joking,' he said.

'No!'

'No? No?' said Alex with utter incredulity. 'You don't have *any* desire to be the first woman President in the history of the United States? To be the most, the most important woman in the world? How can you possibly say that? That's so insane it's unthinkable.'

'Not to me it isn't. I'm not you. I'm an actress. That's what I like doing.'

'So think of it as your greatest acting challenge. That's what Ronnie did. It's all Presidents ever do. Convincing people you're doing the right thing is ten times more important than actually doing it.'

She smiled wryly. 'You're as cynical as Max was, aren't you?'

'Not at all. I really believe the country could use some-one like you. I mean, constitutionally we're out of kilter. The President has way too much power as things stand. If you win, you'll be able to devote your time to bringing the people together and leave the governing to Congress. You already know the people want you. Jesus, they're even giving you money without you asking for it. In Chicago they're voting for you without you being on the ticket. It's clear that they want someone with a little decency and purity and honesty as a figurehead in the White House. There's nothing remotely cynical about that, Annie. It's democracy at work, and it's an opportunity to bring this country together.'

'Alex! Please listen to me. I–am–an–actress!'

'Why do you keep saying that? Don't you care about this country?'

Annie had to smile at that. 'That's low, Alex Lubotsky, that's really low.'

Alex laughed too. 'All I'm saying is that there must be some things you care about, aren't there?'

'Of course,' she said, thinking how with Jerry and his friends in San Francisco she had spent hours discussing how and why America was going wrong. They had all believed that with a little compassion and humanity, the country could become proud of itself again. 'Of course I do, but they're not Dawn's ideas, they're mine.'

'And you'll be the candidate. We can run with your ideas. What I'm saying is that we'll use Dawn as a platform. We . . .'

The line producer's voice coming through the speaker in the corner of the dressing room interrupted them.

'Vanessa, Dawn, William and Carrie. Scene seven, Studio B.'

'I have to go,' said Annie, checking herself in the mirror.

Alex stood looking at her, blocking her way.

'Alex, please! What do you expect me to say?'

'How about yes?'

'You know,' she said, 'I remember being taken to Washington as a kid, on a tour of Capitol Hill.'

'I did that too.'

'Right. How did it feel?'

'It felt like I never wanted to leave.'

'Well, there you go. I felt like I wanted to go home and play with my toys and my imaginary friends. I thought it felt like a great big boring school. I never dreamed of becoming President. I wanted to be an actress, and that's what I am, and right now I think I'm making a pretty good job of it. I don't want to throw that away.'

Alex looked dejected. He had expected Annie to be surprised and flattered and thrilled. He didn't think he knew anyone else who wouldn't want to be President.

'Just do this, will you?' he pleaded. 'Don't sign your contract for a few days. Just think about this, think about what it would mean. Please. And don't forget that I wouldn't be here if I didn't believe in my heart that we could win.'

Annie stared at him, and then she said, 'Has Vince really suggested a sexual harassment story? Funny! I never took him to be a champion of women's rights.'

'Consuela? Consuela!'

From behind her, Faith Valentine heard the pitter-patter of tiny Mexican feet.

'Sit down, would you?' Faith said, tapping a finger on the rail of one of the ornate chairs that surrounded the Hoopers' glass dining table.

Consuela silently obeyed. Before her was a single sheet of white paper and a pen. 'We writing another letter?' she asked.

'That's right, we are. Put down your sister's address in Queens this time.'

Consuela shrugged her shoulders (Faith had spoken to her about that!) and did as she was asked.

'Very good,' said Faith, looking over Consuela's shoulder. 'Now write Dear Mr Producer, comma, and go down a line. Are we ready?'

The shrug came again. During the years that Consuela had cooked, cleaned and lied for Faith, she had never felt anything but pity for the woman. The only reason that she had not left was that she'd covered the tracks of Faith's adulteries for so long that her silence came at a very high price.

Behind her, Faith was ambling about the room, collecting her thoughts. 'Dear Mr Producer,' she repeated, and then, very slowly, she dictated the rest of the letter. 'Once upon a time I was a big fan of *Unto the Skies*, but not any more. In the old days there were a whole lot of reasons to watch the show. Vanessa was my favourite character. She still is, but I can't watch any more because Vanessa is not on nearly often enough, as she should be. There is too much of the one with the pig face – Dawn – and not enough of Vanessa. Everyone I know likes Vanessa more, and do you think anyone is interested in politics, or something? We want to see people love and cry. I was so bored with all the politics that I stopped watching a long time ago. I watch *The Bold and the Beautiful* which is much better.

'New paragraph, Consuela, then: If you had good stories I would watch. Vanessa and Paolo would make a very attractive couple. She might be older than he is but she doesn't look it. Vanessa would be good at running Brendan Air Lines, if she was given the chance. Yours an ex-viewer. Sign it any old Hispanic name, and then take it to the mailbox. There's a stamp on Mr Hooper's desk.'

'Yes, Mrs Valentine.'

Faith lifted a dying iris from the arrangement above the fire. She snapped it vigorously in half and handed it to Consuela as she passed.

'I think that was rather good, don't you?'

'Yes, Mrs Valentine. They are always very good.'

'Mm, I think so too. I might try my hand at a novel one day.'

20

Remarkably enough it had been a week now, and Annie had said nothing to Barbara about Alex's crazed offer. It was, however, often on her mind, causing her to forget her lines and struggle to sleep. She was also listening with a greater interest than usual to the media coverage of that week's midterm elections. Observing the candidates on TV, she wondered how she might perform herself and whether, if she were to win, the sensation would be any different from the one she'd enjoyed two weeks before when taping Dawn's electoral success. She'd felt a strange satisfaction standing, arms raised, before her supporters on *Unto the Skies*, almost as if the celebrations were for real. Annie was sure it would be exhilarating to be elected a leader of people, and this thought made her consider accepting Alex's bizarre proposal. Were she to say no, she knew she would be burdened for ever with a degree of regret. What would she tell her grandchildren? 'I had a chance to run for President, but I didn't want to be a part of history. I stayed on a soap instead!'

Once or twice, Annie had watched Alex share his opinions on the pundit shows and had wondered how she would feel seeing him defend and support another candidate in the '96 campaign. As the most respected and sought-after campaign manager in the United States, he would surely be employed by someone. Why, then, shouldn't it be she?

There was, of course, an abundance of reasons. For a start, Annie had no desire to change her name to

Dawn Hope. As it was, she could barely remember her days before Dawn. The six writers of *Unto the Skies* had been making things worse by incorporating Annie's actual expressions, characteristics and strengths with those of her screen character. At times she felt she was being asked to act herself, only with different lines coming out of her mouth. And although she remained able to see light between herself and Dawn, she feared that if she ran for President she would become like many of the other cast members who'd been playing their roles for so long that they no longer acted at all. They merely *were*. To win with conviction, she would have to become Dawn and endure the slings and arrows of negative campaigning (the midterms were proving particularly malevolent) while standing as someone other than herself. This in itself was almost enough to make her turn Alex's offer down with no further thought.

Annie had been so distracted by all this that she'd given very little consideration to her dinner with Tom Sterling. Barbara was much more excited. She wanted to be invited to a Hollywood wedding with the tabloid helicopters circling overhead and Liz Taylor crying beside Jacko and Bubbles in the second row.

Tom sent a car to collect Annie from the studio. He had told her not to dress up, but she knew what these stars were like and imagined that Tom's idea of a downmarket joint would be somewhere that displayed prices on its menu. She was more than a little surprised, then, when her limousine stopped outside a shop in the Lower East Side.

'He's inside,' said the driver, gesturing towards Regina's Health Food Store and Café.

'Really?' said Annie. 'Oh.'

Regina's had the musky whiff of mixed herbs and spices that all such outlets shared. This was odd, Annie thought, since vegetarian dishes tended to taste of almost nothing at all. The store was typically earthy. There was sawdust on the floor, and chipboard shelves racked with lentils and rices and dried fruits and every assortment of sugarless, funless organic foods packaged in dreary cellophane and suffering from the lack of gandiness that made supermarket shopping seem almost decadent.

At the back of the store, which was brightly lit by crude fluorescents on the ceiling, there were five or six wooden tables. At one sat a couple. The man was leaning across his bean stew to deep-kiss his lover. At another sat Tom Sterling, his back to the door. He was wearing torn jeans, sneakers and an old brown leather jacket. He was reading a book through his dark glasses.

'Tom?' said Annie.

The actor stood and smiled his perfect smile.

'Aren't you looking chic!' he said, apparently as a compliment. 'I hope you don't mind being here. I didn't want us to be seen together.'

'Oh, right!' said Annie, feeling ridiculous now in her fifteen-hundred-dollar Calvin Klein suit.

'Sit down, please.' He narrowed his eyes. 'We must eat!'

Tom had an actor's habit of imparting the most modest statements with gravity. He used his pauses to great effect, with the result that he managed at all times to keep attention on himself. It was as if he perceived movie cameras perpetually at his side. Now he tapped a finger against the sheet of lime-green paper that served as a menu. 'I ordered something already. To get them off my back. Go ahead, why don't you?'

Annie looked at the menu with more than a little dismay. For some reason, she was overcome with a sudden desire for an inch-thick steak, suitably bloody and rare. The tofu burger on offer simply wouldn't do.

'I'm having the mango and squash soup,' said Tom. 'Then the four-root fricassee. It's not bad.'

Annie shrugged her shoulders and folded the gruesome menu. 'OK. I guess I'll join you.'

'I hope so,' said Tom cryptically.

The waitress, a dour teenager with a face crowded with metal studs and loops, curled a lip towards Annie as if she'd been hooked by an invisible fishing line.

'What beers do you have?' Annie asked.

'Roo— '

'Root beer, right!' interrupted Annie. 'Um, then I'll take a strawberry milkshake.'

'Goat, soya or skimmed?' the girl asked.

'Regular, thanks.'

'Skimmed,' she said, shuffling away.

'Nice place. You come here often?' Annie asked, picking out a brown roll that looked alarmingly normal from the outside.

'When I can,' Tom said humourlessly. 'When I want some quiet.'

'She certainly didn't seem too star-struck, you're right.'

'That type never shows it,' said Tom. 'Whatever they feel. She'll want my autograph later.'

Annie doubted this, but made no comment.

It was Tom who spoke again, 'This,' he said, flattening his hand on top of Dawn Hope's *Selected Speeches*, 'was one of the most moving, inspirational, daring books that I have read in a long time. I was impressed that you had the courage to look America's problems in the eyes.'

'Oh, thank you,' said Annie because it seemed too obvious to point out, yet again, that she wasn't Dawn Hope, that she just looked like her.

'I want to ask you . . .' He was interrupted by the girl bringing the dark orange soup, and he waited until she'd dumped the bowls on the table before continuing, his voice lowered. 'I want to ask you if you would consider stepping into the political arena with me.'

Ripping too hard with the surprise of his question,

Annie sent her wheat crackers flying from their crinkly wrapping. One plopped into her soup. 'Shit!' She lifted the soggy cracker out with her spoon. 'Sorry. Um, I didn't know you wanted to go into politics,' she said.

The actor had picked up his soup bowl. He talked across the top of it, his words, fittingly, passing through the hot steam. 'He may have been the biggest asshole this side of Nixon, but Ronald Reagan is a role model to me.'

'You want to become President?'

Tom breathed in sharply, as if the concept was sexually exciting. 'Let me show you something.' From the inside pocket of his jacket he took a brown rectangle of newspaper, cut from a 1989 edition of the *Washington Post*. It was a report on a nationwide survey carried out among high school pupils. Of those asked, it said, less than a third had been able to name George Bush, yet all knew of Tom Sterling. Even more interesting was the fact that sixty per cent of the kids said they'd like to see a tough guy like Sterling as President.

'They're voters now,' Tom said. 'They listen to everything I say. I mean, if I went on record saying I liked to eat here, then this place would be packed every night. Guaranteed. It's the same with politics. I've got enough fans to take me all the way.'

For a moment, Annie wondered whether Alex was behind this. Had he thought she would find it hard to say no to her favourite movie star? She decided to see how serious Tom actually was. 'Don't you think running just because you're very famous is a little irresponsible?'

'No,' he said with great drama. 'I care about a great many things. I care that there are more black youths in jail than in college. I care about minorities. I care about Tibet, about the murder of elephants in Africa. I worry about the ozone layer and, yes, I think masturbation should be taught in schools as a part of AIDS prevention. I believe it's my duty as a world citizen to use the blessing and

347

support of the American people to make a difference to the way we all live. And I care that I have a running mate with the same strength of purpose, the same ideals and hopes. I've been looking, and now I've found that person. You!'

A week ago Annie would have burst out laughing. Now she was intrigued. Although it was becoming increasingly evident that Tom was full of shit, he remained the most popular movie star in America. The exhilarating, terrifying truth was that together, they would probably win, and she would actually be given the chance to do some good.

'I have never been so moved as I was by this book,' Tom continued. 'My hope is that you and I could create the first Buddhist Administration in America. I'm going to be open about that from the start.'

'I'm not sure that would be wise, would it?'

Tom banged his fist on the table. 'No lies,' he declared. 'No promises we can't fulfil. Nothing but the truth and the whole truth, so help me God.'

Annie thought that if Tom was so keen on the truth, she'd better share a little of hers. 'Tom,' she said, 'I think I should tell you that I didn't write the speeches in my book. They were written for my character.'

Tom looked at her, shaking his head, narrowing his eyes, smiling. Then he took one of her hands in both of his. 'I know that, but no one but you could have thought the thoughts behind the words. I heard the values of a Zen believer on every page. I know we have to admit we don't have any answers, but that in time, they will come, as surely as the grass grows and birds sing in the sky. I'm right, aren't I?'

She said yes because, in truth, he'd lost her. Sensing this, Tom let go of her hand and filled his glass with water. He emptied Annie's into the jug.

'This empty glass,' he said, 'this is you.' He poured some water into it. 'You are ready to receive. But this

one,' he said, touching the rim of his full glass, 'this is
the Washington politicians who are full of their own vain
beliefs.' As Tom poured into the full glass, the water
spilled over the table, splashing onto the floor. Annie
pulled her chair back and held her napkin at the table's
edge. 'You see,' said Tom, 'they cannot listen and learn
when they are already full.'

He leant back, clicked his fingers and told the waitress
there'd been an accident. With a cloth under her foot
she trudged around the table like a retarded folk dancer.
Annie was beginning to doubt Tom's sanity.

'I think I'm going to need time to think,' she said.

'Before the first step is taken the goal is reached, Annie.
Before the tongue is moved the speech is finished. More
than brilliant intuition is needed to find the origin of the
right road, and the crow flies west only in the moonlight.
You shouldn't forget that.'

'How could I?' she said. 'Oh, look, Tom, what a treat.
Here comes our four-root fricassee.'

The following day, was midterm election day across the
whole of the United States. Midway through President
Grant's term, candidates were running for Governors'
seats and for the Senate and House of Representatives
as well as for local office. The weather in the east was
unusually clement for early November, which favoured
the Democrats, and Annie enjoyed her early morning
walk to the polling station. As she sat pulling the levers,
she wondered whether her own name would be included
on the ballot in '96. The idea both frightened and excited
her. At least she had been given some time to think.
Tom Sterling had merely wanted to touch base before
flying to Europe for a new movie. Controversially, he
had beaten a long line of accomplished European actors
to win the lead role in *Ludwig*, a major motion picture
about Beethoven. Alex, too, was being patient. Ideally,

he had said, he would want to announce her candidacy no sooner than late the following summer, when raising the necessary twenty million dollars would begin.

For now, Annie's choices were more simple, with Mario Cuomo for Governor the most obvious. She was sure that he would win easily against his Republican opponent, but she wanted to play her part in that victory.

Yet as the day wore on she heard news that the Democrats were faring even worse than expected. By the end of the day, a Republican rout seemed to be in progress.

Annie was keen to watch the actual results as they started being confirmed after ten, and was preparing to leave her dressing room when there was a polite knock at the door. She opened it to see Vince standing there with, of all things, a smile on his face.

'Hi,' he said, 'how was your day?'

'Long.'

'Things'll slow down now your election's done, don't you worry. Especially when you renounce the governorship.'

'Renounce it?' Annie hadn't seen anything about this in the story projections. 'Dawn only won it today,' she said, though they'd taped two weeks before.

Vince winked, and smiled some more. 'Just an idea we're toying with. To cut down on the politics. It's nothing to worry about, just an idea.'

As Annie leant on the door, it swung half-closed. She wished she could close it altogether. 'Vince, I'm tired, I . . .'

'You want to relax. I understand.'

This willingness to please was unexpected and peculiar. Annie found it disturbing.

'That's right,' she said. 'I need to put my feet up.'

'You'd be very welcome to do just that.'

Annie looked bemused. Did she need permission from the Executive Producer to relax?

'Don't tell me you didn't get my note,' he said.

Annie shook her head.

Vince slapped his hand on his forehead. 'I invited you for a drink.'

She wondered whether she'd been subtly releasing pheromones for the past few weeks. Men kept asking her to dinner or for a drink or to spend the next two years running for the American presidency. She had never been so popular before.

'I'm a little bushed, to be honest.'

Vince opened his mouth to say, 'a little bush can go a long way,' but instead managed to look truly upset when he told her how much he'd wanted to have a relaxed chat about her contract. 'I've got an interesting proposal for you,' he concluded.

'Not another!'

'Excuse me?'

'Oh, nothing,' said Annie, although she was thinking that if G&H Productions had chosen to increase the size of her contract, then it would ease her decision about whether to stay. 'OK, Vince. I'll come for a very quick drink.'

'Great! You take your time,' he said. 'I'll nip back, make things cosy. You know where it is?'

She said she did, and within half an hour she was outside his door. Vince had changed and shaved and was stinking of cologne. He was wearing a burgundy silk shirt, cream-coloured trousers and black velvet loafers. The lights were mysteriously low, and Sinatra was sounding from the stereo.

Once he had taken Annie's coat, Vince gestured towards the love seat beneath his mural. 'What can I get you? You're a vodka lady, aren't you?'

'I'd prefer some white wine?'

'Coming up,' then, from the kitchen, he shouted, 'It's Italian, of course. It's got a nice body!'

He returned with the wine in a cooler, another bourbon for himself and a bowl of garlic bagel chips, and although he sent a customary wink towards Annie as he offered them, she found his manner puzzling. In his gauche way, it seemed he was actually trying to be charming.

'You like Frankie?' he asked, sitting in the armchair closest to her.

'Of course.'

'He's got an enduring talent, Annie. That's not common, believe me. But,' he paused to take a slurp of his drink, 'it's something you've got too.'

'Me?' she said with some surprise.

'Absolutely. There's something about the way you act that makes people watch you.' He uncrossed his legs and, with the glass between his hands, leant forward. 'It makes *me* want to watch you.'

'That's very nice of you, Vince. I thought, I mean you never . . .'

'Are you nervous?'

'No!'

'Good! That's a nice top thing, by the way. Beige suits you.' He smiled at her again, and stared intently. Frank was singing 'I've got you under my skin.'

Annie thought she'd probably leave soon.

'Are you sure you're OK?' he asked, an oddly benevolent look on his face. 'You look like you're maybe a little on edge.'

'I've had a long day!'

'You want something to help you relax?'

'I'm fine.'

Vince held up a finger, smiled again, and then ambled out of the room and into a bathroom that Annie knew had a mirrored ceiling and a bath built to resemble a four-poster bed. When he returned he made fists of both hands. He held them out to her. 'Say the magic word!'

'Vince, really I'm fine with this,' Annie said, holding up her wine glass.

Vince didn't budge. 'Abracadabra,' Vince mouthed.

'Abracadabra,' Annie said solemnly.

'Da-daaaa!' he sang, opening his hands. There was a small, round grey pill in his left and an orange and white capsule in the right. 'It's magic!' he whispered. 'A celestial cocktail of Vincey's old friend, Valium, and his new buddy, Prozac.'

Annie began to laugh. 'Are you taking Prozac? Since when?'

'Since a few days ago. It puts me in a better frame of mind to deal with the things that matter. Like you.'

Now he sat beside her on the love seat, so close that his cologne began to make her eyes itch. She put aside the pills and rubbed at an eye.

'You want to take a nap?' he asked.

'No,' said Annie, rather loudly. 'No, I'm going to go soon. Didn't you say you wanted to discuss my contract?'

On the way from the studio, Annie had resolved to accept the G&H contract if the money was good enough. After all, acting, not politics, was her game.

'I certainly do. I want to tell you that I'm on your side, Annie. I always have been, ever since your audition. I mean, Alex didn't want you, not at all, but I said, "She's our girl." And I was right. You've been great.'

'But . . .'

'But, nothing!' Vince laughed and patted her on the back. 'You funny girl.'

Annie could feel his hand motionless on her back, but there was no way to escape it unless she rose to her feet, which she thought would be a little obvious. She chose, instead, to hurry the conversation along. 'So you want to renew?'

'We might, we might not,' he said. 'Maybe that depends on you.'

Now his hand began gently to stroke her back. If only she had been able to dissociate the sensation from its provider, she would have rather enjoyed it. Whenever she was touched by another these days, she felt the tension flood out, making her aware how much was trapped inside.

She inched forward on the seat until she was almost falling off. Vince's hand followed her.

'See,' he said. 'There are a lot of options. I could let you go now, or I could give you a one- or two-year contract, *or,*' he lifted his hand from her back, 'we could talk about four or five years, about a lot of money.' Now the hand was back on her body, this time tickling its way up her thigh. 'Couldn't we?'

Annie jumped to her feet. She wanted to hear more, to know how much cash he was talking about, but not like this, not with the slug leaving his trail up her leg. 'Excuse me,' she said, 'I have to go to the bathroom.'

She thought she heard Vince say 'Freshen up' as she hurried away, and in the room, in front of the flattering mirror, she stared at her flushed cheeks and hoped he wouldn't mistake the blush for excitement. She decided not to risk it. Her agent could deal with the contract. That's what she paid him for. She didn't have to be stuck here with this creep. She turned on the cold water and was about to splash her face when the lights suddenly went off, and all was utter darkness when she heard the door open. Vince came in. She couldn't make him out at all, but she could smell him – the cologne, the cigarettes and bourbon on his breath – and she could sense him in the tiny space.

'Vince,' she called out, 'what's going on?'

'Ssh,' he said. 'Sssh.'

She tried to move to the door but suddenly his hands were on her waist.

'Get off me!' she screamed out. 'Get off.'

354

'Sssh. Just relax,' he whispered. 'And enjoy.'

With all her might, Annie lifted her knee into Vince's groin. He cried out, 'Fucking bitch!' as she scratched his face with her hand and twisted from his grip.

She found the door and yanked it open and ran, without looking back, through the living room and out into the corridor feeling, though he'd hardly touched her at all, as if she'd actually been raped.

By the time Annie arrived, tired from lack of sleep, at the studio the following morning, she'd decided to tell no one of the incident. She thought she'd rather live with her grotesque little memory than risk having others doubt her motives. It continued to amaze her that after millennia of women being abused, still their culpability was always an issue. If she accused Vince, questions would be asked about why she'd been alone in his flat discussing a matter that belonged in the office.

Annie was met at the studio by Vince's assistant, Dave, who handed her some new pages for the day's taping. It was not uncommon to be given new lines on the morning of shooting. Today, Annie didn't bother looking them over. G&H Productions had recently splashed out on Autocues for the actors, and she knew that making herself familiar with the additional dialogue would not be too demanding. In fact, she forgot all about the new pages until shortly after lunch when, as she was relaxing on set in between takes, Stefano Benedetti came up to her and said, 'Glad to see I get the chance at last.'

'Hi, Paolo.'

Although the Italian was so deeply in love with himself that he assumed the rest of the planet was in love with him too, Annie quite liked him. At least he was no hypocrite, and he usually livened up the day with his flirting.

'What do you mean?' Annie asked.

'The new scene,' said Paolo, sitting beside her on Dawn's living-room couch. 'Between you and me.'

Annie took from him the new pages, and as she read she became increasingly incensed. She could feel herself beginning to shake. 'I don't believe this,' she whispered.

'I know. You are a very lucky lady,' said Paolo.

Annie didn't reply, but marched to see the stage manager instead. 'Monty, get Vince down here, would you?'

'Ooooh, I see a-trouble-a-brewing,' sang Monty with good humour, but although he usually made Annie laugh, now her expression remained stern, so he asked for the Executive Producer to be summoned.

Annie was looking over the new pages once more, pacing around the studio while waiting for Vince to arrive. As he was seldom called to the set, tension had quickly spread, exciting the actors into a huddle of expectation. Faith seemed particularly titillated.

After a few minutes, Vince skittled in, tossing a golf ball from hand to hand. He had a nasty scratch beneath his left eye, and it was clear at once that he'd left his Prozac at home. 'What the fuck's going on?' he said to Monty, deliberately avoiding Annie as he walked by.

'Annie wanted a word.'

She felt like slapping Vince as soon as he turned her way. All her disgust had returned at once. 'I'm not doing this,' she said, holding up the pages. 'There's no way.'

Vince nodded. 'Let's go to my office and discuss it.'

'No. There is nothing to discuss. I am not doing a scene that we don't need.'

Vince jerked his neck from side to side like a cockerel about to crow. 'What the fuck do you know about what we need? I'm the Executive Producer and I say I've got to listen to what Oprah and Donahue and Sally frigging what's-her-name are crapping on about. If they do sexual harassment, *I've* got to do sexual harassment. Now the little viewers can see what the fuck's going

356

on out there, they're getting greedy. See? I need this scene.'

'That's not good enough, Vince,' said Annie. 'Not by a long shot. What I think is that it's in here to satisfy your own little fantasies.'

'Jesus Christ,' said Vince, turning to Monty. 'Give me the fucking script.' He glanced over the dialogue. 'I don't see a problem. Paolo comes into your office, he says you're a very attractive woman, and then he goes again.'

'But that's not all, is it?' shouted Annie. 'He also pushes me into a corner and touches my breasts. Does that ring any bells in your mind? Does it maybe strike a chord? Do I need to spell it out or is this conversation over?'

The studio was now as quiet as a church. For a second, Vince looked alarmed, but then he briskly wiped at the bubbles of sweat on his upper lip and, his voice rising to a whine, answered, 'We cannot screw the whole thing up because you've suddenly decided you're a star. Faith wouldn't act like this.'

Annie suddenly laughed. 'Faith doesn't act like anything, Vince! Faith doesn't act!'

'How dare you?' squealed Faith.

'In fact,' said Annie, feeling the resentment from last night beginning to boil over, 'Faith would like it. She *likes* getting fucked over. I don't.'

'How, I mean, what are you talking about?' spluttered Faith, who'd been enjoying the spectacle thus far.

Suddenly Annie didn't care that there was an audience. She had waited fifteen years for this. She turned to face her co-star. 'I'm talking about the fact that you became Vanessa because you fucked the producer. Bernie Hermann offered the part to me, and you knew it. You *knew* that, didn't you?'

'Keep the camera rolling,' Monty whispered into his headset.

Faith was trying to utter a sentence. 'I, I didn't know him before I . . .'

'Then how come he suddenly changed his mind?' asked Annie. 'Huh? It can't have been anything to do with your acting ability because you never had any. You were the class joke at Cornell Williams, or were you too stupid to realise that?'

Johnson Bell stepped between them. 'Girls, this is embarrassing. Let's stop it!'

Annie, behaving as no one had guessed she could, shoved Johnson out of the way and stepped nearer to Faith. She stared into the made-up eyes. 'I'm right, aren't I? You put out to steal that part from me but you don't have the guts to admit it.'

'She was jealous of me!' Faith told her audience. 'That's all I've ever known.'

'Faith,' Annie said quietly, 'how could anyone ever be jealous of you?' Then she turned to Vince. 'You picked the wrong girl last night, Vince. Try her next time. She's the easiest lay in New York.' Annie started to walk towards the studio exit, past an incredulous Paolo. 'Right, Paolo?'

'Where are you going?' Vince asked. 'People, where's she going?'

'Home,' said Annie.

'You can't!' He trotted after her. 'You can't do this. We're not finished yet.'

'Oh yes we are,' she said, slamming the studio door in the producer's face.

He followed her out, leaving Faith as the centre of attention. For a moment, she considered breaking down in tears but, buoyed by the departure of Annie, she straightened her back, tidied her hair and said, 'There are some people who just cannot handle the pressure. Now, is everyone ready for the next scene because I need to get home to my kids?'

Fearing that Vince might follow her, Annie bypassed her dressing room and ran to the street to hail a cab.

As she'd hoped, Alex was at home. He had decided to keep the headwriting job until Annie had made up her mind.

'I want you to tell me something,' she asked him, breathless still. 'If I agreed to do this, to become a candidate, would I get a real say in what goes on?'

'Annie!' he said, putting a comforting hand on her shoulder. 'You'll be the candidate. Of course you'll get a say.'

'Because I don't like half the things Dawn says,' she said angrily. 'Half the time she sounds like those asshole Republicans who won yesterday.'

The Democrats had suffered humiliating defeats across the country in the elections. The voters had chosen right-wing Republicans whose opinions ran contrary to almost everything Annie believed. She couldn't remember the last time an election had upset her so, and she believed in her heart that a terrible wound to the country had been inflicted by the voters.

'Do you think I'd run you for President on their issues?' Alex asked. 'Do you think I want to see electric chairs on street corners? Or immigrants getting spied on? I've been a Democrat all my life.'

'And you think . . .' she began, but then stopped. She sat on the edge of his sofa, and took a deep breath. Was she really going to go through with it because of one fight with Vince? Did two wrongs make a right?

'What?' Alex asked.

'Do you think I would stand a chance?' she asked 'I mean a real chance.'

'Yes, I do, and this is one thing I happen to know about.'

'Because something's got to be done about what happened yesterday, doesn't it, Al? We can't let these bastards take over the country. I mean,' she said, thinking aloud as

359

she remembered Tom Sterling's words, 'I mean, maybe there's a reason why all this has happened to me. Maybe I should do something about it. Try and do something – something good. I just don't know.' She looked up at him. 'Half of me understands that Dawn is some kind of national heroine and the other half is saying that the idea of Annie Marin becoming President is mad. It's like Elvis coming back to life.'

'No, it's not,' said Alex with fervour. 'This is possible, and that's what politics is all about. It may be the most impossibly possible thing you've ever thought of, but it can happen if you want it.'

'You think?' she asked uneasily.

'I think!'

'But I'd need a running partner, wouldn't I?'

'Yeah, but we'll find somebody.'

'Al,' she said, standing to face him now, 'I think I already have.'

21

S enator Dawn Hope's election as Governor of the state of Illinois on UBC's *Unto the Skies* produced the largest influx of mail ever known by the soap opera staff. Almost to a letter the fans rejoiced in her victory, a victory for common sense, Christian decency and women. And time after time, the correspondents expressed their sadness that there were so few politicians like Dawn. 'She makes you feel proud to be an American,' wrote one woman from Lincoln, Nebraska. 'With more like her, I'd sleep better at night,' said another. Alex could not have been happier. The responses confirmed everything he believed.

The contempt with which the American voters treated the incumbent politicians in the midterm Congressional elections confirmed to Alex that he had read the people right. Dawn Hope was, as a maternal, God-loving, Bible-quoting, jingoistic defender of the Constitution, exactly the sort of politician for whom the people had been voting. She could turn to those Americans troubled by the spectre of a new millennium and let down by stale religion and politics and offer them a simple creed to help make sense of their increasingly complex lives. She loved the sinners, if not the sins. Although the traditional American family was the foundation for her beliefs, she hadn't the heart to turn her back on cries for help from impoverished single mothers. She insisted on showing compassion before anger, understanding before incarceration. In fact, Alex believed Dawn was so loved because there was nothing about her to hate. It was upon this that he wished to build her presidential campaign. He was sure that if she remained suitably unfocused, her critics would have nothing with which to argue. The idea was almost Zen-like in its simplicity.

Yet while Alex was marvelling at the beauty of running a candidate with transparent ideals, Annie was putting together her thoughts for her campaign, now named 'New Dawn'. She did not consider them radical, nor difficult to impose, but saw them as the beliefs of a sensible, conscientious citizen. Rejecting the harsh politics that pandered to market forces and privileged interests, she believed in truth, morality and compassion for the less advantaged. She wanted to stand for the politics of common decency and the common man. Antipolitical politics, Jerry had called it. In fact, as Annie burned the midnight oil she was hearing his conspiracy-crazed, anticapitalist, Zen-believing voice in her head, and writing down words that were his.

Jerry hated the deceit of the nation's politicians, and resented their failure to grapple with the root causes of society's breakdown. He questioned the very structure of modern society, so when Annie wrote that she was interested in 'the questions behind the questions' she was remembering Jerry's phrase, as well as his insistence that crime and drug abuse were caused not by evil men but by the institutional capitalist structures that brought about such a desperate underclass. And it was Jerry who had convinced her that the justice system was designed to keep the public entertained. It was because they derived such pleasure from watching criminals being hunted, tried and incarcerated that the authorities made few attempts to tackle the causes of such lawlessness. Ever since lions were encouraged to have their way with Christians, the public had been hooked on the notion of justice as entertainment. Annie wondered if there might not be another way. She had even suggested a couple of Buddhist koans that touched upon understanding and forgiveness. It would, she knew, please Tom Sterling if he agreed to join her campaign.

Alex had been thrilled to know of Tom's political aspirations, and yet he was also convinced that it was for Dawn Hope, not Tom, that a path had been cleared to the White House. So he invited Tom to a meeting in the bar at the top of one of the World Trade Towers. The two sat at a dimly-lit table looking uptown, Alex with a bourbon, Tom drinking Perrier with extract of ginseng that he'd brought along to mix.

They spoke for a while about Dawn's promise, before Alex gestured towards the sleek Art Deco pinnacle of the Chrysler building, illuminated in the night sky.

'You know in 1930 the Chrysler architects were convinced they'd got the Empire State people beat when they'd finished. They were celebrating for months but then suddenly up came this other spire and that was it. The Empire State was the tallest building in the world, and there was nothing Chrysler could do.'

'But the guys who designed the Empire State had an advantage, didn't they?' said Tom, who was feeling at his most astute tonight. 'They knew what they had to beat.'

'Right,' Alex agreed, turning back from the window to face Tom, 'because they were patient they won the prize. I think the same applies to you.'

'You do? You mean I shouldn't run this time?'

Alex leant closer. 'The election in 2000 is going to define a thousand years,' he said, knowing that it was the language of a movie trailer that would most appeal to the actor. '2000 will be a year for heroes. 2000 will be the year for a candidate who can inspire people to believe in the future. 2000, Tom, 2000 can be yours.'

Tom took a sharp intake of breath and sat more upright

in his chair as he looked once more at the immense beauty of Manhattan.

'If you try in '96 and fail then you won't have a chance,' said Alex. 'People won't want a loser in 2000.'

'Why can't I run in 2000 for my second term?' he asked.

'Because it's a risk you shouldn't take.'

'So you think I should wait for six years?'

Now Alex smiled. 'No. Now's the time to get your experience. I think you should run as Dawn's partner. I think you could make a great Vice President.'

'I don't co-star, Alex.'

Alex nodded as if he understood, but then said, 'Given the choice of an Oscar for Best Supporting Actor or nothing, which would you take?'

Tom Sterling looked deep into Alex's eyes.

'Can she do it?' he asked.

'Yes,' Alex said. 'She will.'

'Then I'll think about it,' he said. 'And we'll talk in a couple of days' time.'

As soon as Tom Sterling agreed to join the ticket, a meeting was convened in Alex's apartment for the few aware of the campaign. Annie, late from the studio, rode the elevator up feeling nothing but pride in her involvement. Something that had seemed absurd and even obscene a mere month before, now, quite simply, felt right. She would be able to rock on her porch in her twilight years and know that, when given a chance, she had tried to make a difference.

'At least one of you made it!' said Alex when he answered the door to her. 'Tom's had to race to Vienna to prepare for *Ludwig*.'

Not long before, Annie would have been devastated by the news that she wouldn't be spending a promised evening with the star, but since the four-root fricassee her opinion of him had taken something of a nose dive. Far from being the most desirable man on earth, he had revealed himself to be merely another self-loving, vain, untrustworthy actor whose talent for absorbing other characters was so great because he was so shallow himself. He was like his own movies – quite entertaining once, but trite and tedious after that.

'Between you and me,' Alex whispered, 'I think it's no bad thing he's not here. We'll get more done.'

In the living room she was introduced to Charlie Canon, who'd been lured into the campaign team by the promise of significant office in the Dawn Hope Administration, Lawrence Michaels, who was to be Finance Chairman, and Sanjiv Smith, who would be in charge of electronic communications. Also present were Bob Fein – who'd been sworn to secrecy – and Rebecca Frear, though Zoë Dunlop (who'd agreed to direct the campaign commercials) had not been able to come.

Alex had moved the kitchen table into the centre of the living room and had placed a number of objects upon it. There was a small plastic replica of the Statue of Liberty, an empty plate with some crumbs on it, a pile of dollar bills and coins, a baseball, a china figure of Marilyn Monroe holding her skirt down against the wind and a miniature TV.

Having replenished the drinks, Alex sat again at the table. 'OK,' he said, 'first things first. Whenever we talk about the campaign I'd like us to refer to Annie as Dawn. It's not something I'm a hundred per cent comfortable with, and nor is Annie, but we'd be insane to waste the name recognition. Dawn's already established a set of values on which she'll be running, and they're values which are held in high esteem at the moment.'

'Except I'm not running with all her ideas, am I?' said Annie, wanting the others to know that she wasn't simply a pawn in her campaign manager's game. She was a candidate with ideas of her own.

'No, but the values won't change.'

Rebecca, whose finger was most on the pulse in Washington, said, 'Everyone's talking about values being the big issue in '96.'

'Then it's our luck that Jack Grant doesn't know what the word means,' said Sanjiv.

Sanjiv had become a friend of Alex's in California. The son of an Indian Professor of Computer Science at Stanford University, he had agreed to become part of the New Dawn campaign primarily for the chance to gauge how much use the information superhighway would be in a presidential campaign. Although he would not admit it to Alex, he expected to vote for the Republican candidate on the day, however much effort he had put into Dawn Hope's bid.

'Don't underestimate Jack,' said Alex.

Although most political commentators had been putting ink to the President's political obituaries since the public's loud rejection of his policies in the midterms, Alex knew that Grant was a master of reinvention. He remained a serious challenge for 1996.

'There's so much to be learnt from last week,' said Alex, 'most importantly that there has not been a time in the whole century when an independent candidate has stood such a good chance of winning. I mean that. This campaign is not going to be an amusing diversion. This is going to be a credible challenge. Listen to this.' From a scrappy heap of papers on the floor, he retrieved a page of notes he'd made on election day ten days before. He remained standing while he spoke. 'This is a poll taken last week, and in it half the people said that it would be a good idea to elect an independent President to break the Washington gridlock. This is our mandate.' He handed the paper to Rebecca and rolled up his sleeves, as if he couldn't wait to get stuck into the fight. 'I'm much less interested in who won last week than in who lost, and the loser was Washington. It was simply bad luck for the Democrats that they were the guys in charge when the voters decided to get uppity. And in a couple of years' time, when Newt and Bob have been running the show, it'll be the Republicans' turn to get their asses kicked. That's where we're going to come in. Dawn and Tom are going to seem like bright shining lights compared with the Beltway politicians. They are going to offer an administration that can be trusted and give the the voters exactly what they want.'

'Which is a woman in control,' said Charlie, who'd been finding it hard to restrain herself from talking.

Annie had to admit that she was less interested in Charlie's opinions than her looks. Her utter self-confidence added immeasurably to her natural beauty. In many ways, Annie thought her a female version of Alex. They both seemed more beautiful because of the strength within. The pair were sitting side by side, and Charlie kept looking at Alex with such affection that Annie began to wonder whether she was his secret lover. She knew the two had flown to San Francisco together, and the feminist was exactly the sort of powerful, independent woman Annie imagined Alex would desire. As Charlie spoke now, Annie tried to remember if the voice matched that of the woman who'd answered Alex's phone late at night. It seemed increasingly, horribly likely, and it made her wonder why it was she who was running, and not Charlie. Especially if Alex and Charlie were lovers.

'There's something to that,' said Alex, who didn't look completely convinced, 'but our greatest hope lies in gut emotions. Bob, can you roll that baseball to me, please.'

Bob Fein, who had been scared into silence so far, managed to say 'Sure,' as he rolled the battered old ball across the table. Everyone followed with their eyes as Alex picked it up and held it in his open hand.

'This was the first gift my dad gave me when we arrived in California,' he said, smoothing his hand over its surface. 'I've got a thousand stories about it which I'll spare you, because what matters is that this,' he said, lifting the ball to eye level, 'was *my America*.' He lowered the ball, but kept it clutched in his right hand. 'Now I can guarantee that every immigrant who's ever come here had his own dreams, and I don't think it matters how many Stallone movies are made or how many killings are reported or how much *we* think we're falling apart, if you go to China or France or Poland and ask someone on the street to name the land of opportunity, the land for dreamers, I bet you they'll say that this is it. America.

'It's only *inside* our borders that the dream's getting shaky, isn't it?, because everyone's after too big a slice of the pie. Dawn and Tom are going to say that the dream is still alive. They're going to say, don't be scared of tomorrow, or of your neighbour, or of the new immigrants moving into town. Don't hate them, don't think they're here to take something away from you but understand that they've come to work *with* you in keeping America what it always was. Do you see what I'm saying, Annie? I'm saying the reason the Democrats lost so badly – even when the economy is doing so well, and inflation is down, and Grant is keeping a pretty good peace in the world – the reason they lost is because the election wasn't about how many cents could be knocked off the tax dollar or spent on nuclear warheads or locking people in jail, it was about searching for the candidates who were most likely to make people believe in themselves. Those Republican kids who won, you know, those prissy little clean-shaven walking haircuts, they didn't have any great ideas but they offered people the chance to work things out by themselves without government getting in the way. I'm saying we take that a step further. I'm saying that Dawn and Tom are going to do the most in the White House if they go in there and say, "We're not here to tell you what to do, we're here to help you do it. We're here to bring the country together." The dream's not dead, but it's in hiding and it needs a real leap of faith to make it come out again. I believe this. We need a new dawn, and we're the ones who can bring that about. So,' he said, smiling, 'there you go, that's my baseball story.'

The sound of the ball rolling along the wooden table was all that could be heard. It came to rest in the pile of dollar bills that were heaped before Sanjiv. He laughed and said, 'That was very nice, Al, but don't you think the ball is telling you something? It's saying, fuck your dreams, *I* want to get rich!'

'Hey, that's why the money's on the table, Sanjiv. It's part of the package. That's why there's the old Statue of Liberty there, and the apple pie I've eaten, and Marilyn – what I'm saying is that we need to look at which things are most embedded in the imagination and see how we can address them. I'm open to all ideas.'

'I've thought of a campaign song,' said Rebecca.

She pulled a sheaf of papers from her case and handed a sheet to each person. On it were written the lyrics to one of the most famous songs in America, Simon and Garfunkel's 'Bridge Over Troubled Water'.

'It's got a special resonance for a lot of people,' she said, 'and I thought it had the right kind of message. And maybe silver girl could even be Dawn's nickname.'

'Absolutely,' Alex said, excited. '"Your dreams are on their way . . ." That could be perfect.'

'I like this second verse,' said Bob. '"When you're down and out, when you're on the street, when evening falls so hard . . ."'

'"I will comfort you,"' said Annie, completing the line. 'I like that too.'

'Do you?' said Charlie dismissively. 'I hardly think "I

will ease your mind" is a very affirmative statement, do you Al?'

'No,' said Alex, grinning. 'But it's the right one. Do you have a shrink, Charlie?'

'No.'

'But you used to.'

'I don't think . . .'

'It doesn't matter. The point is that it's cathartic to free your mind of troubles. If we can convince people we'll ease their minds, that'll free them to get on with their lives. It's what New Dawn has got to be about. I think . . .' He stopped. 'I think I've already said my piece about that. We should probably discuss some of the details. I know Lawrence wants to say something about raising cash, so, Larry, why don't you kick things off?'

Lawrence explained that the New Dawn campaign would have to be launched by the summer of 1995 if there was to be any chance of raising the necessary twenty million dollars. He hoped that Tom Sterling was going to make a significant contribution (he'd already made hints, as well as promising use of his Learjet for the team) and that viewers of *Unto the Skies* would donate heavily. He expected to use much direct mail and believed that money could be saved in advertising through placing Tom and Dawn on the daytime and late-night talk shows. It was agreed by all that, when the announcement came, the candidates would be very hot media property and that there was a risk they might burn out too fast.

'One thing I know for sure,' said Alex, 'is that we mustn't announce until we know the precise direction in which we're heading. Candidates have to be single-minded and convinced that they're right. That's much more important than actually being right, because it makes people believe in you, whatever they think about your ideas.'

For the next two hours they discussed strategy and cash and the occasional political idea and by the end of the meeting the disjointed group that had arrived at the apartment left not only feeling united as a team, but sharing Alex's conviction that Dawn and Tom would beat the Republican and Democratic Goliaths.

It excited Annie to be the centre of Alex's attention. They'd seen much of one another over the past few days, and although she had not forgotten the woman who'd answered his phone late that night, and although she was determined to fight her feelings while they remained unreciprocated, she had been enjoying his company. There'd been no sign, either, of the mystery woman. Not until tonight, that was, when the image of Charlie naked in Alex's arms had planted itself in Annie's mind.

She had not been able to fathom his feelings. Despite being attentive and flirtatious, he had not repeated the display of affection he'd shown after dinner in the West Side Japanese. Once or twice, Annie had caught him staring lovingly at her, and he seemed more than a little jealous when she spoke of other men, yet still he kept his distance.

Annie tried to keep emotionally distant too, but the more Alex became engrossed with the New Dawn campaign, the more calm and confident he seemed to her, the more he appealed. She couldn't explain it. She did not carry with her the memory of a dominant father and she was not by nature submissive, but there was something about the firm order with which he conducted his life that she found oddly sexy. And then, of course, there was his smile. No matter that she'd seen it many times since her brief encounter sixteen years before, still it made her feel weak with desire for him.

What Annie could not know was that Alex was fighting his attraction for her too. He'd made a terrible mistake in falling in love with the First Lady, an error that had blinded his judgment and cost him his job at the White House, and he was determined not to fall for his candidate again. Yet for all his wariness, he could not help wanting to spend time with Annie. She seemed to love life in a simple way that he could not. It was as if she was trying to be happier than everyone else while he was trying to be better, believing still, after forty-three years, that happiness would naturally follow success.

Risking what might happen if they spent the rest of the evening alone, he whispered an invitation to Annie for a late drink as soon as the meeting was over. It was the secrecy as much as the request that excited Annie (she'd noticed Charlie Canon's jealous glance) as she waited for Alex to return from his hallway. He came back smiling.

'You didn't have other plans, did you?' he asked.

They stood rather stiffly, facing each other four feet apart.

'No, not at all.'

He lifted her coat from the back of the door and handed it to her. For just a second, Annie thought she saw him pause as if he was thinking of moving nearer, of taking her in his arms, of . . . No! That was absurd. He wanted a drink to talk about the campaign, that was all.

'A friend of mine just opened a bar on the Upper East Side,' he said, his back to her now as he went looking for his wallet. 'You want to try it?'

'Sure, why not?'

He smiled warmly and they were standing by the door when there was a knock from the other side. Alex opened it to find that Charlie Canon had returned. She looked at him, then at Annie, then back at Alex.

'Oh,' she said, 'were you going somewhere?'

Uncharacteristically, Alex seemed lost for a response.

Charlie continued, 'It's just I made a call and found out my dinner's cancelled so I thought perhaps we could have a celebratory drink.'

Alex looked at Annie.

'After all,' added Charlie, 'I haven't had a chance to meet Annie properly yet.'

Alex shrugged his shoulders. He knew that Charlie Canon was too used to getting her own way to give up. If she hadn't got the message after Pam answered the phone that night, she was hardly likely to leave meekly now. Anyway, maybe it was better if the pleasure of being with Annie was turned to business by Charlie's presence.

'OK,' he said. 'How does Morrison's sound? Annie?'

'Wherever,' she replied. Did it matter where they went now that Charlie had stepped in to spoil the evening?

'Good, let's go,' said Charlie, and as she did so she threaded her arm beneath Alex's and walked him to the elevator, leaving Annie two steps behind.

Morrison's was an old Manhattan bar less than a block from Alex's building. The walls were panelled in dark wood, from which saloon-style lamps curved out like arms raising tankards in a toast. There were candles on each table in green bottles encrusted with craggy layers of wax. Alex, against Charlie's wishes, chose the least conspicuous table in the darkest corner and said, 'What can I get you both?'

'Is the champagne drinkable here?' asked Charlie.

'I should imagine so, and if it isn't then you don't have to drink it.'

'You're my kind of man, Alex Lubotsky,' said Charlie, sliding onto the high-backed wooden bench.

'Good,' he said, though he didn't seem particularly pleased. 'Annie?'

'I'll just have a beer, thanks.'

'Ah! My kind of woman,' he said, with a wicked grin before moving to the bar.

Charlie watched him go. 'It's surprising that his body's in such good shape, isn't it?' she said. 'He eats and drinks like a pig.'

'He plays a lot of tennis,' Annie replied, refusing to be outdone in knowledge of Alex's habits.

'Oh, it's more than that. It's his energy,' Charlie said. She leant across the table. 'He doesn't need to know this, but I have *never* had a lover like him. He just knows which buttons to press. I don't know who taught him, but it's incredible.'

'Really?' said Annie, despising Charlie for saying this. So she had been the one at Alex's that night! All Annie's worst fears were being confirmed.

'Don't look so shocked,' Charlie said. 'I know what you're thinking.'

'Do you?' said Annie, wondering if she was really so transparent; wondering whether Charlie knew how much her gloating hurt.

'You're thinking that because I'm Charlie Canon I must be a man-hater, aren't you? Or even a lesbian. Well, let me tell you that I adore men and I doubly adore their penises. It might be frightening when that raw masculinity's unleashed and it might make you feel vulnerable, but I refuse to give anybody the right to deny my orgasms simply because I'm fighting for our right to power. Anyway,' she said quickly, seeing Alex returning, his tongue peeping from between his lips as he concentrated on the precarious swell of Charlie's champagne, 'you can't really hurt them unless you've fucked them first. Can you?' She looked up at Alex. 'We were just talking about you!'

'Were you now?' said Alex, putting down the drinks.

'Yes, we were!' Charlie patted the seat beside her. 'Sit down and I might be nice enough to tell you what.'

To Annie, the evening had suddenly become a conspiracy against her. She wondered why he had to play this game. Why he had to continue to tempt her and to flirt with her if he was making love to Charlie? A part of Annie had wanted to rise to the challenge of a candidacy to prove her potential to Alex, to put herself up with the

Charlie Canons of the world. But even that had done no good. She had obviously been seeing an affection that had never been there.

'So what were you two gossiping about?'

'You're big-headed enough already!' said Charlie.

'A-ha! So you were saying nice things!' he said, smiling at Annie.

'Not me,' she replied sharply. 'Charlie.'

'Oh!' he said, surprised by Annie's tone. 'Well, you can't win them all!' He took a sip of his beer, and wiped the froth from his top lip. He didn't know what he had done to make Annie avoid his eye, so he asked her, as nicely as he could, 'Have you made any plans for Thanksgiving?'

This first anniversary of Max's suicide was a week away. Alex was dreading spending it alone. Even the smell of a roasting turkey upset him. After the news, the Thanksgiving bird had stood overcooked and uneaten on the stove for three days before Alex had thrown it out. It had seemed an almost unbearable waste at the time, and he'd felt a persistent sense of guilt that the animal should have died without purpose. This year, Pam was joining her family, and together they had thought Alex would be too palpable a reminder of Max and might upset the boys. So he had thought that if Annie was going to be alone, then they might spend the day together.

'I'm going to a friend's in Pittsburgh,' she lied, thinking that, although she had not yet accepted Barbara's invitation, she wasn't going to give Alex the satisfaction of discovering she was lonely. His pity was too disgusting.

'Oh, yeah?' he said. 'That's nice. I . . .'

'What about making Dawn's announcement next Thanksgiving?' interrupted Charlie. 'I'll be finished with my book by then, and it could be a good time to appeal to the united American family.'

'It's an idea,' agreed Alex. 'Definitely.'

Annie hated Charlie's self-satisfied little smirk, as she hated Alex for seeming to love it.

He said, 'You're right that the whole announcement – what we say, where we do it, how we present Dawn and Tom – is going to be very important. I learned from '92 that the speech gets played over and over because it's the one time that you really set out the goals of the campaign. We're going to have to fill it with juicy soundbites for you.'

'Oh!' said Annie, nibbling at a nail.

'By the way,' he added, smiling. 'We're going to have to stop you doing things like that. They make you look nervous.'

Annie jerked her hand away from her mouth. Why had he made her look infantile in front of Charlie? She reddened under the feminist's judgmental scowl. She couldn't believe she'd once admired Charlie. She was clearly so arrogant and condescending and in love with herself.

'You should watch Alex here,' Charlie said, gently pushing back her hair. 'He's always cool under pressure.'

'I think I'll leave the staring to you,' Annie said, trying to soften her wickedness with a smile.

'My pleasure,' Charlie replied.

And then, as if in slow motion, Annie saw Charlie place a hand on Alex's. There was something obscene about it, as if the two were flaunting their sexual union. And even though Charlie had soon lifted her hand away, Annie felt as if she had swallowed a lead weight, and she wasn't listening as Charlie began to talk about using Emily's List, about the legions of female voters who'd vote for Dawn simply because she was a woman, about the mathematics of raising funds from fifty-five million female voters. She was staring into the candle's flame instead, thinking of how Alex had chosen Charlie over her, how Alex touched and loved Charlie instead of her. It was almost too painful to bear.

Suddenly Alex, a pack-a-week smoker, moved the candle to light his smoke. Annie thought his hands beautiful. The fingers were square and strong and made the cigarette look strangely delicate and feminine, the way he was holding it high up, too close to his nails. She wished that, just once, she had felt those fingers upon her. Just once.

'What do you think about that kind of housing for single-parent mothers?' asked Charlie.

'Oh, definitely,' Annie said. 'Let's go with that.'

'But do you believe in it?' Charlie asked.

She's staring at me as if I'm some kind of dumb actress, thought Annie. How dare she?

'Maybe we've had enough policy-making for one night,' Alex said, trying to bring Annie back to his side. 'We've still got a year to sort everything out.'

'It's never too early, Alex,' Charlie said.

With the cigarette in his mouth Alex shook his head, his fingers lit by the sparky orange glow of the drag. 'Much better to have fresh ideas to take onto the road. They come out sounding better.'

He seemed to Annie to be stubbing the cigarette out in slow motion, grinding it dead with his strong fingers.

'Who wants another drink?' he asked.

Annie did. She wanted another drink, and another, and she wanted Charlie to say she was tired and needed to go home so that she herself would be left alone with Alex, so that she could hear it from his lips that he didn't feel anything for her, that all the time she was misreading his signs. But as soon as Charlie said, 'Me, please,' Annie knew she wouldn't be able to bear another half hour. She angled her watch to catch the smoky light.

'I think I'll call it a night,' she said. 'I've got to be up at six.'

'Are you sure?' said Alex, who was standing at the

end of the table. 'You don't have time for a quick one?'

'What kind of candidate are you trying to make her?' said Charlie. 'Another Mayor Barry?'

'Exactly, Alex,' said Annie seriously. 'Dawn's a no-drink, no-sex, no-fun kind of woman. I wouldn't want to do anything to fuck that up.'

She left quickly, pacing from the bar feeling horribly alone, as if something of immeasurable value had been stolen, leaving her the lesser for the rest of her life.

22

Eggnog.

Why, when Bob Fein was happily reading a memo from Alex on New Dawn, his mind should have been deluged with images of eggnog, he would never know. Yet looking back (as he was to do time and time again), he blamed this sudden craving for the mistake that finally led to one of the most exciting political events of 1994.

He remembered it happening like this: it was the Monday after Thanksgiving, early evening, and he had come home from editing scripts with Alex clutching a highly confidential list of objectives for raising money for the New Dawn campaign. Alex's aim was to plant in the minds of *Unto the Skies'* ten million viewers the belief that the only thing holding their beloved Dawn back from the White House was a lack of funds, so that when she actually made her announcement the contributions would flood in. A dollar apiece was all that would be needed, though in his heart Alex hoped they would receive more. Already the largest donation made directly to Annie (and this even before any announcement) had been a cheque for three hundred dollars. In total she had received close to six thousand in contributions for her fictional gubernatorial campaign and, although she had donated most to charity, it had set a sensational precedent.

The plan was that Alex and Bob would write a storyline for *Unto the Skies* about Dawn's presidential aspirations. Between them, they could not imagine either the network or Gardner and Hyde Productions having any objections.

After all, in the build-up to '96, it would keep the show in the news. Of course, Dawn Hope would vanish from the show before Annie made her announcement, but by then Alex hoped that millions would be only too happy to help her on her way.

Bob Fein was looking forward to the challenge. There was no reason then for him to be distracted by this image of thick, rummy eggnog flowing into his open mouth. Yet each time he looked at Alex's plan, the liquid dripped once more. He even imagined that he could smell it. There was nothing for it but to go to the store to satisfy this urge.

He had just stepped onto the street when, to his surprise, he saw Faith Valentine clicking towards him in her high-heeled shoes.

'Oh, drat!' she said. 'Bad timing.'

Bob understood Faith now, knew that she paid him these visits to keep him writing interesting stories for Vanessa. He had felt a fool at first (believing that she had really fallen for him), but then he'd begun to enjoy himself. Now he felt that he was manipulating her, for the less interest he showed in Vanessa's stories the more keen she was to please. They had already hit the sack three times and the experience had blown his mind.

'I should have called,' Faith said.

'I'll be back in five minutes. Here,' he said, handing her the keys, 'it's the red one. Make yourself at home.'

She thanked him and he skipped off to the store, his penis quite aware of what would most probably come. In the 7–11 on Third Avenue he picked up a carton of eggnog and, thinking that Faith might like something else, a tube of Pringles as well. At the front of the line, a homeless man seemed to be taking for ever counting out his bottles for their five-cent refunds. Bob wondered how Faith was making herself at home. Maybe she was loosening her top a little, kicking her feet out of the shoes, reclining on the sofa, waiting for . . .

'Shit!' he said out loud.

Throwing the carton and the chips onto the counter, he raced to the door. His heart was thumping feverishly as he ran towards 10th Street, pushing himself off the lamppost as he took the corner too fast. He sprinted like a victim in a dream. At the door he stupidly threw his hands in his pockets looking for the keys, before stabbing his finger against the bell of his own apartment. There was no reply.

'Come on,' he was whispering, his racing heart making him feel sick. 'Come on!'

Still there was no reply, so he backed out into the middle of the quiet street and shouted Faith's name up at the window. He saw no movement inside, though this time when he buzzed she answered, calmly, as if she had not heard him before. She let him in and he slowed his climb up the stairs and swept a hand through his hair and tried to look composed as he reached her.

'Didn't you hear the bell the first time?' he asked.

'I was in the bathroom, Bob. Is something wrong?'

'I don't know,' he said breathlessly. 'There's something in the living room that . . .'

As she followed him down the corridor he could see the page from Alex where he'd left it, appearing larger and more obvious than it was, like a zit on a teenager's chin.

'It's something that Vince gave me,' he continued. 'A plot that has to be secret for now.'

'Sounds interesting,' said Faith, patting his bottom as they entered the room.

Bob picked up Alex's memo as nonchalantly as he could, and swung it by his side.

'I wish I'd seen it now,' she said, trying to reach for it.

Bob hid it behind his back and she stepped nearer and gave him a quick kiss on his lips. He felt the kiss tickle its way like a fingertip down his body. He smiled at the relief. 'So you didn't see anything?' he asked.

He needed to hear it from her.

'Bob!' she answered, trying to look wounded and twisting away from him. 'For all my faults, I am a woman of integrity and honesty. I do not consider it any of my business to interfere in the private affairs of others.'

This was a speech of Vanessa's – he remembered writing it – but it didn't matter. He believed Faith. It was much more likely that she'd been poking around in his bathroom cabinet.

'So, how was your Thanksgiving?' Bob said, wanting to chat about nothing as he placed the memo face down on his desk. 'It must be about a year since you came here the first time. Remember?'

'I remember your girlfriend coming back, yes.'

'She's away,' Bob said at once.

'Oh! Well, I'm here because there are some things on my mind,' Faith said, her bottom raised in the air as she plumped the cushion on which she was about to place it.

'About Vanessa?' prompted Bob.

'Clever boy,' she said, turning to him. As ever, it was her breasts that seemed to arrive first.

'Well . . .' He pulled his shirt away from his somewhat sticky armpits, 'I think she's coming into a very strong period now. Dawn's taking the back seat for a while.'

'This is not about Dawn!' Faith said angrily. She sat down. 'It's something much more personal, Bob.' Suddenly, to his amazement, her eyelids began to flutter and something close to tears filled her eyes. She lowered her head and covered her face with her hand. Her body shook with a couple of strange-sounding sobs.

'Faith? Are you OK?' Bob asked, moving to sit beside her.

Carefully keeping her face hidden, Faith clumped her head (unusually heavy, Bob thought, since it was so blow-dried and empty) against his chest and continued with the odd sobbing noises. After a while, in a voice empty of tears, she said, 'I was abused. As a child!'

Bob was shocked into silence. What could he say? Never mind? Poor you? Who by? Nothing seemed apt. He settled for, 'You were?' It seemed to do the trick.

'Yes.' She lifted her head. 'But I think I'm strong enough now.'

'Good,' Bob said gently. 'For what?'

'To confront it. In the show. I think Vanessa should admit that it happened to her.' She made a sad whimpering sound, and with a face full of pained grief pressed her head to him again, only this time it continued to fall to his chest, past his stomach and onto his lap. 'I thought that you were someone I could trust, Bob,' she said, the bone of her jaw rubbing against his highly strung member as she spoke.

He swallowed, trying to think about anything but Faith's lips. It was not so much the oral act itself that he feared, as proving himself incapable of controlling his erections. It seemed immature and weak. Hardly helping, Faith exerted an even greater downward pressure as she continued. 'Sex abuse is not something to be ashamed of. It's not something to hide behind. It can eat you up if you don't face it head on. We should deal with it.'

'I don't know, we've just tackled that harassment story,' he said.

He bit at the inside of his lip, though suddenly the battle was lost. He knew she knew. In a second, she showed him how, opening his flies and her lips for him.

When he was suitably, predictably mindless, Faith took hold of his hand and led him, his hard-on jutting out unceremoniously like a diviner's rod, towards the bed in which, naked and boisterous above him, she raised the subject again.

'I'll see what we can do,' Bob said, at which she growled (sometimes Faith forget who liked what) and urged him to take her place on top, slipping to her side as he accepted her generous invitation.

Soon after she had come (at least, he thought she had) with a sound that he feared would disturb the neighbours, Faith rose, insisting that Bob remain sated where he was. She said she liked to see him naked while she dressed.

When he heard the front door, he began to wonder if they would run a child abuse story. Probably not. Then again, Faith sure knew how to make it worth his while. He would have to see how it fitted in with Dawn Hope's story. He smiled – it had been a close shave earlier. He didn't know what Faith would have done if she'd seen anything, though he imagined she was too stupid to have figured what it was about.

Having showered, he decided to look over Alex's notes once more. With a towel around his waist he ambled back to the living room.

'Oh, no,' he said. 'Please no!'

The page wasn't there. He scrabbled through the papers on the table and couch, but knew he was searching in vain. He knew where the memo had been, and he knew that the only place it could now be was in Faith Valentine's devious, painted hands.

Once the excitement over Annie's tantrum had calmed down (and it didn't take long, since soap actors were immune to such volcanic displays), life on the set of *Unto the Skies* resumed as normal. Of course, none of the cast and crew were aware that, within a year, their friend was to launch an unlikely bid for the presidency, but then secrecy was a crucial part of the ploy. For now, Annie was just an actress working like the rest of them.

Today she was wearing a navy suit copied from Susan Grant's inauguration outfit. In the scene being taped, Dawn was discussing with the extended Sheridan family her famous victory. Present were William, Vanessa, Mary, Jamie, Carrie and Shannon. The mood was peachy.

JAMIE
I just feel so proud in my heart to have a sister like you.

DAWN
Thank you. And for calling me sister, Jamie.

MARY
My own daughter making it to Governor, I can't believe it.

DAWN
It's no big shakes, Mom. You wait until I become President!

WILLIAM & MARY
President?

DAWN
That's right. If I could only make all the women in America realise that I'm on their side, that I want what's best for them, well, their support would be all I would need. You might not like it, William, but we're the majority.

JAMIE
I'm sure you could do it, Dawn.

DAWN
Oh, thank you. I owe so much to you. My family. I love you all so very much. .

VANESSA
(WALKING TO THE WINDOW, WHISPERING)
You might have taken my place in the heart of this
family, but you're not going to make it to President!
I can promise you that . . .

'Cut,' boomed Monty. 'Aaand tapes are – good.'

Thankful at reaching the end of another day, the actors
were kissing each other goodnight when they saw Alex
running into the studio and across to Annie.

He put an arm around her shoulder and led her out of
earshot of the others.

'What's happened?'

'It's been leaked. The press know.'

'What?' she said, glancing to her side to see Faith staring
directly at them. 'How?'

'You tell me.'

Together, they walked briskly to Annie's dressing room.
'So do we deny it?' she asked as soon as the door was
closed.

'One thing we don't do is talk to the press. Not a word.
We can't stop this being the *Herald*'s front page tomorrow,
but we can make sure they don't get anything more than
they have.'

'Do they know about Tom?'

'Yuh,' he said with a sigh. 'Maybe he talked. I wouldn't
be surprised.'

'I thought he was in Vienna.'

'So? Journalists have long arms.'

There was a quick rap at the door. Alex shrugged as if
to suggest there was nothing to do but answer it.

'Yes?' said Annie.

The door burst open, followed by Mr Vince Moscardini.

'Oh!' he said to Alex. 'What a surprise! One day I expect
I'll find you two fucking in here!'

If only, thought Alex and Annie at once.

'Hello, Vince,' Alex said coolly.

'I've got journalists up to here,' Vince barked, tapping the side of his hand against his forehead. 'You could have warned me you were about to pull this one.'

Despite his apparent anger, Vince had been in high spirits since Faith had brought him a copy of the stolen New Dawn memo. She had presented the two pages as evidence of the pair's duplicity, convinced that it would spell the end of Annie's career on the show. Vince, however, had seen the memo as a means to remove Alex. He was about to get his show back, his previous suspicions being publicly confirmed in the process. It was close to perfect.

'What are you talking about?' Annie asked him.

'You know, and you know *I* know,' said Vince, who seemed to be bouncing up and down like a puppet on a string.

'You lost me,' said Annie, absolutely calm.

'Did you forget you're about to run for President?'

'No,' she said. 'We taped the scene today.'

'Spare me the crap, and I hope you've figured out a good story for G&H and the network tomorrow. Or we'll be suing your asses off. The meeting's in Shermer's office, ten a.m. Be there. Sharp. Both of you.'

Alex looked worried. 'He's quite a producer when he wants to be.'

Annie poured some cream onto a cotton ball and rubbed it over her face. 'We're going to have to think up a pretty good story, aren't we?' she said.

'I can't,' Alex said solemnly. 'Barry Shermer is one person I can't lie to. Not now.'

'So this is it? We're going to announce?' asked Annie, feeling weak with nervousness. She had expected months to prepare for the legions of reporters who'd advance as soon as the secret was known. Now she felt like a sky diver about to jump without having learnt which cords to pull. 'What should I say?' she wanted to know.

'Don't do anything except smile. There will be a lot of cameras outside your apartment. Ignore them. Just ignore them. We are not going to be made to announce until we're ready.'

Annie, who'd taken off her make-up by now, slipped off her costume in front of Alex. Though she was turned from him, she fancied she could feel him stare into her near-naked back. Having been working out daily with her personal trainer, she was proud of her body now. It hadn't been in such good shape since her early twenties.

They were surprised by another knock at the door.

'Hold it a second,' Annie called out.

Moments later, dressed in her favourite baggy sweater and jeans, she opened the door to find Faith filling the space with the curves of her body.

'Oh!' she said, eyeing Alex. 'Am I disturbing?'

'Only sometimes, Faith,' said Alex.

Faith, looking confused, said, 'Well, I'm not stopping. I wanted to give this to Annie.' She handed over a dollar bill. 'To start her off on the road.'

She winked at them both before moving away along the corridor. Annie slammed the door.

'She's going to really love it if I have to leave the show early,' she said.

'She won't if you win the race,' Alex said, suddenly invigorated. 'Listen, I've just had a thought. Can you take your outfits home?'

'They can't stop me,' she replied.

'So get dressed in that suit again, will you? Starting from now, you've got to look to the world like the next president of the United States.'

The body language said it all. The last time Vince Moscardini had been summoned to the UBC president's office, to hear of Alex's appointment to the show, he had been paranoid and jumpy, curling into himself. He had also been half an hour late. This time, arriving early, he looked his best, dressed in a shiny silk suit, clean-shaven and full of natural vigour. He sat upright and alert, close to Barry Shermer, and watched with glee as the rest of the group filed in.

There was Anne-Marie Stillinger, kempt and efficient as ever. After her came David Wolf, head of G&H Productions, who looked as if he'd been woken in the middle of the night by the noise of a teenage daughter getting laid. With him was Paul Roberts, who seemed to shrink in stature whenever he was with his boss, and next, Bob Fein and Alex Lubotsky. Finally, as if to make a point, Annie arrived alone, a minute late, wearing a green suit that had already been seen on TV, on *Unto the Skies* and the morning news.

Soon Barry Shermer opened the meeting. He had a copy of the morning's *Herald* by his side and the stolen memo on his lap. 'I have not yet had time to speak with Alex about this matter,' he said, 'but I feel I should begin by apologising to you all and to Vincent in particular for being taken in, I suppose, by Alex. I have always done what I can to discourage political bias on this network, and my forceful endorsement of him came only after he'd assured me that he was not motivated by politics in seeking the headwriter's mantle. I was clearly blind, and this,' he lifted the copy of the memo from his lap, 'would seem to confirm it.'

Alex remained expressionless. It was Vince who was excited. 'I did tell you,' he said. 'I definitely did.'

Although he'd been enjoying, both publicly and privately, the recent success of *Unto the Skies*, he hadn't forgiven Alex for forcing his way onto the team or for frequently breaking the sacred chain of command by appealing directly to the network above the Executive Producer's head. Alex had never understood that writers belonged close to the bottom of the heap. Now

Vince's revenge would taste particularly sweet. He could hardly wait to put some zap and sex back into the show.

'However,' Shermer continued, 'I do not see the value of conducting a lengthy postmortem. Rather, I think that we should concentrate on the steps that need to be taken from this point forward.'

'May I suggest that Alex Lubotsky takes some steps out of this room?' said Vince. 'For dicking us around.'

'Vince,' said Alex, unable to remain silent, 'if making *Unto the Skies* the number one soap in America is "dicking you around", I wish you luck with someone who doesn't.'

'Excuse me, now you're taking all the credit? You think you did this by yourself? We happen to be a team. Maybe you should have remembered that.'

Alex did not reply. He didn't want to be drawn into a petty argument with Vince. He assumed that his contribution to the show would be understood well enough by the network and sponsors, and that they would consider him too valuable to be dismissed. He wanted to stay on the soap for a while longer. Dawn needed him.

Paul Roberts coughed to gain attention, and then said, 'I have been asked by Mr Wolf to express to Mr Lubotsky the gratitude of Gardner and Hyde Productions for helping turn around the show's fortunes, but we must add that there has been a very unhealthy shift towards current affairs . . .'

'Too right,' interrupted Vince.

'And away from a view of society that's more fitting to drama of this kind. There has also been considerable concern that with the masculinisation of Dawn Hope we have been alienating those women who prefer more feminine role models. As a result, we feel we have no option but to exercise our right to term—'

'Don't bother, Paul,' said Alex, knowing full well what was coming. 'I quit.'

'Isn't that what you said when President Grant fired you too?' said Vince, looking around for a laugh.

Alex stared at the producer with undisguised contempt.

'Oh, shit,' Vince whispered to Anne-Marie. 'We've been here before! I wouldn't take a ride with him for a while . . .'

Alex missed that gem because his mind was on how myopic he'd been. In thinking he could talk his way into staying with the soap long enough to help Dawn's campaign, he'd utterly failed to take into account the links that the Gardner and Hyde conglomerate had with the Republican Party. It now seemed less odd that he was being fired than that they'd hired him in the first place.

'Then I suggest that Mr Fein becomes headwriter,' said Shermer to David Wolf. 'I realise that he has been aware of these recent manoeuvrings, but I think we'd be cutting off our noses were we to dismiss him too.'

'I agree with Barry,' said Anne-Marie. 'And I'd also like to say that, personally, I appreciate the hard work that Alex has put into the show.'

'Yes, but for what?' said Vince. 'Except himself.'

Shermer, ignoring him, said, 'There remains the issue of what we should do with Miss Marin and her character. Now, there seems little doubt that the show's popularity is closely linked with the success of Dawn as a character. I believe it's in our interests . . .'

'Excuse me,' said Annie, looking from Alex to the UBC President, 'if Alex goes, I go.'

Anne-Marie spoke immediately. 'Annie, I'm afraid your two-year contract is legally binding. If you try to leave we'll have no option other than making your life very uncomfortable indeed.'

Anne-Marie liked Annie, but the last thing any of them wanted was for their top star to abandon *Unto the Skies* so soon after her arrival.

'I haven't signed anything yet,' Annie said proudly.

'You haven't?'

Anne-Marie flashed a look at Vince.

'What I meant when I told you that,' Vince hastily explained, 'was that Annie was, you know, *about* to sign. She was about to sign.'

'No, Vince, you told me she *had* signed.'

'Vince and I had a little disagreement,' said Annie, 'about where he could put his hands.'

'You've had our top star out of contract?' Anne-Marie said in anger and amazement.

Vince scratched at his neck. 'Actresses don't usually disappear to run for President!' he argued. 'Do they? Not when they're winning awards,' he said testily, glaring at Annie.

'Well, I am,' Annie proclaimed. 'So it looks as if I fucked you instead of the other way around. Doesn't it?'

Although there followed a silence during which Annie regretted her words, Alex was smirking. She kept surprising him with her spirit.

After a moment, Shermer, always a clear-headed man, looked at Annie with kindness and said, 'Are you absolutely sure this is something you want to do? Now that we've found ourselves in this position, I have little doubt that we could negotiate a contract to favour both of us.'

'No, I've decided,' she said, 'it's final,' though suddenly the idea of throwing away more than five thousand dollars a week, of turning her back on the role that had changed her life and made her a star, seemed frightening and absurd. Why was she doing it? Did she honestly believe that Miss Annie Marin could make a political difference where most professionals had failed?

'Very well,' said Shermer, 'then I want to do this. I would like to call a press conference in which my network, and I presume G&H as well, will announce that it was *our* decision to release Alex and Annie. I think you'll agree that you owe us that.'

Alex nodded. His greatest regret was that he had misled Shermer. Having spent most of his adult life in politics, Alex had simply assumed that his assurances were made to be broken. As it had been in the show's interest for him to become headwriter, it shouldn't have mattered that he told half-truths to ease Shermer's decision, should it?

Bob, who felt responsible for the whole debacle, said, 'Dawn is due to go on a holiday in a week. We haven't written much for her after her return.'

'Then that would appear to be the most sensible time for the break,' Shermer agreed. 'Annie?'

Shermer flicked open a diary on his desk. 'Then if David agrees, we'll meet with the press on December 10th. Here at UBC Tower. That should give you time to get that frown off your face, Annie. Or, just perhaps, you might change your mind.'

23

Almost at once, Alex decided that Dawn Hope's announcement as a presidential candidate would not be made at the UBC conference, but a week or so later. Tuesday, December 20th had a nice festive ring to it, giving him longer to write Dawn's speech and prepare Annie for her most important role. After that, he imagined she would need to go abroad for a while, to minimise the damage caused by early announcement. If she was sent on a fact-finding mission to Europe (it would actually be a holiday paid for by Sterling, who'd committed a massive eight million dollars to the campaign), then there would be less pressure to keep the momentum going.

As the presidential election was not until November 1996, Alex feared that his greatest challenge would be to keep Dawn an appealing prospect for those twenty-three months. Having lost the forum of *Unto the Skies*, this was going to be difficult. One idea was to make her a kind of national agony aunt, with a syndicated column in which she would maintain her reputation as the people's politician and as a nurturing mother figure. With the press contacts Alex had established over the years, he could persuade the editors on a good number of important papers to take her on. Her fee would be minimal, with all the writing done by himself.

At the moment, however, there were more pressing concerns. Alex had accompanied Annie back to her apartment, wishing the press to see the two of them together. The more speculation there was about her

candidacy, the more exposure she would get. He had
been surprised, however, by the number of journalists
packed around the steps to her building (sometimes he
forgot what a star he'd created), and so he resolved to
move her to a hotel away from the media. Untrained
as she was, she could not be expected to manage them
without making some damaging mistakes.

Annie was checked in, then, to the Truman Suite in the
Grahame Hotel, sixteen floors from the nearest rat with a
camera or minitape. The suite was large enough for twenty
people, which Alex thought was probably right. With time
before the announcement so short, he needed all the help
he could get to help him transform Annie from a talented
actress into a great candidate.

Rebecca, fortunately, had just resigned from the First
Lady's office in Washington and had moved into a midtown apartment. She was going to work with Alex on the
announcement speech, day and night if necessary. Justin
Hathwaite, an old friend of Alex from his days at Oxford,
had been flown in from London to help Annie with her
personal presentation and style. A large TV screen had
been positioned in the suite so she could view videos and
learn how best to walk, talk, wave and smile.

The suite was also going to serve as campaign centre
for the meetings with the graphic designers, hairstylists,
lawyers, make-up artists, wardrobe advisers, speechwrit-
ers, financial consultants and other helpers who were to
be drafted in. As far as Alex was concerned, there was no
point in doing things by halves. Either Annie was going
to step out on that podium (Christ, they didn't even know
where or when yet) and astound the nation and the world,
or else she would appear like every other independent, as
an amusing diversion from the real candidates.

Alex had less than three weeks in which to polish Annie
until she was so shiny she would dazzle from Anchorage
to New Mexico. He had to be subtle in making her appear

more serious than she had on the soap while no less glamorous. It was a matter, he believed, of varying the type and colouring of her outfits, of giving her a slightly more formal hairstyle, less make-up and some ideas that were less conservative than those heard from Dawn on *Unto the Skies*.

He could not, of course, send Annie out with the radical opinions that she'd presented him with. They had been a surprise, to say the least, and he was wondering how best to break it to her that she wouldn't have a hope of victory if she let the people know what she really believed. Instead, he had to produce a candidate so perfect that voters would believe a redeeming angel had landed on their shores.

For the moment, Annie had little to do. Today was free for her to enjoy the benefits of the Grahame. She could order whatever she liked from the five-star menu whenever she wanted. She knew there was a private gym in the basement and a personal trainer on his way. And she'd been told that if ever she needed anything, just to say the word, not to worry, but to relax, get in the mood and keep looking her best. She, Alex kept reminding her, was what mattered. She was the candidate.

So far it was the breakfasts Annie had enjoyed. This Sunday morning she was trying the eggs benedict, with hot chocolate *and* coffee and croissants. A young waiter, so discreet she'd figured she could have been fucking a donkey on the floor and still he would have slid silently by, had just left the tray on the bed when Alex rang. Justin Hathwaite had arrived, he said, and the two of them were on their way to the hotel.

She had to dress quickly and forget about eating, and she was still only half awake when she heard the knock on the door in the adjacent room. She opened it to find Alex with Justin Hathwaite. Justin was a fairly short man, Annie's height, with an almost shaven head and a solid, shiny forehead. Had he not been nattily dressed in a chalk-striped suit, he might have been taken for one of those British soccer hooligans who were so good at exposing the true temperament of the nation's people. He was in his early forties, but his full cheeks made him seem younger. The commando soles on his polished black shoes, Annie noticed, gave him an extra inch in height.

Annie took his hand. 'Hi!'

Justin's handshake was brisk and strong. 'Right,' he said, 'can you do that again, only this time try standing straighter when you open the door, smile when you see me – just enough to show that you're comfortable – then shake my hand when it's closer to *my* body than to yours. Squeeze it tight, one shake, up, down, and let it go first. Do you think you've got that?'

For a second, Annie was speechless. Did she really have to do this? She glanced at Alex, looking for help.

'I'm going to leave you to it,' he said. 'Annie, trust this man. He's the best.'

'Oh! OK, see you.'

Justin backed away, shut the door and knocked again.

Again, Annie hesitated. What was going on? Did she really have to learn how to open a door? Presidents had doors opened for them, didn't they? It was one of the perks, like being on the bridge of the Starship *Enterprise*. She wondered how long Justin would wait. He probably thinks I'm preparing myself for the role, Annie decided. Like a Method actress. But Annie didn't feel she needed to prepare. She could be confident and assured if she wanted to be. It was easy. It was acting. She decided to play along.

She opened the door and smiled. 'You must be Justin.' She took his hand. 'Come in.' She released her grip, and held an arm out for him to step inside.

He did so, and dropped his case down by the door. 'Great. Ten times better,' he said. 'Did you feel it?'

'Sure. It just wasn't very me.'

'That's why I'm here. It's got to be you, all the time. It has to become second nature to you. Don't even relax with your friends. Always shake hands like that and you won't slip up.'

'God, this is like *My Fair Lady*, or something,' Annie said with a laugh. 'Have you two taken a bet over me?'

Justin said nothing, which Annie thought rude of him. Wasn't she the important one, the candidate? Alex had warned her that Justin was blunt, but she'd not expected this.

Now he had lifted his case onto the gilded chaise longue. The click of the metal clasps simultaneously springing back reminded her of the doctor who'd visited her often when she was a child, and she felt suddenly nervous, as if she was about to be operated on against her will.

'Is there a bulletin board in here?' he asked, looking around.

'I don't think so.'

'There should be.'

As he called the front desk with his request he began to toss a selection of large manilla envelopes onto the bed. On each had been written the names of various political leaders. REAGAN, R; KENNEDY, JF; GRANT, S; KENNEDY, JACKIE; THATCHER, M; BERLUSCONI, S; GRANT, J; MITTERRAND, F. After these, like a magician with his tricks, Justin took from the case a camera with a large flash attachment, a small stack of videotapes, legal pads and a child's doll.

'I'm sorry if some of this is going to seem basic,' he said, 'but I'm here to eliminate the cock-ups. OK, Dawn?'

'Yeah,' she replied, finding it hard to hear that name, knowing she'd have to get used to it. The legal process of discarding her own had begun.

Justin now sat in the window's alcove, rubbing his chin as he read from a list of his notes. He raised his eyes. 'Let's watch a video before the others arrive, shall we?' he said.

'Sure,' replied Annie, stupidly thinking that he meant they'd be watching a movie. Instead, the image that came up on the large screen was of Ronald Reagan walking through a crowd of children gathered on the South Lawn of the White House.

Justin had pulled up a chair beside hers, three feet from the TV. He held the remote control in his hand and paused the image almost immediately. Reagan was left in limbo, smiling perfectly. 'Remember,' he said, 'Ronnie was king. He was the best we've had in years. All right? I want you to forget his politics.'

'Like he did?' she said.

Justin didn't respond, but said, 'Look what I'm going to do.' He forwarded the tape, then stopped and froze the image. 'See now?' he said. Again, he did the same. 'And now?' He repeated the process, three, four, five times, before asking Annie if she'd noticed what united every frame.

'I don't know, Reagan's smile?'

'Yes, good. But more important is that he was aware of the cameras. Always. What you're seeing is what made him a two-term President, because once he'd got his performance right he never changed it.' Justin set the tape in motion again. He spoke as Annie watched. 'Look at his walk. It's sturdy, it's purposeful, he knows where he's going, his shoulders are back and relaxed. Now look,' Justin said, his eyes transfixed by the image. He was shaking his head in apparent wonderment. '*Look* at that!' Reagan had bent down to pinch a little girl's cheek. 'See? That isn't the way that most of us play with a child. We would squat down and joke around. He's keeping his head up and a little in profile because he knows the camera is here.' Justin fanned out his fingers and held his hand close to Annie's right cheek. 'And he also knows that too many things can go wrong if he bends down low. He could slip, he could lose his balance, he could get a kid's finger in his eye, and then it's not that one camera he's got to worry about but every single lens in the White House grounds and every front page in the country. Do you see?'

'Yes, I do,' Annie said.

'Learning how to do that is more important than everything else combined, believe me. Everything. Now, I wouldn't be here if I hadn't been impressed with what I saw on those *Unto the Skies* tapes, but out of character you're a mess. You're jumpy, you bite your nails, you're a bit giggly and that's fine in real life, even endearing, but it'll mean death, *death*, in any campaign.'

Annie sighed. What right did Justin have to call her jumpy and giggly? He surprised her with a hand on her arm.

'Don't look so worried. Nine out of ten people are like you when I start with them.'

'That's not what bothers me,' she said. 'I'm worried about what I'll be like when you've finished.'

They were interrupted by a knock at the door. Annie answered it to a busboy delivering a two-by-two-foot bulletin board. She scrabbled about in her purse for a dollar tip, gave it, and closed the door.

'Great,' said Justin, 'you were already standing more upright. Only next time you tip someone, give them the first note that comes to hand. Reach in, take it out, hand it over.' He clapped his hands. 'One, two, three. You're the boss, bam, they're gone. OK?'

Justin was pleased to have the board. From the envelopes he took out some photographs of the leaders and started to pin them up. 'This is what I mean about the slip-up.' To the board he pinned a photograph of President Grant screwing up his face as if reacting to a bad smell. Justin explained, 'This was when Yeltsin was at the White House. He was being a buffoon, as usual, drinking out of the dog's bowl, or something crazy, and Grant was so desperate to be in on the act that he forgot how a true

President should behave. And it was this face that made
every Russian front page, right above an article saying
that Grant was being intransigent and pig-headed about
Yeltsin's nuclear proposals. He undermined the whole
process with one mistake. Do you see?'

As the hour progressed, so Justin pointed out the
strengths and flaws of the political figures he had chosen. Besides Reagan, the man with whom he was most
impressed was Silvio Berlusconi, the recently elected
President of Italy. 'If he stays out of jail and in government,' Justin said, tapping a finger against a glossy colour
photograph of the leader, 'this man could out-Reagan
Reagan. Did you know Berlusconi used to be a nightclub
crooner?'

Annie said that she didn't.

'You look at any of his early political photos and you'll
see he's got a very lazy way of standing, always with a hand
in his jacket pocket. That's classic Sinatra, but Berlusconi
made it classic Berlusconi. That's what we need for you. A
mannerism that's specifically yours, that's fundamentally
Dawn.'

Annie nodded. What had he just said? Something
about being like Sinatra? The words had been coming
so fast during the hour there'd been a pile-up on one
of the lanes into her mind, and now nothing was getting through at all. She wanted to pull into a mental
service station, have a coffee away from the clamour.
She was tired of Justin hammering away at her imper-
fections. She had spent thirty-six years becoming Annie
Marin, and up until now had been pleased with the
result. It didn't seem right that this man should take
her apart.

She was about to demand a break when Alex returned
to the room. Annie was relieved. She had been feeling like the new girl at school, alone with the head-
master.

'So what do you think of America's first female President, Jay?' Alex asked.

'Not as much as I'm going to think of her when we're finished,' Justin replied, to Annie's annoyance.

'Well, I've got some backup troops. There's a hair whatever-you-call-him, a hair person, called Bradley Peters in the lobby, and then a friend of a friend who works at *Vogue* is coming in about twenty minutes and after that I thought we'd have Dawn read out some old speeches, practise on that for a while. Oh, and I just heard that Tom Sterling's flying in from Vienna on Wednesday, but he's gone on Thursday, so we'll have a big get-together on Wednesday evening.'

'Can't make it,' Annie said.

Alex laughed. 'I think we should put Dawn through a really tough press test, yeah Justin? With lights. There should be enough of us here for that.'

'Good idea.'

'I can't make it,' Annie said again.

'Why not?'

'Because I can't. I'm doing something else.'

'Don't be stupid,' he said with impatience.

'Then stop treating me like I'm stupid, and start treating me with a little respect. Both of you!' she snapped, genuinely upset so that she had to use all her acting skill to keep the anger down.

'What I meant . . .'

'I don't care, Alex. The next time you want to hold a meeting, ask me first. I don't like being treated like some kind of whore you can do what you like with.'

Alex smiled, and patted Justin's shoulder. 'I always forget how good you are, Jay. Have you two been working on assertiveness?'

Justin was shaking his head.

'No,' Annie replied, standing up and heading for the door. 'We were working on killing off Annie Marin.' She lifted her jacket off a peg. 'And I suggest you get some lessons in saying sorry when I'm gone or you're going to have to look for another candidate.'

On her way out she slammed the door, leaving Justin and Alex alone.

'Thank God,' Justin said, flopping down into the chair. 'I was beginning to worry she hadn't got what it takes.'

'What have you been doing with her?' Alex asked angrily.

'Nothing,' Justin protested, smiling still. 'The usual, what I'd do with anybody.'

'Annie's not just anybody,' Alex said, and then he too was out of the door and running down the corridor. He caught up with her waiting by the elevators. She turned to look at him, and then pressed the down button.

'Annie,' he said, 'I'm sorry if . . .'

'I'm not your plaything, Al. OK?' she said, hitting the button again. 'I'm not your plaything.'

'I know it seems as if we're . . .'

With a ting, the elevator arrived. They stepped in, but as there was another couple inside, said nothing until they were on the ground floor. Annie left first, through the lobby and onto the street.

She had needed to get outside the room, to know she could escape if she wanted to, but Alex had caught up with her and had a hand around her arm as if trying to drag her back inside.

'Annie, please listen.'

She stopped, and he moved to stand in front of her.

'Thank you. Now I'm sorry if we're going very fast, but we haven't got any choice. Either we take this campaign seriously or we should forget it right now.'

'Don't give me that, Al. Like I was some kind of child. You know I want to take it seriously. Didn't you read those ideas I wrote down for you?'

'Yes, I did.'

'They were serious, weren't they? *I* thought so.'

Alex hesitated before saying, 'We're not talking about the speech. We're talking about you being serious as a challenger. If we had a couple of years you could learn by yourself what confident leadership looks and feels like, but we haven't. We've got two weeks.'

She paused, and then said, 'Walk with me?' before setting off. They were silent for a moment, aware of being noticed in the busy Manhattan streets, but then Annie said, 'I'm not interested in running for President just because we *can*, Alex. I mean, if this is some big joke to see if you can wrap the voters around your little finger then I don't want to play.'

'Of course it isn't.'

'Then why all the acting? Why don't you just let me be? I didn't need all this coaching to play Dawn on set, did I?'

'No, but you're not like most actresses I know, Annie. You stop acting when you come off set, and that's not going to work in the election. You've got to be comfortable being Dawn all day.'

'So it *is* all sham!' she said.

'No! It's the only way to get you elected. It's our means towards a good end.'

They'd reached the dazzling windows of the famous toyshop FAO Schwartz on Fifth Avenue, its Christmas jingles mashed together with the yapping of battery dogs and children and wives. Annie pointed to a group of figures beyond Disney's *Lion King* merchandise.

'Do you know how they sell toys these days, Al?' she asked him. 'They make TV cartoons of them. They show Ninja Turtles or Power Rangers or whatever the latest one is, and then they market these toys in their billions because all the advertising's been done without kids knowing that's what they've been watching. They just think they're buying their screen heroes.' Now she looked at him. 'When I read about that I thought it sounded familiar. Doesn't it? Now

I've been advertised I'm becoming the toy, aren't I? All dolled up with shiny hair and fluttering eyelids. Is that what I am, Al? A Barbie doll?'

Alex shook his head and put his arm around her shoulders. 'No, not at all. But you've got to understand that for the real you to come out, for Annie Marin who cares and thinks and who's better than ninety-nine per cent of the people who'll ever run for President, for *that* person to come out, you have to be someone else for a while. But people want you to run. They see you as a symbol of the America we want to believe in, not the America that is. It's like when you step out on stage in costume – they're on you're side. They want to believe you're capable of changing their lives and we will, when we get there we will.'

'Will we?' she asked. 'Really?'

'Yes,' he said. 'We will,' and he opened his arms and gave Annie a hug, and she thought that, for a moment, the two of them must have looked to the world like a couple in love, standing outside FAO Schwartz before going inside to buy Christmas toys for their kids.

24

The following Thursday was Annie's big day. In the evening, the first important campaign meeting was taking place in her hotel suite, and during the day she was required on set, to tape her final appearance as Dawn Hope on *Unto the Skies*.

Ten extraordinary months had passed since she had taken her first nervous steps, feeling like a trespasser, into the bed and living rooms of Hill Way's troubled residents. Having become a part of their lives and of the lives of eleven million fans (not to mention the twenty million plus who watched in dubbed versions overseas), she was now about to leave as suddenly as she'd arrived.

She felt a certain amount of sadness and guilt. She knew that many of the show's fans would be mortified. Her stalker, who Annie hadn't seen since moving to the Grahame, was only a more obsessive and dedicated version of an ordinary fan. The woman (her name, Annie had discovered, was Karen) had taken her devotion a step too far, but there were millions of others who would experience genuine depression and grief when news of Dawn's death, or disappearance, was shared. Sales of Prozac were bound to rise.

The producers had made it harder for themselves by deciding, so Alex had heard, not to cast a new actress in the role. Casting new actors in old roles was standard in daytime drama, and although the transition period was usually difficult when the character returned from hospital or holiday with a new face, the fans would forgive plastic surgery sooner than death. Once Dawn's disappearance became known, Annie expected mass desertions to the more consistently exciting soaps.

She wandered into Studio C. A love scene between the characters Mandy Cranborne and Pierce Brenner was being taped in a bedroom at the far end of the space. As Annie softly stepped towards the action, she had the odd sensation of being in a church. Obviously the thought came to her because of the requisite hush and the exaggerated echo of background noise, yet there was also a sense in which she was witnessing a new religion. Did not the emotional and spiritual mayhem of these ceaseless soap scenes provide for millions the simple moral lessons once given through religion? *Unto the Skies* was no different from any other soap in being concerned with offences against the natural order, and here, as in the ideal world of religion, sinners never escaped punishment.

Annie watched the lovers kiss, and the house lights rose.

'Annie, my lovely pearl,' said Monty. 'I see you are bursting at the seams to start your scene-a-rooni.'

'If anyone's bursting around here, it's you,' she said, poking the stage manager's beer gut.

A few of the grips joined in the joking. They were a vulgar crowd of men, Italian blood relatives mostly, but it was precisely because this overweight, oversexed, misogynistic and macho group, for whom style was a lumberjack shirt and humour a reverberating fart, was not the kind in which Annie would expect to find friends again, that she knew she would miss them once she was back in the big world. On the set, they were her family. She would miss most of the cast too, even the vain studs in their cowboy boots, with their large heads like walking caricatures, and even the self-important tarts who somehow passed off as actresses.

Many of her closest friends were on set that day, as they

were taping the scene before Dawn's departure on holiday with Dale Irving. The actors, none of whom had believed the tabloid stories about Annie's presidential bid, thought she would be back after the vacation. Only Annie knew differently.

The scene was in Hill Way's top restaurant, run by the resident joker Sammy, and with Dawn were all of the Sheridans, as well as Paolo, whose conviction had suddenly been quashed on appeal, and Shannon de Salle.

The characters were seated at a long table eating the bowls of pasta that had been standard fare for many of the show's thirty years. There was much pretend frivolity and, with so many characters together, the cameras could focus on different groups and keep the viewers up to date on almost all of the storylines. Yet the party was in Dawn's honour, and the final words were left to her.

JAMIE
Go on, sis, say something!

MARY
I think Dawn must be bored of speeches.

VANESSA
(TO SHANNON)
I don't think Dawn ever gets bored of hearing herself speak, do you?

SHANNON
I hope she never comes back to Hill Way!

WILLIAM
Go on, Dawn. Your mother would like it.

MARY
Yes, and I don't want to hear you say I shouldn't have . . .

DAWN
(STANDING AT HEAD OF TABLE)
Really, you shouldn't have done all this on my account!

MARY
(TO WILLIAM)
I knew she'd say that.

DAWN
I don't have much to say but thank you. Thank you for making me feel so at home in Hill Way. I don't think that with all the pressures a job like mine brings, I'd have been able to get through these months without you, my family and my friends. And without Dale. He thinks I'm his Juliet. Well, you're my Romeo, every day of the week.

DALE
(RAISING HIS GLASS)
Thank you, my love.

DAWN
I only wish in my heart that everyone could discover the kind of happiness you've brought me.

MARY
You've brought it to us too.

DAWN
I'm only going away for two weeks, but it's going to feel like longer!

Annie looked down the table at her friends. Dawn was right – it was going to feel a whole lot longer. She paused in her speech, the emotion honest.

DAWN
Anyway, that's all I wanted to say. As some of you know, I'm thinking of running for President one day, so I'll be hurrying back from the Caribbean.

CARRIE
(ASIDE TO JAMIE)
And if you ask me, she'll be wearing a wedding band.

SHANNON
I don't think so, Carrie. If only you knew what Dale told me.

'That's a wrap, my lovelies,' said Monty.

The actors were standing from the table when Annie, raising her arms, asked them if they would wait. They sat and looked up at her as they had while taping the scene.

'Christ!' muttered Faith under her breath. 'She thinks we love her in real life!'

Annie stabbed her fork into the sticky, cold pasta and looked up. 'As some of you know, I'm thinking of running for President one day!' she said, repeating Dawn's lines. 'The only difference is that I won't be hurrying back. Actually, this really is a goodbye.'

Some of the actors, forgetting that the cameras weren't rolling, looked back and forth at the actress with exaggerated consternation.

'Now I know this is going to sound kind of gushy but, like Dawn, you did make me feel a part of your family right from the start. It's been fun, and it's been a surprise that it's been fun and, well, I'll visit you soon. So that's it. That's what I wanted to say.'

411

Annie sat down and looked at the faces around her. She certainly saw shock, but she thought she saw kindness, sorrow and friendship too. What she could not perceive was how the cast was feeling inside. The kindly demeanours were hiding the jealousy, spite and envy that was a part of each actor's make-up. Not one was happy that Annie was moving on to become an even bigger star, and it was precisely because of this, because they hated her with all their hearts, that, raising their glasses in a toast, they all did what they'd been trained to do – they smiled.

Annie returned to the Truman Suite not long before the meeting was to begin. She had come dressed in the outfit she'd been wearing on set, which would do until her new clothes arrived. A stylist from *Vogue*, a Brit called Cecilia, had promised to collect outfits from designers who'd be 'chuffed to bits' to see their creations on global display. For Dawn's announcement a bright colour was decided upon. A yellow or blue ('even a subtle red,' Cecilia had wondered), though certainly, definitely, pink received a hefty no. Pink would be seen as too feminine and flimsy. The cut and the colour had to be strong and womanly and 'say a lot without giving too much away' which, oddly enough, was how Alex and Rebecca were approaching the speech as well. Cecilia, dressed in black jodhpurs, black boots and a black Nicole Farhi jacket, had revealed she was 'big on colours right now' and had even suggested 'something that says *America*' before crinkling her brow and sucking on her Mont Blanc pen.

Annie rode the hotel elevator with Justin. She had warmed to him during the past few days and now found her lessons quite amusing. The night before, they had been studying photographs and videos of the sublime Jackie O during the Camelot days. Annie had spent a whole hour trying, with a low chair, to mirror the natural curve of Jackie's arm as she embraced her son by her side. Alex had insisted that children's issues were to be a major focus of Dawn's campaign, and that if she wasn't physically comfortable with them, then the race might be lost.

A hush fell among the members of the campaign team as Annie entered her suite. They were young volunteers, mostly, who'd joined New Dawn to work beside the great Alex Lubotsky and to meet Tom Sterling and Annie. All were keen to do a first-rate job putting across Dawn's Message of Hope, but few knew its details (meaning they weren't yet aware there were none), nor did they feel any urgency to discover any. It was the process that interested and intrigued them, as well as the chance to mix with some majorly cool dudes.

Annie was introduced to those she hadn't met by a watchful Justin, and she was about to grab a five-minute lie-down in her bedroom when Rebecca burst in.

'Tom's arrived,' she told Alex. 'And there's a problem.'

'He's worried we're spending too much, isn't he?' Alex said.

Everything was being paid for with cash from his eight-million-dollar campaign fund.

'I don't think so. He's developed a hearing problem because of *Ludwig*. He thinks he's going deaf.'

'You're fucking kidding me,' Alex laughed, sharing his surprise with the others in the room.

'Nope,' Rebecca replied, smiling too.

'So why's he here at all? He must have been freaked out by the airplane, wasn't he?'

'I presume he'll be taking everything in, even if he says he isn't. And Laurel says you can write him notes.'

'In German?' Annie asked.

'No, he reads English.'

Alex shook his head, and then shrugged his shoulders. 'What can we do? I'll call and tell him we're ready.'

'No telephones, dumbo,' Rebecca said, tapping her forehead. 'I'll go and fetch him.'

Alex turned to Zoë, who'd decided to film the meetings for a possible fly-on-the-wall documentary about New Dawn. She knew how the BBC loved to bolster dented British egos by transmitting programmes about nations more ridiculous than its own.

'I don't think we need that on film,' said Alex, waving a hand in front of the lens of her 16mm camera.

'Alex, sweetie,' Zoë said, lowering the camera, 'let me do my job! We can edit it out later.'

Moments later, Tom Sterling appeared. He was wearing a curious mix of eighteenth- and twentieth-century clothing, black jeans and cowboy boots worn with a white ruffled shirt. It made him look like a 1970s' glam rock star, especially now that his grey hair had been dyed black and permed. Saying nothing, Alex advanced to shake Tom's hand before producing a chair, happily enough a gilded reproduction of an early nineteenth-century design. In fact the entire room, with its excess of gilt, its gaudy draped swag above the deep red curtains, its plaster cornices as thick as wedding-cake icing and its plentiful gold-and-red-striped silk-covered chairs, should have made Tom feel comfortable. But they didn't seem to help, for he kept frowning and rapidly shaking his head, and once or twice he was heard to grunt, like a drunken man in his sleep.

His loyal assistant, Laurel, was beside him, pen and paper at hand. Alex was standing beside a large board covered with a white sheet. Justin, dapper in pinstripes, was beside him.

'OK,' said Alex. 'Thanks for coming, everyone. In case any of you don't know who everyone is, I'll do some quick introductions. We all know Dawn, our future President.'

Alex said the words 'future President' without any irony whatsoever. Yet perhaps more surprising and pleasing to

Justin, no emotion showed on Annie's resolute face when she was so introduced. Gone was the coyness that would have followed such words before. Now her response was a very slight nod.

'To my right here,' Alex continued, 'is Justin Hathwaite, who is – what do you call yourself, Jay?'

'Image consultant.'

'OK. Anyway, he's done great things putting Britain's Labour Party on the road to victory and he's here to help all of us. Can I request that in the interests of maintaining a sharp focus, all suggestions about style go through Justin to Dawn. We've all got our own ideas about what looks and works best, and I want to hear them, but we have to settle on an image and stick with it. The same applies to.Tom Sterling, who I'm sure needs no introduction but to say that he'll make an exemplary Vice President.'

The assembled company watched Laurel write 'exceptional Vice President' on a piece of paper. She showed it to Tom.

In a heavy German accent, he said, 'Thank you,' before, surprisingly, smacking together his hands in applause.

'OK, we may be the front men but . . .'

'And women,' interrupted Annie.

'And women,' conceded Alex, 'but all of you, and I mean this, all of us are vital to our success. Now, this is Rebecca Frear who's the second-best campaign manager in the country.'

'Show-off,' she said.

'Rebecca's our Director of Issues. Gary and Ben have been designing some images and you'll be hearing from them in a moment, Lawrence is our Finance Chairman, Harvey is one of our distinguished attorneys, Sanjiv is our computer and Internet whizzo, Dean, Alicia, Craig and . . .'

Alex clicked his fingers.

'Bobby!' the man said.

'That's right, sorry, and *Bobby* are the embryo of a grassroots organisation that's going to spread very, very fast after the announcement. Oh, while I remember, we're going to be investing heavily in direct mail and I want you all to carry the literature and sign people up if they express *any interest whatsoever*. Get their names, addresses and details. New Dawn has to work like a sort of political Amway. I don't want a single supporter lost through the net because of slackness. All right? Now, moving on, Laurel is Tom's assistant, Debra is from the women's group, Enabling Eve, and Zoë Dunlop will be directing some of the most modern, innovative campaign commercials that have ever been seen. As you know, Dawn and Tom are not ordinary candidates and we're going to have to take full advantage of their differences before they're thrown at us as criticisms. What is going to be very important is to make it clear that they're not tainted by Washington politics, OK? They're clean and . . .'

He was interrupted by the arrival of Charlie Canon.

'Excuse me, I was taping public radio,' she said self-importantly, as she made straight for Tom Sterling's chair.

'Great to see you, Tom,' she said. 'You look well.'

He stared at her quizzically, and then, after a shake of the head, shouted in a German accent, 'Louder!'

Charlie looked absolutely lost.

'Unfortunately, Ludwig is losing his hearing,' explained the po-faced Laurel.

'Oh! I said it was great to see you,' Charlie shouted, leaning close to Tom's left ear.

Suddenly he nodded and kissed her hand, and she took her seat only to hear him turn to Laurel and shout, 'Who was that woman?'

Alex continued. 'Charlie and Debra will be working together to help us secure the female vote. We're looking at over fifty per cent of the electorate in every state who could vote for Dawn on the strength of her gender and . . .'

Charlie, who got terribly jealous if she saw anyone else playing with her favourite statistics, held up a finger and said, 'The important point, Alex, is that it's an advantage to be a woman running for office at this moment in history. We can say, "Look at the facts, men have screwed up long enough, it's time to pass the baton and give women the chance they deserve at the highest level." It's impossible to argue with that.'

'I think Charlie's right,' said Alex, 'but if we may, I'd like to keep this discussion focused on the announcement. Now, on Saturday, Dawn and I will meet the press over our decision to leave *Unto the Skies*. We're going to put it about that she'll *probably* announce her candidacy then. However,' he said, pausing to take a sip of water, keeping his team on edge as he hoped to do to the media, 'we're not going to announce then. Absolutely not. What we're going to do is use the event to publicise the actual date, which is Tuesday the 20th.'

'Where?' asked Craig.

'That's one of the reasons we're here. We need some suggestions.'

'What about from the Brooklyn Bridge?' Alicia asked. 'To tie in with the theme tune.'

She had meant to say 'campaign song' but anyway, Alex said no. It had to be somewhere indoors because of the weather and because Dawn's hair needed to be perfect. After a few suggestions, it was agreed upon that no decision would be agreed upon until the weekend.

'Now,' said Alex, 'what's the story with the campaign song? Did anyone contact Simon and Garfunkel's people?'

'We've got permission,' said Harvey.

'I meant about singing "Bridge" live.'

'Are those two talking?' Lawrence asked.

'I don't know,' said Alex. 'Are they're talking or fighting? Anyone?' There was silence. 'Well, come on,' he said impatiently, clapping his hands. 'You should be on top of things like that. I don't want to have to do all the thinking for you.'

'Did Alicia tell you about the Paul Simon impersonator?' said Rebecca.

Apparently Alicia knew of a man, the spitting image of Paul Simon, who'd be willing to make an appearance at the announcement. He wouldn't sing, but walk behind Dawn so that the press would notice him without having a chance to see him as a phoney.

Alex agreed that it was a good idea if the real duo could not be persuaded to sing or talk to one another. 'That's more like it,' he said. 'Now, I'm going to hand you over briefly to Gary and Ben to explain what they've done so far.'

Gary, a button-down, white-shirted kind of UCLA graduate, was bearded, sincere, married, in his late thirties and head of the graphic design company hired by the New Dawn team. 'Hi, everyone,' he said. 'It's great to be here and a part of the team. We spent some time trying to work with images of bridges, naturally, to link in with the song, but in fact we've since come up with something that I hope you'll like. Ben has it all here on his PC, but we've gone ahead and blown up a couple of images for you to look at. It's – well, I'll let you judge for yourselves.' He lifted the covering from the board to reveal an image showing two-thirds of a giant, luscious orange sun rising above the sea. Clearly defined rays of light emanated from its heart. At the top of the poster were the words, 'A NEW DAWN'. Gary flipped to the next image, which was identical but for the header. This time, the phrase was one gleaned from *Selected Speeches*. 'LET'S RISE TOGETHER', it said. 'Of course,' Gary continued, 'there are an almost infinite number of colour combinations, but what we like about this is that it's focused, it's going to be clearly identifiable and it gives the right signals of warmth, of renewal and of the essential quality of sunlight. And a rising sun is a hopeful symbol, I'm sure you'll agree.'

'Could it be seen as Japanese?' wondered Rebecca.

It was Ben who replied. 'Their flag shows a complete sphere whereas here the sun is rising out of the water. I think it's an optimistic vision for all our tomorrows, like Gary said, and I can see it working well on buttons, on the outside of campaign literature and especially on T-shirts.'

'Justin?' said Alex.

Justin was staring rather sternly at the image. 'I worry that it's too obvious,' he said. 'It's the sort of poster they'd produce for a made-for-TV film about a political candidate.'

'Nothing wrong with TV,' said Alex. 'I like the look. Dawn is, as we know, a very warm person and I'd like people to have the impression that having her as President will be like feeling the sun on their backs.'

Alex was writing 'Tom, do you like it?' on a piece of paper. He handed it to the vice-presidential candidate, who read it, nodded, twitched, and then shouted, 'Good! I am liking of this much now.'

Annie bit on her lower lip. This was one of the habits that Justin was trying to break, but the more she saw Tom the more she worried he might ruin all their hard work. She hoped to God he didn't feel the need to research another part while they were campaigning.

'Thanks, then, Gary,' said Alex. 'We'll work with that for the moment. Now, I want to spend a few moments explaining how we're going to win this campaign from the bottom up. I don't see us winning by knocking on doors, OK? Dawn and Tom are going to win using that,' he said, pointing at the TV. 'And as both are fantastic at using it, that means no one else is going to stand a chance.'

*   *   *

Two days later, with her hand clutching a Gideon Bible, Annie stood before the mirror in her hotel bathroom and looked with approval at her new hairstyle.

Then she spoke. 'I do solemnly swear that I . . . No, too girly!' She began again. 'I do solemnly swear,' this sounds better, she thought, straightening her back as Justin had taught, 'that I will faithfully execute the office of President of the United States, and will to the best of my ability, preserve, protect and defend the Constitution of . . .'

'Knock, knock,' came a voice from the bedroom.

'Damn!' Annie whispered, blushing instantly. The door to the bathroom was open, and although Alex had not come far enough into the bedroom for Annie to see him, she knew it was he, and that he could have heard.

'I'll be right out,' she said breezily.

She pulled her T-shirt as low as she could over her underwear and returned to the bedroom, but Alex had retreated to the adjoining room so she climbed back into bed, and called for him to come in.

'Sorry,' he said. 'I used my key.'

Alex had a key to the suite so the team could work while Annie was on the soap opera set.

'No problem,' she said, bending her knees and lifting them under her chin. She felt as if she was exposing herself to him and wondered what he would do if she flipped the blankets away and asked him to join her. Then again, he wasn't at his most appealing, unshaven and in the same clothes he'd worn the day before.

'You look like shit, Al!' she told him.

He poured some cold coffee into Annie's abandoned breakfast cup. 'I've been at Rebecca's all night,' he explained, pulling up a lush red winged chair.

Annie's heart jumped in alarm until he added, 'Writing your announcement speech.'

'Is it done?' she asked excitedly.

420

'Yup. I'll give you a copy after the press conference. Oh, by the way, it's already in the papers that you're leaving *Unto the Skies*. Someone must have talked.'

'You know what, Alex?' she said. 'I mentioned it to a couple of friends on the set. Does it matter a lot?'

'To us? No, not at all. It's UBC who won't be so happy now their secret's out. But that's their problem. Anyway, it'll all be official in a couple of hours. Your fans are going to go nuts. How are you feeling, by the way?'

'Better since you asked me, thanks.'

'Your hair looks nice,' he said now.

Bradley Peters had cut it the day before. It had been dyed also, to a deeper reddy-brown. Annie felt it with her hand and said, 'I almost didn't recognise myself in the mirror this morning.'

'Oh, good. Then we must be doing something right,' Alex replied, suddenly yawning. He got to his feet. 'Listen, I'm going to go and make myself presentable.'

'You can use the shower here,' said Annie.

'No thanks,' he answered. 'Who knows what I might do if I found myself naked in your bedroom?'

'I'll risk it,' she said, her heart thumping.

He was looking at her as if he was considering the option. Was this really the time? Annie wondered. After all, there'd been no need for him to come around so soon before they were scheduled to meet. Had he been looking for an excuse? She thought, once again, of throwing back the covers, of finding out once and for all, but Alex broke the silence.

'It's never a good idea,' he said, 'if it's not strictly business,' and if Annie detected a hint of regret in his voice, she would have been right. He kept asking himself whether he was fighting a losing battle, and often wondered whether he'd be able to run an objective campaign for a lover.

'Then I'll see you at UBC,' said Annie.

'Right,' Alex answered. 'See you there.'

*   *   *

The press conference Shermer had called to announce the departure of his star performer and headwriter was very unusual. A great many actors and actresses had left *Unto the Skies* with only the journalists from the soap opera magazines showing any interest. Once or twice an actor of some notoriety had been tempted to shrink his or her reputation onto the small screen and the surrounding interest had warranted a word or two in the entertainment pages of the national newspapers, but no one could remember anything like this.

The truth was, of course, that Annie Marin – or Dawn Hope, as she was now to be known – was much more than the most popular soap actress in America. She was the authoress of a book of speeches and sayings that remained in the top five of the bestseller lists, and a likely candidate for the world's most important job. As yet, nothing had been confirmed, and it was because of this (and because Alex had been onto his network of press connections) that so many reporters arrived at UBC Tower on this chilly December morning.

Annie was led to a table lined with microphones, behind which sat the UBC President with David Wolf, Anne-Marie, Vince and Alex. At least sixty reporters were in the auditorium, and almost as many cameramen, although UBC had reserved sole televisual rights. Annie was the focus of attention, although it was some time before she was asked to speak. Meanwhile, Shermer had confirmed the rumours that Annie was leaving the show, adding that a new star had been put under contract who might or might not be filling Annie's shoes in playing Illinois's Governor. This was clever, for it would keep the viewers tuned in, hopeful of Dawn's return.

Following Shermer, David Wolf said a couple of words, Vince managed to insult Alex and the ex-headwriter replied by saying that Dawn was as much a product of the people as of the writers and producers of *Unto the Skies*. Finally, Annie was allowed her say. At her first smile there was a simultaneous fluttering of camera shutters, like a flock of birds disturbed at once by a noise. Then she was bombarded with questions, not about her future career as an actress, but about her possible candidacy, about Tom Sterling, about whether she'd held public office and if she would change her name to Dawn.

Her skill in responding made Alex proud. She was handling the questions like a professional, never giving too much away, staying controlled without seeming arrogant and presenting herself as a legitimate candidate for office. So when the meeting was called to a close, Alex made his way to Annie to congratulate her.

She was talking to Shermer when Alex joined them.

'Barry,' he said. 'Thanks for your understanding.'

'Who says I understand?' said Shermer before he left the two alone.

'He doesn't like losing you,' Alex told Annie, 'and I don't blame him. You did a great job.'

'Did I?' she said, grinning.

'Yes. So good, I'm going to take you out to lunch. We can talk about this,' he said, handing her a copy of the speech.

'You're on!'

'Let's leave at the front,' he said.

A substantial crowd had gathered in UBC Square, hoping to catch a glimpse of their favourite star and political hopeful. Alex wanted Annie to meet with her fans as practice for the larger, potentially hostile masses she would encounter on the campaign trail. He had already decided that, from Tuesday onwards, she would be protected by burly bodyguards, as Madonna always was. The more it could be suggested that she was in need of protection, the more valuable she would appear.

They were close to the exit when they heard a sarcastic little whine from behind.

'Going to meet your fans and voters, are you?' It was Vince. 'I'm sorry for saying this, but what you guys are doing looks to me a lot like jerking off in public. You know? Like Perot with tits.'

'Thank you, Vince,' said Alex. 'Astute as ever.'

'Hey, don't say I didn't warn you, Annie. Because, you know, I never minded you.' He winked. 'Bye-bye now!'

He patted Annie's bum as he walked out into the bright sunshine in UBC Square.

It felt good to be outside. Christmas in New York simply made Annie feel happy. Now, the sounds of a Salvation Army band playing carols reached her through the shiny, frozen air. UBC Square had taken on a fresh aspect, with its thirty Christmas trees ribbed with tiny vertebrae of white lights and a massive red bow positioned above the grand, Art Deco entrance to the tower.

As soon as Annie stepped into view, a crowd of almost two hundred fans pushed forward. Some of the photo journalists had followed her from the hall too, and two TV stations had sent teams to keep up to the minute on Dawn's candidacy. Within moments, Annie was surrounded. A couple of UBC security guards were loitering close by, but since it was mainly female fans jostling her, they saw no need to hold them back. The women were wanting to know why Dawn was leaving and if she would run, and whether she cared for Mary, her mother, and how she could possibly have left Dale Irving behind lounging in the Caribbean thinking he'd found love at last.

Vince, wanting in, muscled his way to Annie's side and patting from his face a placard reading 'Dawn, Don't leave!', he said, 'Don't worry, ladies, *Unto the Skies* will keep coming to you every day at three. Life goes on.'

As he was speaking, Annie noticed her friendly stalker, Karen, standing very still towards the front of the group, wearing an overcoat that seemed a few sizes too big and looking more than a little resentful. Annie assumed that it was because of the move to the Grahame. She nodded in the stalker's direction and a strange expression came over Karen's face, neither sorrow nor malice, but something closer to shock. Then, her eyes fixed on Annie, she plunged her hand into her pocket.

Suddenly, a TV camera was pointed at Annie's face and she lifted her hand to shield her eyes from the glare. Rudely, Vince pushed in front of her to speak with the reporter and as he did so a shot sounded, and another and another and another and Annie felt a hot, terrible pain in her leg and stomach and she fell, her eyes open in panic, her mind unable to believe that she'd been hit, that her hands were covered in blood, that, dizzy, she'd fallen, landing on something soft. Amid the screams and shouts she saw a bright, white light filling her eyes and she wanted to scream out, *No, not now, not this, not now*, but no sound came from her mouth and there was only a deep throbbing in her ears and the taste of blood in her mouth.

Alex was shouting, 'Get back! Back off!'

He pushed away the TV crew and fell to his knees and took Annie in his arms and pressed his cheek against hers and began to whisper, 'It's OK, it's OK. You're OK,' but to him she didn't feel OK, she didn't feel alive, and her neck looked so delicate and soft as her head rolled backwards, heavy in his hands. Bright blood from Annie's wounds were pouring into her clothes and onto his hands, but he couldn't tell where she'd been hit or how badly, and he couldn't see any life in her, even with his cheek against her lips as he tried to sense her breath. He heaved the air into his own lungs and then cried out for the people and cameras to move back again.

He had pictured this scene before, with President Grant. A friendly crowd, a tableaux of smiles, a sudden burst of noise and panic and a body on the ground and always, every time, he had seen himself as he liked to be, calm and in control and even excited to know that he was where history was being made. But now there was no order to his mind. He was sitting on the ground. There was another body beside him – Vince's maybe, he didn't know – and he had Annie on his lap and his tears were mixing with her blood on his cheeks and he hadn't had the guts to tell her he loved her because he'd been scared to, for Christ's sake, because he'd been scared. It wasn't because he didn't think about her, and it wasn't because he didn't love her, he did; it was because he'd been scared. But why, when he loved her enough to have stepped in front of the bullets if only he hadn't been where he always was, watching, a step behind, carefully sizing up the scene before doing anything at all?

More guards from UBC had arrived and were keeping the fans away, though a large crowd had swarmed to the drama. The TV crews were inside the ring because they had a right to see the suffering, they were the eyes of the world. Alex knew they were there, but still he pressed his lips to Annie's ear and whispered, 'I'm sorry. Annie, can you hear me? I'm sorry. Talk to me. Can you hear? Please, Annie, please God. I love you, Annie. I love you.' Suddenly he looked up to the flash of cameras. 'Where's the ambulance? Where's the fucking ambulance?'

Moments later the police were clearing a circle around the victims, and the crews of two ambulances had run in with stretchers.

'Sir, are you injured, sir?'

A pool of blood had formed around Alex's legs, and his hands and face were wet with it. 'She is. Not me.'

One paramedic leant over Annie as another pulled Alex away. With trembling hands, he let go of her and it felt as if he was leaving her, betraying her. As he watched the three men checking her pulse and looking beneath her eyelids, he couldn't free his mind from the horror that he was to blame, that he might as well have fired the shot himself because he'd put her in the firing line so that he could climb back to the top.

'How is she?' he asked. 'How is she?'

'Sir, please step back,' the ambulance man said.

'But she's OK, isn't she?'

An oxygen mask was being strapped over Annie's beautiful, soft face and within seconds she was on the stretcher and they were running beside her, wheeling through the scattering pigeons and towards the ambulance. Alex ran after her, blocking out the faces all around. He needed to see her open her eyes. He needed to hear that she was alive.

The door of the ambulance was shut behind him, and through the tiny window he could have seen, if he had been able to take his eyes off Annie's silent face, a circle of women formed in prayer for Dawn Hope's life, a crowd of kids, high with the thrill, jumping to see blood, and Vince being loaded onto another stretcher, though they seemed to be taking more time with him, because he was injured either less, or more.

What Alex could not have seen from so far away was that one of Annie's signed publicity shots, herself as Dawn in a glittering silver dress, had fallen from a fan's hand and fluttered in the wind to lie, face up, in a slick sheen of bright blood among the pages of the announcement speech she'd been clutching in her hand as the bullets had thudded into her unsuspecting flesh.

25

Like a raindrop on water, the circle made by the linked hands of the women praying for Dawn Hope's life in UBC Square widened through the States and beyond, to those countries where *Unto the Skies* was watched by millions of devoted fans. The shock felt was all the greater since Dawn's assailant existed outside soapland's screen borders, and thus could not be expected to suffer the severe ignominy and punishment that would have befallen the perpetrator of such a crime in Hill Way. An enduring joy of soap opera was that evil was never unpunished, that the natural order was never unsettled for long, and though Dawn's attacker was sure to be sent to trial, it was bitter cruelty indeed that those viewers without cable TV would not be able to tune into the court channel to see justice meted out.

Alex was surprised that Dawn's shooting became the top story, not only on the local news, but on the national news as well. Although reporters were keen to make the crime politically motivated (such acts carried greater historical weight, set apart as they were, from the common or garden acts of human baseness), the truth was more simple. Karen Clare, Dawn's persistent stalker, had shot her heroine for the same reason that Mark Chapman shot Lennon and Jeffrey Dahmer made ragout of young hustlers: because she was crazy. The departure of a much-loved character from a top soap opera was always a deeply sad occasion for millions of people, but this grief was most commonly swallowed, not shot through the barrel of a gun.

It was, of course, greatly to Vince Moscardini's misfortune that his hunger for publicity should have led him towards the lights of a TV camera at exactly the moment when Karen chose to express this insanity. As he'd passed Annie, he was hit once and, successful where so many humans had failed, the bullet found its way directly to his heart. The paramedics had been unable to do anything to revive him and he died where he fell. And although Vince was not a popular man, not with the two women who'd once been his wives, nor with the cast and crew who worked for him, it was generally considered that he didn't deserve to die. Had he been on *Unto the Skies*, a punishment more fitting to his crimes would have been found.

Alex was not so harsh a man as to have wished for Vince's death, but now, as he checked the pockets of the suit he was about to throw out, he did feel that some kind of retribution had been made for Max's suicide. There was a certain dramatic symmetry, a soap opera neatness, to the producer's demise. Still, Alex felt some guilt about the incident. Had he never created Dawn, then Vince would not have found himself in UBC Square the day before and he would have been alive. It was, of course, pointless to trace events back to their sources, but Alex was aware that he'd been sprinting so fast towards his imagined finish line that others had been carelessly knocked off the course.

When Alex had returned to the apartment to change his clothes the night before, he'd thrown the suit in the bathtub and forgotten it was there until he'd stepped, already naked, into the shower this morning. Having rescued what hadn't been ruined from the trousers, and curled them into a bin liner, now he checked the jacket. The fabric was damp from Annie's blood. The day before, he had been in an utter panic at the amount flooding from Annie's wounds.

In the ambulance they had staunched the flow, tending

her with staggering efficiency despite the tumbling ride over Manhattan's cavernous asphalt. Then, Annie was alive. She was breathing well through the oxygen mask, they'd assured him, and because the wounds seemed to be in the lower limbs they were unlikely to be fatal. One of the medics had shouted out that the femoral artery was punctured, which accounted for the large loss of blood, and he'd comforted Alex by saying it probably looked worse than it was, though for now they couldn't see. She was stable, and that was the best for which they could hope.

Alex tied the bag shut and rinsed his hands. Then he brushed his teeth in front of the mirror. The blood seemed to have soaked even to his eyeballs. He was looking forward to catching up on the sleep he'd lost, not only last night but the night before, when he'd chosen to stay up writing the announcement speech that would never be heard. It was all wasted now.

He was about to drop into bed when the doorman buzzed up from below. 'It's a Mr Hathwaite,' he was told.

'OK, send him up,' said Alex.

At the door in his bathrobe, he welcomed a smiling Justin. 'I'm half-asleep, Jay, so . . .'

'Don't worry,' Justin said, slapping Alex on the arm, 'I'm only here for a moment.' He helped himself to juice from the fridge, the thin glass a delicate slice of orange in his hand. 'But I had an idea I wanted to tell you. How do you like "A Star is Dawn"?'

Alex flopped onto the sofa and lifted his feet to the coffee table. 'Justin, Vince Moscardini was killed.'

'I know that.'

'That shot would have hit Annie,' Alex snapped, his exhaustion making him short-tempered. 'As it was, one of the bullets got embedded in a rib. If that hadn't happened, she could have died.'

'But she didn't, did she? I thought you said she was going to recover quite quickly.'

'She is, I mean, she should.'

'So it gives us some breathing space, Al. God's obviously on our side!'

A spike of pain stabbed into the back of Alex's eyes, as if he was being punished for Justin's insensitivity. 'If there's a God he was on Annie's side, and as far as going on with the campaign, forget it. It's over, Jay. It's over.'

Justin laughed gently. 'I know you too well to believe that. Why don't you get some sleep and we'll talk about it tomorrow.'

As soon as Justin had discovered that Annie was expected to make a full recovery, he'd begun to see the shooting for its immense PR potential.

She had absorbed so much so fast that he had become genuinely concerned that, with her pretty face and pristine teeth and immaculate outfits, she would be too perfect and telegenic to appeal to the demanding voters of the mid-nineties. President Grant was suffering from being seen as too slick and smiley, and there was a sense that the voters wanted someone who mixed a little humility and roughness with his or her screen confidence. The shooting, and the invaluable television and print shots of a bloodied Annie being stretchered away, had scratched the gloss off Dawn. More than this, it had made her a female candidate for whom men could vote.

Justin well understood that the women who had planted themselves most deeply in the nation's imagination were those who had publicly suffered. In his home country he'd seen Margaret Thatcher despised not for her many crimes against Britain, but because she had too rarely displayed any vulnerability. Almost the same was true of Susan Grant, who, though feminine, was considered too brilliant and self-assured to capture hearts. No, it was the damaged, the martyred, the unhappy women

432

who were loved. Marilyn with her failed marriages and the drugs tube empty in her plump hand, Jackie Kennedy with Dallas and cancer, and now Dawn with the bullets in her gut. By suffering so, by being seen to be weak, she had earned the sympathy, and probably the votes, of the people.

Justin knew they could lay it on thick in the campaign. The shooting tied in well with 'Bridge Over Troubled Water', too. The silver girl was laying herself down to be trampled over and to protect the people from the muddy waters of modern America. She was willing to take a bullet for the nation. This approach was so appealing that Justin couldn't fathom Alex's stubbornness. He was obviously too fond of the candidate (that much was clear from the raw anguish captured on his face by the cameras), but that surely wouldn't be enough for him to turn his back on this political gift horse. That wasn't Alex Lubotsky's style, and so Justin was sure that after a few hours' sleep his friend would see the light.

'I can see you're not on this planet any more, Al,' he said. 'I'll give you a bell tomorrow.'

As Justin was by the door, Alex said, 'You can count me out. I mean it.'

'I know you do,' said Justin, stepping into the corridor. 'But don't forget, tomorrow's a whole new day.'

As far as Justin Hathwaite was concerned, Saturday had been the perfect day for the shooting, as those papers without Sunday editions ran the story on Monday which effectively gave Dawn double the coverage. Alex had thought nothing of this, having slept for the best part of a day and night, so that when he arrived at the hospital on Monday morning he felt dozy from too much rest, not too little. Annie herself was groggy from the painkillers, but she was fully conscious and sitting up in bed reading about herself.

'Hi!' he said, angling his head around the door.

To see her looking so bright and alive made him think for a second that the weekend had been a nightmare. He had dreamt of her death during his sleep. In the dream she had been conscious after the shooting, staring at him with malice in her eyes. However many kisses he had planted on her face and lips, her expression had remained one of stark and bitter incomprehension, as if she was shocked by some betrayal. And then he'd felt hands on his arms pulling him from her as the paramedics had, but this time they were policemen handcuffing him and taking the gun from his hand, Annie staring all the while and the blood pooling into a lake around herself. Then he'd seen two fingers slide Annie's lifeless eyelids shut as he opened his to let the tears spill silently out.

'It looks as if I'll have to welcome you from my bed again, doesn't it?' she said.

He stepped forward, feeling unsure of himself. He had brought flowers, irises because he Annie mentioning that they had more class than roses. There was, however, scarcely space for more, so like a florist's had the room become.

'How are you feeling?' he asked.

She looked pale, and there was a bruise on her upper left cheek from where it had knocked Vince's head as she fell. Aside from that, he thought she looked remarkably healthy.

She took a sip of her drink. 'I'm going to be fine, so long as I don't leak anywhere.'

'That's great news. I was, um, I was worried.' He seemed strangely nervous as he took a step nearer the patient. 'I was very worried.'

'I know,' she said, staring at him and wondering how much of what she remembered was a dream. She could see Karen, and the look on Karen's face, and the hand in the pocket and an unfamiliar popping sound, but as there'd been no bang, like the bang of a gun in the movies, she had not been able to believe she was shot until the pain and dizziness had come and she'd fallen, the strength gone from her arms, the sense lost of how her limbs worked on her body. And then she remembered strong arms wrapping her, and voices, and, clearly, the words 'I love you.'

Later, having heard that Alex had stayed with her all night in the hospital, she wondered if it had been he.

'Do you feel up to talking?' he asked, standing with the flowers still in his hand.

'Sure,' she replied. 'It's just this fracture hurts when I move. So don't make me laugh.'

He pulled up a chair and said, 'I've never seen so many flowers and cards in one room,' as he looked everywhere but into her eyes.

'I know.'

'Are they from friends or . . .'

'Fans, mainly.'

'There'll be plenty more of those, I'm sure.'

'Yeah. Probably.'

Again, they were silent. Alex squinted to read the tiny blue writing on the side of Annie's intravenous drip. Then he said, 'It's good you're feeling better. I was worried about you.'

'Were you?' she asked this time.

'Yes,' he said, very softly. 'I was.' He reached out to take her hand, and as he did so, she turned it upwards and moved it so that their fingertips were touching. 'I was more than worried. Annie, I . . .'

'What happened to Dawn?' she joked, nervous because she wasn't convinced he would say the one thing she wanted to hear.

'Dawn got shot, I think. Didn't she?'

'Did she?'

'Well that's what I wanted to talk about.' He lifted his hand away and at once seemed to relax, the tension

435

leaving his face. 'We need to decide whether we quit now or later.'

'That doesn't sound very like you,' she said, turning towards him a little and wincing at the pain in her leg. She had been told that her wounds would have been much worse had the gun been fired from a closer range.

'Perhaps I haven't been feeling very like me since Saturday,' he said, avoiding her eyes and pulling a dead petal from the roses bunched carelessly in a blue plastic vase by her bed. 'Sometimes things happen that make you wonder if being you is so great after all.'

'You sound like Max used to,' she said.

'Mm.'

'Al, what happened wasn't your fault. Karen's a crazy. She could have shot me anytime.'

'But you should have been protected.'

'So get me some bodyguards next time,' she said lightly and, seeing the surprise on his face, added, 'I can't let a bullet stop me from running, can I? What would all these people think?' as she looked about her at the cards.

'I think they'd understand.'

'Would they? I think I'd always be seen as the candidate who ran scared.'

'It's OK to be scared of being shot dead, you know. Besides, I don't like the idea of people taking pot shots at you.'

'Lightning doesn't strike the same place twice,' said Annie and then, reaching out across the bed, she added, 'but thanks for thinking of that.' She smiled. 'Are you sure a stray bullet didn't hit you in the head?'

'I'm sure. Annie, there's something I should have said a long time ago. I . . .'

Suddenly the door banged open and a woman came in, holding in front of her face a bar of chocolate the size of Vermont. She was laughing.

'Bra!' Annie shouted.

Alex stood up. Annie thought he looked embarrassed, a mark of humility she had not believed him to possess.

'I hope I was disturbing something,' Barbara said in her husky voice.

She was Annie's age, but looked older. She had what Alex termed a suburban figure. The cellulite had relocated to those areas on her body where it planned to spread out and retire. Her face was as white as plastic, but she retained a wicked glint in her eye and a seductive growl to her voice.

'Alex,' Annie said, 'this is my oldest and best friend Barbara.'

'Alex Lubotsky!' said Barbara, shaking his hand. 'At last I get to meet the man in person. She's been talking about you for long enough!'

'Bra!' Annie complained, feeling herself redden.

Barbara winked, and said to Alex, 'We'll talk later.'

'Maybe I'll take you up on that,' he replied, smiling. 'You can tell me all her secrets while she's trapped here.'

'That's not fair!' said Annie.

'See!' Barbara said. 'She's got plenty to hide.'

'I'm sure she has,' said Alex. 'I think I'd better leave you two alone. Annie, we'll talk. Bye, Barbara.'

'Bye. *We'll* talk, too,' she said with a wink which she followed with another hearty laugh.

'OK!'

As soon as he'd gone, Barbara sat on Annie's bed and cut a groove in the chocolate's wrapping with her nail. 'So, Miss-top-story-on-the-nightly-news-with-Dan-Cramer,' she said, 'how does it feel to be shot?'

Annie was staring at the door. 'He said he loved me.'

'Alex did?' Barbara, too, looked at the door. She knew so much about Annie's frustrated attempts to get closer to the man that she felt as if she knew him already. 'When? Now?'

'No, when I was shot. It was the last thing I heard.'

'Has he said it again?'

'No,' Annie replied, adding, almost to herself, 'And I'm not sure he ever will.'

'It was a shock to the system,' Rebecca told Alex as the two of them sat waiting for Justin in Annie's Truman Suite. 'What do you expect?'

Alex shook his head. 'I don't know. Not this.'

He'd been explaining that it felt as if something inside him had been shot when Karen fired her gun. Despite Annie's insistence that the campaign should go on, his own resolve had crumbled. Now, three days after the shooting, he could find no enthusiasm for New Dawn. He thought that to continue would be like pushing her into the firing line once again.

'Besides, what else have you got to do?' Rebecca asked.

'That's not the point,' he said, too harshly.

Alex lifted from the table the Marilyn figure he'd bought. Would Annie be destroyed because America couldn't let go of the people she loved? Wouldn't it be better to lead her away from the public's gaze? These thoughts were interrupted by Justin, who was in a terrific mood.

'Sorry I'm late. I dropped in at the hospital.'

'To see Annie?' said Alex.

He had not yet visited her this morning, and he felt an unfamiliar jealousy that another should have been there.

'For a minute, yeah, but I really went to see the administrator. Listen to this: you know the President's coming to New York the day after tomorrow, well, he's scheduled to visit a new AIDS ward at Annie's hospital that afternoon. The place'll be packed with media. Why don't we have the announcement then?'

'Justin, I'm not sure about this,' said Alex.

'Of course you're not, but in a couple of days you'll be

seeing this in a totally different light. I know you too well. Don't you think, Becca?'

Rebecca said nothing. She had guessed the truth. When she looked at Alex she saw a man who couldn't tolerate the thought of putting a woman he loved through a presidential campaign. And yet he was also the man for whom the political game had always come first. Which of his loves, the new or the old, would win the day, she couldn't say, though she suspected that he might find it harder to reject the chance of victory in 1996.

'It's not for me to say,' she told Justin, who was taking down the leaders' photographs from the bulletin board, as if he knew the campaign was over. In fact, it was because he believed Annie had learnt enough by now. 'Well, I've spoken to Annie and she wants to go on, so I don't think we can afford to stall. People will see her as a martyr if she's in hospital, and she's not likely to be there again, unless someone else takes a shot.'

'Exactly,' said Alex. 'They may.'

'Al, listen, let's use this opportunity and, if you still feel like this in a couple of weeks, then we'll quit.'

After a few moments, Alex agreed, saying, 'So long as she's happy with that.'

'Oh, she is,' said Justin. 'She definitely is. She's suddenly got the fight in her blood.'

Two days wasn't much time, so Justin set about his task as if his life depended upon it. The hospital administrators agreed (after some financial persuasion) to allow the announcement an hour before the President's arrival on Thursday. It was agreed that Annie's bed would be wheeled into an old lecture hall on the third floor. Justin was adamant that Dawn should be seen to be suffering, that it should be understood by all that she had taken the bullets for the good of the nation.

Cecilia from *Vogue* was summoned again, and the yellow outfit that had originally been chosen was discarded in favour of a thick white Dior bathrobe which Annie would wear above an ivory silk camisole. Justin was after what he called the fucked virgin look, as perfected by Linda Evans, a.k.a. Mrs Blake Carrington in *Dynasty*. Frequently, she had risen from her husband's bed emanating both complete satisfaction (Blake was all man) and purity. Dawn too had to be both sexually irresistible and morally chaste. As an added touch, a small gold crucifix was to be worn round her neck. With luck, she would appear almost angelic, a notion enhanced by her miraculous escape from death.

Simon and Garfunkel had declined the invitation to sing, so Justin hired a gospel choir to perform its rendition of 'Bridge Over Troubled Water'. It was his belief that the lumpy, white masses in the Midwest to whom Dawn was largely speaking (it wouldn't matter how ugly her majority was, so long as it was a majority) would not be alienated by the presence of blacks as entertainers, while the African–Americans themselves would appreciate their superior singing talents being recognised. The choir would stand in a semicircle behind a selection of the flowers and cards.

Alex was woken on the morning before the announcement by the smug stutter of a fax coming through next door. He climbed out of bed feeling brighter than he had for days.

The fax was from Justin, saying that Annie had finally read the speech written by Alex and was angry that none of her own ideas had been included. Alex, of course, had done all he could to make the speech emotionally powerful through being intellectually weak. Having laboured to wash the colour from the speech until it was all but transparent, he was proud of his achievement. If, as Justin went on to suggest, Annie rewrote the speech to include her own populist ideas, all the hard work would be wasted.

The announcement wasn't going to move people unless it was wholly empty of political substance. To make matters even worse, Justin ended by saying that CNN had agreed to broadcast the event live.

In the shower, Alex wondered what he should do. If Annie made an announcement speech that went as far as attacking capitalism itself for digging up its own moral foundations (one of Jerry's ideas that she'd put down on paper), then she would destroy any chance of receiving the vital backing of the business community. She seemed unable to understand how damaging it was to have ideas that challenged the status quo.

He turned to feel the spray on his face. Maybe the answer was to let Annie go in a blaze of glory, let her have her say and kill New Dawn in the process. Yet when he pictured her on TV, saw the excitement in her face turn to disappointment as her ideas were torn apart, he became aware that he couldn't let that happen. If she was going to carry on, there was no point in him standing by, watching her make mistakes. Justin was a brilliant image consultant, but he had too little experience at producing media events. Perhaps the shooting had come as a test of their resolve, and now that they had all survived, the path to great glory was clear.

He dressed quickly, in a suit and tie for the first time since Saturday, and made it to the hospital in less than half an hour. He felt as full of energy and enthusiasm as he could remember. He was looking forward to seeing Annie, too, and thought it was good that he cared for her, good that he wanted the best for her, but beyond that there was no choice but to keep the relationship professional. It was lucky he hadn't given anything away since the shooting. Only if they were partners, not lovers, would the campaign be a success.

'Well, look at you,' said Annie when Alex came into the room. 'Business as usual, is it?'

There was an undeniable smirk on his face. 'I thought I better give Justin a little hand.'

'So he told you about the speech?' said Annie, folding her arms like a stubborn matron.

'Yuh, he faxed me,' Alex replied, looking at Annie and thinking how beautiful she was today, her face clear of the lurid make-up she'd worn on the show, her eyes porcelain white and shiny.

'And?' prompted Annie.

With his hands in his pockets, Alex ambled to the other side of the room. 'Remember that conversation we had outside FAO Schwartz? When I said we had to do some things we didn't like so that you could get elected and start doing the things you cared about?'

Annie nodded.

He walked to stand beside her. 'This speech I wrote is something we've got to do.'

Annie lowered her eyes to neaten the sheet over the fold of blankets. A new set of linen was arriving for the announcement, something more chic than the hospital cotton. She spoke without looking up, 'Tell me something. Is that the speech you'd have given Susan Grant? Or is it some kind of watered-down soap opera version? Because I can't imagine her saying the things you wrote.'

'And I can't imagine her winning if she didn't. Why do you think I'm here with you instead of her?' he asked, sitting on the side of the bed.

She smiled wryly when she looked at him. 'Sometimes I wonder how stupid you think I am. It wasn't just a coincidence that you ran down to Washington the day the President was cleared of Cochabamba, was it? You thought he wouldn't be able to stand again until that happened. And then you decided his wife wasn't such a good bet after all. Is that right? Didn't you suddenly need a new candidate so that all your hard work wouldn't go to waste?'

'No,' he said, staring intently into her eyes. 'I thought you were better. I thought you were much better.'

'So why do I have to read a speech that makes me out to be a fool?'

'Because it'll *move* people, Annie. You've got to understand that. It's how it has to be. You've got some wonderful ideas, and I agree with them, but you've got to be patient. *After* we've won the people's confidence, after the speech, we'll be able to get serious, because by then you'll have millions of supporters and supporters only listen to the ideas they agree with. But you've got to get that power first. That's the trade-off. If you're a candidate you have to say and do things you don't like so you can get into a position to do some good.'

'So when does it end, Al?' asked Annie. 'When do I get to do those things?'

'When we've got the power. When we win. You're going to have to trust me. You're going to have to believe that I wouldn't do anything that wasn't right for you.'

'So I read the speech you wrote?'

'If you can. I don't think you'll look a fool. I think you'll look like – the future.'

'Will you help me, then?' She picked up the speech, and flicked through the pages. 'Help me make it sound right?'

'I could,' he said, 'but I don't think I'm the right person. Do you have an acting coach?'

'For *Unto the Skies*?' she said, sounding astounded. 'No.'

'And there's no one you know like that?'

For a moment, Annie was silent, and then an idea came into her mind.

26

Sixteen years had passed since student and teacher had last seen one another, though it felt as if a lifetime had folded over. Annie had not been surprised to discover that Bea Shellenburger was still teaching at Cornell Williams, and she was excited at the thought of seeing her again. Not many of the students who passed through Bea's class could have climbed to Annie's dizzy heights, and it made her feel proud of how far she had come.

It was early in the morning of announcement day when Bea was led into the hospital room. She had aged almost imperceptibly, remaining where Annie had put her when they'd first met, in late middle age, a woman with short, straight hair (still no grey) and a face that would, taut and frown-free, have surely been pretty in its youth. Perhaps the slim, high cheekbones did Bea less good in these later years, the shadow they invited more sorrowful than striking. Yet her energy seemed undiminished. She wasted little time with pleasantries and was soon asking Annie to read out the speech.

It had taken a cheque, and not even a large one, to persuade Bea to spend three hours with her ex-student. The colour of Dawn's politics was not discussed, Bea's instructions being very simple. She had to ensure that Annie would squeeze every last drop of emotion from the written words.

To begin with, the teacher did what she could to produce the kind of conditions in which Annie might find herself later in the day. She drew the blinds and positioned the

Anglepoise above the bed to shine onto the candidate's
face. She also removed the shade from another lamp,
and pointed it towards Annie. Then she withdrew into
the relative darkness and said, 'Whenever you're ready,
imagine there are hundreds of people and cameras out
here, and then you can begin.'

Annie took a deep breath, did as she'd been asked, and
then read the speech from beginning to end. When she'd
finished there was a short silence before Bea moved, her
body slowly illuminated as she approached the light, her
face looking skeletal, lit by the lamps below.

'Was it OK?' Annie asked.

She felt pretty good about it. Now that she'd had a night
to sleep on Alex's edited words, she was resolved to give
it all she'd got.

'I want to tell you something that Cornell used to say
to his students,' Bea said. 'He used to say that the one
thing the audience will never forgive you for is if you
step on that stage and say your lines as if you don't mean
them. OK? That's why actors need training, because when
you're up there you've got to have the passion inside
you.' Bea held her hands to her head, as if in anguish.
Slowly, she returned her eyes to Annie. 'That's got to
come from inside. There's nothing worse for an actress
than holding back because you're too scared to let the
passion out, because you're too worried how you might
look, or what others might think of you. Is that what's
happening here?'

'No,' Annie insisted. 'I thought I showed passion,
didn't I?'

'Once or twice, yes,' said Bea. 'But it didn't sound as if
you believed what you were saying. Do you?'

Annie hesitated.

'Do you?' Bea repeated.

'Yes.'

'No, you don't. You don't believe a word.'

'Absolutely, I do.'

'Then show it to me,' Bea said, firmly grasping Annie's hand. 'Can I have that?' Bea asked, taking the speech. 'OK, this speech has a beginning you can really get your teeth into. You began like you were reading a newspaper article on cooking apple pie. That's no good, that's no good at all. Now, listen to me.' Bea composed herself, snared Annie's attention by staring her in the eye, and began:

'Ladies and gentlemen, after you've looked down the barrel of a gun, life seems very precious indeed.' Then she paused. 'Less than a week ago I came face to face with terrible violence. I was shot, and I was wounded, and I saw a friend die before my eyes.' Again Bea paused. She looked as if she might burst into tears, but Annie couldn't deny that she was hooked, that she felt the intensity of the words.

'You see what I mean?' said Bea. 'You can grab them right from the start, then they're going to be on your side. Can you do it for me like that?'

'Yes,' said Annie, keen to try now. If there was one thing she was sure of, it was that she could act. She knew she could act.

'Good,' said Bea. 'I think you can too. But I want to hear it. I want to hear the passion, from your stomach and heart, not from your head. If there's any time when I think you're saying something you don't believe, I'm going to walk right out of that door. Understand?'

'You're on,' said Annie, and this time when she read it she knew how much better it was, knew the sensation from those times on stage when she'd surprised even herself with words she'd heard many times, as if her conscious self was beyond the footlights, observing the performance.

Bea looked happier too. 'How do you feel?' she asked. 'It was better, wasn't it?'

'I mean you yourself,' she said, taking from her mouth her unlit cigarillo. 'Does it hurt? Is it difficult to speak?'

'No, I'm fine, really. The painkillers are so good I keep forgetting I've been shot.'

'Don't forget!' declared Bea, both fists clenched and held before her. 'Don't forget the pain. I want you to feel it, and I want you to make me feel it too. I want you to make everyone who's listening feel it. Now try that.'

Annie began again, and this time she kept interrupting the speech to cough, or to clutch at the wound in her stomach, her face creasing with pain. Bea clapped her hands to make Annie stop before picking up a glass of water from the tray that spanned the bed.

'Use this, OK? You're going to need some water sometimes. But don't overdo it. Did I ever tell you how I act drunk on stage?'

'Yeah,' Annie said, remembering not only the advice, but the very class in which it had been given. 'You said that drunk people think they're sober.'

'That's right,' said Bea. She tried to put the glass back on a clear space on the tray, but kept knocking it against one of Annie's books. She was swaying slightly, too. 'They think they're sober,' she slurred, 'but we can see they're not.' Now she stopped performing and stood straight. 'I want you to act as if you're trying to hide the pain. Don't make a big song and dance about it, but,' Bea paused, and took a sharp intake of breath, which she held in her lungs, 'but talk through it, show you can beat it. Drop those little hints and they won't think you're looking for sympathy.'

'OK,' said Annie, hoping she was a good enough actress to hide pain that she wasn't feeling at all. 'OK.'

'Good, now run through it again, and we'll see if you're ready to show it to the world.'

Whether or not she was ready for the world, the world was ready for her. Now, with half an hour to go before the speech, Annie could see from her hospital window the TV vans lined on the pavement below, curled cables

448

slapping the aerials like halyards in the wind. She thought these would serve well as the flags of Dawn's nation. Her citizens were camped around McLuhan's fire. They had seen Dawn born in a Chicago hospital, concerned for her mother's health, and now they would witness her rebirth, her metamorphosis from a fictional woman in a fictional ward to a real person in a New York hospital before the refracted eyes of the world. Yet even as the bustle on the street below seemed strangely foreign since her incarceration in the hospital, so Annie doubted that Dawn could exist without her TV life-support machine. It worried her that Dawn was too much of a TV magician, that her tricks would be transparent without the blinkered half-vision of the cameras. It worried her that she might not be up to the challenge of excelling beyond the screen.

'Turn this way,' said Bradley Peters.

The hairstylist was putting the finishing touches to his creation (soft and natural yet innately glamorous, to match the delicate tones of the make-up), and Cecilia was steaming the bathrobe to rid it of wrinkles. The bed had been plumped and looked inviting to Annie, who was sitting on a chair by the window when Alex burst in.

'I'm sorry, you guys,' he said. 'I need two minutes alone with Dawn, please.'

Once the stylists had gone, Alex sat on his haunches before her. 'I've got good and bad news.'

'I only want the good,' she said.

Having been listening to the echoing commotion in the high-ceilinged corridors outside, Annie was suffering from stage fright. She didn't want to hear anything to worry her more.

'We're going to be on *Window on Washington* tonight,' he said. 'You, me and Charlie.'

UBC's daily half-hour show was the most popular political show on weekday TV. As guests were always invited into the studio, Annie wanted to know how she could possibly be on.

'They're going to set up a camera and monitor in here,' Alex explained. 'The bad news is that I've got to fly down to Washington before your speech.'

'You're not going to be here?' she said with alarm.

He comforted her by his presence alone.

'No, but you'll be fine.' He took hold of her hand, and though worried by how cold it felt, said nothing of that. 'I've told Justin to make sure there are no questions afterwards. You'll come straight back here.'

'But what about tonight? There'll be questions then, won't there?'

'Don't worry, I'll be in the studio. Just do what you did on the street that time. Just act as Dawn, and I know you'll be perfect.'

'But they're so nasty, those guys.'

He stood and gave her a kiss on the forehead. 'They're not going to crucify an invalid, now, are they?'

Once he'd wished her good luck, he left to catch his plane. Soon after, she was back in bed, Justin and Rebecca standing by her side, and four nurses ready to wheel her out for the performance of her life.

As they left the room, passing various members of the campaign team who'd gathered to wish her luck, Annie thought it fitting that she was being pushed towards the media, as if incapable even of walking alone. She closed her eyes and said a silent prayer and then the burble of voices told her how near she was, and the next thing she knew the cameras were flashing, and the TV lights were on her so she could barely see how many people were gathered inside the large hall. She smiled, as she'd been told to, and the bed was turned so now she faced the press.

She had expected – feared – terror, but at once she felt a calmness that must have come from knowing that this was

what she did well. Annie Marin had been able to perform
for as long as she could remember, and it didn't matter if
there were one or a hundred thousand people watching.
She could do this. She could hold any audience in the palm
of her hand.

A hush fell when Justin and Rebecca swung the table
of microphones across Annie's bed and stepped back. She
looked down at her speech, lifted her eyes until there was
absolute silence, and then began to speak.

'Ladies and gentlemen, after you've looked down the
barrel of a gun, life seems very precious indeed. Less than
one week ago I came face to face with terrible violence. I
was shot, and I was wounded, and I saw a friend die before
my eyes. And although I cannot bring Vince Moscardini
back, although we cannot bring back the lives of the
thousands of victims of violence who die tragically and
needlessly each year, I want to say this: there is hope. I
was shot, but I am alive. I was hurt, but now I am strong.
This great and noble nation of ours has been wounded too,
but together we can nurse her back to health. If we can
accept our weaknesses, then we can rebuild our shattered
communities and broken hearts. I see brightness on the
horizon. I see a new dawn of hope and happiness and
prosperity for America. But to reach that light we need
to take a great step of faith.

'My fellow Americans, I offer you my hand and ask
you to follow. It is with the greatest pride and hope in
my heart that I announce my candidacy for the presidency
of the United States.'

Annie paused, and briefly shut her eyes as if fighting
the pain. Tens of camera shutters clicked, and continued
to click as, with a slight smile, she carried on. 'Ladies and
gentlemen, it is all too easy to forget that we are a young
nation, that we continue to search for the best and truest
way to live decent, honest lives. Compared with many
other countries, ours is still a child.

'But what kind of child is this? Is America like little Robert Sandifer, the eleven-year-old boy gunned down for murdering a girl barely older than himself? Is she like Sandra Millars, who was so tragically raped and stabbed in her own schoolyard? Is she like the teenage girls who grow up using crack cocaine and giving birth to unwanted babies in inner-city drug dens? Is this the kind of child we have produced?' A child too scared to ride a new bicycle for fear of being mugged, too scared to go to school to study, or to walk in the parks, or to sleep at night while the guns rage outside? Some will say yes, some will say this is the America I know. Is it?' asked Annie, catching the eye of a young man in the front row of journalists. She held his stare for a few seconds. 'Is it?'

'No! This is not my America. My America is a land that has been built brick by brick by generations of immigrants of every race and creed and colour. My America is a land where a kid from the slums can become a hero, where people are not judged by the colour of their skin or the language of their beliefs. This is a land built by dreamers for people with dreams. It is not too late to make those dreams come true.

'And yet,' said Annie, softening her voice and lifting her eyes to the back of the hall, 'and yet "if a house be divided against itself, that house cannot stand." We are becoming a divided nation and our house will fall unless we can unite. I want that to be the goal of my presidency. My vision begins with each and every one of us taking the time to acknowledge that what we have is too good to waste. I want us to consider the lilies. I want us to take time to look out of the window and see that this is a beautiful land, a land that belongs to us all.'

Now Annie began to speak more loudly. Taking Bea's advice, she had occasionally touched her wounded leg, but now she wanted to speak without interruption and with all the passion she could muster.

'I will not be a President answering to the special interests of politicians and lobbyists. I will be a President of the people and for the people. I don't want to impose a government of red tape and paperwork and bureaucracy. I want to be the head of an Administration that will value people as human beings. I want to bake a new cake, with every loyal American, young and old, black and white, as part of the ingredients. That cake will be the new American family. We cannot write laws to make families sit together at the dining-room table. We cannot turn back the clock. Yet as we stand at the crossroads of a new millennium, we can make a choice about which direction to take. We can choose to go forward with love and understanding in our hearts. We can choose not to close our doors, but to open them as they were open in the past. We can choose to put something back into the communities of which we are all members. It is not only for others that I ask this to be done. It is for ourselves, for all our tomorrows.

'As your President, I want to be a bridge across the troubled waters of this glorious land. I want to rise above the pettiness of partisan fighting like a new sun. I want to make America warm again, so we can ease our minds and sleep well at night, proud and confident that with tomorrow's dawn a new and better day will arrive. It can be done. It can.

'And so I am here to offer myself as a servant, not to Washington interests but to you, to every one of you, the people of America, my brothers and sisters, my neighbours and friends. My children.

'I say we can look down the barrel of this gun and see whatever we choose. Hope, not despair. Tolerance, not hatred. A dawn, not a darkening of the skies. Together we can grow and flourish and walk with pride and strength

towards a new and better day. I say it's not too late
to remember what America means, and to build our
dream again.

'Thank you very much. God bless you all.'

As soon as Annie had finished, the questions began to
rain down. Rebecca stepped in at once.

'I regret to say that Miss Hope's doctors have requested
that no questions be asked. I guarantee there will be plenty
of opportunities in the next twenty-three months. Instead,
I'd like you to listen to our campaign song.'

As Annie posed for the cameras, feeling jubilant about
the speech, the United Harlem Peace Singers began to
sing of weariness and tears, rough times and friendliness,
ending their moving rendition of Paul Simon's song with
words to sum up the New Dawn campaign. 'If you need
a friend,' they promised, 'I'm sailing right behind. Like a
bridge over troubled water I will ease your mind . . .'

The announcement speech was received well by the people
who mattered, namely the television commentators. Bea
Shellenburger had brought a large bunch of flowers, and
Justin had arrived grinning from ear to ear. Of course, in
singing Dawn's praises, both knew they were congratulating themselves. Dawn Hope belonged to them all.

Most admired had been the candidate's great courage.
It was decided by the opinion brokers that Dawn was a
selfless woman entering the political ring not out of vanity
or crude ambition but from a love of country. She was a
woman willing to sacrifice herself for the common good.
Already, donations were pouring in.

Despite Annie's acting during the speech, all the excitement had taken its toll of her, and as soon as the crew
from *Window on Washington* had set up a camera and
monitor in the room, she asked if she might be allowed
some peace to recuperate before her appearance on TV.
However, no sooner had the last person left than she was

disturbed by the noise of two helicopters flying close to the building, their massive searchlights skimming the rooftops nearby. Then from the streets came a chorus of sirens. She wondered whether there had been an explosion, or if a dangerous fugitive had escaped. Suddenly the sirens stopped and the helicopters seemed to be coming so close to the building that she thought they might crash.

For ten minutes or so, all was quiet, but then she heard people running in the corridor, seemingly towards her room. After a brief knock, Justin came in. He was looking excited. 'Jack Grant's in the hospital and wants to see you.'

'You're kidding!'

'No, I'm not. Will you see him? His people don't want pictures, but it'll make great press anyway.'

'Um, yeah, of course I will. When?'

'In about five minutes.'

'Oh, my God,' said Annie.

She was, as she'd been so often since this roller-coaster year had begun, scared and excited by the prospect. She wondered why the President wanted to see her, especially since she'd just announced she was after his job.

Justin left her alone to ponder this, but seconds later three armed (and apologetic) policemen came into the room to check for danger. They requested the blinds be drawn, which Annie agreed to, and as she looked out of the window she saw two police snipers on the roof of the neighbouring building. Then she was alone again, wondering whether all this would be done for her if she was to succeed.

After a few minutes, she heard what she guessed was the presidential party approaching and, after a polite knock, Jack Grant himself was in her room, approaching her bed.

He was taller than she'd imagined, with less perfect skin. Yet he possessed an immediate aura and presence that many more handsome men were denied. He walked towards the bed and, taking her hand in his, said, 'I hope you'll forgive me for barging in.'

'Of course.'

He looked around the room. 'You seem to be keeping Manhattan's florists busy.'

'Yuh,' she said, feeling awkward with him standing there, holding her hand as if they were lovers.

The President walked to the window ledge. He sat facing her. 'He's very good, isn't he?'

'Excuse me, sir?'

'Alex Lubotsky. He's good at what he does.'

'Oh, yes! Yes, he is.'

They were silent for a moment before Grant said, 'Do you like him?'

The question surprised her. She could have said, *Yes, I love him,* but settled for 'Yeah!' instead.

'Good. Still, I'm prepared to guarantee you'll hate him during the campaign.'

How could I? Annie thought to herself. How could I?

'I remember one week during the primaries he made me travel over ten thousand miles and it was the same story every time I got off the plane – you know, I'd shake a thousand hands, meet local staff, give the same speech to thirty people who couldn't care what I was talking about, and then when my hands were frozen stiff and all I wanted was to go home to my own bed for once and sleep for a thousand years, Alex would put me on another plane and we'd take off for a dinner in somewhere like Cedar Rapids which wouldn't end until midnight because everyone there wanted a picture taken with "the guy from the TV". And every time I'd ask for a minute to myself, Alex said no, because a minute on my own was a minute spent with someone who'd already decided which way to vote.' The President sighed. 'Still,' he added, picking something off the sleeve of his jacket, 'that's the game, isn't it, Annie?

'And you know what's strange?' he said. 'When I got to the White House nothing changed. They still try to run your life.' Grant smiled a weary smile. 'Anyway, why am I telling you this? I'm sure Alex has explained it all.'

'Actually, he, he kind of suggested that he'd run the show until after the campaign, and then . . .'

'And then you'd get a chance?' the President guessed.

'Something like that.'

Grant moved to sit in the chair by Annie's bed. She thought it strange to be looking down at the President, as if he was paying her homage.

'It seems easy from a distance, doesn't it? I can't remember a time when I didn't want to be President – you're probably the same – and I always dreamt that if I had the courage and the will I'd be able to legislate and inspire people to change America for the better. You know, right a few of the wrongs. I believed that from when I was little boy right until the time I found myself in the Oval Office and I looked out of the window and all I saw was rows and rows of people wanting to cut me down. They don't even listen to you, half of them. And that comes as quite a surprise, let me tell you – that it's not about how good your intentions are, or what you feel in your heart, it's about whether you can duck in time. Because you're only put there because people want someone they can throw apples at. Do you know what I mean?'

'I think so, Mr President.'

Like millions of others, Annie had voted for President Grant in 1992 believing he had the vision to reverse the nation's decline. It was because he'd raised hopes so high that his failure seemed so great.

'Sir,' she said, 'may I ask you something?'

'Sure.'

'If it's pointless, why do it? Why run again?'

His smile was wide and genuine. 'I can't give up just because it isn't the party I thought it'd be, can I? I made a promise to the people of America that I meant and which I intend to honour. Besides,' he said, rising to his feet, 'after a while you get used to the apples.'

He held out his hand and she took it.

'I'm afraid I've done all the talking, but I did want to wish you luck, Annie. There's nothing pleasant about running for office, I know that. But we do it because we can't live with ourselves if we don't, isn't that right?'

She said nothing, knowing how easy it would be to live with herself if she didn't run. She suddenly felt she had no right to challenge this man just because she was a TV star. It wasn't enough, was it?

'Well,' he patted Annie's hand. 'Get better soon, won't you.'

'I'll try, sir. Thank you.'

He smiled at her, and then he was gone. Within seconds, Justin was back inside.

'What did he say? Quick! We need the story.'

Annie was staring at the door.

'Annie? What'd he say?'

She blinked at Justin. 'He said he was tired of the apples, Jay.'

'What?'

'He wished me luck, OK?' she said impatiently.

'That's it? That's all?'

'I think so,' she said distractedly. 'Yeah.'

Though Justin wasn't happy, Annie would say no more, and in minutes they were joined by a UBC sound engineer and a camera technician who'd come to establish the sound and picture links with the studio in DC.

Running at thirty minutes, *Window on Washington* was similar to CNN's *Crossfire*. One presenter, the slick Patrick Morell, was an ex-Chairman of the Democratic National Committee. The other, Lear Cooper, a grey-haired bulldog of a man, was a right-wing political journalist from *The Washington Times*. They had been chosen not so much for their insight and intellect but because they were both opinionated showmen. Their function was to make politics entertaining, and it was with this in mind that the producers chose guests who could be counted upon to bray loudly. Deliberate thought was as welcome as bipartisan agreement. What the producers sought and the audience craved was the fanatical, stubborn intransigence provided by conservative, religious right-wingers and Democratic ideologues.

Annie had enjoyed the show for years. Never had she imagined that she would be a guest on it. Now, with a microphone attached to her robe and the link established, she was powdered again, a glass of water was brought and before she really had time to compose herself (it had been the same all day, like skidding on ice) she heard the opening music from the show and saw the titles on her small monitor, the Capitol Dome illuminated through a window, and then the studio lights came up to reveal Lear Cooper and Patrick Morell and Alex and Charlie sitting round a wooden table, all looking as if they were about to discuss the end of the world.

Cooper began angrily. 'Today on *Window on Washington*, Dawn Hope! What does she stand for, what are her passions, what does she believe? Is there anything behind the gloss? With me are two people who'll have us believe there is, ex-Grant guru Alex Lubotsky, and the woman voted feminist with the most beautiful hair, Miss Charlie Canon.'

Charlie looked furious as the camera moved to her and then to Morell. 'Later in the programme we'll be talking to defeated Republican challenger Oliver North about his own presidential aspirations, and we also go live to New York to speak to Dawn Hope herself.'

A light went on above Annie's camera and once she'd been seen, Morell was on air again.

'But I want to begin by asking Alex Lubotsky this

question: Al, can we glue our fragmented society together with cookie dough, or is Dawn Hope baking a cake that's never going to rise?'

Alex looked quite smug when he said, 'If you're asking whether Dawn Hope is a credible candidate, the answer is definitely yes. She's a remarkable woman who has a positive vision of community that transcends partisan squabbling.'

'OK,' Cooper interjected. 'I understand that on her soap opera, Dawn Hope is a prominent Senator sitting on several important committees. But in fact, what we're being presented with is a candidate who's a TV actress. Is that what the nation needs?'

'Lear,' said Alex with a smile. 'I can think of a hero of yours who was an actor before he became President.'

'Reagan had held public office,' Cooper said aggressively. 'Your candidate hasn't.'

'So? She's not claiming to be anything she isn't. What she's doing is saying, "Here I am, I have a vision of a caring, pragmatic *non-partisan* Administration and I want to grapple with the large issues facing us – now take me or leave me." And you shouldn't forget,' said Alex, leaning back in his chair, 'that the Chief Executive is in fact Article Two of the Constitution. That means . . .'

Cooper, taking a cue from his producer, interrupted, his voice raised, 'Isn't it the case that you're trying to dupe the electorate into voting for Dawn Hope and movie idol Tom Sterling so that you yourself can return to the White House?'

Alex and Cooper were old friends, if political rivals, and both had played their parts often enough for the public. But it was rare for Lear to sail this close to the wind. He was breaking an unwritten rule.

'That is absolutely not the case,' said Alex. 'The clear message that came through from the midterm elections is that . . .'

'Is that people are sick of the last candidate you were responsible for putting in the White House,' yelled Cooper. 'Why should they trust you this time? Leopards don't change their spots.'

Alex's voice maintained a pitch of perfect equanimity. 'The message is that voters are confused about the future and have totally lost faith in government to provide the answers. What Dawn Hope and Tom Sterling will be saying is that ordinary citizens can run for office and that ordinary people still matter. They want to create a government of and for the people.'

'You're a good friend, Al,' said Morell, 'but you're sounding a lot like a mixture between an old Perotist and a new Newtist. Are you?'

House Speaker-elect Newt Gingrich was the Republican most credited for what was being termed America's second revolution following the midterm elections. One of his missions was to dismantle the large, intrusive government of which Democrats such as Alex were traditionally so fond.

'How *I* sound should not be an issue. It's the candidates you should be listening to, and they're both in favour of a responsive government that can intercede to enable all Americans to live full, just lives. If that means a slight change in the role of government, so be it. It's because Dawn Hope is not tied to any party or ideology that she's able to make the right choices for America. She believes politics is more than a game.'

'What?' hollered Cooper. 'Now you're getting silly.'

Charlie butted in. 'Listen to you! If anything's laughable, Mr Cooper, it's the way you're hopelessly trying to cling onto the autocratic, straight, white male power structure. Dawn Hope is an agent of change.'

'Are you trying to suggest that voters should choose Dawn Hope simply because she's a woman?' said Cooper, as if the idea was intolerably anarchic.

Charlie swept back her hair and looked sternly at the presenter. 'No, because she'll be the best candidate. Of course, that's partly because men have squandered their right to govern.'

There was a brief silence. For a horrible second, Annie thought it was her turn to speak. She didn't know what she'd do if she was asked about pragmatism or Article Two. Justin had coached her on some of the likeliest questions, but since the President's visit she'd been feeling frighteningly out of her depth and place. There was a whole world beyond the learned smiles and poses which she didn't understand. And what chance could she possibly have to make a difference where President Grant had failed? It was a kind of madness to think she had a hope.

'Another thing troubling me,' Morell was saying, 'is that we're being presented with Dawn Hope, not Annie Marin. Does that mean this is all an act?'

'A degree of performance is inevitable in politics,' argued Alex as confidently as he could, because he knew how thin this ice was.

Morell shook his head. 'But there's a difference between being the best you can be, and being something that you're not.'

'It's clear to me,' said Charlie Canon, 'that you can't tolerate the idea of a female President.'

Cooper swung his chair to face camera two. 'Is this a matter of Dawn Hope's gender, or is there something more sinister going on? Join us after the break, when we talk to the candidate herself.'

In her hospital room, Annie could not remember feeling this nervous ever before.

'What if they ask me something I don't know?' she said to Justin.

'Do as I said and steer around the issue. Remember that game we played, where you had to talk for ten minutes without using various words?'

Annie nodded, and bit on her nail. Without apologising, Justin pushed the hand from her mouth.

'So imagine you're doing that. They'll move on fast enough.'

'But what . . .?'

'Thirty seconds,' said the technician.

'You'll be fine,' Justin said, giving her hand a squeeze. 'I'm sure we've covered most of the questions anyway.'

Annie wasn't so convinced. Although she'd been memorising facts and figures, she felt as if she was about to sit an exam in a language she didn't understand, but there was no turning back because through her earplug she could hear the producer counting down to her cue and seconds later the red light of her camera was illuminated. As she concentrated on the black lens, Justin and Rebecca watched the monitor. The screen had been split, with Annie on the right and Lear Cooper on the left.

He was speaking, fast and aggressively, as if filing a report from a war zone. 'Welcome back. From her New York hospital bed we have presidential candidate Annie Marin. Miss Marin, I hope you don't mind me using your real name.'

Annie said that she didn't, which judging from Justin's grimace was an inauspicious start.

Cooper continued, 'I want to congratulate you on a speech made in difficult circumstances. We all wish you a speedy recovery.'

'Thank you,' said Annie, though she'd already been warned of the dangers of taking Cooper's kindness at face value since, as Rebecca had said, 'With Lear, you never know which face you're looking at.'

'I was wondering,' Lear continued, 'whether your resolve was shaken at all after the attempt on your life.'

'No,' said Annie, happy to be able to begin with a truth, 'quite the contrary. I have become even more determined to look for ways in which we might tackle this kind of violence.'

'So are we to presume that your speech was more than a show of eloquence? More than just an act?'

'If I wanted to act, Mr Cooper, I'd have stayed on the stage.'

In the studio, Alex couldn't suppress a smile. He was aware that he was taking a huge risk in allowing Annie to appear on the show that even skilled politicians feared, but she had begun well.

'All the same,' Morell suggested, 'I didn't get a great sense that the promises you made were particularly tectonic. Are they?'

Annie put a hand to her earphone. 'Excuse me? Um, did you say teutonic?'

'No, *tec*tonic.'

Annie nodded but her mind was in a whirl. How could she talk her way round this when she had no clue what tectonic meant? Suddenly she felt a surge of heat to her cheeks and the prickle of sweat on her forehead. The seconds were feeling like minutes and in desperation she glanced to her left, to where Rebecca was mouthing, 'Yes, say yes!'

'Yes,' said Annie, 'they are.'

Alex, clearly sensing Annie's distress, cleverly said, 'The reason we can build upon her promises . . .' before he was interrupted by Cooper, as he'd known he would be.

'I'd prefer it if we could hear from the candidate herself.'

After a deep breath which hurt her fractured rib, Annie said, 'I'm sure Alex was going to say that we can build America again if we reconstruct the foundations of our society through a combination of community action, individual responsibility and government intervention. I don't think we can hand the entire nation's soul over to the business community, as some people seem to want.'

At the end of the bed, Justin and Rebecca visibly relaxed. That had been a close call, but Annie had remembered her lines and come out on top.

'Point taken,' said Cooper, 'but even if you find the miracle tonic that's been eluding all the professionals, how do you think your brand of homely truths is going to work in the international community? Have you had time to think about, say, the continuing crisis in Bosnia?'

Annie nodded with more confidence than she felt. Truth was that she had had time to talk about Bosnia (though she'd certainly done none of the thinking), but now she couldn't remember what she was supposed to say. Who *were* the good guys? The Serbs? The Croats? The Bosnians? The Serbo-Bosnians? The Croat-Serbs? The Bosno-Croats? And what about the Yugoslavs? Weren't there any people out there calling themselves Yugoslavs any more? What had happened to Goran, the cute teen-ager she'd had her way with on a beach near Trieste?

She decided to take Justin's advice and swerve. 'I've certainly spent a lot of time thinking about that situation and you know, it's very clear to me that, that it's a situation that's been going on for far too long and I think definitely that we have to ask ourselves what is our role, how can we get involved either through the United Nations or else in a more direct military capacity, and . . .?'

'On whose side?' Patrick Morell wanted to know.

Again Annie paused, but Justin was spinning his hand to encourage her on. He thought she was doing just fine.

'I think what's dangerous is getting too involved in a dispute that has, after all, a long history. You know, this isn't a new conflict, and, and, and in many ways we need to be cautious. It would be a mistake to try to police the world like that and also it could be damaging to the whole peace process if we said we were going to support the Serbians or the Croatians or the Muslims or, you know, any other faction.'

'So you'd advocate sitting on the fence?'

'Um, no, I would take whatever action the situation demanded,' said Annie, who felt she was really flying now. Justin had been right. All she had to do was pretend she knew what she was talking about.

For a moment, no one said anything but then, as Justin had predicted, Cooper moved on. 'OK, let's come back home. I guess the issue everyone likes to have defined for them is taxation. Are you a tax-and-spend liberal, Miss Marin? Do you want to put your hand in my pocket?'

'I'd rather not, Mr Cooper, but seriously I think if we're going to get anything substantial achieved we have to be brave enough to cut spending and raise taxes.'

'No!' Justin whispered to Rebecca.

'No!' Alex blurted out in the studio.

Cooper swung around in his chair, sensing blood. He pointed at Alex. 'Are you disagreeing with your *own* candidate, Al?' he hurriedly asked.

Alex knew he had to remain cool, however much damage he feared Annie had inflicted. In his eyes, any tiny hint of increased taxation, however prudent in fiscal terms, was politically disastrous.

'No, Lear,' he said, 'Dawn is keen to examine all budgetary options, but I'm sure she was about to point out that we haven't finalised our economic platform at such an early stage.'

'Is that right, Miss Marin, did you get your lines wrong?'

'Yes,' she said, then seeing Justin put a hand to his forehead, added, 'I mean, I meant that we have to be . careful, I . . .'

'Could it be the case, Miss Marin, that you don't have an opinion on this subject?' Cooper suggested.

For just a second, Annie closed her eyes. Yes, she did have an opinion. She agreed with Jerry that higher taxation was not the crime conservatives made it out to be, that you couldn't throw society into the marketplace and see if it survived. But Alex had said the idea wouldn't fly. He'd said that Dawn wasn't that kind of candidate.

'Of course I have an opinion,' she said.

And it wasn't just this she had an opinion about, she had pages of opinions that she wasn't allowed to share because Alex said she had to be patient and Alex said they had to do it his way and Alex said that Dawn Hope could only win if they raised twenty million dollars from people who didn't want to be challenged or made to think. But Annie wasn't sure she could spend the next two years telling people only what they wanted to hear, because nothing would ever get done if nobody faced up to the truth.

'And that perhaps,' Lear continued, ignoring Annie's reply, 'you are simply a very talented actress speaking lines written by Mr Lubotsky.'

Now Alex was angry, 'Lear, you have no right to act as judge and jury on this matter when you haven't given Dawn a chance to tell us what she believes.'

'I know what I see and I know what I'm hearing and I don't think our society is well-served by this pretence, by . . .'

'You mean by a woman with an independent mind?' Charlie butted in.

'No, by someone who appears simply to be going through the motions, who . . .'

Now Morell joined the fray, his voice raised above the others. 'Miss Marin, perhaps we can clear this up by asking you your opinion on a very hot issue. What are your thoughts about balancing the budget?'

There was silence. For a moment, Annie closed her eyes and bowed her head. What was she doing here? Was she nothing more than someone to throw apples at, as the President had said? Wasn't it time to throw the apples back? Yes, she was an actress spouting lines! Why couldn't she tell the truth?

In the studio, Alex found Annie's silence almost painful. Yet this was not the pain he would have expected. He was not suffering because his candidate was damaging her prospects on national TV. Instead, all the shame he'd felt after the shooting had flooded back and more than anything he wanted to take Annie in his arms and away from all this, away from the firing line of journalists and commentators and citizens who thought they could do better. This was just the start! There'd be twenty-three more months of attack and criticism and then, if by some miracle she succeeded, years of torment. Did he have any right to do this to her? Hadn't he proved his point to Jack and Susan and the world by now? Yes, he was the best spin doctor around, but so what? So what, when it hurt the person he loved?

'Annie,' he said, and she looked up as if they were alone and not being watched by millions, 'tell us what you believe. Tell us what you wrote.'

'You mean . . . ?'

'The ideas you wrote for me.'

'At last,' said Morell, 'we're going to get some answers. Join us after these messages.'

Though Rebecca and Justin were offering advice during the break, Annie wasn't listening. All she was wondering was whether Alex had meant what he said.

'Ten seconds,' warned the technician.

Annie heard the countdown in her earplug and then Morell said, 'We're back with the founding members of the New Dawn campaign and in her New York hospital room we have an exclusive chance to talk with the presidential hopeful herself. Miss Marin, you left us on the edge of our seats during the break. Do you have a unique budgetary plan you want to share with us?'

Annie paused. She wished she could see Alex. She would know what he wanted if she could see his face.

'Have you forgotten?' asked Cooper.

'No,' she answered quietly. 'But, then, I don't think it matters what I say, does it? I've got a whole list of figures I could give you about the budget, but no one's interested because they won't believe me anyway. They're just waiting to see how you'll lay into me when I'm finished. That's why most people watch this garbage, isn't it? Because it's like slowing down to look at a car crash. There's always a chance you might see some blood.'

'We're simply interested in establishing the truth,' said Patrick Morell, who was a little taken aback.

'Whose truth?' she said, suddenly angry. 'Yours? Lear Cooper's? Because you're never going to agree, are you? One of you can always be counted on to turn any conversation into a slanging match, and if you ask me that's pretty damaging to how people view politics. It's because of creeps like you that nobody believes the President even when he's telling the truth. Why do you always have to be *against* everything he does, even when he gets it right?'

'Miss Marin, this is a free democracy,' said Cooper, folding his arms and leaning back in his chair. He was willing to take a little flak if it would help raise ratings. 'We're supposed to speak up when we see our President making mistakes.'

Annie laughed. 'You'll never admit that you're part of the problem, will you? But the way I see it, you are *most* of the problem, Mr Cooper, because if you spend your whole life hacking down the people who are trying to do some good for this country and, yes, I think President Grant is one of those people,' she said, pointing to her side as if Jack Grant was still in the room, 'then you turn politicians into criminals. And if the little guys are told not to trust the big guys then everything starts to crumble. Personally, I don't think shooting people down with words is a million miles away from shooting them with guns. It's the same in the end because everybody's being taught they have to be *against* something, and if we're going to put ourselves together again it's about time we started being *for* things instead.'

She paused, quite breathless. Where had all that come from? At the end of the bed Justin was no longer looking at the monitor but was pacing back and forth, staring at Annie like a malicious prosecutor.

'And what is it that you're standing for, Miss Marin?' asked Cooper. 'Cooking lessons?'

'No, Mr Morell, I'm for plenty of things. I'm for giving people a chance. I'm for saying that this country belongs to all of us and not just the guys who run the system. I'm for saying that we'd better look at other ways of treating criminals because locking people up still isn't working. I'm for telling Americans to start giving the banks a hard time for screwing the Third World for every cent it's got. I'm for Congressmen being allowed to talk about the things that matter instead of going in circles arguing about who's responsible for this mess we're in. And I'm for saying that if we keep on playing these stupid games, if we keep on throwing billions of dollars away in negative campaign commercials when there are guys living in cardboard boxes then God help us, because . . .'

'Miss Marin, I'm sorry, but . . .'

'And what really pisses me off is that all you people on TV pretend you're so responsible and important when really you're . . .'

'Miss Marin,' Morell said again, 'I'm very sorry but we're right out of time. I want to thank you very much, and we hope you get better soon.'

'Oh, ah, thanks,' said Annie, and suddenly the light on her camera went off, and the sound technician was stepping forward to take her mike and everything was going on as if she'd conducted any normal interview, as if she hadn't been on the verge of quitting the race on national TV.

On the monitor, Cooper was thanking Charlie and Alex, before he turned to Morell, and said, 'Patrick, wouldn't you agree that it's because Jack Grant is a dithering incompetent that loyal Americans like Annie Marin think they can do a better job?'

'Lear,' said Morell through his grin, 'you're talking out of you-know-where again. I'd say it was because sane people are out to stop the new Republican army before it's too late. Thank God that democracy's still alive and well.'

Cooper again, 'Join us after the break, when we'll be talking to Oliver North.'

In the studio, Charlie was angrily whispering to Alex, 'What the hell was she playing at?'

He looked at her, and then stood. 'Nothing,' he said, with a smile. 'Get it?'

In the hospital room, the atmosphere was tense and unpleasant. Rebecca was staring out of the window while behind her the technicians packed up.

Justin was packing papers into his briefcase. No one was speaking. After a while, the UBC men shook Annie's hand and left.

Justin looked into her eyes. 'What happened? Did you forget everything I taught you?'

Slowly, Annie shook her head.

Justin continued to stare at her. There was nothing kind or forgiving about his expression. 'We even went through what to do if you found yourself trapped like that. Didn't we, Annie?'

'Yes, Justin, we did.'

'So what? You just lost your mind?'

Now she smiled. 'No, I think I found it.'

It seemed after that he couldn't even look at her. He swung the briefcase off the table, and said, 'Becca, let's go.'

Rebecca's glance at Annie was more sympathetic, but

she revealed much by saying nothing. At the door, Justin turned. 'You know it's over, don't you?' he said before the two of them walked from the room.

A minute passed, then ten, twenty, thirty. No one came in or called. The whole hospital seemed unusually quiet. Annie followed the second hand of the electric clock.

Alex knew the number. She was sure he would call soon. She was sure.

She'd done the right thing, hadn't she? To say what she felt. Alex had told her to, hadn't he? He'd seen that it was useless and wrong to go on? Yet as the minutes piled up, no one came or called, leaving Annie all alone to wonder what her life would hold now that she'd thrown it all away.

27

Nighttime and still no word from Alex. Images of the day were spinning in Annie's mind like an orbiting alphabet soup, fragments of recent memory forming sentences of thought before disintegrating once more. The quiet was almost overpowering, and more than once she switched on the light (her fingers having learned the route to the switches in this foreign space), surprised to find she had not been sleeping long.

Even now it was before eleven. Annie's too-hot body, awake from inaction, was battling her mind which, in a state of excited, dizzy exhaustion, could not let go the events of the day.

It had been the most extraordinary of her life. She had met a President, spoken to a nation, destroyed a dream, upset a cart of apples. In her sleep she had even pictured the fruit being hurled at a man like Sebastian's arrows. This man was neither Grant nor Alex. He was younger. Strangely, he looked most of all like Max.

Annie had received no visitors, though food had come which she'd poked at from boredom, and then the pills which made her feel this way. Sometimes during previous nights she'd woken forgetting that bullets had torn holes into her, and when she'd turned she was surprised by the discomfort. Right now, though, she felt little pain at all. Instead, she felt a deep and surprising calm as she had on the night her father had died. It must have been then what it was now, relief to be free from something that had become more of a burden than a love.

Annie knew that, had she been a disciple of Bea Shellenburger, of Cornell Williams and the method technique, she would have wanted to absorb Dawn's self so deeply that it might have become impossible to leap from the race that Dawn would have wanted to win. But as she lay thinking about what she'd thrown away she realised that she herself had never wanted with her heart – not like she'd wanted to act and love and be loved – to stand where Alex would have put her, a hand raised in the squalling January winds, swearing to defend a Constitution when she wouldn't have been able to defend her actions to herself.

Only the theatre of the moment appealed. She smiled to herself as she thought of it now, knowing that it had been possible, she could have become President. She could have kept her head and lied on TV. And yet after Jack Grant's visit she lost the will to win. Whether or not that was the President's intent, she didn't care. She was glad to be free. The only fear was that now she'd be alone, because still Alex had not rung.

The hospital pillows were filled with some kind of washable foam and uncomfortable. She threw one to the floor and curled the end of the other to sleep on the corner of its fold. In the corridor, from which light teased her under the door, she heard heavy steps which pulled her into wider consciousness, but they passed and she nestled back down, low into the bed. Her heartbeat throbbed deep in her ear and she felt herself floating away on the rhythm, back down canals into her mind.

The half-dreams came again. She was looking at rows of journalists writing so fast that their pens fell off the pages. Even though she was talking gibberish, they were scribbling down every word. Now the studio: Lear Cooper's face rounding into a baby's, Alex solemn and staring, then Justin whispering something to Rebecca. Alex again! She imagined him touching her neck, his hands soft and warm as they always were in her dreams.

His lips against her cheek. Alex, please forgive me for doing what I did. I do love you! He whispered back her name and she snuggled into a ball, warmed by the sound. She imagined him curled into her belly.

She heard her name came again. Aaaneeeee. Aaaneeeee.

'Annie?'

She opened her eyes. In the darkness she made out the figure of a man standing by her bed, holding a pillow.

'You dropped this,' he whispered.

'Alex?' she asked, her voice cracked and dry.

He smiled at her. 'Hi, there.'

'Alex, you're here!'

She pulled herself up. Though the room was dark, light threaded beneath the door and through the slats of the blinds, making him half-visible as if he remained in her dream.

'I'm sorry about what happened,' she said. 'I . . . do you hate me?'

'What do you think?'

She shook her head. 'I don't know. I don't know what to think. I've been having strange dreams.'

'Me too.'

When he smiled at her she thought she was back sixteen years before, when she'd first seen his face in Cornell Williams.

'You've got a lovely smile,' she said.

It widened.

'Do you know where I first saw it?'

'Tell me,' he said, gently lifting her fingers into his hand.

His gesture gave her courage. 'In the hallway at Cornell Williams. I was late for my class and I ran straight into you, and you smiled at me and I thought— ' She stopped.

'You thought what?'

She looked away from him. 'I guess I thought I was in love but it was silly because I only saw you for five seconds and you probably didn't even notice me and . . .'

'Green,' he said.

'What?'

'You were wearing this green, I don't know, this wrap, this shawl thing and it was green, wasn't it?'

'I,' she laughed, 'I have no idea. I don't, I have no idea. But you think you . . .?'

'I was waiting for Max and you almost winded me and I wanted to follow you into your class.'

'So you do remember!'

'I told Max to look out for you, but I think he was into . . .'

'Breasts. He was into Faith's breasts,' she said, her happiness bubbling into a laugh.

'Probably. His mistake, huh?'

'Was it?'

'I think so.'

In the silence, she felt herself trembling beneath her skin. Nervously, she said, 'Alex, maybe you don't have to make the same, I mean just because he . . .'

She would have gone on, but he silenced her by pressing his lips to hers. Very slowly, she opened her mouth and felt for the tip of his tongue. Gently, he slid his arms behind her back and pulled her towards him.

'Alex . . .'

'Ssh, sssh. We've done too much talking.'

They kissed again. She longed for him to climb into the bed with her. She wanted to be naked with him, nothing more. It would be enough to hold him by her side for ever.

'So what happens now?' she asked him in a whisper.

'Now now?'

'No, tomorrow now.'

'I don't know,' he said. 'You tell me.'

'What about the campaign?' she asked.

'Yesterday. That's definitely yesterday.'

'And us?'

He kissed her. 'Yeah, that's tomorrow. And the next day.'

'And the next?' she asked through her smile.

'I hope so.'

'What about Charlie?'

'I think she's got ideas about taking your place. I think she wants me to run a campaign for her but honestly I can't see . . .'

'I meant you and Charlie. I thought you were together.'

The notion made him laugh. 'Are you kidding?'

'But I thought . . .'

'Ssh,' he said, kissing her again. 'Don't be silly.'

After a while she said, 'Al, when I was shot I thought I heard you say something. I thought I heard you . . .'

'I love you.'

She grinned. 'Yeah, I thought I heard . . .'

'I love you. I said I love you.'

'Right, so.'

'I can't even remember the last time I said that to anyone, but I mean it more than anything I've ever meant. I love you.'

'Oh, Al.' She stroked a hand across his forehead. 'Me too. I mean you!'

'We took our time saying it, didn't we?'

'Sixteen years,' she joked.

'And we've taken a pretty odd route, haven't we?'

Annie reached across and turned on the light. The brightness made her blink, but she wanted to see this man she loved. He was looking so handsome, so perfect.

'Remember how you said to me the other day that the world could be mine?'

Alex shook his head. 'Let's not talk about that. I should have stopped it sooner, I . . .'

She put a finger to his lips. 'Well, it is. At least, that's the way it feels.'

There were no regrets. Not for a moment did Annie wish she hadn't done what she did, and nothing could make her change her belief that everything that had happened was for the best. How could she think anything else when what she had now was a dream come true?

Out of hospital but not yet strong, she was invited to spend Christmas with Alex at Pam's Titusville home, while Pam and the boys spent the holiday in Georgia. Pam had been doing all she could to encourage the affair, quite unaware that it needed no encouragement at all.

The young lovers (as they called themselves, though neither had known love like this when they were young) bought a little tree and too many presents for one another. Among those Annie collected for Alex were two framed front pages from *The New York Times*. The first was from the day after her appearance on *Window on Washington*, the headline reading 'Actors confirm Presidential bid. In announcing, Dawn Hope speaks of renewal'. But it was not for this that she'd had the page framed, but for the article beneath, the headline of which ran, 'On television, candidate's candor seen as inspired politics'.

The media's reaction to Annie's outburst against Lear Cooper had been stunning. It was claimed that she had already stamped her mark on the '96 campaign by having the courage to stand on principles that were usually untouchable. The people had asked for honesty and been given it. Even Alex had been surprised by the media's endorsement of Dawn, though he had not been tempted to restart the campaign. The happiness he'd felt after visiting Annie late at night in the hospital was as great as any he'd known, and he wanted it to last. Besides, it was evident that she had little desire to fit into the shoes he'd been crafting for her, and this alone was enough to make him glad the campaign was over. So a day after her announcement speech, she declared that she was stepping out of the race, endorsing President Grant in the process.

The second front page, from which Alex was tearing the wrapping paper as they sat beside the glorious fire, had caused Alex and Annie even more amusement than the first. It was from an edition only three days before. This time the headline read, 'Hollywood star keeps campaign alive with new running mate'. Underneath the headline was a photograph of Tom Sterling and Charlie Canon together before a row of microphones. Justin Hathwaite, it was revealed, had been appointed their campaign manager.

Annie, wearing a thick Shetland sweater given her by Alex, limped across to sit by him, and together they looked at the article.

'You know they're eleven points above Grant,' she said. 'Do you think they'll go all the way?'

'Nah, they haven't got a hope.'

'Haven't they? I thought you said before that Tom was such a big star they couldn't lose?'

'Well, I mean if *I* was running their campaign . . .'

'Arrogant bastard!' she said, poking him in the ribs.

'No, I mean it,' he said.

And he did. The obvious mistakes that Justin had been making had given Alex itchy fingers to get back in the ring. There was so much he could do with Charlie and Tom that wasn't being done, and so many flaws he would tear apart were he spinning for a rival candidate. In fact, he believed it would only be a matter of time before he returned to the circus to manage someone else's act better, he trusted, than anyone else could.

'You watch,' he told Annie, 'these two are about to blow the biggest lead in election history and it'll all be because they won't be able to keep their opinions to themselves.'

'Charlie won't like that.'

'Good,' he said.

'Meany!'

'I know. But then,' he bent to kiss her, 'I hate her,' (he kissed again), 'for keeping me,' (and again), 'from you for so long. Think of all those hours we missed!' Now he lowered his hand to Annie's waist and up inside her sweater. "Mmm, it's toasty in here."

"That's nice," she said as he began to caress her breasts.

Making love to Alex had been everything she'd hoped it would be. The first time, after he'd carried her up three flights of stairs and over the threshold of the apartment she'd not seen for a month, had been filled with a romance and patience unusual for a first night. This was not because they possessed souls more beautiful than those of other men and women, nor even because their love was more special, though both felt it to be, but rather because wild abandon was impossible while Annie remained weak and wounded. So with great tenderness, Alex had kissed her body from head to foot and up again, and it was almost an hour before he had entered her.

Now, hardening yet again, he began to fondle Annie's breasts with a greater urgency. They had already celebrated most of Christmas day in bed, but Annie couldn't get enough of this man. She wanted all of him, she wanted to possess a part of him.

On the day they had arrived in Titusville, they had resolved that there was no need to wait, no need to think of marriage and houses and jobs, but that they should try for a child, two children, ten, as soon as they could, whenever they could. The thrill that each time might be the one filled their lovemaking with a pleasure that was new. Both of them believed there was magic in the air.

'You're like a teenager,' said Annie, feeling him through his trousers.

'And what would you know about teenagers?'

'Not nearly enough,' she said.

They kissed again, and then he stood and pulled her hand, wanting to lead her upstairs.

'Hey,' she whispered, 'Why don't we do it here, in front of the fire?'

'Won't you be cold?'

'Not if you get some more logs, caveman!' she said, slapping the outside of his leg.

'Can you resist me that long?'

'Try me!'

He left and she watched him through the window, looking the loyal husband as he lifted the logs into his curled arm. She was lucky, there was no question of that. She was lucky that she possessed no doubts at all, that she was utterly convinced that here was the man with whom she'd be happy for the rest of her days. It had not been so long before that she'd questioned her future and wondered whether the racing years might race on by, leaving her unsatisfied and unhappy. Those fears seemed a lifetime ago now. Since Alex had come to her in the hospital, she had been feeling nothing but joy. And although her love for him brought with it an optimism about the future (great roles, starring parts, happy kids), she also felt that it wouldn't matter what else happened in her life, so long as she was with him.

He turned, arms laden, to walk up the lawn. Quickly she climbed the stairs, hardly feeling the healing wound in her leg, to collect the duvet and pillows from the bed. Coming back down, she was surprised to see him back in the room, warming his hands in front of the fire. He turned, grinning broadly.

'Where are the logs?' she asked when she reached the bottom step, and then suddenly she heard the screen door snap shut in the kitchen.

She turned to look and heard Alex cry out, 'Wilma, I'm home!'

Her head snapped back to where the figure had been, but now the space was empty.

'Hey!' said Alex, 'are you OK? You look pale.'

'Alex, I . . .?' Annie began, remaining motionless at the foot of the stairs.

'What?' he said, passing her to tip the logs into the basket.

Annie took a deep breath.

'Nothing,' she said. 'It's just I thought I saw – no, it was nothing.'

'Actresses!' Alex said.

A galaxy of sparks crackled up the chimney as Alex threw a log onto the fire.

Of course, thought Annie, the clothes were different. But the face had been the same. Definitely the face had been the same.

'You're always imagining things that aren't there!' continued Alex in his mocking tone. He straightened his back and slapped the bark off his hands. 'Now weren't you the one who thought you were someone else?' he said. 'I seem to remember . . .'

'You shush!' said Annie, slapping his arm.' And count yourself lucky you've got Annie Marin at all.'

'Oh I do,' said Alex, taking her in his arms. 'I know I'm the luckiest man alive.'

She leant her head against his shoulder and closed her eyes and thought, for just a second, that she felt the brisk caress of a cool gust across her face before deciding that Alex was right, and that it was all in her mind.

What mattered to Annie was what she could feel and see. This was real – this man, this feeling, this touch of his hands, and it made her as happy as she'd been at any time in the thirty-six years of her life.

Epilogue

S OAP OPERA NEWS, Volume 5, Issue 21.

Editor's notes,
   by Jayne-Anne Lipke

TWO PIECES OF GOOD NEWS FOR DAWN HOPE SPELL DISAPPOINTMENT FOR HER FANS

After the blistering storms and hurricanes of 1994, the waters have been calmer for UBC's flagship soap, *Unto the Skies*, in the first few months of 1995. But there's still a swell to the sea!

The bitter court battle raging between the executors of the late Ned Hooper's will and *UTS* star Faith Valentine is hotting up. Attorneys for the star, who is entering her seventeenth year of playing Vanessa on the show, are claiming that her husband was not of sound mind when he left his entire estate to their long-serving maid, Consuela Martinez. A verdict is expected next week, and we'll keep you posted.

In happier news, veteran actor Lanny Mason has joined the show (which has now settled at a healthy 7.9 rating) as an ex-con who, headwriter Bob Fein says, will set the cat among the pigeons in Brendan Air. I can't wait!

And last weekend, many friends and family of ex-*UTS*

headwriter Max Lubotsky gathered at a joyful ceremony in Savannah, Georgia to celebrate the marriage of his beautiful, widowed wife, Pam. Among the revellers was Annie Marin, who swept all of us off our feet with her masterly performance as Senator Dawn Hope last year. She was accompanied by her partner, ex-*UTS* headwriter and presidential buddy, Alex Lubotsky. Annie Marin, looking vibrant in emerald green, promises that she'll be back on our screens in *The Bubble that Burst*, a TV movie about Dawn Hope to be directed by Zoë (ex-*UTS* director) Dunlop.

'But the fans will have to be patient!' Annie told me with a sparkle in her eyes.

Shooting of the project, scheduled for August, has been delayed for a further four months. Why the wait?

'For the two best reasons in the world!' said Marin cryptically.

Staying true to the wonderful partnership that brought Dawn Hope to the world, Annie Marin and Alex Lubotsky are promising a new production in September. Annie was grinning from ear to ear when she revealed one final twist to the tale. 'I'm having twins!' she said, adding jokily, 'and I already know what they'll be when they grow up! One's going to be an actor and the other's going to be President of the United States!'

And on that joyous note, I'm signing off until next week's off-set update.

Always remember: keep that smile on your face!

Jayne-Anne.

TIM GEARY

EGO

It's never been done, so Saul Weissman decides to do it. The century's greatest retailer is going to create the first ever male supermodel to launch his new cologne.

All employee Miles Jensen has to do is go and find the perfect man.

Two weeks, twenty-four time zones and countless agencies and nightclubs later Miles returns to New York with six possibles – among them an Italian playboy, a British ex-army officer and a Brazilian Casanova.

They may be worlds apart but they're all hungry for the six million dollar contract. Some of them want it more badly than others. One will stop at nothing to get it.

HODDER AND STOUGHTON PAPERBACKS

FIONA WALKER

FRENCH RELATIONS

It's a summer of lust, bed-hopping, unresolved sexual tension, horses, dogs, bolshy kids – and lots of bad behaviour. And in the midst of bedlam, at least two people fall in love . . .

'Romps along with plenty of self-deprecating wit'
The Sunday Times

'A sizzling summer read of love, sex, passion and soaring temperatures'
Sun

'Walker has a nicely epigrammatic turn of phrase and she understands how love can make normally sensible adults behave like imbeciles'
Daily Express

'Raunchy: [an] explosive debut'
Daily Mail

'The bonkbusting read of the summer'
For Women

'Romantic, intelligent, steamy and really rather wise'
Bookcase

Fiona Walker's new novel, *Kiss Chase*, is out now in hardback.

HODDER AND STOUGHTON PAPERBACKS

EDWINA CURRIE

A PARLIAMENTARY AFFAIR

Where politics equals sex, power and ambition.

'*War and Peace* in black suspenders'
Today

'Superior in almost every respect . . . there is real feeling here and real energy in the narrative . . . and through it all runs the excitement of lived experience. The books paints a fresh and absorbing portrait of the parliamentary world; it is better than Archer, much, much better than Dobbs.'
Sunday Telegraph

'An absorbing tale of obsessive ambitions amongst the political classes, with credible characters . . . you will not readily put this book down.'
Sunday Express

'A riveting insight into the malice, friendships, backbiting, infighting, political intrigue and seduction that goes on at the House of Commons . . . And never was a book published at a more appropriate time.'
Daily Mail

'An extremely timely and graphic novel – an uncomfortable amalgam of truth and fiction.'
Independent Magazine

HODDER AND STOUGHTON PAPERBACKS